LOVE ON A SMALL ISLAND

More Tales of New York

by

Judy Pomeranz

Library of Congress Cataloging-in-Publication Data

Judy Pomeranz, What Lies Beneath: Tales of New York, novellas and stories

Summary: Tied together only by the common setting of Manhattan and the urban experience that implies, Judy's disparate characters are variously confident, insecure, tough, fragile, bold, timid, tormented, serene, guarded, or open, and occasionally all the above. Like the rest of us, they put one foot in front of the other and hope to reach a place that feels good and right. Also like the rest of us, they rarely quite get there, and when they do it rarely lasts.

ISBN: 978-1-939282-41-5

Published by Miniver Press, LLC, McLean Virginia
Copyright 2018 Judy Pomeranz

First edition March 2018

For George, with thanks for forty-five years of inspiration and all the rest

TABLE OF CONTENTS

10

PREFACE

The seven stories in this collection are tied together by a common setting—New York City and its suburbs—and by a common theme: the power of love and its impact on the human condition.

This Metropolitan area is a region blessed or cursed by vast socio-economic and cultural disparities, which greatly influence the way people live, think, feel, and react. Love runs through the stories as the single and most important motivating force, but that love takes a multitude of forms, and manifests in hugely different ways from story to story and character to character.

We see love and its loss as a powerful force for good in the world, for redemption, and for heightened awareness in the individual. But we also see it as a destructive, dislocating, dystonic, or frightening force. In each story, we see the flip side of love: the impact of its loss, which is either ultimately positive or devastatingly negative. We see love lifting characters to great heights of joy and plunging others into depths of sorrow, despair, and self-destruction. We see how love can expand one character's worldview while causing other characters to collapse into themselves or run for cover into tiny emotional corners.

Love can be dramatic or subtle, intense or gentle, true or false, and in these stories, it manifests in all these ways. Regardless of the manifestation, in the end love is always the most important driver of humanity that exists in fiction, and in the real world.

LIES BENEATH THE SURFACE

Judy Pomeranz

Chapter One
Fallen Hero

I first learned of my father's hospitalization from Dan Rather on the CBS Evening News. It was the late fall of 1987, and I had the television on to provide white noise and a kind of companionship while I worked on an art review, trying to meet a looming deadline for ART-NY magazine. Though I wasn't really listening, the anchorman's words, delivered in his characteristically dramatic monotone, grabbed my attention:

> *Renowned American artist Sam Jackson, age sixty-two, was admitted to Three Pines Convalescent Center in Sag Harbor today, lending credence to long-standing speculation that he has been suffering from a tragic case of early-onset dementia, which sources say may have been caused or exacerbated by drug and alcohol use. He is said to be gravely ill.*

Cut away from a recent still photo of my father's face to a tape of the artist at work in the mid-1950's.

> *Celebrated for the stunningly original paintings that helped put New York on the art world map in the post-World-War-II period, Jackson was born and raised on a farm in central Illinois.*

Judy Pomeranz

Cut to black and white image of the artist as a young man in short pants, a cropped jacket, and string tie, posed stiffly in a picture with his parents.

> *He came to New York in the 1940's to study at the Art Students' League, but left the school within months, reportedly due to "philosophical differences" with the school's administration. Jackson nonetheless remained in the city, working in poverty and obscurity until he emerged onto the scene with his signature "cutaway" style, a conceit that charmed and ignited the passions of gallery owners, collectors, critics, and curators.*

Cut to Mayor Ed Koch of New York City.

> *"Sam has done us all an enormous service by creating art that exemplifies the inventiveness and dynamism of our great city. He is a civic treasure, and I am proud to have counted him as a personal friend."*

Cut to Susan Dailey, *New York Post* art critic.

> *"If I could afford to, I'd wallpaper my house with Sam Jackson's work."*

Cut to Bart Rosenberg, best-selling author and professor of philosophy at Columbia University.

> *"Sam imbued his canvases with more than aesthetics. His art bespoke a uniquely personal philosophy that he would never verbalize or define, but instead invited the world to decode. He was a conceptual, technical, and stylistic genius."*

Cut to George H.W. Bush, Vice President of the United States.

> *"Sam was not only a great artist, but a decent human being. His foundation for children with learning disabilities has helped youngsters across this great country of ours maximize their God-given talents and live productive and fulfilling lives."*

Cut to Jonathon Van Cleef, Director of the National Gallery of Art.

> *"I'm going to make a bold statement here when I say the paintings of Sam Jackson are without equal in the history of twentieth-century American art. I'm a big fan of Rothko, Pollock, Newman, Johns, Rauschenberg—God knows I love that whole mid-twentieth-century coterie. But Sam Jackson gave us a unique something derived from his personal presence. He was larger than life, and his legacy will be as well.*

I stared at the TV screen long after the news ended, thinking how peculiar it was that the assembled celebrities had talked about Sam in the past tense and with the kind of wildly exaggerated paeans to his goodness and importance one usually employed only with reference to the dead. I tried to feel something, anything that would elevate me above or beyond this state my therapist would refer to as "without affect." This was my father, for God's sake. Despite the disaffection and years of estrangement, I wanted to feel grief or compassion or at least pity for this man who was slipping away from reality, or into his own new version of it. This man who might be dying. But I could conjure no feelings, only dull, empty depression provoked by my own emotional inadequacy.

I finally turned the TV off, wishing I had done so before having heard the report I could neither assimilate nor forget. I went to the kitchen to pour a double Glenfiddich on the rocks into a cut crystal glass. Though I shunned luxuries, and eschewed conspicuous consumption, I appreciated my single malts, along with the glassware and rituals that made them taste and feel the way they should.

I brought the full glass, along with the bottle, into the living room, and looked over my collection of CDs. I pulled out an Ella Fitzgerald disc, slipped it into the stereo, then settled myself on the sofa. I took a long pull on the Scotch, letting Ella's smooth vocal tones wash over me as I focused on the warm path the alcohol cut through my system, sliding from my mouth into my throat, down through my esophagus, past my heart, and down into my deepest core. It was a familiar and ineffably pleasant sensation, a prelude to the anesthetizing process. I took another sip. Paused. Then another. My shoulder muscles gradually unclenched. I dropped my head, lifted it, and turned it to loosen the tight cords in my neck. Some people meditate; I drink Scotch.

When Ella began her classic rendition of "Someone to Watch Over Me," I topped off my glass. I leaned back into the sofa, brought the cold crystal to my lips, and allowed the music to transport me back to Greenwich Village, where I had listened to the same number sung by the same vocal genius filling the air of my father's studio—a dingy, cramped space under a pitched roof on the fifth floor of the decrepit brownstone in which he, my mother, and I had shared a small apartment.

I was five years old, a tiny child with soft pink skin, a mop of red curls, and a smattering of pale freckles across my nose. My mother always said I was adorable, and my godfather Irv agreed; he said I looked like Raggedy Ann. I wore a yellow sweater that day, which Irv's partner Wilson had knitted for me; it was my favorite because of its plastic, duck-shaped buttons. Beneath the sweater I wore miniature blue jeans and a T-shirt, because I always insisted on dressing like my father, whom I vaguely feared but utterly idolized.

The air of the studio smelled of linseed oil, turpentine, cigarettes, Scotch, and sweat. The music blasted, shaking the windows; my father loved jazz and he loved it turned up loud. He stood in front of a canvas, propped up against the wall, which was a head taller than he and eight feet across. After a moment's consideration, he slathered the center with layer upon layer of hot reds, oranges, and yellows in great sweeping strokes of a broad brush. The circles emanated concentrically but irregularly out to the canvas's edges.

I stood beside him. "It's beautiful, Daddy," I whispered. I knew from experience that complete silence was preferred, and that a quiet voice, while a distant second, was the next best thing.

Sam didn't look away from his work, nor did he respond, except to frown. He filled a brush with the bright purple he had mixed on his palette and painted heavy strokes over a wide area of red, then moved back to examine the result. As he studied the painting, I retired to my favorite place in the studio, a cozy crease where the sloping roof met the wood-plank floor, a comfy space only I could fit into.

I loved the way Sam's brush moved across the canvas, hopping or pirouetting in sprightly, quick steps, leaving dashes, dots, squiggles, and flickers in its wake, and other times dragging or slogging heavily through mounds of thick, rich impasto, producing snaky troughs, or heavy, dense fields of saturated color. The brush seemed to pull Sam's arm behind it as it arced, twisted, circled, and zipped through the air, bringing his whole body into motion.

As I lay on my side, I found my own arm pulled by the rhythm of his. It mimicked his movements, making tiny parallel gestures in the air, then taking flight and aping Sam's motions on a grand scale that dragged me into a standing position and made my body move and dance to the strains of his gestures and the jazz tunes that filled the air. I swirled and twirled in a state of pure grace, gliding across the floor, following Sam's lead on my own small scale, pretending I was the artist.

All the while, I imagined the picture my gestures would produce. Like my father's, it was bold and crashingly modern, but unlike his, mine contained recognizable imagery, like twisting vines; huge, leafy plants; pudgy, adorable animals; scrawny, scary ones; and fantastic creatures born of ancient myths and fairytales. In my mind, the images cavorted across a canvas the size of Manhattan, producing a tangled web of animated figures created of and trapped in a cage of brushstrokes.

Dizzy from the movement and lightheaded from the smell of paint and my own visions, I twirled right into my father. I grabbed the loose denim of his jeans to regain my balance, stood on the toe of his boot, and hugged his enormous leg as tightly as I could. Either playing along with me or oblivious to my attachment, Sam continued his own movements, lifting me with his leg and dragging me around with him as he continued to work.

But when he came to a sudden stop to dig his palette knife into a pile of oily blue pigment, I lost my balance, along with my grip, twisted around, and fell forward, hitting my forehead against the canvas.

"Ouch!" I cried, though the touch of the soft fabric and squishy paint didn't hurt as much as startle me. I looked up at my father, saw the rage flaring in his eyes, and whimpered.

"Jesus Christ, Dawn!" Sam roared, staring at the place where my head had smudged the canvas. "You've ruined my god-damned painting."

"I fell," I murmured. I ran my hand across my sticky forehead, looked at the mess of red, blue, and orange that covered my hand, and began to cry in earnest.

Judy Pomeranz

"Why the hell can't you stay out of my—" Sam stopped mid-sentence and gazed at the sticky mess on my fingers; his sudden silence, which was entirely unfamiliar, frightened me more than the yelling had. He grabbed my wrist with his giant hand, yanked it toward the canvas, and pressed my palm against the lower left corner of the painting, next to the smudge my forehead had made.

He dropped my hand, stepped back, and looked at the passage he had created. A tiny handprint, dappled with color and heavy with texture, rode peacefully upon the surface of a dynamic roil of paint. Sam stared as if in a trance at this small figurative element in the otherwise entirely abstract work.

I held my breath, knowing I was awaiting an important verdict. I steeled myself for outrage.

But Sam grinned. It was a beatific smile I had not seen on my father's face before, nor would I ever again.

"You're a goddam genius, Dawn," he said, still smiling. "It's like a portrait." He lifted me up and gave me a fat, wet kiss on the cheek, not noticing or caring that I held onto his stubbly, whiskered face with paint-smeared hands, sullying the artist with his own art. For the briefest moment, those bright blue eyes favored me alone.

But as soon as he set me down on the floor, I rushed to the safety of my nook under the eaves. I knew, even then, that what was genius now could revert back to my having ruined the goddam painting.

***

I shook off the memory as I poured myself another Scotch, then tried to turn my attention back to the review I was writing of the Metropolitan Museum's Pre-Raphaelite show. I turned the pages of the catalogue, fixated on the lithe young women whose crinkly, flowing tresses looked as if they'd been pressed between pairs of washboards. I tried to formulate a clever sentence that would allude to the neurotic sameness and banality of the artists' subject matter while acknowledging the intrinsic beauty of the paintings and undeniable technical skill of their creators. And I tried to forget what I'd heard about my father.

It was only with great effort that I restrained myself from drawing invidious comparisons between the talent exhibited by the

20

artists represented in this show and the shtick relied upon by so many painters of my father's generation. I knew that, to make such a case in my review, no matter how personally satisfying, would be unwise; it would be perceived as a politically incorrect jab at modernism and, worse yet, recognized by anyone who knew me as a petty and gratuitous slap in Sam Jackson's face, delivered as a purely retributive gesture.

I pulled my hair back and twisted it into a knot, an old nervous gesture, then poised my fingers over the laptop's keyboard and waited for the brilliant words to flow. But it wasn't happening. I couldn't free my mind of the disturbingly incongruous image of the blustery, venerable, gigantic Sam Jackson as a helpless nursing home resident.

I was still awaiting the muse when the phone rang. I grabbed it, grateful for any reprieve from both my writer's block and jumbled thoughts.

"Hey, sweetie," came the voice from the other end. It was my godfather, Irv. "I'm guessing you've heard the news by now." He sounded concerned.

"You guessed right."

"I'm sorry I wasn't the one to tell you, Dawn, but I didn't know, myself, until after he was checked in."

"Who did it?"

"Julia and Daisy," Irv said, referring to Sam's current wife and their daughter.

"Was it necessary?" I asked, not that I wanted to know, or to prolong the conversation about Sam.

"He's gotten a lot worse. He won't eat, and he's stopped talking. Won't say a word. You know, it's funny, Julia was okay with home care when he was loud and a pain in the ass, but when he got quiet, it scared the hell out of her. It was just so…"

"Unlike him," I said, completing the thought.

"Yeah, so damn unlike him," Irv said with a chuckle, but I could tell he was trying not to cry. "You okay, sweetie?" he finally managed.

"I'm fine."

"You're a tough one, kid. Want to go see him? I'll take you out there this weekend."

"No thanks. You knew the answer to that before you asked."

He was quiet for a moment. "Would you do it for me?"

21

"Jesus, Irv. Please don't do this."

Irv was the one person in the world I honestly adored, and the one person I could count on to selflessly, and often senselessly, adore me back. He had always supported me in whatever I wanted to do, and had never made a single demand. As far as I could recall, he had never even made a request of me. So I knew my going to Sag Harbor was immensely important to him, which is the one and only reason I found myself agreeing to ride out to the tip of Long Island the following Saturday morning.

Chapter Two
A Proposal

"I have a proposition to pass along," Irv said as we headed east on the Long Island Expressway in his vintage Range Rover. His tone was breezy, but I recognized the lightness as forced.

I stared out the window at the scruffy, sunburned brown plantings that lined the road. They provided intermittent but depressing bits of nature to complement the strip-mall landscape we sped past.

"Sounds ominous." I looked to see if I could read anything in his expression, but all I saw behind his aviator sunglasses and neatly trimmed silver beard was a practiced poker face.

"I'm only the messenger." He turned to me with a grin. "I know what you're going to think when you hear this, but try to keep an open mind, okay?"

"Ominous."

Irv smiled but kept his eyes on the road. "Jack Rambo at FineArts Press has a project he'd like you to consider."

"A project?" These words would have been music to any freelance writer's ears, and mine were no exception, but I sensed a catch. "What kind of project?"

"A biography." Irv's eyes shifted from the road to me and back again.

"Why? I've never done one."

"Because you know the subject better than anyone else."

"Oh Jesus, Irv." I twisted my hair into a tight knot. "Not Sam's biography."

He looked at me and nodded.

I took deep breaths to retain or regain composure. Irv *was* only the messenger. "I assume you told them how I'd feel about their proposal and where they could put it?"

"I told them I'd raise it with you."

"Jesus." I slapped the Range Rover's wooden dashboard. "You know there's no way—"

"It might be good—"

"Forget it." I crossed my arms in a posture I knew was childish but hoped would end the discussion.

"This could be the break you've been waiting for." Irv risked a look in my direction. "How many art book ideas have you pitched? Here's one that falls right into your lap, one you could write better than anyone on the planet. How can you not consider it?"

"You know how hard I've worked to get Sam and his demons out of my life. I'd have to be insane to take on a project like that."

"You could handle it," Irv said. "Besides, this might be a way for you to finally deal with those demons, and with Sam, and make peace with the whole thing. To get to know about him and understand his motivations and why he is the way he is—but just be on paper, where he poses no threat. It might be a purgative, and could be healthier than spending all your energy trying to pretend he never existed."

I looked out the window again at the blighted landscape that zipped past us.

"I'm scared," Irv said, "that you'll always regret it if Sam dies before you get this thing worked out."

***

As soon as we walked into the nursing home I knew I had made a mistake in agreeing to come here. I wanted to get the hell out. It wasn't only the thought of seeing my father, but the place itself was making me sick.

It was sparkling clean and smelled of orange-soda antiseptic. It was cheery; the lighting was bright, the décor pastel blues and pinks, and the matronly front desk attendant as sweet as sugar. It could have been a nursery school. It *should* have been a nursery school. The thought of my father living in a place like this—along with the thought of having to see him—made me nauseous. I scanned the environs for a Ladies' Room, fearing I might need one.

"Mr. Jackson is in room 324," the receptionist said, after Irv had told her who we were and who we wanted to see. "Take the back elevator to the third floor, and the nurses will direct you from there. He has strict limitations on visitors, so I'm sure he'll be happy to see you." She beamed at both of us.

"Thank you," Irv said.

He looked at me somberly. "You ready?"

I didn't answer.

"You okay?"

I shrugged, and grabbed his arm. We walked the interminable hall leading to the elevator. We passed an aviary populated with tiny, brilliantly colored birds, and a wall-sized aquarium in which neon fish of all sizes swam and frolicked. I concentrated on putting one foot in front of the other. We reached the end of the corridor, and stepped onto the elevator, which rose slowly to the third floor.

When we got off we found ourselves in another world, a place decorated with handmade paper flowers; photos of ancient people in funny hats hamming for the camera; posters that talked about being happy and counting your blessings; and a whiteboard featuring the date, the day of the week, and a listing of activities, which included Bingo, sing-along, movie time, reminiscences, and crafts. The air was filled with tinny music emanating from a piano in a lounge area on our right.

The pianist was a heavyset, jolly, blonde woman of indeterminate age in a rosy pink smock. She was surrounded by grizzled, gray-haired people, most of whom were in wheelchairs. They all held songbooks, but the vast majority just sat there with their mouths open; some tapped their fingers or toes to the beat, as if rhythm was instinctive. To our left was a nurse's station, where we found an aide who directed us down a hallway to Sam's room.

Irv knocked on the closed door of room 324. No one answered. He waited, then turned the knob and pushed the door open. I followed him into the room, and noticed first the neatly made-up, empty bed, which made me wonder if my father had died. Then I saw the shriveled husk of a man propped up on a chair near the window.

"Hi Sam," Irv said quietly. He walked over to my father and bent down to plant a kiss on his pasty, papery cheek, a gesture my father would once have treated with disdain but now seemed not to notice. "Good to see you, my friend." Irv gently rubbed Sam's shoulders. Then he pulled another couple of chairs over near Sam's, and sat down.

He chatted with Sam, shooting the breeze, bringing him up to date on who was doing what, what the weather was like, what the local sports teams were doing, as if the shell in front of him could possibly comprehend or care.

I couldn't bring myself to touch my father or even sit near him. I stood behind Irv and gazed into Sam's vacant eyes, searching for a glimmer of the man who once occupied the weak little body before us, the man who once created works of art the critics described as *Revolutionary! Ingenious! Titanic! Gutsy! Bold!*

These same words had also been used to characterize the artist himself. Sam Jackson had been an individual defined by superlatives, made for exclamation points. When he entered a room, his presence had filled it entirely, leaving neither space nor air for anyone else.

Sam had been huge in every way. In his prime he had stood six feet four inches tall and weighed a solid 240. His head sat on a tree trunk neck and his hands were like lion paws, massive with stubby fingers and salad plate palms. But, for all his bulk, his limbs were long, and I remembered how surprisingly graceful his choreography had been as he moved in front of his giant canvases. His legs would take on a balletic ease of motion and his arms a simian sweep when he slathered paint with a brush or cut through mounds of impasto with his palette knife.

He had also been loud; his baritone voice had boomed and echoed even when he tried to speak softly; it had resonated and set up vibrations even when he whispered. And his eyes had been as striking as his voice. Everyone talked about those amazing blue eyes that seemed almost as large as the rest of him. They were neither the bright blue eyes of a Hollywood idol nor the pale translucent blue ones of a magazine model. They were lapis lazuli, a blue so deep they were nearly black, if the angle and lighting were right. And they were so expressive my mother once told a reporter they were like windows into his soul. She had added, with a nervous laugh, that Sam could never hide anything from her because his eyes revealed everything.

She was wrong about that. And I suspect she knew it at the time.

But there had been a spark in those eyes, a glow of intense, frantic animation, which, while seductively irresistible, was not always welcoming. It could be challenging or intimidating, even frightening in its intensity. The spark rarely dimmed but often turned away, like a light seeking an object worthy of illumination. If and when it found such an object, it would rest on it for only a moment before moving on, leaving the original object in the dark.

But now, the light was gone. The eyes I peered into were grey and watery, dim with a blurry cast; they looked more like inert slugs than organs of sight. Perhaps now, more than ever, they were windows into his soul.

Judy Pomeranz

Chapter Three
Plunging into the Abyss

For days after visiting what was left of my father in Sag Harbor, I could barely eat or sleep, though I longed for a respite from the images that played in my mind. While I still had no real feelings for Sam, other than disgusted pity, I was haunted by what I had seen and equally so by the flood of unwelcome memories the whole event provoked. I spent those days taking long walks around the city; watching mindless sitcoms on TV; drinking copious amounts of Scotch; talking with Irv; and writing, but only non-fiction. Though poetry was my favored genre, I didn't write any for a long time after that visit. Diversion—cold, calculated distraction—was what I needed; I couldn't risk sitting alone with my thoughts or doing anything that might allow my subconscious to kick in, never mind risk exploring its inner reaches.

After a week of passing my days in these aimless mental and ambulatory meanderings, I decided to attack the pile of unattended mail. I propped pillows on the sofa in my tiny living room, lay against them, and slashed envelopes open. I tossed aside offers of credit cards, pleas from charities, and postcards from realtors wanting to sell my home despite the fact that I was a renter. I put the phone bill, along with a renewal card for *Poetry* magazine, on the coffee table, then turned to the last piece of mail, an envelope from FineArts Press. I almost threw it into the pile on the floor of never-to-be-opened junk mail until I noticed the first-class postage, which piqued my curiosity. So I slit it open and pulled out a neatly typed letter on crisp, white stationary, from the Press's CEO, Jack Rambo.

The letter was a personal one, and one I should have expected. It was a missive which offered me a hefty sum to write the biography of Sam Jackson, a book Jack believed would be of the "utmost importance to both scholars and the lay reader." Rambo assured me his operation would put "substantial resources and the full weight of our marketing force" behind the book. In a proposal that was courteous, yet brief and to the point, he promised I would have editorial freedom in framing and structuring the biography. While he thought time would be of the essence (no doubt wanting to cash in on my father's illness or imminent death), he would offer flexibility in terms of deadline. Clearly, Irv had not passed my disinterest in this project along to the people who mattered.

As I stared at the letter, a dread washed over me. The money was the tip-off. The only reason a publisher would offer such a prodigious sum was if he expected to have a best-seller on his hands, and the only way an artist's biography would become a best-seller was if it offered a personal, insider, tell-all story that would spill the beans about the artist's dissipated lifestyle from the point of view of the alienated, misanthropic daughter.

I got up off the sofa, plunked myself down in front of the laptop I kept on my kitchen table, and began to type.

I told Mr. Rambo that while I appreciated his offer, I had neither time for nor interest in pursuing such a project, and implied I was skeptical about why such a prestigious press would solicit an unknown art critic to produce a book about which they felt so strongly. If they owed Irv a favor, I said, they'd have to find another way to repay him. If they merely wanted the artist's daughter's name on the cover, I wasn't interested in obliging. If they thought I had insider information to contribute, I wouldn't be able to deliver, since I hadn't spoken to my father in more than two decades.

Needing to feel that this chapter was closed, never to be reopened, and hoping some outside air would blow the grimy, sticky layer of dread off me, I printed the letter, addressed an envelope, kicked off my fuzzy slippers, and put on my running shoes to walk the three blocks down to my local FedEx, where I requested overnight service. Then I came home, lay down on the sofa, and took a long, sound nap that lasted until the next morning.

***

Despite my curt response, and much to my surprise, Rambo proved persistent. Two days after I sent my letter, his next one arrived, by express mail. In terms that were irresistibly seductive to a freelance writer who, like most in the business, believed she was under-published, under-read, and, of course, under-appreciated, he asked me to reconsider:

The book I envision, Rambo wrote, *would be both scholarly and personal; it would capture Sam Jackson as a husband and father, but most importantly as a public figure who influenced the development of the art and social mores of our time. It must be written from the perspective of one with access to primary sources and the skill to use them properly. It must also contain a thorough analysis of Sam's work: its foundations, its evolution, its meaning, and its place in the grand continuum of art history.*

You, Dawn, are the person who can write the biography I have in mind. I have read your criticism and essays, works in which you demonstrate the reporting, analytical, and contemplative skills we need for this job. I have also read your poetry, which suggests you have the temperament and the literary skills to carry this off with great elegance. The fact that you are the artist's daughter is incidental.

***

It was difficult not to be won over by this man who claimed to be among the dozen or so people in the known world I figured had actually read my poetry. But, as delightful as his letter was to read and, yes, reread, I remained fearful. I had put myself through enough grueling years of analysis to know that ripping open the sores of the past could be dangerous, particularly when performed unassisted.

So, despite a recent and revolutionary resolve to live my life without outside counsel or over-analysis—a resolve born of emotional exhaustion and boredom with what my friend Tom referred to as mental masturbation—I made an appointment to touch base with the psychotherapist with whom I had worked for more years than I cared to remember.

During those long years, I had developed a love-hate connection with Dr. Sally Steinbrenner, based not only on my acknowledged dependence, the thought of which I detested, but also an unspoken mutual respect. I would persist in asking questions, fully recognizing how profoundly I would resent her answers, then generally follow her advice. But this time, I expected her to support my instinct.

***

"And don't you dare ask me what *I* think I should do," I warned as I concluded my rambling narrative about Jack Rambo's offer. I leaned into Dr. Steinbrenner's sofa, which I always refused to lie down on, fearing I would turn into a Woody Allen character.

"Okay, then, if you want my honest opinion, I think it would be a healthy project." Dr. Steinbrenner spoke in her irritatingly pert manner, from the comfort of her high-backed, severe, brown leather armchair.

"What do you mean, 'healthy'?" I asked, prepared to do battle.

"As the root of the word would imply, it could help you heal."

"Heal from what?" I asked, as if there were any question.

"Your obsession with your father."

"Jesus, Doctor, I'm past all that."

Even though I knew it wasn't true, I felt compelled to say it. It was part of our carefully scripted dialogue.

"Then why is it that, no matter where we begin, we always end up talking about him?"

I glared at her, then looked at the floor. Why had I ever chosen a psychoanalyst over a good, old-fashioned, pill-pushing shrink who would just prescribe some mind-numbing drug instead of indulging in all this talk? Particularly irritating was that I was here voluntarily, and paying dearly for the privilege. What did that say about *me*?

"Let's face it, Dawn," Dr. Steinbrenner said, "you've worshipped your father and you've detested him, but you've never been indifferent to him, and you've never let go of him. This project would force you to immerse yourself in the details of his life, and, in doing so, to maybe finally face and grapple with your own anxieties. By uprooting them, exposing them to light and air, measuring them, and butting up against them, you might conquer them. But you'll never conquer what you don't confront."

***

I asked Irv to meet me that evening for a drink at our favorite rendezvous spot, Sir Harry's Bar at the Waldorf-Astoria. Besides being on neutral Midtown territory between Irv's Chelsea home and my apartment on the way-too-far-east-to-be-fashionable part of the Upper East Side, Sir Harry's was dark, crowded, and noisy, with a tiny edge of dissipation, no matter what time of day or night you showed up. It exuded urban intimacy laced with anonymity, which meant it was a great place to escape the real world. And they poured an honest drink.

I found Irv at a small table in the back, nursing a Manhattan, a drink I'd never before seen him order. Irv is ecumenical when it comes to food and drink, and happily ingests just about anything. I, on the other hand, am a woman of narrow tastes and strong loyalties, with no gastronomic sense of adventure, which is why he had already ordered me a Glenfiddich, neat.

"Hey, Babycakes." Irv stood to peck me on the cheek. He had graced me with that name when I was a child, and couldn't get over the habit of pulling it out.

I gave him a fat kiss in return, enjoying the familiar scratchy feel of his beard, then sat down and took a long drink of my Scotch.

"I'm thinking about going ahead with the biography," I said, abruptly. I never have been good at small talk.

"I'm glad," he said softly, favoring me with a gentle smile.

"I knew you would be, but it doesn't make sense."

"Why not?"

"You're Sam's best friend."

"So?"

"So, why would you want someone like me to write his biography? You know I can't stand him, and you know I'm not going to be the most objective reporter. You know I'll be tempted to get back at him by trashing his reputation. Doesn't that bother you?"

Irv pulled the cherry out of his drink and sucked on it before popping it off the stem and eating it. "No, because I know you'll be fair," he said with annoying calm and utter confidence. "You're a person of integrity, and you'll write it as you see it after you've done your research." He smiled at me. "God knows, Sam's not perfect, and any biography will reflect that; it has to. But he's not all bad."

I rolled my eyes and took another long pull on my drink while glaring over the rim of my glass at a man at the next table who was clearly enjoying eavesdropping on our conversation.

Judy Pomeranz

"You might learn some things about Sam that'll make you view him with more sympathy," Irv said, "and I know you'll reflect those things, because you're a damn good writer and an honest human being."

"Why do you think I'm going to learn anything new? Considering that the press has been relentless in following Sam, I'm not sure why anyone thinks I'd have anything to contribute that's not already out there."

"I guess we'll find out."

Partly amused, partly annoyed, and partly terrified, I swirled the Scotch in my glass and stared into the vortex it made. "And you don't think this enterprise will make me crazier than I am?"

"Who knows?" Irv said with a sweet grin. "Maybe it will."

"And you think I should do it anyway?"

"Yes," he said seriously. "Absolutely yes."

Irv's serenity made me edgier than ever. "But where do I begin? How am I supposed to learn all there is to know about a man I've so assiduously avoided knowing anything about?"

"You begin with me," He reached across the table to touch my hand, which calmed me. "No one knows your father better, so I'll be your first interview. Come by in the morning and we'll talk."

Chapter Four
Genesis

And so it was that I found myself snuggled into the chintz-covered settee that dominated the solarium of the red brick, federal-style townhome Irv shared with his partner, Wilson Grantly. I sipped Earl Grey from a translucent Limoges cup, and surveyed the elegant, tranquil little Chelsea paradise that surrounded me, a place filled with leather-bound books, treasures from travels around the world, and brightly-colored yet intensely soothing fabrics and wall coverings. Irv's place was the polar opposite of the basic, unadorned apartment in which I lived and the neutral spaces in which I had grown up, yet being here lowered my blood pressure.

Whenever I was in Irv's world, I wondered how two men as different as he and my father had ever become such good friends. Irv was serene, cultured, erudite, unassuming, sensitive, and charming; my father was loud, uneducated, boorish, narcissistic, and obnoxious. Irv was concerned with making the people in his sphere happy and comfortable; my father was concerned only with how the people in his circle could make *him* happy and comfortable. Even the physical contrasts were stark. Irv was thin, fair, delicate-featured, and manicured; my father was large, dark, and sloppy. Irv was gay, and my father famously insatiably heterosexual. So, it was with great interest that I set up my tape recorder and settled in to listen to Irv's description of their first encounter.

"It was 1949 when Sam and I met," Irv began. "Thirty-eight years ago.

"I was twenty-one years old and a newly-minted graduate of Columbia College when I met my darling Wilson at Turncoats Bar, a sleazy nightspot in the Village and one of only a few gay bars I knew of. I was waiting tables at Sarah's Diner on the Lower East Side, living at my parents' home in Brooklyn, and making art in their basement at night. Wilson was a few years older than I, and was a smart, handsome Wall Street lawyer on the fast track to becoming partner. He was also one of the kindest and funniest people I had ever encountered. I fell in love with him instantly and was gratified and amazed to realize my feelings were reciprocated.

"Just weeks after we met, I moved in with him, and he insisted I give up my day job so I could paint fulltime. He not only provided me with the financial wherewithal to do it—sweetly saying he considered it an investment—he also provided me with the security and confidence I needed to create art all day long, telling me 'posterity deserved no less.' How could I not fall in love with a man like that?"

I grinned at the smitten man across from me; even I was in love with Wilson, and God knows I'm a tough customer.

"So," Irv went on, "I answered an ad for shared studio space down in the Bowery and signed up for a deal that allowed me to use the studio from eight a.m. until eight p.m., leaving it free for another tenant who paid a reduced rate to make his art at night.

"The studio was a drafty warehouse space with concrete floors, bare plaster walls, and a residual reek of urine, but it was cheap, reasonably large, and, most important, had perfect north light that filtered in through huge, if filthy, windows. I moved in with an easel, a couple of folding chairs, and my art supplies, and immediately began painting with great soul and eagerness, reveling in the luxury of working for hours on end, day after day." Irv paused and looked at me. "Is this more than you want to know?"

"Not a bit. I'm fascinated. Why didn't you ever tell me this before?"

"You never asked."

"I am now. Please go on."

So Irv proceeded. "Much as I loved painting all day and doing work I felt was important and on the verge of evolving into something meaningful, I felt less enthusiastic about my own art when I paid attention to the work left behind by the night tenant. His paintings were incredibly varied in style and content, yet they didn't seem to come from a rookie seeking an artistic voice. They had an assurance, an energy, almost a swagger that gave them a life of their own and suggested a grand confidence on the part of their maker, a quality I greatly envied.

"One thing my fellow tenant wasn't, however, was neat. Each morning, I would find a riot of canvases propped up or tossed around the room. Splashes and drips of paint covered the floor and walls; tubes and cans were strewn everywhere. The man apparently worked from frenzied inspiration, not from the careful preliminary drawings and warm-up exercises I indulged in. But my God, the result was fantastic. Each day, I would study the additions and amendments he had made to his paintings the night before. I wanted to understand how he did what he did and to divine what manner of godly inspiration or muse he relied on, because I desperately wanted access to it. It was always hard for me to return to my own canvases after studying his. Mine seemed so amateurish and tentative by comparison.

"Then, one morning, I walked into the studio and found a message scrawled in red paint on the plaster wall opposite the windows:

" 'NICE USE OF COBALT IN THE UPPER LEFT CORNER,' the message read. An arrow pointed down toward my picture. 'TAKE THE DAMN THING OFF THE EASEL AND DON'T TOUCH IT. IT'S FINISHED.'

"Puzzled, even frightened, I finally decided the message was a compliment.

" '**Thanks**,' I printed in neat blue letters under the red scrawl, '**I'm grateful, because I admire your work.**'

" 'WHAT THE HELL ARE YOU, A GODDAM CRITIC?' I found the following morning.

" '**Do you have a problem with praise?**' I responded, this time larger and in purple, getting into the spirit of the thing.

" 'SO NOW YOU'RE A GODDAM SHRINK. EVEN WORSE. I LIKE THE SURREAL THING YOU HAVE GOING ON IN THAT NEW PAINTING. REMINDS ME OF MIRO.'

" '**Are you calling me derivative?**' I wrote back in jest.

" '**YOU'RE PARANOID! I WAS BEING GENEROUS.**'

"And so the dialogue-on-the-wall went, on and off, for several weeks, as we painted our way around the room. Then, one morning I found this message:

" 'IF YOU'RE GOING TO TALK ABOUT MY WORK, I WANT TO SEE YOUR GODDAM FACE. MEET ME AT THE THREE OAKS BAR. I WORK THERE FROM NOON TO EIGHT.'

"And that, Dawn, was my initial encounter with your father."

I shook my head, unable to respond. It was so totally like him.

Irv smiled at me, sipped his tea, and wiped his mouth with a linen napkin. "Even then, he spoke in capital letters. I did go to the Three Oaks. It was the first of many visits I would make there over the years. But, as good an artist as your dad was, he was a lousy bartender." Irv shook his head slowly. "He was rude to the customers and ridiculously arrogant."

"No surprise there," I said.

"He'd slam drinks down in front of his sad coterie of regulars and sneer at them as he waited for payment, but he was lavish with free drinks for the few people who managed to amuse him. He was mad as hell that he had to work at a job like that when he knew he should be painting. He knew it even then, though he was only eighteen at the time. He was a kid. But he was right.

"You asked what initially drew me to Sam and what continues to attract me. I suppose that very thing is a big part of it. He's not only a genius at making art, but he's one of the rare creatures in this world who knows exactly and beyond question what he's meant to be doing. There's something majestic about being in the company of a person like that. Probably like being around Churchill or Hemingway or Pollock. While people like that aren't necessarily pleasant, they're bigger than the rest of us, and we can sense it being near them.

"The problem is they become frustrated if anything interferes with their mission, which is why they don't play well with others. They're so focused that they can't see anything outside their viewfinder, so they come across as self-centered. But I don't think self is what it's about. It's about knowing they have something to do, a finite amount of time on this earth, and a need to get it done." Irv sipped his tea and pondered his own words.

"In spite of their neurotic fixations, these people are among the world's great seducers, and I'm not talking sexually, at least not exclusively. When someone like Sam pays attention to you, you're powerless to do anything but please him. You know that about your father, Dawn. You've been there. It's like a divine gift when he shares a tiny corner of himself." Irv looked at me for agreement, which I didn't feel like giving.

"The funny thing is, I don't think your father ever considered himself a genius, or even a great artist. Yes, he acted like he did, but that was probably out of insecurity. I think his harshness came from a subliminal sense that he was capable of something truly and exceptionally great but that he couldn't quite get there."

Irv got up and poured us each another cup of tea from a silver art deco pot, carefully removing the leaves with a fine mesh strainer, one of dozens he had collected over the years.

"Sam favored me with his attention," Irv said as he sat back down. "Maybe it was because I took his art seriously before other people did. Maybe because I let him be the way he was. Maybe because I was the only one around. Or maybe he knew he was different and felt a kinship with another outsider."

"What do you mean 'another outsider'?" I asked.

"You have to remember, Dawn, society was cruel in those days to people like Wilson and me. This was way before Stonewall. I lost my family because of naïve honesty about our relationship, and Wilson had to be extremely careful because of the firm—there was no way he could come out of the closet and expect to ever become a partner. We had to keep a low profile, and we spent a lot of energy either evading the truth or dancing around its edges. It's a horribly ego-dystonic and isolating way to live.

"As a result, we had few close friends who weren't gay. But Sam, that macho thug who could be so bigoted, biased, and close-minded, was, ironically, the exception. He's called me a faggot, a queen, a pansy, a patsy, and a lot worse over the years, but it's just talk, just his shtick, just part of the package you buy into with Sam. In the end, he's always been there for me, and for Wilson."

Irv paused, took a deep breath, fiddled with the teapot, and wiped his brow with his white handkerchief. Then he looked at me as if assessing my capacity to deal with more tales of Sam, or his own capacity to deliver them. "Before you leave, I have one more story to tell you that might shed light on what motivated Sam. And that question—of what motivated him, what made him do what he did all his life—is the main puzzle you'll have to solve in this *magnum opus* of yours. I don't think anyone has fully figured out what gave Sam his relentless drive to obsessively make art."

"Go on," I said.

"This happened a few months or a year after we met. We were having a drink in the Cedar Tavern with other artists when the subject turned, as it often did, to the issues of 'philistine commercialism' and the 'inherent unfairness' of the art market, topics that inevitably led to a discussion of Jackson Pollock, whom most of us viewed alternately as either a god or a sellout, depending on our mood. Pollock annoyed the hell out of Sam. Still does, all these decades after Pollock's death.

" 'Why the hell should Pollock be in the Hamptons, living off Castelli,' Sam shouted to the barroom at large that evening, 'while we're sweating in the tenements? He does nothing but spill god-damn paint on canvas'."

" 'Actually,' our friend Daniel said, 'Jackson's method involves more thought and planning than you might imagine. He takes a good deal of time between colors to decide—' "

" 'Jesus Christ, Danny,' Sam interrupted, 'all the world needs is another Pollock apologist.' Then Sam slammed his glass down so hard it shattered, spraying Scotch and sharp fragments across the tabletop and onto the floor. 'And don't tell us about his so-called method. Thanks to Namuth's film and *Life* magazine, every middle-class idiot in America knows how that motherfucker works. That's what I mean about commercialism. Could you create art on command? For a fucking audience? It's not art—it's a circus, a scam'."

" 'That's not fair,' Daniel said quietly. 'Pollock's done something new, something uniquely his own, which is more than any of us can say.'

"Sam's face turned a horrible shade of magenta. That vein in his neck throbbed." Irv leaned his forehead on his fingertips as he recalled that night. "He picked up a jagged shard of glass and ran its point cleanly across the palm of his hand, making a bright red line. Then he slashed his palm from the other direction, creating a red X that turned into a pool of blood.

" 'Do you like it?' he said to Daniel. 'It's new and original. It's all mine.' He smiled as if possessed by something I hope I'll never understand. 'There's only one problem. It's not portable. To get the work you have to buy the artist, and I, unlike Pollock, am not for sale.'

"Sam wiped his hand on a cocktail napkin, folded the napkin over, then opened it and held the bloody thing up. 'Voila!' he crowed.

'A portable work of art. Fresh and original, a new goddamn methodology. The artist is a genius'."

"Daniel and I stared at Sam while the bartender, who had seen much worse in this establishment that catered to artists, calmly dropped a couple of Band-Aids and a glass of water on the table. I thanked him and cleaned Sam's palm, dipping the napkin in the water and gagging as I felt the depth of the wound.

"Daniel dropped a couple of dollars on the table and left.

" 'Stigmata,' Sam mumbled as I swabbed."

Irv stared at his own left palm, and fell silent.

"That's it?" I said after what a long time had passed. "That's the end of the story?"

Irv nodded, still looking at his hand.

"But you said this would tell me something about what made Sam tick. What am I supposed to learn from it?"

Irv looked up at me before shrugging and responding apologetically, "I don't know. Maybe that his art's in his blood? Maybe that it's his life? Maybe that the artist is the art?"

"Or maybe that he's insane," I said, knowing my response was meaner than necessary.

"Maybe," Irv replied. His eyelids drooped and his head hung down heavily, as if the telling alone had drained him. "There's one more thing you should know. That god-forsaken Bowery studio I told you about? It was Sam's home. He'd go there from the bar every night, sleep a couple of hours, work until morning, then head back to the bar where he'd hang out until it was time to open the place and start serving. All he ever spent money on was paint and canvas, and a couple of drinks when he couldn't get someone else to pick up the tab—that's how badly your father needed to paint."

***

Irv sat back in his cushioned wicker chair and stared at me, his eyes barely focusing. Then he closed them and massaged his temples. I'd never seen him look so old. "God, that was so long ago. Another world. I can't stand to think that that brash young man with so much promise, so much bravado, is the same person we saw out at Sag Harbor."

41

Judy Pomeranz

I flipped off the tape recorder and nodded. "Thanks, Irv," I said quietly. "We've done enough for today." I stood up to leave.

Irv pushed himself up out of his chair with some difficulty, walked me to the foyer, and helped me on with my coat. Then he took a folded piece of heavy ivory paper from the breast pocket of his camel jacket and handed it to me.

"I put together a list of a few people, mostly friends of Sam, who you might want to talk to."

I unfolded the page to find a neatly handwritten roster of names and phone numbers accompanied by notes indicating each person's relationship to Sam. A quick scan revealed not one of the names was familiar to me. I really didn't know my father.

Irv then turned to the satinwood chest that had stood in his foyer for as long as I could remember and pulled open the deep bottom drawer. He took out a key and a faded Thom McAn shoebox. He held the key out to me. "It's to his studio. He wanted you to have it."

I involuntarily backed away from the proffered gift. "Why?"

"Because you're his daughter," Irv said, as if it were that simple. "He loves you," he added quietly. "Or he did when he was capable of feeling."

"I don't believe that."

"Take it or leave it," Irv said wearily.

"The key or the statement?"

"Both. Sam told me a couple of years ago that you should have anything you wanted in the studio if anything happened to him." Irv cleared his throat. "I guess this counts as something happening."

"I still can't believe he'd—"

"Remember," Irv interrupted, "the estrangement was your idea, not Sam's. Don't forget how long and hard he tried to see you, talk with you, have some kind of relationship with you. He never stopped trying to—"

"To give me money," I said, finishing what I figured was Irv's thought. "I still get checks every month, and I still send them back unopened. I don't want to be bought off." I regretted how mean and petty the words sounded as soon as they left my mouth.

Irv started to respond, but I cut him off. "Can we drop it?"

"Of course. I'm sorry. I'm not here to make a case. I just want to help you with the book. And I'm just giving you the key because that's what Sam wanted."

"I know." I squeezed Irv's wiry, tightly muscled forearm through the soft cashmere coat sleeve. "And I'm not here to be a bitch, so I'll take the key with thanks."

Irv dropped it into my palm then stared at the old shoebox and touched its lid lightly before handing it to me. The cardboard smelled musty and felt cool, as if it had been in a cellar. "Some souvenirs of your mother."

I sat down in the Chippendale side chair next to the chest and lifted the lid. The box was filled with old photos, scraps of paper, scribbled notes, and carefully penned letters on yellowed stationary.

"She and I used to leave notes for each other on a beautiful little antique desk Sam installed for her in our Bowery Studio," Irv said. "She started it as a riff on the messages Sam and I scrawled on the walls, a practice she thought was insane." He smiled. "Your mother and I both loved literature, but we never had a chance to talk about it when Sam was around. You know—"

"Yes, I know." No one talked about much of anything but Sam when Sam was around.

"So, this was our way. These little notes. I saved all the ones she wrote, and found out years later that she'd saved mine too. She gave them to me weeks before she died."

Irv didn't take his eyes off the box, and I didn't know what to say.

"You've always looked exactly like her." Irv sank into the chair on the other side of the chest. "You're tiny like she was— you only weighed six pounds when you were born. And you had fine blonde hair that turned her coppery red by the time you were two. You did have Sam's blue eyes at first, but even those turned into her green ones. You were one hundred percent her baby, though you never had her gentle personality." A little smile crossed his face.

I wanted to protest but couldn't bear to break the spell.

"Your disposition was Sam's," he said. "You were born demanding—you always needed to be coddled and cajoled. We were all only too happy to accommodate. Even Sam spoiled you, in his way. He was awed by you."

"He had a funny way of showing it."

"I know you felt he neglected you."

"Not just me. He was crueler to my mother than he was to me."

Irv leaned forward and put his elbows on his knees; his clasped hands supported his chin. "There were days you don't remember, days when Sam was both mother *and* father to you."

"Oh, please, Irv. Don't exaggerate his goodness. I don't recall a day when he was even a remote facsimile of a father to me."

Irv looked up at the ceiling and seemed to ponder whether he should dignify my statement with a response. "There's so much you don't know," he finally said. "When Aurora came home from the hospital with you, she was ecstatic, utterly exuberant about you and her new role as your mother. But within days, she became overwhelmed by being entrusted with the care of a fully dependent little being. She became edgy, depressed, and ultimately frightened to the point of incapacity. She couldn't eat or sleep. She wouldn't touch you for fear you would break. None of us could talk her out of it, and she refused to see a doctor."

Irv gazed at the small English landscape on the opposite wall. "There were whole weeks when she wouldn't get out of bed. She would lie on her back, tears flowing down that beautiful, pale face, and she would weep without making a sound. I used to wash her hair to try to make her feel better."

"Jesus," I murmured. "Post-partum depression?"

"That was part of it, but she had a lot more going on, things that weren't so readily dealt with or treated back then."

"And you're telling me *Sam* took care of me?"

"He took care of both of you. Wilson and I helped as much as we could, but Sam did the heavy lifting. There were days when he didn't even touch a paintbrush, which might not seem like a big deal to you, but it was the ultimate sacrifice for him, one that spoke volumes about how he felt about you and your mother."

"Why have I never heard this before?"

"Because Sam didn't want you to feel insecure or unloved, or to think less of Aurora. He knew it wasn't her fault, and he knew she loved you desperately. He never wanted you to have any reason to think otherwise."

Chapter Five
The Muse

I decided to walk home from Irv's in the hope that the blast of cold air would clear my head and the locomotion would make me feel like I could walk away from everything I was involved in. I buttoned the top button of my heavy wool coat and wrapped my scarf around my neck a second time.

Irv's final revelation threatened to upset my simple ability to self-righteously detest my father, a construct upon which my entire adult life had been built. As much as I wanted to, I couldn't dismiss Irv's story about my mother or shake the unsettled feeling it gave me, because it resonated at a deep level. Hearing it coaxed a long-forgotten memory of my own to the surface.

As I rounded the corner onto Fifth Avenue at the top of Union Square, I recalled how, as I child, I had loved being sick. Fever, headache, sore throat, sweating, vomiting, chills, whatever. I welcomed it all. If I couldn't come by it honestly, I'd bring on symptoms by ingesting noxious substances, sticking my wrists under hot water, or walking outside without a coat. More often, I'd fake it, complaining dramatically of non-existent aches and pains.

I also loved being injured. I'd fall from my bike and scrape a knee, pull a door open into my forehead, or drop a book on my toe. I'd slit a finger with a kitchen knife, fall from a swing, or bump my head on the pavement. And I knew, even at that time, exactly why I did it; it was for the most classically Freudian of reasons.

I pulled my cashmere scarf more tightly around my neck and picked up my pace, shuddering at the thought of what Dr. Steinbrenner would have to say about these recollections.

My warmest memories of my father were rooted in times when my body was maimed or uncomfortable. He would rise to the occasion. He would carry his enormous bulk ever so softly, ever so quietly, ever so gently, into my bedroom. He would touch my forehead with his callused fingertips, press his chapped lips against my cheek in a feathery suggestion of a kiss. His eyes would be filled with concern, his speech soft and calm. "How's my princess?" he would whisper.

I would shrug my shoulders, believing that speaking would break the spell. For a moment, he was Robert Young and I lived in the world of *Father Knows Best*. I would act wearier than I felt; I would sigh and draw a forearm across my brow. I was a regular Sarah Bernhardt, but he never called me out on it or made fun of my drama.

"You gonna be okay, baby?" he would say.

I would look into his eyes, relishing that they were trained on me, alone.

I wanted the illness or injury to last forever, and I was a good enough actor that I eventually became known not as a fraud but as a "delicate" child.

Picking up my pace against the bracing air, I wondered why Sam had been so good with me only when I was sick or hurt, and seemed so neglectful when I was healthy. How odd it was—and unfair—that I had forgotten those moments of Sam's uncharacteristic tenderness, choosing instead to focus on the all the other times when he didn't seem to care if I lived or died. And how interesting to learn that Sam had also taken care of my mother when she was sick. Perhaps that's why she too was considered "delicate" of constitution.

***

By the time I got home, my nose was red, my cheeks were numb, and my hands felt frostbitten. Fall was turning quickly to winter. I was exhausted from the cold and the long walk, which had not served to get Sam out of my system but had only given me time to obsess about what Irv had told me.

I tossed my coat, scarf, and gloves onto the living room sofa, went to the kitchen to put up a pot of coffee, and sat at the small oak kitchen table, where I furiously typed notes. When I needed to get my ideas down before they disappeared, and elegance of expression was not an issue, my treasured Montegrappa pen was too slow.

The conversation with Irv had convinced me that I would have to make my mother a major piece of the framework I was building to analyze the life of Sam, no matter how painful it might be. Their lives were inextricably intertwined, and they had defined each other.

I poured my stream-of-consciousness memories into the computer:

My mother's name was Aurora. She was the opposite of my father in nearly every respect. She was soft-spoken and timid, built like a wisp, so thin she seemed breakable. When I first gained a crude knowledge of the logistics of sex, I had nightmares of her breaking in half or being crushed under the weight of my enormous father.

She died when I was nine.

I understand that children commonly canonize parents who die young, but my mother really was a saint, a martyr to my father's holy image. Everyone loved her, but no one noticed her when Sam was around. Not even me.

Before she married, she wrote poetry. She also wrote profiles, essays, articles, and reviews. Those paid the bills. But it was poetry she loved.

After she died, Irv showed me her early poems. They were about nature, art, and solitude—the last being a favorite subject of hers. And they were as delicate as she was, but with an inner strength and generosity of spirit I'd like to think attracted my father, though it was more likely her looks that initially got his attention. Sam was a sucker for beautiful women, and had little use for others.

Sam and Aurora met when she was writing an article on emerging artists for Art Scene *magazine. She had heard about Sam and Irv from a mutual friend and had come to the Bowery to see their shared studio and their work. Shortly after she died, Irv told me the whole story.*

He said Sam fell for my mother as soon as she walked in the door. Although she was almost twenty, she looked fifteen, with her long red hair flowing loose and a shapeless dress of sea green, gauzy fabric covering her thin frame. She smelled of lilies of the valley, and wore sandals that made her look like a nymph from Greek mythology. A willowy being plucked right out of a pre-Raphaelite painting, she seemed utterly out of place in the graffitied, litter-strewn studio. According to Irv, every man who met her—himself included—fell in love and wanted to wrap her in soft, heavy layers of protection, though once she opened her mouth, it became clear that she was as bright and marvelously articulate as she was beautiful.

Irv gave me a copy of the article she wrote following that visit, and he laughed at how tentative she was with regard to his painting. I've read it so many times, I still remember the quotes:

"While Irving Golden's work is daring and worth keeping an eye on, it has the sharp charge an artist can rarely sustain over time. I fear his artistic career may not live up to his youthful promise."

As cautious as she was with regard to Irv, she was lavish in her praise of Sam's work, many years before anyone else noticed him:

"Sam Jackson's paintings have a flash of sheer brilliance, an indefinable yet indefatigable quality that spiritually disarms the viewer. One doesn't merely look at these paintings, one falls completely under their spell. Though they are abstract, they speak clearly and directly, communicating something at once unknowable and irresistible. This largely self-trained, unheralded artist is a force to be reckoned with."

According to modern mythology, akin to revisionist history, as soon as Sam read her article, he declared he was going to marry her.

***

I stopped writing and pondered a question so obvious I wondered why it had never occurred to me before: What had my mother seen in Sam? It was easy to understand, given her beauty and the attention she lavished on him, why he would have been attracted to her, but what about the other half of the equation? After Sam made his mark—and, not incidentally, his money—he had his choice of beautiful women. That I understood: the obvious charms of money and fame and power. But what had attracted Aurora to this gruff, bluff, wannabe artist, so many years before all that?

I recalled what Irv had said about the magnetism exuded by a person like Sam, who knew where he belonged in the world. That must have been a powerful pull for someone like my mother, who was never sure of her own place. Though she had everything going for her, she was always diffident. Not afraid, but timid. Perhaps being in Sam's orbit gave her a sense of purpose, a feeling that she shared in the grand mission he had defined for himself. And maybe that was enough for her. For a while.

I needed to know more. Speculation wouldn't cut it for a serious biography. If I was going to engage in this crazy enterprise, I had to do it right. To understand Sam, I needed to know what she had seen in him back then.

So, on a wing and a prayer, figuring this is what biographers were supposed to do, I picked up the phone and dialed *Art Scene* magazine. After being passed from person to person and office to office, I finally hit upon an editor who had been there long enough to have known my mother. His name was Jake Parinsky, and he too had been a young reviewer at the time.

"I've heard all about you," Parinsky said. "You were one of your mother's favorite topics of conversation." His voice was pleasant, gravelly, and grandfatherly.

"So, you stayed in touch with her after she left the magazine?" I asked.

"In a limited way."

"When did she leave?"

"I don't recall the year, but it was shortly after she met your dad."

"Why?"

"We all wondered. She was an amazing critic. Damned clever, insightful, had a great eye and a rare ability to translate that into prose. Given a few more years of staff experience, she could have worked for any magazine in the country."

"So, what happened?"

He paused; it sounded like he was puffing on a pipe. "Why are you asking now, after all this time?"

"I've been asked to write my father's biography, and there's a lot I don't know about him and my mother."

"A biography, eh? That should be juicy," he said in as kind a way as those words could be uttered. "You're brave to undertake that."

"I don't know about that," I said curtly, not wanting to revisit my decision, "but I'm doing it. So, why did my mother leave the magazine?"

"Well," he said, stretching the word out, pausing for thought. "She never told us, but I don't think your dad wanted her to work. He didn't mind if she freelanced from home—they needed the money. But he wanted her around, where he could see her, if you know what I mean."

"I'm not sure I do. Was he jealous of her being with other people, or sexist about women working?"

"I don't think so," he said slowly, as if weighing his words. "No, not exactly either of those. He just needed to have her there," he said simply. "She was his muse."

I laughed at the quaint notion. "His muse?"

"I got to know Sam a little, through your mother, and he was dependent on her. He worshiped her."

"He had an odd way of showing it," I blurted out.

"I couldn't agree more," Jake said. "He was always full of bullshit and bluster, he acted more self-assured than anyone in the city of New York, but he needed that woman. After he met her, his work changed dramatically. Look at the before and after paintings and see if you agree. There was roughness before—there was a bravado and flashiness—but no subtlety, no lyricism. After he met Aurora, it all changed. It changed again after he lost her, but by then it didn't matter—he was established."

"Did he ever acknowledge his debt to her?"

"I doubt it." Jake chuckled. "But it was there, and he knew it. He needed her around to do his best work." I could hear him puffing on the pipe again. "Do you have time for a story?"

"Of course."

"I was in their neighborhood one afternoon, and dropped in unannounced to see if your mother wanted to go out for a cup of tea. This was after they had moved into that dreadful brownstone in the Village, the one with the studio all the way upstairs. I got no answer when I pounded on the door, but I heard music coming from the studio windows, so I let myself in and went on up. I found your mother working at the little rolltop desk she had up there. Do you remember it?"

"Yes."

"It was a gift from Sam, she told me. A pretty little piece of furniture. She was sitting there working on an article or a poem, or maybe paying bills. And Sam was painting. Neither one noticed when I came in, so I observed the scene. It was as if Sam was painting your mother, as if she was his model. He would look back and forth between her and his canvas, as an artist does when he's painting a portrait. But this was no portrait, not even an arguably abstracted one. Still, he kept looking at her."

"How did she react?"

"She seemed not to notice," Parinsky said. "I finally said hello, and she gave me a kiss on the cheek, a peck so damn chaste she might have been my sister. Sam ignored me and kept working. I asked her if she'd like to take a break and have a cup of tea. She said she would, very much. But your father—who I didn't even think was tuned in on the conversation—said he needed her in the studio."

"What did she say?"

"Not a word. While Sam's tone of voice was benign, his look didn't leave room for discussion. It wasn't an angry look, or frightening. It was severe determination with an edge of desperation."

Jake paused, and I heard the puffing again. "Then he looked away from Aurora and went back to his painting, confident he'd made his point. Your mother said maybe we could do it some other time and I agreed. I was so damn uncomfortable I couldn't wait to get the hell out of there. Those few moments made such an impression on me that I never contacted her again. We only spoke when she took the initiative to get in touch with me, which was infrequently, and only much later, after Sam was famous and otherwise occupied much of the time."

"Did she ever say how she felt about her marriage or her role in it?" I tried to phrase the question as an objective biographer might, rather than as a curious daughter or voyeur.

"Never. She would talk on and on about Sam's work and how brilliant he was, but she never revealed anything personal about their relationship, and I wasn't about to ask."

Judy Pomeranz

Chapter Six
Correspondents

I thanked Jake Parinsky for being so forthcoming, hung up the phone, and poured myself another cup of coffee. I wished, as I almost never did, that I had someone to talk to.

I was cordial to my neighbors and to the people I worked with on freelance projects, and I had lunch or went to the movies with an acquaintance occasionally, but I had never sought or cultivated friendships. For as long as I could remember, my only confidants had been Irv, Wilson, and Dr. Steinbrenner, and that had been enough. I preferred being alone.

But now I wanted someone to bounce all this strange new information off of, someone uninvolved who didn't know my past or my future, someone reasonable and objective who could tell me what was normal, what was troublesome, and what was nuts. I wanted to talk with someone who cared about what I had to say, but didn't have to, like a perfectly attentive airplane seatmate.

Before the conversation with Parinsky, it had never occurred to me that my own existence mirrored my mother's. She had had me, Irv, Wilson, and my father in her life. Beyond the three of us, I knew of no one to whom she was close, not even her sister, whom I met only twice because my father didn't like having her around. I suppose he was jealous of her.

My mother had always put on a good show for Sam's friends and, later on, for his army of admirers. She had entertained all comers, was quietly charming at gallery openings, and hosted dinners as required by the odd conventions of the upper class Bohemia in which we eventually resided. But I never knew her to go out with the girls, have friends for coffee, chat on the phone, or do any of the things June Cleaver or Donna Reed did with their pals.

The talks with Irv and Parinsky, and my own recollections, left me physically and emotionally drained. My body wanted nothing more than to collapse into bed and remain there for the foreseeable future. But something perverse drew me to the shoebox Irv had given me, the one he'd said contained "souvenirs of your mother."

I pulled the box out of the *Dean and Deluca* bag Irv had put it in for my walk home, set it on the kitchen table, and lifted the lid. On top of the pile of papers inside was a creased black-and-white photo from which youthful versions of my parents and Wilson stared out at me. My mother wore dark shorts and a light sleeveless shirt; her long hair was pulled back into a ponytail. She stood between my father and Wilson, mugging for the camera in a forced, manic effort to appear jolly. Wilson, in khakis and a polo shirt, grinned broadly as he draped his arm across my mother's thin shoulder. My father, in his trademark jeans and tee shirt, stood slightly off to the side, looking at the camera but seeming perplexed or preoccupied. Behind them all, I could make out a rickety frame cottage on a lake.

Beneath that picture was another taken on the same lake. In the foreground, my mother smiled at Irv, who helped her out of a rowboat onto a dock. She wore the same clothes as in the first picture, but her hair fell loosely around her shoulders and her smile was not forced, but sweet and relaxed. Irv held two bamboo fishing poles in one hand and my mother's elbow in the other. I placed the two photos side-by-side on the table, and stared at them, fascinated by how different my mother looked in these two shots apparently taken on the same day.

Then I pulled from the box a sheaf of small sheets and scraps of paper bound together with a red ribbon. These were the notes Irv and Aurora had left for each other in the old Bowery studio. I untied the ribbon and unfolded the top sheet, a dull coral-colored piece of paper that had a rough top edge, as if it had been torn from a pad.

Irv, it said in my mother's elegant, spidery, left-slanting handwriting, *I finished de Profundis and found it saddening, maddening, beautiful, terrible, and so perfectly articulate. I think Oscar Wilde might be the most sensitive man who ever lived.*

Below that was a creamy note card covered with Irv's small, neat writing: *My dear Aurora, Wilde's a clever fellow, but he's a whiner in that monstrous bit of self-serving fluff. Articulate, yes, and sometimes wise. But he wore out with age. He was so much better as a young man. If you want to talk about a gay writer who aged gracefully, how about James Baldwin?*

Then, on a scrap of white paper: *Irv dear, we can agree on something. I adored <u>Notes of a Native Son</u>. Did you read <u>Giovanni's Room</u>? Unbearably sad. Perfectly expressive.*

Followed by another heavy, ivory card: *Aurora, why are you so drawn to sadness, even melodrama? I love Baldwin but G.R. was over the top. By the way, have you and Sam seen the new Rothko show at Smallerts Gallery?*

In reply on a pink notecard: *The Rothko exhibit is lovely. We went last week. Those extraordinary veils of color and feathery edges make the shapes float off the wall. But Sam declared it "phony, formulaic pap."*

And an ivory card: *Speaking of phony, my dear, what do you think of these new poets, Koch and O'Hara? Words, words, and words for the sake of words. What is it all about?*

Then on a piece of wide-ruled notebook paper: *Irv, you philistine! Koch and O'Hara are the voices of today. They throw words at you, and freaky images, but no more than modern life throws stimuli at you. Maybe both make sense, maybe neither does, but it doesn't matter because it's all real, as real as abstract art. Go with the music of it, the craziness of it. That's hard for you because you're so stiff, but I adore you anyway.*

The final note in the pile, written on an otherwise empty ivory card said simply: *And I you.*

I dumped my coffee in the sink and poured myself a Scotch, then I sat down and reread the notes, one by one, slowly, thinking about each word and the two remarkable people who had written them. I brushed a tear off my cheek, closed my eyes and took a deep breath. I wanted desperately to dive into these words and thoughts and soak them in, but feared I might never emerge. I wanted to think about Irv and my mother, not my father.

I finally restacked the notes in the order in which I had found them, tied the faded red ribbon back around them, took the last sip of my drink, and got ready to crawl into bed, feeling melancholy about the lost potential of wasted lives, but oddly better about the world.

Judy Pomeranz

Chapter Seven
The Artist's Models

I awoke early the next morning, anxious to return to my work. I threw on my old terrycloth bathrobe, brewed a big pot of Jamaica Blue Mountain coffee, picked up the newspaper outside my door, and concentrated on the front page while filling my system with caffeine. This had long been my morning ritual, one that was so soothing I believed it essential to maintaining my equilibrium. Besides, I'd been told that freelancers needed to beware of starting work before breakfast, that there lay the road toward letting work take over their lives.

But the *Times* couldn't compete today with the Thom McAn box that was calling to me. So I pushed aside the newspaper, lifted the lid of the shoebox I had left on the kitchen table, and dumped out the contents. A pale blue envelope caught my eye. It was addressed, in my mother's writing, to Irv. Unlike the pile of notes I had read the night before, this was an actual letter, complete with street number and canceled stamp. The return address revealed it had been sent after my mother and father had moved into the brownstone, so Sam and Irv's shared Bowery Studio would have been a thing of the past.

I took the thin blue sheet of stationary from the envelope and read:

Dear Irv,

I hope it's a girl. Though I will adore any creature who happens to pop out, I would love to have a little female compatriot. Sam says he'll take whatever comes, and that's a healthier attitude, so I haven't told him I have a preference.

What do you think? (Be careful how you answer; when Wilson told me he's betting on twins, I banished him from the apartment for the duration.) More important than her sex, I hope she has her godfather's sweet and mellow temperament instead of my neuroses or Sam's bluster.

I don't agree with you that Dr. Spock is an idiot (though I do agree that Camus might do me as much good). I need all the help I can get. I'm so scared I'll mess this baby up. Sam's not concerned… he says it's all about instinct and that I'm being paranoid, which is no doubt the case. But I wonder if we're up to this. It's a human being, for God's sake, and I've never even been good with pets.

I've become so attached to this mysterious, magical child I have yet to meet that the responsibility feels very, very heavy. As my love grows, so does my fear. Tell me you'll help me with this. Promise me, Irv, that you'll spend time with this baby and help us make her into a happy, sane little being.

Hugs to you and Wilson,
Aurora

It was unnerving to see myself referred to as a heavy burden, as disturbing as listening to Irv relate the story of my mother's post-partum depression. Having believed so fervently and for so long that my father was the singular evil figure who had driven my mother to illness and to a much-too-early death, the notion that I might have been partly to blame was not only surprising, but unsettling. What was not surprising was that she, like I, had turned to Irv in her moments of distress. Not to Sam.

I put the thin blue page back into its envelope. How sad it was that my mother and Irv had been compelled to communicate through notes and letters. I understood from firsthand experience that no one talked about anything serious or personal in Sam's presence, if it did not involve Sam himself. And, as I had confirmed in my conversation with Jake Parinsky, Aurora spent little time outside of Sam's presence.

The notes were better than nothing as a means of communication and intellectual release. Irv must have cherished them as much as she, to have held onto them for all these years.

***

Like Proust's Madeleines, the letters stirred up my own long-repressed memories of life in our gritty little brownstone, the decrepit place in the Village we called home until I was eight.

Our fourth-floor, walk-up apartment consisted of two minuscule bedrooms; a Pullman kitchen; a small but well-lit living room; and a bathroom with pale green, cracked tile on the walls and a claw-foot bathtub that took up most of the floor space. My mother had made it homey. She had painted my bedroom ceiling deep blue and stenciled on stars. She had papered the living room with a horrid cabbage-rose print even she admitted was a mistake. She had scrubbed the permanently stained, green linoleum on the kitchen floor so hard it peeled. And she had hung the bedroom windows with ecru lace curtains my father said made us look like "goddam Irish immigrants."

Even Sam had contributed to the décor. One memorable night, he came home staggeringly drunk from the Cedar Tavern and painted wild and amazing jungle creatures all over my bedroom walls, while I looked on from my bed in stunned delight and my mother stood paralyzed at the bedroom door.

Sam's studio was on the fifth floor, which he referred to as "the penthouse." Due to the house's pitched roof, he could only stand upright in the center, but a couple of dormer windows and a skylight made it a decent place to work. The studio held great intrigue for me because my father could be found there whenever he was at home, and because magical things were produced there. But it was most intriguing because it was off-limits to me. On the rare occasions when I was granted entry, I adored not only watching him work but surveying the cluttered, filthy mess, for no one was allowed to touch anything in his space, not even to clean.

I recall coming home from school one day to an unusually quiet apartment. I was six. I went to the kitchen, where my mother usually waited for me, but she wasn't there. I grabbed an apple and looked for her in the living room and bedrooms. I called out to her, but got no response. Retracing my steps through the whole apartment, I neither saw nor heard anything until I reached the stairway to Sam's studio. From there, I heard a low moan that seemed to come from some haunted or animalistic version of my mother. The eerie sound was followed immediately by my father's booming voice.

"Just stay put and keep quiet."

I'd known my father to be self-involved, arrogant, bullyish, and harsh, but I'd never before heard such frightening anger seething in his voice.

Though I knew better than to enter the sanctum without being invited, I couldn't help following the sounds. I crept halfway up the narrow staircase as quietly as I could. The studio door was ajar but no sounds now emanated from within, other than those made by a brush slashing roughly across canvas. I moved softly up the last few steps, placing my feet carefully on the treads so as not to cause any creaks. I peered into the studio and saw my mother sitting on the hard, cold wooden floor. Completely naked.

Her legs were spread open in front of her, and she leaned back on her hands with her head tilted up so that her red hair fell back almost to her waist. Tears stained her face, which I saw only from the side. She looked so exposed in that horribly open position I had to fight to keep from crying along with her.

My father stood in front of a gigantic canvas. He squirted paint from a tube directly onto the stretched cloth, then slathered it violently with his brush.

I was so stunned by the scene that I forgot the prohibition, stepped into the room, and watched as my father pushed his loaded brush with such a bold energy I could hardly bear the contrast between his strength and her vulnerability. I stood there watching for a minute before my father's eyes riveted on me.

I couldn't move. I wanted to run, to bound down the steps in one leap, head out the front door, and never come back, but I stood immobile as I waited for the inevitable rebuke which I was sure would be accompanied by corporal punishment.

"Hey, Dawn," my father said cheerfully, "how was school?"

My mother slammed her legs together, pulled a long, thin arm across her breasts, and turned toward me. She tried to smile but it didn't work. Instead she looked like she was going to be sick.

I didn't answer, but simply watched as her legs snapped into her torso as if pulled by external force, her arms clamped around her legs, and her head tucked into her knees in a perfect fetal position. My mother turned into a ball.

"Want to see the picture I'm painting of your mom?" Sam seemed unaware of anything untoward in this scene.

I nodded, but stayed where I was.

"Come on over."

I walked slowly toward my father, but kept my eyes on my mother, hoping she was still somewhere in that ball.

"You didn't tell me how school was," Sam said.

"Fine," I whispered.

When I got within arms length, he lifted me up and we stood in front of the canvas. "So, what do you think?"

Heavy swirls of fleshy tones covered the surface. They were punctuated by incised and painted red slits from which emerged scores of wispy, reddish-brown lines.

"Where's mommy?" I asked.

"All over the canvas, baby. This is her portrait."

"It doesn't look like her," I ventured cautiously, hoping he wouldn't take it as a criticism.

"It's a different kind of portrait. I'm painting her as I see her."

"Oh." I looked at my mother who was still wrapped in a ball. "Mommy?"

No response.

"What's wrong with her?" I asked.

"Nothing, baby, she's just resting," Sam replied lightly. "It's hard work being my model."

"Does she like the picture?"

"She hasn't seen it yet."

"Why?"

"I won't let her look at it until it's finished. Only you and I have seen it. It's our secret."

While I was thrilled to think that we shared a confidence, I felt like a traitor to my mother. "When will it be finished?"

"When it's done, we'll know it."

"Is she okay?"

"I told you, Dawn, she's fine." He spoke impatiently, and I could tell that was the last question he would answer with grace. "Now, go on downstairs. She'll be right down."

I moved toward the steps, but turned and took one last look at the scene I was leaving. Sam had gone back to his painting; Aurora remained wrapped up in herself. No one seemed to notice I was still there.

As I walked down the steps, I heard my father's voice. "Get the hell up off the floor, Aurora, and take care of your kid."

I sat at the kitchen table and stared out the window, idly polishing the apple for which I now had no appetite. I looked down at an old, gray-haired woman sitting on a front stoop, two boys chasing a ball down the street, and a hunched-over rabbi strolling along the sidewalk. I wished I was anywhere out there. Anywhere but here.

"Hi sweetie." My mother spoke in a fuzzy voice as she walked into the kitchen wearing her faded red silk bathrobe. Her eyes were out of focus and her gait was labored; she walked as if she was as heavy as Sam.

"How was school?" she asked in a dull monotone.

"Fine."

I wanted to ask why she'd been crying. I wanted to understand what I'd seen. I wanted to cry. I wanted to scream. But I said nothing, and she walked on through the kitchen and into her bedroom.

We never talked about what had gone on upstairs. Never. I knew better. But I have seen that painting many times since. It now hangs in the Museum of Modern Art under the title, "Portrait of a Whore."

***

It was not long after that day in the studio that I began to model for my father.

One Saturday morning, before my mother woke up, I was watching cartoons and munching on dry Cheerios when my father appeared in the living room.

"What's up, angel?"

I loved it when he called me that. That's when he seemed most like Robert Young.

"Just watching cartoons," I said, hoping he'd join me.

"Want to help me in the studio?"

"Really?" I was afraid to get too excited, in case I had misunderstood.

"Really," he said with one of those big smiles. "Come on."

And so, still clutching my bowl of cereal, I padded up the stairs behind him. When we got to the top, he took my hand and walked me over to his big, paint-spattered recliner. He sat me down and told me to flip my legs over the chair's arm, which I did.

"Now look up at me over your knees," he said.

Which I did.

He took a fake dahlia and stuck it behind my right ear, then stood back to observe the scene before opening the top two snaps of my pink flannel pajamas and pulling the neckline open far enough to expose most of one shoulder.

"Perfect," he said. "Hold it right there."

And I did.

Thus began our Saturday morning ritual. I adored posing for him, even when my limbs would tingle and my neck grow stiff from holding positions too long. I loved being the center of his attention, and I loved the way he manipulated me. He would move an arm or a leg, tilt my head just so, bend a finger or adjust a foot. He would pull a pant leg up, yank a sleeve down, remove a hairpin, a bracelet, or a blouse. He would dress me in costumes, put fruit on my head, and glue pearls to my ear lobes. Once he even put a red wax tongue in my mouth.

Thinking back on it from this distance, it all seems bizarre, even Nabokovian, though he never did anything really inappropriate. For me, these sessions were all about being entirely his, the center of his world, for a few ethereal moments. For him, it was about the work. It was always about the work. On some level, I understood, even then, that I could just as well have been a landscape or a bowl of fruit.

Judy Pomeranz

Chapter Eight
Making It

The days when I had craved my father's attention and lived for the privilege of entering that old Greenwich Village studio were ancient history. I now stood across the street from the building in SoHo which housed his current studio, a four-story, iron-façade structure with a cornerstone bearing the date "1889." I stared at the key Irv had given me. I was not sure I had the fortitude to visit this place I'd seen only in a PBS special, but an exploration was part of the deal I'd bought into in agreeing to write the biography, so I threw back my shoulders with feigned confidence, and approached the building as if I belonged there.

The ground floor housed an upscale Italian restaurant from which a heavy garlic smell emanated, cutting the chilly late-morning air. I unlocked the door adjacent to the restaurant entrance and found myself in a narrow, dark entryway facing a wrought-iron cage elevator, into which I stepped, with trepidation.

The heavy doors clanged shut behind me, making me feel like a death row inmate, and the elevator slowly climbed to the second floor. It groaned to a stop, the cage opened, and I stepped out, dazzled by one huge, open, sunlit space punctuated only by graceful, white-painted iron pillars and a circular iron staircase. The walls were white, and the windows along the front façade were twelve feet high, cut into eighteen-foot walls. Large, unfinished paintings were propped up in a long row against one wall; smaller ones stood on easels. Sleek maple tables held hundreds of compulsively arranged paint tubes, as well as palettes, oils, brushes, pencils, and knives. Sky-high bookcases crammed with art tomes lined an entire wall.

It was all astonishingly pristine. I knew my father now had an army of assistants, but I wouldn't have thought anyone could bring order to his working life. Of course, I didn't know how long it had been since he had actually worked here himself.

I wound my way up the spiral steps to the second level, where I found something more in keeping with what I had expected. It was a vastly larger and far more costly version of what I remembered from my childhood. The downstairs must have been for show and for assistants. This, I had no doubt, was where my father had done his work.

Here was the chaos I knew so well. The paint spatters, the mess of mangled tubes, the tangle of crusty brushes and rusted palette knives scattered across flimsy metal tables. Yes, it was enormous, brilliantly lit, white, and glorious, and God knows it was expensive, but, in all important respects, it was that little garret in the Village.

It was also a case of eerily suspended animation. But for the dryness of the paint on the palette, Sam might have just stepped away for a break.

Resisting the urge to lay my hands on these tools of the trade that had for so long been off-limits to me, I climbed the last circular flight to the top floor, where the ceilings were lower, the space more intimate. A sofa and three cushy easy chairs formed a pleasant grouping in one bright corner, but the rest of the space was devoted to storage.

Finished, signed paintings, propped upright and stacked five or six deep, occupied all available wall space. Works on paper lay stacked in wire bins, separated by tissue and heavy poster board that protected them and kept them flat. Sketchbooks filled maple bookcases, and one hidden, partitioned-off area housed semi-figurative wax sculptures, an art form I never even knew my father had worked in.

I wandered around this upper floor for an hour, flipping through and gazing at scores of paintings that spanned decades and myriad stylistic periods. The one common element they shared was energy. Most were abstract, some vaguely figurative, but all bore the mark of Sam's high-impact style and personality; each was overwhelming and irresistible.

As I was finishing my circuit of the upper floor, I came across two paintings that brought me to an abrupt stop. Two paintings as familiar as my signature. Two paintings I thought I would never see again.

They were tucked away near the wax sculptures, all by themselves. They were not hidden in piles, like the others, nor were they out on display. Each was simply propped up against a wall that was plainly visible from the little sitting area. Was that placement intentional, or chance? Did my father like to sit and look at these?

On the right-hand side was *Window on the World*, the painting that bore my handprint, a work created long before Sam Jackson became **Sam Jackson**, the work that had provoked my father to declare me, at age five, a genius. On the left was his first Cutaway painting, entitled *Slay it Again, Sam*. I recalled reading a *New York Times* report some years ago that Sam had spent millions of dollars buying that painting back for himself at auction.

So much of my childhood was contained in these two paintings.

***

Irv had brought the gallery owner to our home one afternoon not long after my father completed the picture that bore my handprint. I knew the man was important because of the way my mother, dressed up in a breezy pink cotton dress and clean white sandals, greeted him with ceremony and an evident case of nerves. Only much later would I understand why she was so nervous, that this man possessed the power to give my father a real show, to pluck him from the vast pool of unknown artists and expose him to the public.

"It's a pleasure to meet you," my mother said to the man, who wore a crisp gray suit and red tie, and carried himself with great authority.

"The pleasure is mine," he said formally and without a smile, but I could see admiration in the way he looked at her.

"Sam's upstairs," she said.

The man nodded, then looked in my direction but didn't acknowledge me.

"Let's go on up, Adrian" Irv said. "You're going to like what you see."

So, the man's name was Adrian. I remember thinking it was a peculiar name for a man, since my ballet teacher was called Mademoiselle Adrianne.

The three adults walked up the steep flight of wooden steps to the studio; I trailed along behind, having been neither encouraged to join them nor prohibited from it.

"Sam," Irv said when we arrived in the studio to find my father in the midst of work on an almost blank canvas, "this is Adrian Stapleton of the Stapleton Gallery."

Sam barely acknowledged the man's presence with a nod, keeping his eyes on his work.

"Sam and I are so pleased you took the time to stop by," my mother said more loudly than usual, as if delivering a message to my father. "Aren't we, Sam?"

Again he nodded, and, after a dramatic flourish of green paint, stuck his brush head-up in a coffee can, tossed his palette onto a paint-spattered metal table, and came over to shake hands with our visitor, who seemed less than thrilled at taking Sam's dirty hand in his own clean, manicured one.

Irv, who was also dressed in a gray suit, directed Adrian Stapleton's attention to a painting my godfather loved. It was called, for reasons beyond me, *Washerwoman Reading Euripides*. Featuring an off-center mass of sky blue surrounded by gradations of cream and white, it was an unusually peaceful picture, easy to look at.

"It's quite ethereal, isn't it?" Irv said.

Mr. Adrian Stapleton looked at it but didn't respond.

"Take a look at this one," Sam said abruptly. He took Stapleton by the elbow and led him to the canvas that featured my handprint. "What do you think about this? My assistant here helped me make it." He tousled my hair, a gesture that seemed staged, since it was hardly common. "It's called *Window on the World*."

Mr. Stapleton looked at it. I watched his eyes travel across the canvas, then up and down. None of us spoke or moved. I doubt that anyone even drew a breath.

"It's good," Mr. Stapleton finally pronounced. "Very good. This is the real thing."

"You think?" Sam said.

The gallery owner nodded without looking away from the picture. "It's bold, it's got guts, but it's not overwhelmed by those qualities. It's got soul, sweetness." Each phrase came out slowly, cautiously. "It's very moving."

"You like the handprint?" Sam said with a broad smile.

"I do. It's a great riff on Pollock." Stapleton's face betrayed a hint of a grin. "A nice touch."

"What do you mean, riff on Pollock?" Sam said harshly.

I recognized the look on my father's face.

"A nice play on *Lavender Mist*," Stapleton said. "It's clever the way you refer to the handprints he put in the upper corners of that work."

Sam's face turned red; my mother's turned white.

"Sam, he didn't mean—" Irv began. But that's as far as he got.

"This has nothing to do with Pollock," Sam shouted. "Why the hell does everything come back to him? I've never seen any god-damn *Lavender Mist*, and if I did, I wouldn't copy it."

"I didn't say you'd copied it," Mr. Stapleton said quickly. "I meant I could see your inspiration. That's not a bad thing. I admire clever appropriations and variations on a theme. Homages, you know, part of the great tradition of art history. I did not intend it as a criticism."

Instead of watching him explode, as I had expected, we all watched Sam implode. His face flushed, his teeth ground audibly, and his eyes flamed as he picked up a tube of brown paint and squeezed a large, mushy pile onto the lower left corner of the canvas. Then he smeared it with his palm over my handprint, obliterating the print entirely. My eyes filled with tears as I saw my work of "genius" become a mud puddle. In a final dramatic gesture, Sam dragged his filthy, paint-covered hand diagonally across the whole canvas.

"There," he said, turning to face Mr. Adrian Stapleton, "I believe I've taken care of any possibility this might be deemed derivative."

He set the paint tube back down on the little table and walked out of the studio. I still remember the sound of his heavy boots on the steps as he bounded down the four flights to street level. I also remember the silence that prevailed in the studio as we all stared at the defiled painting and understood—yes, even I understood—that my father was possessed by a self-destructive demon that would, absent a miracle, forever prevent him from assuming his rightful position in the pantheon of art history.

∗∗∗

The miracle in question came a few years later and resulted in the painting that stood next to *Window on the World* here in Sam's SoHo studio. *Slay it Again, Sam* was a landmark work which came into being when I was six years old. This painting changed everything for us.

I've always liked to think that the story of this painting began the day I came home from school carrying an art project of which I was inordinately proud.

"Look what I did today," I said to my mother, running into her bedroom, where I often found her writing in her journal. I yanked the book bag off my back, pulled out the art project, and held it up for her to admire. "Mr. Simons said mine was the best in the class."

Mother scrutinized my masterpiece quietly for a moment before declaring, "it's beautiful, sweetie."

"Do you think Daddy will like it?" Since he was harder to please, his approval meant proportionately more.

"Of course he will. How could he not?" As she spoke, my mother's eyes traveled back to the open page of her journal, as if she longed to get back to it.

"See, first we colored this paper with lots of crayons." I held up the page and pointed. "Just colors. No shapes or anything."

She nodded.

"Then we took black crayons and covered up all the colors. See?"

"I see."

"So, for a while it was all black. But we knew there were colors underneath."

"Sometimes that happens in life," my mother said absently. "Sometimes it looks black but you know there are colors underneath."

I dismissed her statement and continued. "Then we took sharp things and scraped away the black. Mr. Simons said we could use the wrong end of a brush for a skinny line, or our fingernails or a ruler for a fatter one, or a scissors for in-between-size lines. I mostly used my fingernail." I held it up to show off the black still embedded under it. "When we scraped away the black, the colors came popping back out. It was like magic."

"Very magical," Mother said dreamily, "and very beautiful." She kissed the top of my head. "Just like you."

But I wasn't finished. "See, here I scraped away the black in the shape of a sunshine, and the colors underneath look like the sunrise.

Don't they?" I pointed to the image in question. "Mr. Simons said it was clever of me to make a dawn because it was like signing my name without really signing it. Like some guy used to sign his paintings with a butterfly instead of his name."

"Whistler," my mother said softly, her eyes fixed on the journal. "Why don't you tape your picture up in Daddy's studio so he'll see it when he gets back from Uncle Irv's. He'll be so proud of you."

So, I did just that. But my father never said a word about it. Not ever.

***

Not even nine months later—just long enough for gestation—when Sam's first one-man show opened at the Gavalia Gallery on East Fifty-Seventh Street to rave reviews. Critics from publications as diverse as *The Partisan Review* and *The New York Times* hailed the exhibition and "Sam Jackson's fabulous new 'cutaway' style" as a stunning highlight of the season:
Completely original!
Moving, compelling, thought provoking!
A perfect marriage of aesthetics and message.
A bold, knock-your-socks-off style.
Sam Jackson is here to stay.
And indeed he was. Suddenly, the critics who had ignored him for decades not only noticed but loved my father. So did the gallery owners and collectors. With that show, he became the wave to ride. Just like that. When Sam finally leapt, he leapt big, directly from the slagheap into the stratosphere.

Unbeatable, said the *Washington Post*.

That he was. By the end of the show's first week, eight of the ten large works on display sported red dots, and reporters of all stripes begged for face time.

One prominent journalist, who insisted on interviewing my father at home, was so delighted by our hovel's "romantic Bohemianism" (read, poverty) that he asked to photograph not only the artist but also his "beautiful family" on the living room sofa, in front of the first cutaway, *Slay it Again, Sam,* which he had borrowed from the gallery for the purpose. And that is how it came to pass that I was in attendance—on my father's lap—when he answered the following question:

"Mr. Jackson, I wonder if you would share the genesis of this new style. It's so unlike your previous work, such a bold and, if I may say so, risky departure. While I'm not privy to your methods," he said, pointing over his shoulder at the picture, "it would appear you have covered the canvas in colors, covered the colors in black, and cut into the black to reveal the tonalities below. It also appears—and forgive me if I'm being too literal —that, in each of these vastly different pictures, you've included a sunrise. It's simple, but brilliant and dazzlingly expressive. May I ask what manner of inspiration led you to this new place?"

I smiled broadly at the interviewer, proud and pleased to know what my father's answer would be. I straightened the green bow in my hair, ready for the camera to turn to me.

"I can't claim full credit," Sam responded with uncharacteristic modesty. "I did have an inspiration." He smiled down at me, and I beamed at him as I watched his lips form the words, "Max Ernst."

"The surrealist?" said the reporter, clearly pleased that the grand continuum of art history was being perpetuated. "You got this from him?"

"I wouldn't say 'got this'," my father said, laughing his booming laugh to make it clear that the notion of his appropriating a style was absurd. "I was inspired." He leaned back into the sofa, hands behind his head, as if preparing to share wisdom with a student. "I've always spent time studying the masters, old and contemporary. Though I haven't had a lot of formal training, I'm an inveterate museum-goer and reader."

I've never known him to be either.

"I've long been a fan of the surrealists, Ernst in particular, and I'm fond of a picture of his called *A Moment of Calm*. That got me started down this path."

"Fascinating," the reporter said. "Can you tell me exactly—"

"That's all I'd like to say about it at the moment," my father said as he lifted me off his lap and stood up, "except that I've decided to give this painting to my beautiful little girl." He gestured toward me and smiled in a grand sign of noblesse oblige, then gave my fanny a pat, a signal that it was time for me to go.

***

In spite of my father's generous statement, I never did see that painting again. Until now. As I stared at it, I could feel my face reddening from the anger and hurt I felt at Sam's betrayal.

In an effort to suppress the memory, I looked back at the painting beside it, *Window on the World*, and that's when I realized someone had carefully, tediously, and perhaps even lovingly labored to strip away the brown paint from the lower left corner to reveal one tiny, perfect handprint.

Judy Pomeranz

Chapter Nine: The Good Life

Slay It Again, Sam.

As I left my father's SoHo studio, I thought about how that painting had changed the course of art history—or so the sycophants said—not to mention the course of our lives. From the moment my father showed the enormous canvas covered in black and punctuated with peek-a-boo slits that hinted at roiling, kaleidoscopic worlds underneath, he could do no wrong. He dominated the art world, and so did we.

Dealers, collectors, and curators alike hailed his new style, praising his ability to "pierce the darkness and reveal hidden worlds." They spoke of the "spiritualism" that characterized his new work, the "depth of meaning" inherent in each and every canvas, and the "socio-psycho-theological dramas" played out on their surfaces. Where did they get this stuff?

My father had loved it and played it for all it was worth. He dazzled the press and the art world with his "startling blue eyes," his "delightfully irreverent and cocky *joie de vivre*," his "grand and imposing stature," his "monumental pronouncements on all things artistic," and his "beautiful little family." The great irony was that he out-Pollocked his detested Pollock, even years after the great man's death. He was a star, my mother and I were his props, and nothing would ever be the same again.

In some ways, they were better. Our grungy walk-up apartment off Seventh Avenue gave way to a grand townhouse on St. Luke's Place and a weekend home in East Hampton. We went from noshing at the corner deli and eating my mother's chicken soup to dining at Delmonico's and being fed French cuisine by Nell, our new cook. My blue jeans and tee shirts were traded for fluttery, flowery frocks my father's press agent deemed photogenic.

Other things were more complicated. I found myself suddenly and surprisingly in great demand at my little progressive public school in the Village. A solitary being by nature, I had always preferred books to people, so I was taken aback by this peculiar notion that everyone wanted to be my friend. The phenomenon fed my tender ego but also made me uncomfortable as I tried to negotiate a path that would allow me to deflect the encroachments on my privacy while retaining the gratifying popularity that provoked them. Even I was a minor star in the firmament.

Before long, inevitably, my father faded out of our lives. He still frequented the Cedar Tavern, loudly proclaiming to anyone who would listen that he would "never forget his roots," but he was now in demand far beyond Greenwich Village. He hobnobbed at parties in Larchmont and Scarsdale, was feted by glamorous hostesses on the Upper East Side, and jetted across the country at the slightest provocation. He spent time in wondrous places like St. Moritz and Paris and London and Barcelona, and on tropical islands like St. Thomas and Tahiti, and he gamboled and gambled in Monte Carlo and Evian. All without us. My mother and I stayed home learning geography by following his travels on my brand new globe, a gift from Irv.

He didn't want to upset our lifestyle, he told my mother.

How thoughtful.

And still I idolized him. More than ever, because his attention was even harder to capture. I lived for the rare but exhilarating moments when he would give me a wet kiss on the cheek, pick me up and swing me around, ask me to pose, or call to say hello.

***

When I couldn't have the man, I doted on the image. I clipped my father's face from newspapers and magazines with my blunt-tipped scissors and pasted the pictures on the walls of my new pink-painted room. That way, I reasoned, I could have him all to myself. He didn't turn away from me then, nor did he walk away or tell me he was too busy. He just stared out at me from the walls, paying me his full and undivided attention. It was glorious. And, for a while, it was enough.

I noticed that, in almost every picture, Sam was accompanied by a beautiful woman. Not one in particular, at first, but a host of them, a different one in every venue. I found this curious, since I had previously only known my father to consort with male friends. But I knew better than to raise the issue with my mother, especially when the same strawberry blonde appeared over and over again.

The women in Sam's life were not the only things I was uncomfortable discussing with my mother. Many topics seemed, all of a sudden, to be inappropriate. Though I had been exceptionally close to her throughout my younger years, I instinctively grew wary of our interactions. More than once, I saw a tear creep down her delicate white cheek as she flipped through magazine photo spreads of Sam or caught his image on the television news. More than once, I found her lying in bed in the middle of the afternoon, wide awake. Often, my godfather Irv asked me to be gentle with her, saying she was going through a "rough patch."

One day, I found her sitting at the old desk Sam had bought for her, so many years earlier, to use in his Bowery studio. She ran her fingers over the fine grain of the wood and stared into a void only she could appreciate.

I watched her for ten minutes before speaking. "Why aren't you writing, Mama?"

She looked in my direction, but didn't make eye contact.

"Mama?"

"Hm?"

"Why are you at your desk if you're not writing?"

"I don't do that anymore," she said, matter-of-factly.

"Why not?"

"I can't."

"Why can't you?"

"I don't know," she said in a tone that ended the conversation.

She sat there at her desk through dinner time, through bath time, through reading time, and through the time when I could keep my eyes open no longer and put myself to bed.

***

Not long after that— my disorientation surrounding that period became so profound I couldn't have said whether it was weeks or a year—Irv picked me up at school and told me my mother had gone away for a while.

"Where's she gone?" I asked as we walked home.

"You'll have to ask your daddy, Babycakes." Irv stopped to tighten the wool scarf around my neck as a cold wind kicked up around us; he still treated me as younger than I was, and I didn't object. "He's coming home."

"He *is*?" I hadn't seen my father in ages, and was so excited at the prospect that I forgot all about my mother. "When?"

"Soon," Irv said with a sad look I found troubling. "He's due in from London tomorrow afternoon. He should be here by the time you get home from school."

I smiled broadly and skipped down the pavement, mentally selecting my wardrobe for the next day. I would wear the plaid jumper he liked, knee sox, red loafers, and my white blouse with the ruffled collar. Maybe if I were sufficiently attractive, I'd get him to stick around for a while.

"But, Irv." I stopped in mid-skip and ran back to him. "If he's not coming until tomorrow, and Mama's not home, who's going to be there tonight? Will I be alone?" The thought partly excited and partly terrified me.

Irv crouched down so our faces were at the same level; I could smell his musky aftershave and the fresh, cool aroma of his cashmere coat. He put his hands on my narrow shoulders, looked me in the eye, and spoke with great seriousness. "Do you think Wilson and I would leave you alone?"

I shook my head slowly.

"You're coming to our house," he said.

"I *am*? Overnight? On a school night?" Spending the night with the two of them was a world-class slumber party.

"You bet." Irv stood up, took my hand, and we walked down the street, a happy couple—or so I thought. "We will *never* leave you alone."

Judy Pomeranz

Chapter Ten
She's Gone to Paris

"Your mother's gone to Paris."

My father blurted out the words as I walked through the door after school the next day. He was like an actor spilling out his lines before he forgot them or lost his nerve.

"Hi, Daddy," I said timidly, more interested in his rare appearance in New York than in my mother's whereabouts.

When Irv, who stood by his side, elbowed him in the ribs, he stooped down, opened his arms wide, and waited for me to fly into them, which I did with glee. I hugged him as tightly as I could, and he hugged me so hard I felt I might burst open. I'd never felt that kind of intensity from my father, and I didn't want it to end.

But it did, and the news of my mother sank in. I stepped back and looked at him. "Paris?" It was the kind of place my father would go, but I had never known my mother to venture further than Long Island. "Why?"

He looked blankly at Irv, then at me, shifted his weight uneasily, and sat at the kitchen table. Sunlight filtered through his graying hair and bounced off the midnight blue of his irises as he stared at the ceiling. He looked old, and unaccountably sad, but as handsome as I'd ever seen him.

"She needs time to herself," he finally said.

"Why?"

"A, uh… project. She's working on a big project. She's writing—"

"Why in Paris?"

"It's… some people… some research. She has to be there."

"Why don't we *all* go?" I asked, growing excited at the prospect. I had heard my father's friends talk of Paris as a Mecca, a mythical place, a castle in the air.

"No," Sam said quickly. "This is something your mother has to do on her own." He walked to the window; I sat on a chair at the kitchen table.

We were silent, and I wondered if my mother had left us for good. Maybe she had found another man, with a daughter she liked better. A lump formed in my throat at the thought that I might have driven her away and would never see her again.

But then my always-vivid imagination kicked in, and I conjured the implications of such a disaster. If my mother were not around, my father would have to stay home with me, and I would be the woman of the house. I would entertain Sam's friends, I would gently critique his paintings, I would be there when he got up in the morning and when he went to bed at night; I would make sure Nell prepared his favorite meals, wait up for him when he went to the Cedar Tavern, and sit with him—like this—every afternoon. I would watch the sunlight make a halo around his head, and I would be blessed.

"Are you okay?" Irv said.

"I'm fine." I threw my father a big smile.

Sam's shoulders relaxed and the tension lifted from his features. "You're a sport, babe. And just for that, I've got a big treat for you."

"What?" My smile broadened.

"I'm going to send you to a fancy-schmancy boarding school up in Connecticut."

I stopped smiling.

Sam looked away.

I turned to Irv, who looked back at me with compassion in his eyes.

"But I don't want—"

"You're gonna love it. They've got a ton of land, tennis, a pool, trees… hell, they've even got horses."

"But, I don't want…"

"It's god-damn gorgeous up there."

"But I like it here."

Sam didn't seem to hear me; he continued extolling the virtues of this sylvan paradise. He didn't seem to know that I didn't swim, play tennis or lacrosse, climb rocks, hike, or ski, and that I didn't want to learn. He didn't seem to care that I'd rather be here in the city, with my books, my museums, and him.

He went to the ceramic cookie jar one of his sculptor friends had made and pulled out an oatmeal cookie, Nell's specialty.

"Catch!" He tossed it in my direction. "That's for being a sport."

"When's Mom coming home?" I asked, looking at the cookie in my hand.

"I don't know, kiddo." He whistled a Miles Davis tune as he walked to the hallway.

"Why didn't she say goodbye?"

Irv stared sadly at the door as my father left the room.

Sam didn't even hear the question.

***

After Irv left the room, I crumbled the oatmeal cookie into tiny pieces and spread them across the kitchen table, dragging the crumbs with my fingers, making swirling paths through them, smashing the raisins into the shiny oak tabletop.

"Did you hear Mom's in Paris?" I asked Nell, not bothering to look up.

"I did, honey."

"She left awfully suddenly."

"Yes, she did."

"She didn't say goodbye."

"I'm sure she wanted to, she just didn't have a chance. She told me to tell you she loves you and she'll miss you."

I didn't know whether to believe that, but chose to.

"Did you know I'm going to boarding school?"

She nodded. "That's wonderful, honey. Connecticut's beautiful."

"It stinks."

"Your daddy wants to do something special for you."

"He wants to get rid of me." I pouted. "Why didn't she say goodbye herself?"

81

Judy Pomeranz

Sam came back into the kitchen, wearing his coat. He grabbed another cookie from the jar and walked towards the back door.

"Why didn't Dawn's mother have time to say goodbye?" Nell asked him pointedly.

"She was in a hurry," he said.

"I didn't have a chance to tell her goodbye," I said.

"So, write her a letter," Sam said offhandedly, chomping on the cookie and dropping crumbs all over the floor. "I'll address it for you." He kissed the top of my head. "See you later, kiddo."

***

I did write a letter, sweet and kind, in my best third-grade penmanship, on my good blue stationary. I wrote how much I loved her and how much I missed her and how I longed for her quick return. I told her about Connecticut, about boarding school, about how beautiful it was supposed to be, and about how I was being taken away from everything and everyone I knew and loved. I told her how I hated it.

Then I tore it up and started over on a clean sheet:

Dear Mama,

Why did you leave us? Why did you go to Paris alone and make me go to Connecticut? Why couldn't we all go to Paris together, like a real family? Why are you tearing us apart?

I used to love you. I used to think you were beautiful and sweet, but now I know you are selfish and mean. Now I have to go to Connecticut and play stupid sports with a bunch of bad, stupid girls. Who else goes to boarding school? Why are you ruining my life and why didn't you say goodbye?

I hope you never come back. I want to be alone with Daddy, anyway.

Dawn

I folded the note and put it into an envelope which I sealed with red wax I'd been given by a schoolmate who'd gone to Colonial Williamsburg in Virginia. I shoved the little rose stamp into the red wax, let it dry, and pulled it out. My secret note was ready for my father to address.

***

On the day I was due to leave for Connecticut, a couple of weeks after I gave my father the letter and he promised to make sure it was delivered, Irv came to see me. I was sitting on the front steps when his red Thunderbird pulled up.

"What are you doing here?" I asked in a sulk, for we had already said our goodbyes the night before.

He pulled me to a standing position and held me without saying a word.

I wriggled myself free of his embrace and repeated the question.

"You're going to stay with Wilson and me for a while."

"I don't have to go to Connecticut?"

"Not now."

Though I didn't want to look a gift horse in the mouth, I couldn't resist asking why.

"Where are your bags?" Irv replied, ignoring my question.

We went inside and picked up my suitcases, which, thanks to Nell, were packed and ready for Connecticut.

"Why are we—?"

But Irv just hauled the four suitcases, one under each arm and one in each hand, to the car, stashed them in the trunk, and held the front door for me.

When we got to his place, Wilson made me a cup of sweet, steamy hot chocolate topped with tiny marshmallows, while the three of us waited for my father.

***

We had eaten an unusually quiet dinner and were watching TV sitcoms when my father finally arrived. I could tell by the way he walked that he'd been drinking.

"Your mother had an accident," he said, slurring the words. "A car—"

"In Paris?" I asked.

"Yes, in Paris," Sam said. "It was a bad one."

"So, she's not coming home?"

"No."

I looked at my father, who betrayed no particular emotion; all I could see was drunkenness. I felt like I was going to throw up. "Why isn't she coming home?"

"She's dead." He walked to the liquor cabinet to pour himself a bourbon, which he knocked back in one smooth motion. Then he poured another. "I've got to go," he said to Irv.

"Listen, buddy," Irv nodded toward me. "Can't you—"

"I gotta go."

And he did.

***

I stayed with Irv and Wilson for a full month. Though they wouldn't let me turn on the television, they pampered me in every other way. They catered to me, read to me, cried with me, and even prayed with me when I asked them to, for my Catholic friend Patty Martin had once told me that was the way to get what you wanted. And I wanted my mother back.

I also wanted my letter back. I couldn't stop thinking about it.

I was plagued by a terrible guilt and an emptiness that lingered and lurked, precluding sleep, impeding appetite, and, worst of all, preventing my feelings of loss and sadness from flowering into a full, purifying bereavement. I asked Irv how long it would take for a letter to get to Paris.

"A pretty long time," he said. "If it was an airmail letter, five or six days. If it was regular mail, it could take weeks."

That made me feel better; I could hope my father had sent it regular mail. But I would never know, and the relentless anxiety persisted. My grief wouldn't take hold until much, much later, and even when it did, it would never be an unadulterated, purgative sorrow, but a profound melancholy tainted by a culpability that would weigh heavily on my shoulders.

Chapter Eleven
Revelation

When I got home from my father's SoHo studio, I went straight to my storage bin in the basement of my apartment building, and dug out a green metal file box I hadn't touched since I put it there when I moved in. I brought the box upstairs, set it on the kitchen table, and fetched the key from my jewelry box.

I had trouble getting the key into the lock because a layer of rust had formed deep inside the keyhole, which struck me as oddly but appropriately metaphorical. When I finally managed to cram the key into the hole and turn it, the lid sprang open, exposing files which contained assorted bits and pieces of my youth: old school papers, report cards, notes and letters, poems my mother had written, and, finally—in the back—an article I had ripped from the pages of a once reputable but now defunct newsmagazine.

I had come across it in the course of doing research at my Connecticut boarding school, for a sixth grade library assignment designed to teach us how to use the *Reader's Guide to Periodic Literature*. We were each to choose a topic and find as many articles on it as we could. I had chosen my father as my subject, and quickly completed the project by amassing a huge compilation of citations. Although we were not required to actually retrieve the cited articles, one item on my list had sounded sufficiently intriguing to send me to the magazine archives. It was dated two years earlier and entitled, "Did Sam Jackson Drive Her Crazy?"

The librarian, pleased that the project had made me "quite the little researcher," was more than happy to take me to the basement to dredge up the issue that dated back almost four years.

Flipping through the magazine to the page indicated by the *Guide*, I was surprised to see a picture not of my father but of my mother, who had died several months before the article's publication date. I sat at one of the large, refectory-style wooden tables in the old school library and read quickly through the story. Then I read it again, more slowly. And yet again.

According to the writer, my mother had not gone to Paris at all, as I had been told, but to Belmont, Massachusetts. She hadn't been working on a writing project, but had been locked up in a high-class insane asylum benignly known as McLean Hospital. She hadn't died in an accident, but had killed herself two weeks after her admission and moments after her first visit from my father, who had, incidentally, been seen in Boston with one Julia Chirac, the strawberry blonde he had appeared with in so many of the pictures on my bedroom wall in New York. My mother had hanged herself with a rope of braided and tied nylon stockings.

I took the magazine deep into the library stacks and carefully tore out the two pages on which the story appeared, then returned the magazine to the librarian with great and formal thanks. I ran back to the dorm, locked myself into a bathroom stall, and read the story over and over again, hoping it would change.

How had no one ever told me about this? Not even hinted at it? How could I have been stupid enough to have lived in my bubble of oblivion all this time? I sat on the toilet seat and hung my head, which felt as if a twenty-pound weight had been attached to it. I was angry and ineffably sad, but I couldn't cry, hard as I tried. It was like wanting to throw up, knowing you would feel better afterwards, but not being able to.

I sat in that stall all afternoon, until the dorm monitor forced me to come out for dinner. By that time, I was certain of what my father had brought on his first and only visit to my mother in her elegant loony bin. My letter. I was sure, beyond any doubt, that he had delivered it, as he had promised he would. The beautifully sealed, carefully disguised, noxiously nasty bombshell I had passed off as a missive from a loving daughter who missed her mother. No wonder she killed herself. He arrived in town with a beautiful blonde on his right arm and a hateful note from a detestable daughter in his left hand, a note that said "I hope you never come back."

We had killed my mother.

I had ignored, not noticed, or forgiven countless instances of insensitivity, neglect, and cruelty on my father's part, but I knew that I would never, ever forgive him for the lies and deceit that had made me an accomplice in my own mother's murder. Nor would I ever forgive myself.

Even after all these years, the memory of that eternally long day in the bathroom stall remained unspeakably awful.

I put the article back into the metal file box without reading it, slammed the lid shut, and poured myself a heavy Glenfiddich, which I knocked back like a sailor.

Judy Pomeranz

Chapter Twelve
Ego the Size of New York

I awoke to my alarm the next morning with a raging headache and a queasy stomach. My own fault. Classically hung over. I forced myself out of bed and headed for the shower because I had an interview scheduled for ten a.m.

The appointment was with one Gerald Hopley, a man whose name appeared on Irv's list of my father's acquaintances. Hopley had attended classes with Sam at the Art Students League, and to say that he was not excited by the prospect of meeting me would be a gross understatement.

"You're Sam Jacksons' daughter?" he had said when I called a couple days earlier, his voice sharp with hostility.

"I am, and I'm writing his biography."

"So, I suppose you're going to show the world what a great artist and grand human being your father was." Hopley's tone shifted from hostile to sarcastic.

"That's not my intention. My father was a deeply flawed man, and I intend to show him in all his aspects.

Hopley paused. "He was a shit."

"I know. Can we talk?"

Again, a long pause. "I'll decide when I see you."

We agreed that I would come by today at ten.

I knew by his tone that this was not a chance I was likely to get again, so I couldn't blow it. I showered, drank two cups of strong coffee, forced down a half-piece of dry toast and headed for the subway, which took me to Astoria, Queens.

Judy Pomeranz

I found Hopley's ochre brick rowhouse in a modest neighborhood. Some of the houses on the block appeared abandoned, with boarded windows, peeling paint, and scruffy, weedy front yards. Others seemed tenderly cared for, with the wilted remains of sweet little annuals in their yards, along with trolls or cement frogs, and even the occasional polychromed Virgin Mary. Hopley's house fell in between—occupied, but barely. The front door, sprayed with black-and-white graffiti, was partly hidden by a torn screen door.

I opened the screen door and knocked. A wizened, gray specter of a man with an angry visage composed of what were once probably attractive, classical features opened the door and stared out at me.

"So, you're Sam Jackson's daughter." Hopley's voice was gruff and raspy

"Yes, I'm Dawn."

"You don't look anything like him," Hopley responded flatly.

"I favor my mother," I said, in an unintended double-entrendre of which Dr. Steinbrenner would have made much.

"Damn good thing," Hopley replied, finally opening the screen door to let me in.

I put out my hand to shake his, a gesture he chose to ignore.

He preceded me into a room piled so high with magazines, newspapers, and sketchbooks it was hard to take it all in at a glance. He moved a pile of *National Geographic*'s from a faded red sofa to the floor, and gestured for me to sit, which I did. I could feel a spring covered by only the thinnest layer of fabric poking into my thigh.

"What kind of art do you make, Mr. Hopley?" I asked, in an attempt at polite patter, something I've never been good at.

"Are you kidding? I've spent my whole life as a plumber."

"Didn't you study with Sam?"

"Hell, yes, but no one in that class made a living at it. Other than your old man. Art was a damn pipe dream for the rest of us." He chewed on the corner of his lower lip.

"It's a tough business," I said.

"Don't patronize me."

"I didn't mean—"

"What do you want from me?"

"I'm writing Sam's biography, and I need to understand what he was like as a young man." Sensing the kind of reaction my tape recorder was likely to elicit, I pulled out a small pad and pencil instead.

"He was a pain in the ass," Hopley mumbled.

Comforted by the knowledge that some things in life are constant, I smiled. "How so?"

"Damn full of himself. Ego the size of New York."

"Why do you say that?"

"He was cocky as hell, wouldn't have anything to do with the rest of us. Acted like he was above us. I had ten years on him, but that didn't make any difference." Hopley gnawed on his raw lower lip. "Insecurity, if you ask me."

"What do you mean?"

"He was pissed off and embarrassed that he had no talent. Same reason he got himself kicked out of the League."

Sam had always referred to his departure from New York's premier art school as having been caused by "philosophical differences."

"Why was that?" I asked, trying to sound casual.

"You don't know?"

I shook my head.

"He copied Pollock."

"But, I thought Pollock was out of the League by the time Sam got there."

"He was. Long gone."

"So, what happened?"

Hopley didn't respond for a while, trying to determine the real motives behind my questions.

"Your father arrived in New York as this damn cocky kid from out in God's country who knew how to make idiotic little figurative pictures, and that was all. He was good at it, mind you, but his stuff was workmanlike. Nothing personal, nothing unusual, no art. Just copying what he sees. But he thinks he's God's gift, you know?"

I nodded. I knew.

"It was the late forties." Hopley settled into his memories and leaned back against a pile of old *New Yorker* magazines. "We were so young, your father especially so. There had been the war—everything was a frigging mess. The old art didn't cut it anymore. It didn't address the shit happening in the world. So, all of us were looking for something new that would reflect the chaos. People were doing crazy things. Gutsy things. But old Sam was over in the corner making little representational pictures.

"So, he got razzed all the time. We all made fun of him, which he asked for by being so full of himself. And the next thing you know, he brings in this drip painting. This amazing thing." Hopley's eyes grew big with the recollection. "We all thought we were doing stuff that was out there on the edge, but none of us had thought of losing the easel, losing the paint tubes, even the brushes, damn it, and letting gravity do the work. It was brilliant."

I nodded.

"We were blown away—the students, the instructors, all of us. So, suddenly Sam goes from being the butt of our jokes to being the biggest thing around. Just like that. The pathetic kid from the Midwest got what he came to New York for. For a few days, he was it."

"Why a few days?" I asked.

"Because it was all over when one of the instructors went to a gallery and saw Pollock's first drip paintings. He realized Sam had seen them, and understood this twit at the League was not a hot new thing after all. He had copied Pollock."

"What did the school do about it?" I asked.

"They told Sam there was nothing wrong with being influenced or derivative, but there was something big wrong with passing someone else's ideas off as your own."

"Could they prove Sam didn't come up with it on his own?"

" 'Course not, but it's so damn obvious. What are the odds of these two guys coming up with the exact same thing at the same time? How stupid did he think we were?"

Hopley looked at me as if he expected an answer.

I shrugged.

"Pretty damn stupid," he said. "So, we let Sam know we were onto him and that we thought his game was cheap." He spat the last word out bitterly. "Then he got crazy pissed at everyone, denied he copied anything, and took a swing at one of the instructors." Hopley stopped to take a breath, having worked himself into a frenzy. "That's when he got his ass kicked out of the League."

"I never knew—" I began.

" 'Course not. Nobody does. No one cared at the time. He was a damn twit. Then, when he gets to be someone who somebody might care about, no one has the nerve to mess with him. League likes being associated with him. No one's going to believe a guy like me. End of story."

Chapter Thirteen
Peeling the Onion

The encounter with Gerald Hopley confirmed my hunch that, to understand the man my father ultimately became, I'd have to get a fix on the younger one who had arrived in New York with a chip already on his shoulder.

My knowledge of Sam's family history consisted of exactly two facts: that he was an only child and that his parents had both died when he was young. Despite my occasional questioning, and cautious prodding once when I had to put together a family tree for school, he had never been willing to discuss anything beyond those basics. I had attributed his reticence to his native narcissism, figuring he preferred to perpetrate a myth of having sprung full-blown and phoenix-like onto the earth with no human intervention and no familial baggage. But, after talking with Mr. Hopley, I wondered whether there was more to it, a trauma or pain lurking in his past which he feared resurrecting.

Sam had grown up in a small farming community in central Illinois called Shepherdsville. His address was "Box 23, Route 610," which I knew only because it appeared in bold, penciled print on the inside cover of an old grammar book I ran across when I was a child. The address appeared beneath the name "Marlissa Jackson," whom Sam told me was his mother, my late grandmother. When I asked why his mother had a grammar book, he said she had been a teacher. End of story.

With nothing more to go on, I decided to set off for Shepherdsville. I knew neither what I was seeking nor what I might find, making it a venture Sam would have called a crapshoot. When I told Irv of my plans, he offered to come along, pressing the matter when I demurred, as if he was unsure I could handle it alone. But I wanted to do this myself. For myself and by myself. I needed to.

***

After checking into the Shepherdville Inn, the sole choice of lodging in my father's tiny, rural hometown, I headed for the nearby public library, a small, neat, blue-painted Victorian frame building located across the quiet, tree-filled town square. This would be a good place to search for information on the town's renowned native son.

The library's main room housed an oak card catalogue, walls lined with oak book cases holding reference tomes and others I couldn't distinguish, along with a large oak desk where a sturdy woman of indeterminate age and gray-flecked mousy brown hair sat behind a brass nameplate that said "Miss Barnett" in bold block letters.

"Good afternoon," Miss Barnett said. "What can we do for you?"

"I'm Dawn Jackson." I held my hand out to her. "I'm working on a biography of my father Sam, and was hoping you might help me with information on his childhood."

"Oh my goodness, it's such an honor to meet you." Miss Barnett stood and shook my hand with a smile. "We're so proud of your father. He's our most famous citizen." She put her hand on her heart as if about to swoon or say the Pledge of Allegiance. "If you came into town from the south, you saw the sign that says 'Shepherdsville: Boyhood Home of Sam Jackson'."

I hadn't seen it, but nodded nonetheless, fascinated that a quiet little place would admit to association with a man like Sam. "Do you know of anyone still here in town who might have known my father or his family?"

"That goes back quite a ways," Miss Barnett said.

I nodded.

"You might want to talk with Jack Peets. He always brags about having known your father and his sister—says they all went to school together."

"He must be thinking of someone else. My father was an only child."

Miss Barnett gave me a sideways look. "No…" she elongated the word as if stalling for time. "I've been here my whole life, and I know this place." She put her hands on her substantial hips. "I also happen to be in charge of our newspaper archives."

"I didn't mean to offend you, but this is the first I've heard about a sister."

"Her name was Marlissa," Miss Beasley said as if to prove her point.

"Same name as my grandmother," I replied meekly, wanting to show I wasn't entirely ignorant of my family history.

"No, the mother's name was Jane. Waita minute."

She waddled away, leaving me alone and befuddled, wondering which of us was completely off base and fearing I knew.

She soon returned with a film canister containing issues of the *Shepherdsville Courier* dating back to 1947, the summer of my father's fifteenth year. She took out the spool of film, threaded it into a microfiche reader, and scrolled through it. When she found what she was looking for, she offered me her stool and pointed to a brief notice that read:

We are sad to announce that our dear Marlissa Jackson died yesterday at the age of ten. She is survived by her loving parents, William and Jane, and by her older brother Samuel. Services will be at the First Methodist Church on Wednesday, at noon.

"What did she die of?" I managed to ask Miss Barnett.

"I think it was pneumonia, but I'm not sure. They never said, officially." She tucked a loose hank of scraggly hair behind her ear.

"How could I find out? Would there be hospital records?"

"She wasn't in the hospital. She died at home."

***

I left the library and followed Miss Barnett's directions to the tidy Cape Cod cottage of Jack Peets, a handsome man with white hair, bright green eyes, a lovely smile, and a firm handshake. I introduced myself, and he invited me into his cozy living room and directed me to have a seat in a wingchair next to the fireplace.

"Miss Barnett told me you had some questions," he said kindly. "What can I help you with?"

Judy Pomeranz

"To tell you the truth, I've just now learned that my father had a sister." I averted my gaze and stared at the fire, embarrassed at revealing this degree of ignorance of my own family. "So I'm starting at the beginning. I'd like to know more about her, and the family, and anything you remember about what my father was like back then."

"You didn't know your father had a sister?" Mr. Peets lowered himself into a brown recliner that was patched in three places with silver duct tape. Clearly his favorite chair. "That seems right odd."

"My father was never communicative." I recognized that sounded like an absurd understatement in this town where everyone knew everything about everyone else's family, not to mention their own.

"Weren't you curious? Didn't you ask him anything?"

I squirmed in my chair, uncomfortable at having to defend myself to this man I'd never seen before but liked. "I asked him something at some point, but he didn't like talking about his past."

Mr. Peets nodded, but looked skeptical.

"So, what happened to her?" I asked. "The sister."

"Close as I can tell, she got pneumonia, but no one ever took care of it. That's the long and short of it. I heard the parents thought she was faking or exaggerating, to keep from going to school. You know how kids can be. I recall Sam was right concerned—he worshiped that beautiful little redheaded girl—but no one paid him any heed. They thought he was taking her side, like always."

I stared at Mr. Peets, not quite able to assimilate what I was hearing, but remembering the loving care Sam used to shower on me when I was sick.

"So, she died," Peets said. "Just like that. No doctor, no hospital. Right there at home. And that's when your father turned."

"Turned?"

"Sure." Mr. Peets scratched his bald scalp. "Can't hardly blame him, can you?"

"For what?"

"For how he turned out. He was a fine boy at first. A nice boy. Always liked to draw, even though his father didn't much care for that. The father naturally wanted his son to carry on the family farm. He thought drawing was a girly thing." Mr. Peets winked and waved a floppy wrist at me. "You know?"

"So, Sam was a nice boy?" I needed to grab onto that.

96

"Sure, until the thing with Marlissa. After that, he got mean, dark. He blamed his parents for the little girl's death, and everyone else in town, too. He became nasty."

"In what way?"

"He stopped talking to everyone. He knew that if someone had taken care of her, she wouldn't have died. He resented that something awful. If you ask me, he probably hated himself for not making her well. Hate to sound like one of those TV shrinks but that's how it seems to me."

Mr. Peets pushed himself up off his chair, walked over to a walnut cabinet, pulled out two glasses, and poured a healthy slug of bourbon into each. "You look like you need this."

"Thanks," I said weakly, and took a sip as Mr. Peets continued his story.

"Pretty soon, it got so we were all afraid of Sam, he was so angry and quiet and unto himself. Then he up and left town. He couldn't have been more than sixteen. Didn't tell his parents or anyone else where he was going. None of us knew till he turned famous, and by then the parents were gone, though not by much. Too bad they couldn't have lived to see him make it."

"But didn't his parents die when he was young?"

"Depends on how you define young." Mr. Peets chuckled. "Seems young now, but he wasn't a kid. Must have been in his mid-twenties when his mother passed, and his daddy followed her by not more than a year."

I stared. "Did he come back for the funeral?"

He shook his head. "No, and that was a sad thing, them dying like that, as if they had no children to follow along behind them."

I took a gulp of bourbon so large it burned my throat and emptied the glass. "Didn't he have any friends when he lived here? Anyone he could talk to?"

"Not so far as I know. What with school and chores, kids didn't have much free time in those days. And if Sam did have a minute, he'd be drawing. I remember that clear as yesterday. No, the only friend he had was that little sister of his. Loved her to death."

Judy Pomeranz

Chapter Fourteen
The Perfect Family

My trip to Shepherdsville produced nothing beyond what Miss Barnett and Jack Peets had to offer. The town had been devastated back in the early 1970's by the closing of the local tannery and the overtaking of small family farms by agribusiness, so the population was sparse; almost everyone who had known my father's family had either moved on or died.

But even these limited new insights had brought Sam's younger years into a dim and dismal new focus that caught me off-guard and made me realize I needed to get a better feel for the broader arc of his life before digging into the details. I needed perspective, and a feel for the totality of what I would be dealing with.

While I now had a skeletal outline of Sam's early days and personal knowledge of the middle years, I still had no clear sense of the man called Sam Jackson who succeeded the one I grew up with: the man who married a woman named Julia and had a daughter called Daisy; the Sam Jackson with whom I had refused to have any communication after my eighteenth birthday, the year of my majority—or, as I had always considered it, my liberation. I knew all about his public image, all about the artist created and defined by the press, but I knew nothing of the man himself. I needed to fast-forward.

After giving myself a day off to assimilate—or recover from— what I had learned in Shepherdsville, I scanned the roster of contacts Irv had prepared for me. I allowed my eyes to rest briefly on the name of one of the two people I most dreaded meeting: Julia Jackson, the person I needed to talk with above all others. Though I had never met her, I felt a connection with her, for she was the strawberry blonde who appeared on my father's arm in all those magazine images I had clipped; hers was the heart-shaped, star-struck face that had stared out at me from the photo-covered walls of my room on St. Luke's Place. Over the years since my mother's death, I had come to resent Julia almost as much as Sam.

But not as much as Daisy, that glorious little replica of Julia the press couldn't get enough of. I hated her most of all, for she was the daughter who had gotten the best of Sam Jackson, a fact made plain in dozens of magazine spreads, news stories, and art reviews that lauded Sam's work and the little angel so often credited with inspiring the best of it.

Despite my heroic efforts at avoidance, I had been bombarded with TV and magazine coverage of that perfect little family throughout my adult life. I had seen them on the beach, in their Architectural Digest home, in a multitude of European capitals, and in the Presidential Box at the Kennedy Center on the night Sam was inducted into the American Academy of Arts and Letters, an award that made me want to relinquish my citizenship. Through it all, I had watched this person—my own half-sister—grow from a little fairy child into a beautiful young woman. I had seen pictures of her wedding and, not a year later, photos of her own beautiful baby girl. The family was everywhere; the coverage was relentless. They were unavoidable.

They were also the people who defined the "mature" Sam Jackson, the man whose biography I had agreed to write. That being the case, they were the people with whom I would now have to deal.

***

Thankfully, Irv agreed to provide moral support, and this time I took him up on the offer. He also provided transportation to Sam and Julia's East Hampton summer home, where Julia had been staying since Sam had entered the Three Pines Convalescent Center in nearby Sag Harbor.

"Are you sure you're ready for this?" Irv asked as we drove up a driveway lined with columns of towering hedgerows leading to an enormous, rambling gray shingle structure.

I didn't answer.

"We can still turn around." He glanced in my direction.

I shook my head and straightened my spine as if preparing for battle.

Irv pulled the Range Rover into a small parking area beside the house. He squeezed my hand as we walked to the front door.

The moment Julia opened the door, I stared into the face of a gracefully aged version of my own mother. I had never noticed in the photos how much Sam's two wives resembled one another; I could only imagine how much they both resembled little redheaded Marlissa Jackson, Sam's sister, whom I now wondered if Julia knew anything about.

Judy Pomeranz

Chapter Fifteen
I Assumed You Knew

"Hello, Irv." Julia held the door open as we walked into a black-and-white marble-floored foyer. She gave him a soft peck on the cheek, not the air kiss I might have expected, but a true show of affection. It was a small gesture that made me feel a little better about her.

"Julia." He smiled warmly, clasping her hand, "it's so good to see you."

There was no question he meant it; I could see they genuinely liked one another, which was one more point in her favor.

"And Dawn." Julia looked me straight in the eye with neither a smile nor a frown, but a direct, guileless gaze that held a measure of caution. "I can't tell you how happy I am to finally meet you."

She was pretty, in an uncluttered way, and pleasant in an honest one. She seemed so much like my own mother—only stronger—that a wave of sadness swept over me. I took her proffered hand and embarrassed myself by holding onto it longer and more tightly than I had intended.

"I'm pleased to meet you, as well," I said timidly, certain she was privy to every nasty thought I had harbored about her over the years.

We passed through the foyer into a light-filled room that ran along the back of the house and overlooked the ocean. The surf, which reflected a cerulean sky, crashed against a sea wall and fell in a spray of twinkling droplets onto a sand strip beyond the precisely mowed lawn. I was looking at the inspiration for one of my father's paintings, an expressionist work he called *Morning Blue* that hung in a gallery all its own at the Art Institute of Chicago.

"Please, have a seat." Julia pointed us toward two easy chairs and a long sofa upholstered in celadon-and-white-checked chintz.

I took a chair; she and Irv shared the sofa.

"What can I get you to drink?" she asked. "Coffee? Tea? Iced tea? Wine?"

"Tea would be perfect," Irv said.

"That's fine with me." I tried not to sound as awkward as I felt.

Julia nodded to a blue-uniformed woman who had materialized out of nowhere and disappeared as discreetly.

"Dawn, we have so much to catch up on." Julia leaned forward. "I hope you'll allow us to do that one day soon. But I know you're here with a purpose today, so why don't you tell me what you'd like to know."

"You know I'm writing a biography?"

"Yes, Irv told me. It's a marvelous idea."

"Yes, well, thanks," I murmured. "What I need to know is... I don't have a list of questions. I need to know about your life with Sam."

"You want to know what it's like being married to him? Living with him?"

I nodded.

"I think you have some sense of that," she said with a grin.

I nodded again. "But my experience might not be the same as yours."

"A valid point. So, where shall I begin?"

I noticed a silver-framed snapshot on an end table by her elbow. It depicted Julia's daughter Daisy holding her own baby, whose name was Heather. I seized on the photo as an opportunity to buy time while trying to come up with an intelligent question.

"She's lovely." I nodded toward the picture. "They both are."

"Thank you," Julia said. "I happen to think so too."

"She looks just like you," I said.

Irv shifted in his seat, which I took to indicate boredom or embarrassment at my inability to come up with anything other than mundane chitchat.

"Thank you," Julia said again.

"She doesn't resemble Sam at all," I said, dragging the topic out for all it was worth. If I kept her talking about the family, I was bound to glean something useful.

"Well, she wouldn't, would she?" Julia said rhetorically.

"Why not?"

"You know…" Julia looked at Irv, who subtly shook his head, then looked at me.

"So, Dawn, what questions do you have for Julia?" Irv said nervously. "We don't want to take up her whole afternoon, do we?"

"I'm not in any rush, Irv," Julia said.

"Why wouldn't she look like Sam?" I asked Julia again, ignoring Irv's intervention.

Julia looked back at Irv, who shrugged. But his expression betrayed concern.

"I was artificially inseminated," Julia replied matter-of-factly.

"You mean Sam's not Daisy's father?"

"He most certainly *is* her father," Julia said defensively, almost angrily. "He's been a wonderful father to her, in his way. He's just not her biological father."

"I'm sorry," I mumbled. "I didn't mean…"

"I know you didn't, Dawn. I didn't mean to snap at you. I just assumed you'd know why she couldn't be his biological child."

"Actually, no. I didn't know." I turned to Irv, who was hunched over in his chair, elbows on his knees, staring at the floor. "I still don't."

Julia looked at him too, as if seeking permission to proceed. He glanced up at her, then at me. Then he closed his eyes and dropped his head back down, effectively removing himself from the loop.

"You don't?" Julia said.

I shook my head.

"The oligospermia," she said.

I'm sure I looked as clueless as I felt.

"Sam has an extremely low sperm count," she finally said.

My face burned as I took in this revelation of my father's sexual inadequacy. I'm not sure if I was more embarrassed by the topic itself, by the fact that I had forced Julia to discuss it, or the reality that I was once again completely ignorant of a fundamental fact I was supposed to have known. Nonetheless, I forged on, proving that chutzpah and prurient curiosity trump discretion and good taste.

"What happened to him?" I asked. "Was it the result of an illness? An accident?" I tried to recall whether he had a bout of German measles. It was obviously something that would have happened after I was born.

"Not that I know of," Julia said.

Now she looked uncomfortable. I don't suppose she had intended to open up a discussion of sexual dysfunction with her innocent response to my remark about family resemblances.

"It might be a congenital condition," she finally said. "I'm not certain."

Her tone put a close to the conversation in time for the maid to return with a tray carrying three small flowered teapots, three porcelain cups, and three tiny silver spoons, along with delicate pots of sugar, milk, and lemon slices.

How enlightened and civilized we all were.

***

Once we got past those surreal opening moments and dropped the topic of Sam's problem, the afternoon was quite ordinary and even pleasant. Julia was not only charming but low-key, modest, not unintelligent, and definitely not a pushover. She was far better equipped than my mother had been to deal with Sam, or at least to insulate herself from the potential ill effects of his company. Far better equipped than I.

I learned nothing else particularly revelatory that day, and left with the perception that the images of the lovely, happy little family I had been subjected to over the years might have been accurate. That came as a surprise, since I had long assumed that this family, like ours, had worn a pleasant veneer that masked a far more complicated truth.

***

On the drive back to Manhattan, I thanked Irv profusely for coming with me.

"I wouldn't have had the nerve to go alone," I said, "and I'm glad I went."

"She's lovely, isn't she?"

I nodded.

"Maybe we'll go see Daisy one of these days," he said.

"We'll see." Meeting my supposed half-sister remained a frightening prospect in spite of the successful encounter with her mother. "I can't get over that Sam's not her father."

"As Julia said, he's as much her father as he is yours, biology or no biology," Irv said flatly. "He's been an important part of her life and she of his. Don't ever think otherwise."

"So, what's the deal with Sam, anyway?" Now that I was getting used to the idea, I was amused that my quintessentially and often obnoxiously macho father had lost the ability to conceive children. "What happened?"

Irv shrugged. "I don't know."

"It must have been *something*," I persisted. "That doesn't just *happen*, does it? Are you holding out on me?"

"I honestly don't know the nature or the source the Sam's problem with conception," he said impatiently. "How *would* I?"

"But you knew he had one."

Irv nodded. The fact that he was incapable of lying when presented with a direct question or statement had always worked to my benefit.

"And you have no idea what its source was?"

"As Julia said, it was probably congenital."

"But that doesn't make sense. If it was congenital, wouldn't it have manifested before? He managed to conceive *me*, didn't he?"

Irv shrugged again, keeping his eyes glued to the road.

I took a deep breath and sat quietly while the implications of his silence sunk in.

"Good God, Irv, you're not trying to tell me that *my* mother was artificially inseminated, are you?"

"I'm not trying to tell you anything of the kind, Dawn," Irv said in an agitated manner that let me know I was pushing too hard. "I don't know the circumstances of your birth. I've never known, and I don't imagine you or I ever will know, for sure."

"But you've *suspected* I might not be Sam's biological child?"

He kept his eyes on the road and both hands firmly on the steering wheel.

I kept my hands in fists and my lips pursed, to avoid erupting. "How could you have known and not told me?" I tried, without success, to keep my voice in a normal register.

"I didn't *know* anything, and I still don't," he said in a voice that pleaded for mercy.

"But how could you have *imagined* such a thing without—"

"Can we please talk about something else?" he interrupted.

He looked so upset I took pity on him, and tacitly declared a moratorium on the subject for the balance of the silent ride home. But I was unable to put it out of my mind.

Had I come out of a test tube? Had such a thing been feasible all those years ago? It was impossible to imagine that I was the product of anything or anyone other than Sam and Aurora Jackson. I looked exactly like one of them, thank God, and had been told I acted way too much like the other. No, only the biological child of Sam Jackson could be as neurotic as I was being right now.

***

Irv pulled into an illegal parking spot in front of my building and turned off the motor. He looked at me hard, trying to see through me or inside me. In the dim evening light, the fine wrinkles that radiated out from his eyes and the sides of his mouth became pronounced. He looked old.

"Are you okay, babe?"

I nodded slowly. "I'm fine."

"It's been a hell of a day. You've learned things you probably didn't care to know and questioned things you thought you did know. That's never easy."

"I can handle it," I said, partly reflexively, partly snidely, and partly hoping he wouldn't believe me and would make it all make sense.

"You can handle anything—you always could. That doesn't mean you're all right with it." He continued to stare at me. "You're a tough one. Sometimes too tough."

"Meaning?"

"It's not bad to ask for help or admit you're hurt or confused."

"What brought that on?"

He smiled meekly. "Maybe reading too much pop psychology. Remember I'm here if you need to talk."

"That's not what you said an hour ago."

"I know. " He touched my arm. "Do you want to talk?"

108

"Not now. There's not much to say, assuming you're not holding out on me. Besides, no matter how much we talk, we're not going to resolve anything tonight, are we?"

He shook his head.

"Maybe not ever," I said.

"Probably not," he agreed.

"But I'll always wonder—"

"Why is it so important?"

"—if I'm Sam Jackson's daughter."

"You *are* Sam's daughter," he reiterated firmly. "You always were and always will be."

"Biologically."

"Does it matter?"

"To me it does."

We were both quiet.

"So, what's next?" He tried to sound chipper. "Do you want me to set something up with Daisy?"

Judy Pomeranz

Chapter Sixteen
Ignorance is Bliss

Oligospermia. Low sperm count. I pronounced the word slowly, trying to wrap my tongue around the soft vowel sounds and my brain around the concept. Impotence. There was irony that my father, a man of imposing stature and inordinate ability to co-opt and appropriate the hearts and minds of his fellow human beings, should be, in this fundamental way, impotent. Powerless to reproduce. Incapable of populating the world with creatures created in his own image. There might be a God after all, one with a sense of humor.

Though the temptation to be flip was irresistible, the more poignant powerlessness imposed on Sam by Alzheimer's made this new revelation less satisfying. There was also the nagging question of my own conception. Was it possible Sam had been unable to father children even back then?

I had no reason to believe my parents had desired my entry into the world so fervently as to have taken Herculean measures to ensure it, nor had I any reason to believe that my appearance had been accompanied by either high drama or high technology. No, the only thing that made sense was that Sam's impotence postdated my birth. But what had caused it?

***

The question was on my mind as Irv drove me to the home of Sam's daughter, Daisy Blackburn.

Daisy lived in Westchester County. Larchmont. Of course she would. She was the good daughter. The nice daughter. The pretty daughter. The daughter who had married well and produced a granddaughter. The daughter who had stayed in touch with her father until he was old and senile and who would be there, even now, to support him in his hour of need.

Dr. Steinbrenner might have been right that petty sarcasm did not become me.

"I'm not sure of the etiquette on greeting a grown-up half-sibling for the first time." I stared out the window at the bleak gray high-rise housing projects of the Bronx whizzing past us.

Irv was smart enough not to answer.

"You like her, don't you?" I said.

"She's got hang-ups, as we all do, but she's a lovely girl."

"Hardly a girl anymore," I said.

"You know what I mean."

"Is she anything like me?" I asked.

Irv pondered the question. "I'll let you be the judge of that.".

"Is she anything like Sam?"

"No," Irv said immediately. "Nothing like Sam."

"Am I?" I shot back.

He nodded, but was smart enough not to elaborate.

***

The Blackburn house was constructed of rough brown stone in an architecturally ambiguous style designed to impress. It occupied a large, densely treed lot with a wooden swing set tucked into a copse on the far left side. Dozens of bushes that would produce full, blazing spring blossoms filled beds running across the front of the house, and clusters of evergreens were scattered artfully throughout the yard. The quintessence of upper middle class America, the whole scene reminded me of a movie set, down to the black Mercedes convertible parked in the driveway.

And Daisy herself was right out of Central Casting. She greeted us at the front door in tennis whites that accentuated her muscular frame, blonde-streaked hair, and perfectly even tan I soon learned she had acquired in St. Bart's. Of course.

Once the awkward introductions were out of the way, Daisy ushered us into an extraneous but elegant side room, which, in an earlier era, might have been called a parlor.

"Can I get you something to drink?" Clearly, she had been well trained by her mother, but I could feel her scrutinizing me as she awaited my response.

"No, I'm fine," I said, which was not true except in the context of drinks. I was more uncomfortable than I had expected to be, as my mind busied itself making invidious comparisons. She seemed so graceful and at ease, while I felt like a disaffected oaf.

"Irv?" she offered.

"I'm good too, sweetie, thanks."

"It's so nice to finally meet you." Daisy turned her attention back to me, though I didn't hear conviction in her voice.

"You too," I said meekly.

"I hear you're writing our father's biography."

I nodded. "I'm just getting started."

"How can I help?"

I took that as my cue to launch into innocuous preliminary questions I had designed to elicit how much information she might share. Although she never failed to respond kindly, chattering at great and tedious length, she never came close to revealing anything personal about herself or Sam.

While she was relating a particularly "droll" (according to her) and endless (according to me) anecdote involving our father and one of her professors at Smith College, a tiny, curly-haired, strawberry-blonde girl minced into the room and slipped up onto Irv's lap. I knew from photos the girl was Daisy's daughter, Heather.

Ignored by her mother and quietly smooched by Irv, Heather plainly understood and practiced discretion, almost to the point of invisibility. I smiled at her as her mother rambled on, and she rewarded me with the quickest little grin before burying her head in Irv's beige cashmere cardigan. She pulled her head back and smiled at Irv. An angelic smile. Then she fiddled with the leather buttons on his sweater.

"Aren't you going to say hello to our guest?" Daisy said to the girl after she finished her story.

"Hello," the child said in a squeaky little voice, then pressed her head against Irv's chest.

113

"Heather," her mother said sternly, "get down off Uncle Irv and greet our guest properly. This is Ms. Jackson."

Heather reluctantly slipped off Irv's lap and stuck her thumb into her mouth. "Hello Ms. Jackson," she mumbled, speaking around the obstacle until her mother pulled her hand roughly away from her face.

My heart ached for this child. She looked so much in need of Irv's lap. Almost as much as I had once been.

"Nice to meet you, Heather." I smiled at her. "You can call me Dawn."

Daisy shook her head at me in reprimand, while Heather climbed onto Irv and gave him as powerful a hug as her thin arms would permit. When he responded with a loud, smacking kiss on her right cheek, she giggled, climbed down, and ran out of the room like a little sprite.

"She's adorable," I said to Daisy. "How old is she?"

"Three. Not an easy age." She shook her head and rolled her eyes as if I would understand, then corrected herself. "Oh, but you don't have children, do you?"

"No."

Daisy looked at her gold Rolex, gasped dramatically at "how late" it was and "how quickly" the time had passed. "It just flew by," she said. "I've so enjoyed meeting you, but I'm due at the club for a tennis game in ten minutes. I'll walk you out."

Which she did. She hopped into the convertible and put down the top. "Let's do this again," she said cheerfully. Then she drove off.

I wasn't sure where that left Heather, though it was fair to assume a nanny was on the premises. Still, her mother might have said goodbye to her.

But then, her mother had Sam as a role model.

***

When we got back to Manhattan, Irv treated me to lunch at E.A.T., the upscale deli on Madison Avenue. I was a fan of their matzo ball soup, and he adored their omelets, so we didn't mind paying the ridiculously inflated prices.

"That little girl is a doll." I ritualistically cut the huge matzoh ball up with my spoon so the rich chicken broth would penetrate its spongy dough.

Irv nodded, munching on a piece of walnut-raisin bread. "She's the best. What did you think of her mother?"

I shrugged. "I'm not sure."

"She's a good person, underneath the suburban matron. She's had a complicated life."

"I can imagine."

"There's more than you know. Her husband's the investment banker equivalent of Sam. Quieter, but in charge, when he's around."

"So, how did Heather turn out so well?"

"How did *you*?" Irv said with a puckish grin.

"Good point. Must have been my exceptional godfather."

"Yeah, must have been."

We ate without talking for a while.

"You've been uncharacteristically quiet since we left Scarsdale," Irv finally broke the silence. "What's up?"

"That little girl looked so timid in her own house, with her own mother. It made me sad."

Irv put down his fork. His eyes shimmered with tears.

"What did I say?" I asked.

He took a moment, then responded slowly and deliberately. "Do you know how long it's been since I've heard you say something made you sad?"

I shook my head.

"Ages. Decades. You've been so defensive for so long, so intent on protecting yourself from being hurt, that you haven't let yourself feel much of anything. This is new."

"I thought you didn't like pop psychology."

"I mean it. This is real progress."

"You're glad I'm sad."

He nodded.

"Thanks a lot."

Irv smiled. "The honorable Dr. Steinbrenner would call this 'appropriate and healthy affect.' I'd call it human. And yes, it does make me glad, if a little sad."

"You're not making sense, but while we're psychoanalyzing, I'd say you've been distracted, yourself, today."

Irv took a swig of coffee and looked out the big plate glass window onto Madison Avenue.

***

As we pulled up in front of my apartment building, a legal parking space big enough for a Range Rover opened up ten feet ahead of us. Any New Yorker would recognize this as divine intervention, not to be taken lightly.

"Want to come up? It's fate."

Irv stared at the departing car.

"Did you hear me?"

He shook his head.

"Are you okay?" I said.

"Yes, I'm fine. And sure, I will come up." He pulled the Range Rover neatly into the vacated spot and shifted into park, but made no move to get out of the vehicle. "I have something for you. I had planned to let you look at it on your own, but maybe I should be there with you."

"What are you talking about?"

Irv snapped off his seatbelt, climbed out of the vehicle, and came around to open my door. As I got out, he opened the back door and took a worn, black leather notebook off the backseat.

"It's your mother's journal." He closed the back door, then my door.

"Where did you get it?" As I touched the book softly with my index finger, a bit of leather flaked off and fell into the gutter.

"From Sam, years ago."

We walked up the sidewalk to the front door of my building.

"After she died?" I asked.

"No, before."

I stopped and faced him. "Why did he have it? Why didn't she—?"

"I'll explain upstairs."

***

We settled into our usual spots in the living room, me on the sofa, Irv in his favorite armchair.

"Can I have a Scotch?" Irv asked.

"Sure," I said, though it was odd for him to ask for one so early in the day.

"You might want one too," he said.

I poured two doubles, neat, and handed one to Irv. Clutching my own, I sat on the sofa. "What's this about?"

He took a sip before responding. "Please remember I'm not doing this to hurt you. I'd never hurt you."

"You're scaring me." I reached for the black leather book that sat on the coffee table, but Irv grabbed it and held it against his chest.

"You know your father's painting at the Museum of Modern Art, 'Portrait of a Whore'?"

I nodded, recalling the terrible afternoon when my father had first shown it to me. "He said it was a portrait of my mother."

Irv nodded slowly, his eyes closed. "Sam gave me this journal right after he painted that picture, the same evening."

"But I thought you said it was my *mother's* journal."

"It is. Sam found it that day and read it. That's why he painted the picture."

"He had no right to read—"

"I agree, but it's too late for that. Way too late." He drew in a breath so deep I was afraid he would pass out. "He did read it, and didn't like what he read. That's putting it mildly."

"Why? What's in there?"

"I'll let you see for yourself. I hope you can someday understand what it was all about. How it happened. And why. That's the most important thing—the why."

I was beginning to think I'd rather not know what my mother had written. Ignorance had always been bliss for me, so why mess with it?

"You have to understand, we loved each other," Irv said so quietly I could barely hear him.

"I know you were always best friends."

"I'm not talking about Sam," Irv said.

"Who then?"

"Aurora."

"I know you loved each other. I knew it even before I read your notes. She needed you for a million reasons. I've always known. What are you driving at?"

He handed me the journal. "Turn to the entry for June twenty-fifth."

I opened the book and saw it began with an entry for January 1st of the year before I was born. I flipped to June 25 and read silently:

This lake is magical. I adore being away from the city. The silence here is astonishing, as are the sunsets and the stars, the trees and the water. It's all so perfectly seductive, and so wonderful being in the company of those I love—Sam, Wilson, and Irv. Would that it were for more than a weekend.

Last night's dinner was three scrawny fish Irv and I had caught in the afternoon. Never has a meal tasted better. After eating, we sat in front of the fireplace with our drinks. Sam had his Scotch, as always. Wilson, Irv, and I drank two bottles of a perfectly smooth French red wine Wilson brought back from a business trip to Paris. Sam pronounced it Frog Juice and said he'd drink it when the French thanked us properly for our help in the war, and not before.

Soon enough, Sam snored in his armchair and Wilson headed off to bed, pleading jet lag, so Irv and I decided to take a walk around the small lake.

That's when I realized how many stars there are. They lit the sky like glitter. We held hands and circled the whole lake without speaking a word, then we ended up back at the little dock in front of our cottage.

I lay down on the warm wood of the dock so I could look up at the stars. Irv lay beside me. He reached for my hand, and we gazed up toward the heavens in beautiful utter silence, interrupted only by the gentle lapping of water against the dock posts.

I turned to him and kissed him. It wasn't the kind of kiss I'd given him, and he me, many times in the past, and I'm not sure why I did it. I did it without thinking, without planning. He rolled over so we were facing each other, and we stared at one other in that brilliant starlight.

I don't know who touched whom first, or exactly how it unfolded, nor does it matter, but what ensued was the most natural event imaginable. Also the most inevitable.

I suppose we should feel sordid or evil, but I only feel peaceful. Perfectly peaceful.

That's where the entry ended.

I sat on the sofa with my mouth hanging open. I didn't know whether to be angry or sad, to be happy for Irv and my mother or outraged at the infidelity toward my father. I even wondered if I was misinterpreting what I had read.

"That was the only time," Irv said softly.

I turned to him. "Sam read this?"

He nodded.

"And you're still alive?" I said.

"He was angry at both of us. He threw the journal at me that night, after he found it—threw it as hard as he could. That's how he let me know he knew about it, eight years after it had happened. He couldn't even say the words. God, he was so damn hurt. So mad." Irv put his head in his hands. "It took us all a long time—a lot of years—to get over this. I guess we never did. How could we? How could things ever be the same again?"

"I never knew—"

"We all behaved in front of you, most of the time." He looked up. "God only knows how. None of us wanted you to be stuck in the middle. I imagine Sam would have left Aurora, but for you. He certainly would have liked to jettison me from his life. But we all got past it because of our common interest in you."

"What about Wilson?"

"I told him right after it happened," Irv said, "so by the time Sam found out all those years later, it was old news. Wilson actually understood. He was sad and hurt, but he knew it didn't mean I loved him any less. The man is a saint."

I hardly heard what Irv was saying because the import penetrated my thick skull. I was born in March of the following year. I could tell Irv knew exactly what I was thinking.

"Are you?" I whispered.

He didn't respond.

"Are you my father?"

Judy Pomeranz

Chapter Seventeen
Sick or Saintly?

"I don't know," Irv finally said.

"Jesus," I muttered. "How can you *not know if you're my father?*"

"Does it matter?" Irv's facial muscles tensed.

I slapped the end table beside me so hard my palm stung. "How can you ask that?" I shouted. I stood up and paced. "It's no wonder I'm so screwed up."

Irv appeared dwarfed by the armchair he sank further into, and I could tell he had no idea what to say. I felt sorry for him, but no less angry. I sat on the sofa and closed my eyes, trying to regain my equanimity.

"Listen, Irv, you know I love you, in spite of this whole mess and in spite of whatever the truth may be. But hell, yes, *this is important to me.* What the fuck do you *think?*"

"What do you want me to do?" His voice was soft and weak.

"I don't know."

"Sam thought I was your father," he said quietly.

"He did?"

Irv nodded wearily. "He made it abundantly clear the day he threw Aurora's journal at me. In the course of his ranting, he let it slip that he had long suspected he might have a problem because he'd slept with so many women—both before your mother and while they were married—and never impregnated one. Then you were conceived and he figured he had it in him, after all. So, for all those years afterward, he felt newly empowered. More than that, he felt he had this little person all his own, an actual part of him, whom he loved more than he loved himself. But when he read the journal and learned about that night at the lake, all the pieces fell into place."

"So, you're telling me Sam has treated me as his daughter for all the years since then, even though he believed I was your child?"

"Not that you were my child, exactly, just that I was your biological father. He was always your father."

I shook my head; that sounded way too pat, but there was nothing left to say. I couldn't believe Sam Jackson had lived with me, raised me, tried to have a civil relationship with me as an adult, and even now sent me checks each month, checks I continued to return unopened and unacknowledged, all the while believing I was the child of his wife's lover. Was that incredibly sick or saintly?

I, in return, had shunned him, hated him, for being insufficiently fatherly (the irony was killing) and for trying to protect me from the knowledge of my mother's suicide. I had hated him for the years of cruel and insensitive behavior I was sure had led to my mother's depression, behavior I had assumed was entirely unprovoked and unwarranted.

Now the deck was reshuffled. I no longer had any idea who was saint and who was sinner. Nor did I know where I stood in the whole mess.

Chapter Eighteen
It's the Way Life Works

Two days later, I rented a car and drove out to the nursing home in Sag Harbor. I did it on my own, without Irv's help. It was time I acted grown-up.

Sam looked more shrunken and vacant than he had the last time I saw him. He lay in bed with his eyes wide open, but showed no awareness that he had a visitor. His breathing was raspy and labored, his complexion sallow, and his eyes duller than before.

I sat carefully on the edge of the bed, lifted his hand, and let it lay heavily in my own. I thought about the brushes this hand had held, the clay it had dug into, the Scotch it had knocked back, the women it had fondled, the children whose curls it had tousled.

"You're his daughter?"

I was startled by the voice, and turned to see a young woman in a powder blue uniform standing near the door.

"Yes... I mean, I guess... I did sign in..."

"I know." woman came closer. "I wanted you to know he's been declining precipitously these last two or three days."

"His wife called me."

"We didn't have a phone number for you. I'm sorry. I don't think it'll be long."

"He's dying?"

She nodded and smiled sadly. "I'm going to miss him. He was a hoot when we first met him, back when he first moved in. He flirted with everyone in sight, on his good days. He's always been a lady's man, huh?"

I nodded. "When's he—what do you anticipate…?"

"Time-wise? I don't know. Maybe a week, maybe a day or two. The family—the rest of the family—has ordered hospice care."

"Thank you," I murmured.

"I'll leave you alone." The woman quietly closed the door behind her.

I looked at the body on the bed and thought about the man who had supported me all those years—not heroically, God knows, but by doing what he knew how to do and as well as he was able.

More saintly, on balance, than sick.

As I stood over him, I saw a tear creep down his cheek. It took me a moment to realize it was mine.

"Thank you," I whispered. I pretended he responded with a nod and a smile.

***

The funeral was held a week later. It was an enormous affair filled with flowers, glowing tributes, paeans, and eulogies delivered by the high and mighty. Press coverage was relentless and inaccurate, exemplified by such screaming headlines as:

PRODIGAL DAUGHTER COMES HOME

INSIDE SCOOP ON ARTIST'S $$$ ESTATE

BATTLE BETWEEN THE DAUGHTERS

There was no prodigality, no inside scoop, and no battle between the daughters. My contact with Daisy in the days leading up to the funeral was minimal and civil. I had, however, spent a good deal of time with Julia, who provided me great comfort by listening to my lengthy, guilt-ridden ramblings, graciously excusing my behavior toward Sam, and assuring me that he had always blamed himself and his own shortcomings for the estrangement.

"He knew he was not the best father, Dawn. He knew he wasn't there for you when he should have been. He tried hard to make up for that in raising Daisy and was so dedicated to it, I'm afraid he spoiled her." She put her finger on her lower lip as if to stop its

124

trembling. "They loved each other so desperately. And Sam adored little Heather."

"I can understand why," I said.

***

As I walked alone to my rental car after the private burial service, Irv came up alongside me and took my elbow gently. "Doing okay?"

I nodded. "How about you?" In spite of the several messages he had left on my answering machine, I hadn't spoken with him since the day he showed me my mother's journal.

"I've had better days, but I'm okay."

"Where's Wilson?"

"I told him to go on home. I'd like to talk with you, if you'll let me."

"About what?"

"I know you're angry that I didn't tell you about Aurora and me sooner, but I thought it was better that way for everyone. I now see I was wrong, and I'm so sorry."

"Why *did* you finally tell me?"

"You were going to find out soon enough, with all the poking around you were doing, especially after Julia mentioned Sam's fertility problem."

"You had to know that would happen when you urged me to do this biography in the first place," I said. "How could you not?"

"I should have figured on that. Maybe that's why I wanted you to do it. Maybe some part of me wanted you to know. I only wish I'd told you sooner. I'm so sorry to have hurt you."

I stopped walking and turned to face him. "I *was* hurt, Irv, and angry. But now I don't know what to think or feel. I'm not mad at you right now, or at my mother. I'm not even angry with Sam, which is totally disorienting. I don't know what to do with all the energy I've always devoted to hating him. He gave me an excuse to be pissed off at everything in my life, and without that, I don't know how to approach the world."

Irv squeezed my elbow, and we walked again.

"I do feel angry about one thing, though: that Sam died before I had a chance to work things out with him."

"God, I know. I'm so sorry."

"I'm not looking for an apology. It's just the way life works."

I opened my car door and slipped into the driver's seat.

"Meet me at Sir Harry's?" Irv said.

I didn't answer. I'd decide as I drove.

***

I looked around Sir Harry's, waiting for my eyes to adjust to the darkness, and found Irv in the back sipping something pink; a Glenfiddich waited for me.

"What's the iridescent drink?" I asked in mock disgust.

"A Cosmopolitan. You know I'm a slave to trends."

I smiled at him cautiously, comforted by the resumption of our old inane but familiar repartee.

Irv held his glass up in a toast. "To Sam." His voice quivered.

I held my glass up to his and clinked.

"Nothing will ever be the same without him," he said.

I nodded, and we each drank.

Then Irv drew in a deep breath and said, "I want to talk about Aurora."

"I don't. There's nothing left to say. Let's move on."

"I want you to understand—"

"I'm not a child. I understand how these things happen."

"But it wasn't one of 'these things.' It was different."

I took another sip of Scotch.

"Have you ever heard of 'courtly love'?" he asked.

I rolled my eyes. "Please, Irv, not a lecture—"

"Have you?" he persisted.

"Only in a medieval context," I said, resigned to the discourse that would inevitably follow.

"Right, but it describes my relationship with your mother. I admired her, worshiped her. She was so bright, clever, articulate, and so beautiful. But so painfully human. Our relationship was based on shared intellectual interests and an unspoken knowledge that we brought out the best in each other. We were each wittier, more sparkling, in the presence of the other. That was hardly the effect Sam had on any of us."

"Hardly," I agreed.

"What happened on the dock was not about sexual attraction precisely, though there was an element of that." He paused, thinking. "It certainly wasn't planned, and it never happened again. That wasn't what our relationship was about.

"The oddest thing, is that, when Aurora became pregnant, she and I never once discussed the possibility that the baby—you—might have been created that night. I always wondered, and she probably did too, but we never talked about it. When you were born, you looked just like your mother, which was a great relief, so the issue became, as Wilson would say, moot. Ultimately, I stopped thinking about it, and maybe your mother did too, though it's hard to say since she agonized quietly over so many things."

I nodded, staring at the table.

"So was happy being your godfather and having the best of you. I didn't need to know if you were my biological child. I didn't want to. Neither of us wanted to hurt Sam. But we did."

"How did he find the journal?" I asked.

"Your mother was out, and Sam needed scissors. He went into Aurora's desk. That's when he came across it."

"And read it," I said.

"He had no compunctions about privacy."

"God, it must have been awful when she got home."

"I can only imagine." Irv drank the last of his Cosmopolitan and signaled the waiter for another round.

"I still remember coming home from school to find her 'modeling' for him that afternoon," I said. "It was unbelievably horrible."

"So I heard. She was devastated that you saw her like that. She was a changed woman from that moment on."

"I don't understand how you and Sam could have remained friends after that."

"I don't understand it myself," Irv said. "It was rough. He exploded. He punched a hole in my living room wall to keep from punching me. Then, for a long time, we didn't speak. But things returned to normalcy. It amazed me, but I was so damned grateful they did. The months I spent without you and Sam and your mother were the worst of my life. I'd become dependent on all three of you. You were family to me and Wilson, and I couldn't bear to lose another family." He looked at the ceiling and paused. "One of the things I

127

admired most about your father is that he put it all behind him, or appeared to. I don't know how, and I don't think many men could have or would have. I'm sure he did it for you."

I didn't have the energy to cross-examine him on that point and, for once, didn't feel the need for either an argument or a conclusive answer.

Chapter Nineteen
Dispositions

Two months after the funeral, on a cool, sunny afternoon, I opened the door for a deliveryman who arrived with two large crates containing paintings by Sam Jackson.

My father's will had provided that I would inherit the full contents of his studio, including everything, as the lawyer put it, from pencils to paintings. After weeks of sifting through mountains of stuff, I took home a carload of sketchbooks, drawings, and art books, along with old brushes and cans I was certain I remembered from my childhood. Beyond that, all I wanted were the two paintings in whose creation I had played a part: *Washerwoman Reading Euripides*, which bore my handprint, and *Slay it Again, Sam*, the first of the seminal Cutaways, whose style was inspired by my school assignment, though my father never stopped attributing his inspiration to the surrealist Max Ernst.

I invited Julia and Daisy to take whatever they wanted from the rest of the studio's contents, then let Sam's assistants divide the remainder amongst themselves. They had played a far greater role in the creation of all these works than I had. Besides, having consistently refused my father's charity in the past, I suppose I was continuing to do so out of habit.

The deliveryman carefully pried open the first wooden crate, pulled out a large package, and unwrapped layer upon layer of cushioning material to reveal the strikingly expressive *Washerwoman*, which he leaned against the wall. As he went to work on the next crate, I stared at the small handprint in the corner, a print still slightly obscured by streaky remnants of the brown paint my father had slashed on then scraped away. I pressed my large, open hand against it, amazed that such a tiny, delicate mark had once been made by me.

I stepped back and gazed at the painting from across the room. It was perfect right there; I would hang it on that living room wall.

I turned my attention to the picture emerging from the second crate, the Cutaway painting. As the deliveryman pulled away the last bits of downy wrapping, the intensely joyful under layer of colors flew out at me. The magic was still there. And the little sunrise symbol—I couldn't take my eyes off it. I stared and stared and smiled, or perhaps cried. All I know was that I heard, with great clarity, my father's words to the reporter: "I've decided to give this painting to my beautiful little girl."

After sending the deliveryman on his way, I stood in front of that painting and pondered where to hang it. It had to be a special place. I wandered through my apartment seeking the right wall. The bedroom? Living room? Hallway? I dragged the large canvas from place to place, trying it out against every wall large enough to accommodate it. Space was no problem, as I had little art and expansive walls. Color was not an issue, as the painting had every hue known to man, and my décor was neutral. But no placement seemed right. No wall was perfect for this painting that had finally, after all these long years, come home.

***

That night, I leaned the painting against my bedroom wall before crawling into my four-poster bed. I watched the colors flit and flutter across the canvas as passing cars threw light into the room. Then I fell into a peaceful, dreamless sleep.

When I awoke, I knew where the painting would go, where it would be perfect.

I dragged it into the kitchen, leaned it against the refrigerator, and made myself a big pot of Jamaica Blue Mountain coffee. I sipped a steaming mugfull as I stared at the painting and recalled how, as a child, I had made up stories about what was going on behind the perforated film of darkness. I had seen rain forests there, fairy kingdoms, palaces, and all forms of paradise.

Before I could change my mind, I walked over to the phone and called the delivery company; I arranged for expedited service. The painting would be picked up this morning. I wound the soft packing materials around and around and around the picture until it finally disappeared; I pulled it into the heavy crate it had come in. Then I sat down and waited.

The same deliveryman who had brought it to me the day before soon arrived at my door. "Where's it going this time, ma'am?"

I almost lost my nerve and told him to leave it where it was. Instead, I said nothing.

"Ma'am?"

I looked at the package. I looked at him. I looked back at the package.

"It's going to my niece," I whispered.

"Could you be more specific?" he said, poised to fill out the form.

"Heather, Heather Blackburn." I gave him the Larchmont address and left him to fill out the paperwork while I took a heavy cream note card from my desk drawer.

Dear Heather,
This is a gift from your grandfather who adored you. When you miss him, or when you feel lonely or a little sad, look at the colors and the sunshine he made, and think about the worlds of wonder underneath the black surface.
Love,
Aunt Dawn

I stuck the note into the crate before the deliveryman sealed it shut.

I hated watching that painting disappear. Again. But I was more disturbed by how saccharine I felt. This was not me; I was neither sentimental nor noble. The concepts didn't suit me, and the vulnerability they implied frightened me. I believed, even then, I had done the right thing, but I yearned for my old familiar, cranky self, which I trusted would return soon enough.

THE END

Judy Pomeranz

ELEGY

Judy Pomeranz

Chapter One
Nocturne

August 19, 1989

Thankfully, most of that day is a blur to me now, but certain details persist vividly in my memory like bits of a dream. I recall slipping off to the window on the far side of the living room, away from the crowd, and fixing my attention on the scene fifteen stories below. There was nothing unusual out there, nothing I hadn't seen on innumerable other occasions, but that brief interlude of observing the larger world constituted a moment of grace which rendered me blessedly oblivious, if only for an instant, to the scene taking place around me.

I set my Scotch on the windowsill and stared down at the idle young men and women sprawled over the front steps of the Metropolitan Museum of Art across the street. Though I had observed these creatures and their compatriots over the course of the twenty-two years I had lived on Fifth Avenue, I had never before taken the time or trouble to consider *why* they would spend their time sitting outdoors on those hard, dirty steps. Were they there by choice or default? Did they enjoy that milieu or were they trying to escape something? Were they happy? Was anyone? Did it matter?

For one strange moment, I imagined myself among them. In my fantasy, I wore tight black jeans, a black tee shirt, a plain black blazer, and a pair of those enormously heavy work boots the young sometimes favored. I half-reclined on the museum steps—like Ingres' *Grande Odalisque*, only more erect—and read a paperback book of poetry. Sylvia Plath. I melded into the crowd so completely that I became an integral part of the urban landscape, an aspect indistinguishable from any other.

I was snapped back to reality by the touch of a hand on my shoulder, which brought the absurdity of my reverie into sharp focus. The sad fact of the matter was, no matter how much black I covered myself with, I would never fit into any environment as naturally, as confidently, and as casually, as these denizens of the steps. I would look stiff, clownish, and, above all, ancient in the midst of such callow characters. For that day, at the age of forty-five, I was the oldest woman in New York.

I turned away from the window to find the hand on my shoulder was attached to my best friend, Mitzi Stone. I started to force a smile, but when I looked past her and saw the roomful of people, I lost the energy to dissemble. My facial muscles collapsed and my knees started to buckle. I grabbed Mitzi's arm for support.

"It's okay," she whispered, and gave me a moment to regain my bearings before gently guiding me to a chintz-covered chair.

As I sank heavily into its cushions, I wondered whether I would ever summon the energy to lift myself back out. Perhaps I would be devoured by this soft, sweet chair, never to be heard from again. I smiled at the notion of spending eternity deep in the embrace of the feathery upholstery.

"Are you all right?" The left corner of Mitzi's mouth pulled down as she spoke, and her right eyelid twitched; I recognized the tics as her peculiar indicators of anxiety, and I knew what she was anxious about. She was afraid her best friend had become *unglued*, as they say. That she had gone *nuts, crazy, insane*. That she was *playing without a full deck*. That *her elevator didn't reach the penthouse*. That she was *one fry short of a Happy Meal*. I continued to smile as these idiotic but apt phrases reeled through my mind.

Mitzi's lips smiled back at me, but her eyelid still twitched. "Can I get you anything?"

"My Scotch. I left it on the windowsill."

"Are you sure you—"

"I'm not drunk. Please, get me my Scotch."

She moved toward the windowsill but stopped to talk with a small clutch of solemn gentlemen dressed in dark suits. As they chatted, each one of them ever so discreetly snuck a surreptitious peek in my direction.

Loony. Out to lunch. Unburdened by sanity. I amused myself by coming up with euphemisms to describe what these people no doubt perceived as my state of mind, but the novelty soon wore off. I wished Mitzi would stop talking and get the drink. I didn't care about drinking it; I just wanted to hold it. The smell reminded me of Charles and of my life. Not this farce in the living room, but my real life, the one that had ended on Tuesday, four days ago.

***

I had been at our home in East Hampton. It was one of those brilliantly sunlit August mornings when the damp air shimmers in a thousand colors, like pointillist brushwork. I had just finished swimming my morning laps, the full fifty. I pulled my goggles off, tossed them onto the deck, lay back in the clear water, and started to do a luxuriously slow backstroke, my reward for finishing the laps in good time. I concentrated on the feel of the cool water sliding across my body and the sun baking the kinks out of my arm muscles, which were still tense from the vigorous stroking. I paddled lazily with one hand and touched my abdomen with the other, enjoying the taut feel of it.

I closed my eyes and pondered the day's schedule. I had lunch with Mitzi and Caroline in Southampton, and then had to pick up a few things at Saks before my three o'clock tennis game with Sally Fromer at the Maidstone Club. Singles. I made a mental note to stop at the florist after that to make sure they had the centerpieces for Saturday night's Great Gatsby Picnic. The tulips *had* to be Dutch, even if they were from a hot house; I was not going to put up with those garish South American ones again this year.

Our annual Gatsby party had frankly become a burden. It was a ridiculous tradition that required more effort every year, but it was an evening people had come to expect. Our friends anticipated it for months, and the local press post-mortemed it for weeks, so while it was far from my idea of a good time, it was non-negotiable.

As I flipped over to do an easy breaststroke, I saw Mitzi standing at the far edge of the pool. Dressed in khaki shorts, an ivory linen camp shirt, and her big Jackie-O sunglasses, she looked into the water without moving. I swam over to where she stood and grabbed the side of the pool.

"I never thought I'd see *you* awake at this hour," I said. "What's up?"

"I have something to tell you." Her voice was oddly flat; she spoke in a monotone that reminded me of a cartoon character under hypnosis.

"So, tell me." I took off my cap and dunked my head back into the water to smooth my hair.

"Get out." Mitzi's statement was neither an invitation nor a request. It was a command.

Puzzled and frightened by her demeanor, I did as I was told. I grabbed one towel and wrapped it around my head, then dried my arms, legs and torso with another. It seemed important that I act as if nothing was the matter.

"What is it?" I propped my foot up on a chair and carefully dried the skin between my toes. "Why are you here?"

"Sit down." It was another command.

I bundled myself into a heavy white terrycloth robe and turned to her. "Would you *please* tell me what this is all about?"

"Sit down."

To avoid prolonging the unpleasantness, I sat on the edge of the padded lounge chair. "What *is* it?"

Mitzi sat down beside me and looked straight ahead. She opened her mouth as if to speak but no words came out, just a squeak. She took my right hand in her left and stared at it with an odd, twisted expression. "It's about Charles."

I shook off her hand and yanked on the ends of my robe sash, tightening it so much I could hardly breathe. "What *about* him?" My husband had returned to Manhattan a week earlier to take care of some business and was due back in East Hampton on Saturday, in time for the party.

"Daniel just called." Mitzi referred to our houseman in Manhattan who had been with Charles longer than I had. "He asked me to tell you."

"*What?*" I stood up and reflexively tugged again on the ends of the sash so hard it cut into my waist. "He asked you to tell me *what?*"

***

That was the moment.

As I reran the scene in my mind, I recognized that particular instant at the pool as the last moment of my real life. The interminable moments since then had constituted a whole new state of being—or non-being. Something entirely unconnected to anything belonging to me.

When Mitzi finally brought my Scotch from the windowsill, I inhaled its aroma before taking a drink. The smoky smell and tinkling sound of the ice cubes were familiar and good. I took a sip and tried to will myself into a kind of Proustian state. If Madeleines could transport one to a world of the past, I reasoned, why not Balvenie?

"Keep them away from me," I said.

Mitzi crouched down so she could speak to me without raising her voice. "Keep who away?"

"All of them."

"But Lauren—"

"Please."

"I'll do what I can." She stood up, took a deep breath, and walked into the crowd of people that filled my living room, the room that used to be Charles'-and-my living room.

I rested my nose on the rim of the glass and inhaled again, slowly and deeply. Though the scent conjured up a vague, indescribable sensation that spoke of Charles, I could capture neither a visual image nor any suggestion of his voice. I could see articles of clothing—the navy blue blazers he wore in the Hamptons, the tweed jackets he wore at home in Manhattan, the tuxedos he wore for benefits, and the ancient, wrinkled khaki pants he wore whenever he could get away with it—but I could not see his features. I could recall words he had spoken at dinner speeches, but could not hear the notes of his voice.

Deeply ensconced in the chair, I tried to create a world in my mind where everything was as it had been before. Once created, I decided, I would live there. I was lucid enough to know that living in such a place—a place with no basis in current, tangible fact—constituted insanity, but that didn't matter.

A man's voice penetrated the borders of my new world. "Lauren, darling, we're so sorry."

I turned toward the voice and found two familiar faces, to which I could attach neither names nor associations. One belonged to an olive-complexioned man wearing pinstripes and a cobalt blue Hermes tie dotted with little yellow clovers; the other was affixed to a female head covered with nicely highlighted hair. As the faces moved toward me to plant wispy air kisses next to my cheek, I viewed them as if through a fish-eye lens. They zoomed in, each face morphing into an enormous conical nose trailed far behind by pinprick eyes.

"He did so much for so many people," the man said. "We'll miss him terribly."

"Thank you so much." The appropriate words and gracious tone of my own voice took me by surprise. To see what would happen, I tried it again: "And thank you for stopping by." Not bad. I sounded almost normal.

"We're here if you need anything, darling," the woman said.

As soon as they walked away, a tall, gray-haired man approached. "I wish I could say something that had some meaning." He touched my shoulder.

"Thank you," I said.

As soon as he stepped away, another platitude-spouting couple appeared, and Mitzi came up behind my chair. "I'm sorry," she whispered. "I tried to keep them away."

I realized I could get through this party—was that what they called it after a funeral?—by sitting here and thanking people. Yes, I would thank them all, regardless of what they said, while pursuing my own thoughts. And so I did, sniffing the Scotch and taking an occasional sip between encounters.

If the past was real, it had to be out there somewhere, for nothing turns to nothing. Wasn't that physics? If that were the case, I should be able to reclaim the past. If the past was *not* real, then I hadn't lost anything. That seemed positive but left me rootless.

When Charles' brother, Findlay, came over to see how I was doing, I asked him to refill my drink. He did so without comment, and brought it back with a small plate of hot canapés, which he placed on the satinwood table beside me. He planted a kiss on top of my head and walked away.

The smell of food made me nauseous; I had not eaten anything but a few crackers since Tuesday. I pushed the plate away but the stench of crabmeat remained in my nostrils. That's what we would have been eating at the Gatsby Picnic. Crab legs. Tonight. I had to give him credit; Charles had finally found a way to get out of that damn party.

***

"*What* did Daniel ask you to tell me?" My voice sounded shrill as it echoed off the ceramic tile wall that ran alongside the pool. My fingers were sore from clutching the terrycloth robe ties so tightly, but I couldn't release them.

Mitzi shook her head; a tear crept out from under the dark lens of her glasses.

"Is Charles sick? Was he in an accident?" I grabbed her by the arms and shook her, as if I could somehow shake a response out of her.

"No."

"What *is* it then?" My voice was an octave too high and far too loud.

"Daniel found him in bed. He's dead." She just said it. Just like that.

"Jesus Christ." I sank down onto the lounge chair. I had heard the word *dead*, but couldn't assimilate its meaning. I watched bits of sunlight dance across the pool's blue water as I tried to absorb the message. "What happened?"

"I'm not sure."

"When—?"

"This morning. Charles didn't come down to breakfast, so Daniel went upstairs to check."

"When did he die?"

"During the night."

"Jesus Christ."

Mitzi draped her arms awkwardly around me.

"What do we do?" The words didn't sound appropriate, but I had no others.

"Jimmy's on his way. He'll take us back to Manhattan."

***

The minister came over to the chintz chair where I sat sniffing and sipping my Scotch. He crouched down so his face was level with mine. "I have to go now." His voice was deep and theatrically somber. "Are you going to be all right?"

I instinctively averted my face so he would not get the full impact of my alcohol-drenched breath. "I'll be fine." That came out surprisingly nicely. "And thank you for everything you've done."

"I've done nothing compared to what Charles did for the church all these years, and for so many others."

This was a twist. Was I supposed to comfort *him* now? Make him feel better about his meager efforts? I gave it a shot. "You've been wonderful to me. I couldn't have done it without you." *Done what?* I wondered as I said it, for I had not done a thing since Tuesday. Nonetheless, I smiled.

The minister returned my smile, rather sadly. "You're so brave." He took my hand. "The mayor did a wonderful job of summing up Charles' generosity in his eulogy. It was a lovely tribute."

I nodded.

"Please remember I'm here for you. I'll call tomorrow."

***

Jimmy Willis arrived in East Hampton around noon, full of kind words and condolences. He helped Mitzi and me into the back seat of the Lincoln, and we took off for Manhattan.

Jimmy had driven Charles and me for over a decade, shuttling us from place to place in Manhattan, and to and from East Hampton. But once he delivered us out here to the far tip of Long Island, away from the gridlock traffic and parking problems of the city, we both enjoyed driving ourselves. I loved to put down the top of my little Mercedes and let the wind blow through my hair. It was one of the few things in my life, like swimming, that made me feel young.

None of us spoke on that dreadful trip to Manhattan until we were well west of the Hamptons, passing through the endless landscape of strip-malls, superstores, and suburban housing tracts that constitute so much of Long Island.

"How did it happen?" I said.

"I beg your pardon, Mrs. Acheson?" Jimmy tilted his head back and to the side, as if to hear better.

"How did Charles die?"

"You don't know?" I caught him sneaking a look at Mitzi in the rearview mirror.

"No, I *don't* know. That's why I'm asking." I regretted my tone of voice, as I was fond of Jimmy.

"I... uh... I don't know either, Mrs. Acheson."

"Tell me."

"You'll have to ask Daniel, ma'am." Jimmy gave the car more gas. "I wasn't there. Daniel called me at home and asked me to come get you."

Mitzi reached across the broad back seat and patted my hand. "We'll be there soon."

"I'm really sorry, Mrs. Acheson," Jimmy murmured.

***

After the minister left, I curled myself more snugly into the soft chintz chair. If not for the company, I would have rolled up into a full fetal position. I nibbled on a tiny quiche, but it made me feel so ill I had to take a swig of Balvenie to push my stomach contents back down.

I looked across the room with detached interest, at the sad expressions on the faces of the few remaining guests. Charles' brother, Findlay, was pale and thinner than usual; he wore an expression so melancholy the corners of his mouth dragged along his jawbone. Mitzi's husband Paul wiped his brow with a linen handkerchief as he talked to a neighbor. Mitzi herself looked ten years older than she had four days ago.

I had yet to shed a tear that I could recall; the past four days were such a blur I didn't know precisely *what* I had done. I was grateful for the oblivion, even though I sensed it was unnatural and inappropriate. This was a time for mourning, and I was supposed to be the chief mourner. So, while I accepted kudos and words of admiration about my "bravery," "courage," and "quiet strength," I knew none of these were accurate characterizations. *Zombie. Completely without affect. Unfeeling. Cold. Heartless. Out-of-it. In a fog.* Those came closer to the mark.

As I lifted my head, Whistler's *Nocturne* came into my line of vision. I had never liked this painting and had only allowed it to be hung in this hidden corner of the living room because it was Charles' favorite. I preferred more decorative works, like the Monet with its blood-red poppies, the golden sunflowers of van Gogh, or the chubby little Renoir girl. I even preferred the seventeenth-century Dutch still-lifes that hung in Charles' library. They had some color, some arguable beauty, and a degree of craftsmanship in the execution that was completely lacking in this Whistler painting of smog.

But now, as I examined it through my own haze, I could vaguely detect an entire, fully imagined scene behind those atmospheric veils of dull color. For the first time, I perceived a living, pulsating city obscured by the fog. How remarkable. If Whistler was a genius, as Charles had contended, perhaps his special gift lay in his understanding that the spark of life could be so deeply buried that it could disappear entirely from human perception.

***

Jimmy got us back to the city by three that afternoon. He escorted Mitzi and me into the co-op, then left. Daniel and Charles' brother Findlay were waiting for us in the library, along with Charles' lawyer and his physician. The four men stood as we entered the room. Each of them gave each of us a kiss on the cheek or a small squeeze in the nature of a weary hug. Each one told me how sorry he was and murmured nice words about Charles. Then we all sat down.

"What happened?" I asked.

All four men were silent. Findlay turned to Mitzi who slowly, almost imperceptibly, shook her head. I looked at the floor and waited.

"Daniel found Charles this morning."

I thought it was the lawyer Gerald talking, but couldn't be sure because my eyes were focused on the delicate rosy pattern of the Persian rug.

"I'm so sorry, ma'am."

That was Daniel.

"It was too late. There was nothing anyone could have done at that point."

That must be the doctor, whose name I couldn't remember.

"Jesus Christ, it's horrific. Unbelievable."

That was poor, dear Findlay.

When I was able to raise my head, I looked at each man, one by one. "How did he die?"

No one answered. I folded my hands in my lap and waited for a response, though the men's demeanor and their stalling had already confirmed my worst suspicions.

"Pills," the doctor finally said.

"What kind of pills was he taking?"

"These were not pills I had prescribed," he said quickly. "They were sleeping pills he had procured on his own."

"I never knew Charles to have trouble sleeping." I'm not sure why I felt compelled to make them verbalize what they didn't want to think about.

"It wasn't an accident."

I stared at him for a long moment, then turned toward the loaded bookcases.

"He swallowed the entire bottle," Findlay said quietly. "He died choking on his own vomit." In an effort to stifle a sob, or in empathy, Findlay gagged.

I wanted to breathe deeply but feared that doing so might open me up to more horrible news, so I kept my breathing shallow and labored. "Why?" It was the only word I could manage.

Once again, the men were silent for a long moment.

"We don't know," Gerald finally said.

"Was there a note?"

"A short one." Findlay pushed himself carefully up off the chair, as if he were very fragile, and walked over to Charles' mahogany desk. He took a piece of heavy ivory paper from the blotter and brought it to me.

I fingered it; I put it to my cheek and felt it. The creamy stock was Crane, the bold pen stroke had been made with Charles' favorite Montblanc, and the writing was definitely his. I held it down close to my lap and explored each twist and turn of the black ink marks, but my eyes wouldn't focus clearly enough to make out the words—or my mind wouldn't.

"Are you all right?" the doctor said.

I nodded, but kept my attention on the note. Each letter was formed like textbook copy for the Palmer Method. Charles's writing was so elegant he had often joked that while he had nothing worthwhile to say, he said it quite beautifully. I stared at the page, willing my mind to make words out of the marks and sense out of the words.

Please forgive me. I just don't know what it's all about, and I am too tired to go on pretending I do.

My first thought, strange as it now seems, was that even in a suicide note, Charles had put the comma in the right place, between the two independent clauses, just as he had once instructed me to do. Then my mind flashed on a profile that had appeared recently in a German magazine, after Charles had purchased a Holbein etching of the Holy Family at auction in Berlin. The headline was "Charles Acheson's Love of Art and Life."

"Can I get you something, ma'am?" Daniel said. "Something to eat? A glass of wine? Brandy?"

I shook my head.

"Would you like to get some rest?" the doctor said.

I nodded.

He asked Mitzi to help me get ready for bed. "And give her two of these." He handed Mitzi a bottle of pills with no apparent recognition of the irony involved in pushing pills at this particular moment.

"I want to go to the blue guest room," I said.

Mitzi guided me upstairs to the largest of the guest bedrooms.

"*Should* I want to go to that bed—our bed—the bed where he died?" I asked as I sat on the side of the guest bed.

"Of course not."

I kicked off my shoes and let my toes dig into the deep carpet pile.

"Can't I get you something to eat?" she said. "Sadie's made Vichyssoise. It might be soothing."

I shook my head. I didn't feel the need to be soothed; I felt calmer than I could ever recall feeling. Frighteningly calm. So calm I vaguely wondered what distinguished that state from death. But there was tentativeness to my tranquility, recognition that if my oblivion were pricked by the smallest of pins, I might explode, like an overblown balloon.

As I sat there on the bed, I wondered what had ever possessed me to create such a ridiculously cheery room. Why had I chosen these saccharine yellow and blue Mario Buatta fabrics? I dug my fingernails into the heavy padding of the quilted bedspread, vowing to redo it all in black if I ever found the energy.

Mitzi left the room, then reappeared with a blue nightie and a glass of water. She started to undress me as if I were a doll, so I responded as such, neither helping nor hindering the operation. She unbuckled my belt and unhooked my trousers, then undid the buttons of my cotton shirt and pulled it off. She coaxed me into a standing position, unzipped my trousers, and let them fall to the floor. She unhooked my bra and set it on the bedside table, but left my lacy panties in place. She slipped the satin nightie over my head and let it slither coolly over my torso.

She handed me the glass of water and two small blue pills, which I carefully placed on my tongue. They tasted bitter, which seemed perfect. "The water," Mitzi reminded me, though one of the pills had already dissolved.

I took a long sip, fascinated by the peculiar sensation of that single, lonely pill swimming around in my mouth. Then I swallowed.

I climbed into the bed linens, savoring the cool crispness of the Pratesi sheets, then lay my head on the pillow and closed my eyes.

***

I took one final swig of Scotch and slumped further down in my chair as the party, or whatever it was, drew to a close. The few remaining guests stopped by with words of comfort and consolation as well as offers of help, company, *anything at all you might need*. I knew it would be difficult to make good on the offers, since everyone would be heading back to the Hamptons now that their unpleasant duty here had been fulfilled. Not that it mattered; I wasn't planning to need anything.

As I nodded, tossed off tiny smiles as gifts, grasped hands, and gave thanks to those who paid me court, I tried to comprehend the notion that life around me would go on as usual. Life *had* been going on as usual since Tuesday. It was only for me, not for the world at large, that life as I knew it had ceased to exist.

After the last guests had said goodbye, when the only people left were Findlay, Mitzi, and the help, I did what I had wanted to do all day long. I curled up in the chair and fell back into that dazed state somewhere between sleep and death, confident that my own fog would not lift any sooner than Whistler's.

Judy Pomeranz

Chapter Two
Where There's A Will

August, 1989

Alone in my rooftop garden the morning after the funeral, my thoughts drifted back to the moment I first laid eyes on Charles Acheson. It was September 21, 1966; I was twenty-two years old.

I had begun my nightly walk from Midtown to my tiny efficiency apartment near Gramercy Park when the sky darkened to the color of slate, and the air became so thick and heavy it was palpable. I picked up my pace and tightened my grip on the brown envelope that held the manuscript I was taking home to review, a document I was certain held the key to my literary career. Though I had begun my job as a typist at the Wylie and Wylie Literary Agency only three weeks earlier, the elder Mr. Wylie had just that afternoon told me, with a wink and an embarrassing squeeze, that because I showed such great promise, I could take first crack at reading a novel from the slush pile. I wasn't sure whether my intelligence or my new mini-skirt was the greater indicator of promise, but I was thrilled to have the opportunity.

As I started to cross Fiftieth Street at Park Avenue, a brilliant flash of yellow illuminated the sky, thunder rumbled in the distance, and rain began. It was not the gentle pitter-patter Gene Kelly might have danced in, but the kind of downpour my father would have called a bladder-buster, and I might have called an omen.

Sticking the precious manuscript inside my cardigan, I ran for the nearest form of cover, which happened to be the silvery Art Deco overhang designed to protect the Waldorf-Astoria's guests from the elements. I knew the Waldorf was among the most elegant hotels in Manhattan, so I felt privileged but mostly intimidated standing in this rarified place.

Taking my cue from the crowd around me, I pretended to wait for a taxi, though I fervently hoped the rain would let up before I reached the head of the line; there was no way I could afford such a luxury. I checked the envelope for water damage and twisted the moisture out of my long hair while surreptitiously inspecting my cohorts. There were fifteen or twenty of them, all men. Most were handsomely dressed in business suits and polished black shoes, and all were well groomed, right down to their manicured nails. But they were surprisingly nondescript, not nearly as separate and apart as I had assumed Waldorf patrons would be. They resembled ordinary human beings, which came as quite a revelation.

One, however, was exceptional. He was at least six feet tall, and slim, with gray-flecked dark hair and strongly defined features arranged into a generous smile as he chatted with the doorman. Having recently discovered the miracle of window-shopping in designer boutiques, I recognized his trench coat and loafers as Burberry and Gucci, respectively, and was prepared to lay money, on the strength of the cuffs alone, that a custom-made English suit lurked beneath the Burberry. "Distinguished" was the word that immediately came to mind; he had the appearance and demeanor one of Wylie and Wylie's first-novelists would have called "patrician." The man met precisely the profile for the extraordinary type of person I would have expected to find outside the Waldorf-Astoria.

But before I could study him further, a long black limousine drove up and took this perfect specimen away. How utterly appropriate.

***

That was so long ago it seemed like ancient history. Prehistory. Almost everything had changed in the interim. The country had gone from being energetic, innocent, chaotic, rebellious, involved, and young, to being conservative, disaffected, mature, staid, and smug. I had done the same. But Charles had gone on, through it all, being simply and relentlessly Charles.

150

I sat up straighter and tried to force these memories from my mind, sensing my incapacity to deal with the emotional overload that would result if they were allowed to persist. I gazed past my prized topiary boxwoods at the monstrous gray air conditioning system of the building next door and recalled that barely a week earlier I had convinced Charles to approach that building's co-op board with an offer to have a decorative barrier installed around the machinery. A trellis on which vines would grow might be nice. I wondered if he had gotten around to that before he...

No, I would not think about that.

Daniel appeared, holding a portable phone.

"I told you I didn't want to talk to anyone," I said.

"I'm sorry, but it's Mr. Bailey. He says it's important."

I glared at Daniel but took the phone, wondering what Charles' lawyer could deem to be of sufficient importance to disturb a grieving widow—for that's what I was now, wasn't I?—the day after the funeral.

"I'm sorry to disturb you." Gerald paused as if waiting for a response.

As he had never been one of my best friends, I chose not to favor him with one.

"We really must get together," he finally said, "sooner rather than later."

"Why?" I brushed a wilted, brown leaf off the glass tabletop and watched it drift down to the tile floor.

"We need to discuss Charles' will."

"I know what's involved."

"You know what he did about the Foundation?"

"We had no secrets." I realized, as soon as the words left my mouth, how pathetic they sounded in view of what Charles had done. "I know he left a great deal of money to the Foundation, along with some other assets... securities, I suppose. That was always his plan, and I certainly had no objection to it. He assured me I would be provided for, as well."

"You have nothing to worry about on that score. He took *very* good care of you, but there are a couple of provisions we need to discuss."

"Such as?"

"I'd rather do this in person."

I didn't have the energy to argue. "How about two this afternoon?" If we had to meet, I wanted to get it over with.

"That's perfect."

I set the phone down on the table and walked over to the wrought iron rail that ran along the roof's edge. I looked out over the top of the Metropolitan Museum into Central Park, a view I normally found comforting, majestic. But today the scene appeared pale, blurred and hazy. The trees were grayish rather than bright green; the joggers moved like oozing blobs of matter, reminding me of the magnified germs one saw on public television; the buildings in the far distance were so indistinct they could have been mountains or storm clouds.

The fuzzy, Whistlerian scene puzzled me. Perhaps the optical oddness was the result of unusually high summer humidity, or smog, or maybe I needed cataract surgery. It was not until I touched my cheek that I realized the problem was of a different nature. It was tears that obscured the view, tears that slid down my face and onto the railing, tears that dropped to the terrace floor and dappled the terra cotta tiles.

They frightened me, these tiny drops of salt water, for I understood they signaled an impending end to my oblivion. Up until now, I had not wept, either for Charles or myself; I had not grasped the dimensions or the quality of my loss, and had hoped I might never do so.

I closed my eyes and tried to regain the state that had, until now, been mine without great effort. But shutting my eyes to the world only left me alone with the most haunting images. *He died choking on his own vomit.*

I snapped my eyes open and looked down at the noisy, dirty, busy, and potentially diverting world of New York. I wiped away the tears. Instead of shutting the world out, I would attempt the opposite. If I focused all my attention on the cacophony of images below, maybe my mind would have no room left to accommodate other thoughts or sensations.

I looked down at the Met and tried to imagine my favorite impressionist paintings that hung inside. Degas' dancers, Monet's poplars, Renoir's portrait of Mme. Charpentier and her children. But instead I saw Charles standing in front of the strange lion painting by Rousseau that always made him smile; Charles accepting his appointment to the museum's Board of Trustees; Charles donating three Monets in honor of the retiring curator of French art; and

Charles wearing the outdated tuxedo I detested to the opening of the Titian show.

I wiped a renegade tear and looked to the left, hoping to be distracted by the bustle of Midtown, the grandeur of the Empire State Building, the stateliness of the just-barely-visible twin towers rising out of the downtown smog. But instead I saw Charles' fifty-eighth floor office at the Acheson Foundation; Charles riding the bus so he "wouldn't lose touch;" and Charles taking me to the Presidential Suite at the Waldorf Towers the day I finally told him how I first observed him on that rainy day in front of the hotel.

In desperation, I followed the rail around to the right, looked down Eighty-second Street toward Madison, and tried to zero in on my favorite shops. But I found my eyes resting instead on Charles' beloved Tuscan restaurant, the one whose chef kept a special supply of snowy, spongy tripe on hand just for him.

There was no escape.

A phrase came to mind that Charles had read to me long ago; it had to do with the scales falling away from one's eyes. I didn't know where the words had come from, nor did I know who had said them; they had seemed ridiculous, at the time.

But now they resonated.

***

At exactly two o'clock, Daniel showed Gerald Bailey and his associate into the library.

"Thanks for seeing us." Gerald bent over to kiss my cheek.

"What's on your mind?" I asked in a peremptory manner.

"I'd like you to meet my associate, Tom Smithson." He motioned toward the pale young man by his side, who nodded shyly but shook my hand surprisingly firmly.

"I'm sorry for your loss," Smithson murmured.

The men gravitated to the mahogany leather wing chairs facing the sofa on which I sat. Smithson perched on the edge of one chair, causing hardly a ripple, while the more substantial Gerald settled heavily into the other.

"I'm pleased to see you looking so well," Gerald said in a smarmy and ridiculously inaccurate appraisal.

"Thank you." I folded my hands and waited.

"I was worried about you yesterday, but today you seem more yourself."

"What would you like to discuss?"

Smithson took a plastic pen and legal pad out of his scratched brown leather briefcase and sat poised, apparently ready to record anything of importance that might transpire. Gerald shifted his formidable weight, making the leather squeal softly, then leaned back and gave me a look of great earnestness.

"It's about the Foundation. You know it meant a great deal to Charles."

"Of course." I pushed the bottom brass button of my St. John jacket in and out of the buttonhole.

Gerald cleared his throat and continued as if giving a speech. "Directing the Foundation's grant program allowed Charles to make a difference in the way people lived their lives and to affect how society functioned. That was important to him."

"I *know*."

"He not only put his family wealth into it, but his life, his time. He spent dozens of hours each week directing the Foundation's operations. It was an enormous job."

"I *know* that, Gerald." I stopped playing with the button and gave him a hard stare. "I'm the wife, remember?"

He proceeded, unfazed. "You know he left substantial resources to the Foundation."

I nodded.

"Do you know how much?"

"Not exactly, but it's not something that greatly interests me." I saw Daniel coming and waved him away before he could offer drinks.

"He left four hundred and ninety three million dollars, in cash and securities." Gerald said the numbers slowly and leaned forward in the chair as if trying to grab my attention.

I nodded; the amount meant nothing. I had no idea of the specifics of Charles' financial status, nor did I wish to. I knew it was all inherited, and I knew there was plenty; that was all I needed to know.

"That is in addition to the three hundred and thirty million dollars the Foundation is already worth." Gerald stressed the numbers, still apparently anxious to provoke a response.

I was careful not to betray one. "Why are you telling me this?"

"The Acheson Foundation will be among the most influential philanthropic institutions in New York. With such vast resources, it will come under tremendous pressure; everyone will want a piece of the pie. The funds must be disbursed according to the Foundation's original mandate."

"So?"

"The mission statement is not terribly specific." Gerald turned to Smithson. "You've got it there, Tom. Read it to us."

Smithson pulled a document from his briefcase and read slowly in a soft tenor: " 'To foster the arts in New York City by providing direct assistance to both emerging and established New York artists—visual, literary, and musical—for specific projects or general living expenses.'" After he finished reading, Smithson fiddled nervously with the edges of the pages.

Weary of interjecting my terse comments and questions on cue into what was effectively a monologue, I decided to wait him out.

"There's a great deal of room for the exercise of discretion in making spending decisions," Gerald concluded.

"That's what the Board's for," I said.

"Exactly," Gerald said triumphantly. "And responsible disbursal of the funds in a manner consistent with Charles' wishes will be a grave responsibility for the Board, one requiring a great deal of time, energy, and study. A tremendous effort."

I looked pointedly at my watch. "What did you come here to discuss?"

He leaned further forward in the chair, resting his elbows on his thick thighs. "He left you in charge."

"He *what?*" I turned from Gerald to Smithson who quickly looked down at his blank legal pad.

"Charles' will stipulates that he wants you to direct the Foundation. It appoints you as his successor as Chairman of the Board of Trustees, which gives you the strongest voice in deciding how the Foundation's assets are to be disbursed."

"Don't I have a say in this?"

Gerald leaned back in his chair. He made a steeple out of his fingers and studied it. "There's nothing to say you can't resign the position, should that be your wish."

"This is a figurehead thing, right?"

"No, you have the same authority that Charles had."

155

"So, I'm supposed to *work* there?"

Gerald smiled indulgently. "You could say that."

"When did Charles make this decision?"

"Week before last," Gerald said.

I massaged my temples in an effort to alleviate an incipient headache. "So, he was planning to… to do what he did? That's why he revised his will?"

"I don't know." Gerald shook his head. "He asked me to make some amendments. I didn't question him."

"There's more?"

"One more, but it's unrelated." He shot a look I couldn't read at Smithson. "Let's make sure we're straight on this first."

"I don't know what he was thinking."

"It's an enormous responsibility and not something you should undertake lightly." Gerald spoke in a comforting tone.

"I have no interest in this. It's not the kind of thing I do. I want to resign. How do I do it?"

Before Gerald could respond, Smithson said, "Take a few days to think about it."

"If Mrs. Acheson wants to resign, that's her right. It's not our place to talk her out of it."

"Of course." Smithson appeared to gain in confidence. "But we owe it to Mr. Acheson to let her give the matter some thought."

I did not appreciate being discussed in the third person. "Why should I *think* about something I don't want to *do*?"

"It's what your husband wanted. He felt strongly it would be good for both you and the Foundation," Smithson said.

"Jesus Christ." I dropped my head into my hands.

"This is not about Charles. It's about Mrs. Acheson's wishes." Gerald spoke sternly to Smithton through tightly pursed lips, then directed his attention to me. "Listen, it's a hell of a big job, and if you don't want it, say the word and I'll prepare the paper work."

Smithson's words tumbled around in my head. *He felt strongly it would be good for both you and the Foundation.* I gazed at the packed bookcases and worn leather desk chair. I smelled Charles' newspaper-and-tweed scent. For the first time in five days, I saw Charles in startling detail. It was a fleeting picture, but vivid and powerful. My throat began to close and my eyes filled with tears, but I asserted control. "I'll let you know. You said there were other provisions you needed to discuss."

"Just one." He pulled a thick document from his black Asprey briefcase and paged through it. "Here it is." He ran his finger down one page. "It's about the books." Gerald gestured at the shelves lining the room.

Having had no idea what to expect after the Foundation bombshell, I felt an exquisite relief and almost laughed out loud. If there was one thing in the universe of Charles' possessions I cared not one whit about, it was the books.

Gerald began, "Charles left you virtually everything other than what went to the Foundation. The house in the Hamptons, this place, all his personal effects, the cash, securities, art—"

"Okay, Gerald. What about the books?"

"Those are the single exception."

"I have no interest in them. He knew that."

"He did," Gerald said in a patronizing tone, "and it's not as if they have great value. They're just old books."

"So, why would he provide for them specifically?"

"I suppose they meant something to him, and he wanted them to go to someone who would appreciate them." Gerald leaned forward. "He wanted you to know this was not intended as any kind of slight. He didn't think you would want them."

"I don't."

"Charles said you would welcome the opportunity to put more attractive objects on these shelves." He smiled, sat up straight, and tightened his bow tie, a signature item of apparel I found affected.

"You can stop treating me with kid gloves. I'm not interested in the books."

"Perfect. Then everyone's happy."

I thought that was an idiotic thing to say at a time like this.

"The firm will arrange to have the books packed up, and we'll get them out of your way as quickly as possible."

"To whom will they be delivered?"

"A friend of his. Sydney Ray Jenkins."

"Who's he?"

"Another avid reader, I gather. Charles told me it was someone he enjoyed discussing books with. That's all I know." Gerald put the papers back into his briefcase.

But now my curiosity was aroused. "I suppose I should meet him, or at least drop him a note. If Charles thought enough of him to leave him the books... Where does he live, here in New York?"

"No, California."

"Would you be good enough to give me an address and phone number?"

The two lawyers glanced at each other. "Sure," Gerald mumbled. "I'll have my secretary call you."

"Good." I stood as if to dismiss them.

"Right," Gerald closed his briefcase and stood too. "By the way, Sydney Ray Jenkins is a young woman." He spoke in his normal tone of voice but avoided eye contact. "Thought you'd want to know before getting in touch."

Chapter Three
We'll Always Have Paris

Summer, 1966

I had been a young woman—impossibly young and ridiculously naïve—when I first met Charles Acheson, shortly after my maiden voyage to Europe. I couldn't help wondering if this Sydney Ray Jenkins, whoever she was, resembled the person I had been then.

***

I had worked all manner of odd and debasing jobs during the four years following my high school graduation, to pay for that trip to Europe in the summer of 1966, the year my best friend Annette finished college. I had been a pink-clad waitress in a greasy diner, a hat-check girl in a men's club, a sales clerk at Woolworth's, a maid in a cheap motel, a babysitter for three screaming monsters, a mop-wielding member of a hospital cleaning crew, and a piece worker in a dress factory. I even did time in the refinery that had once employed my mother. All for the sake of the trip.

Though Annette and I had always talked about our long-planned and greatly anticipated voyage as a modern-day Grand Tour, we knew it would be more in the nature of *Europe on Five Dollars a Day*, but that was all right. Having been no further from my Bayonne, New Jersey home than Baltimore, where Annette attended college, I was thrilled at the prospect of seeing anything beyond the Atlantic shoreline. So, on June 1, we boarded our Icelandic Airlines flight for

Judy Pomeranz

Luxembourg with the intention of seeing as much of Western Europe as humanly possible in the space of three months.

***

As it happened, Annette did see a great deal of the continent, but my Grand Tour ended abruptly in Paris, our second stop, with an artist who painted pastel portraits of tourists on the *Place des Alpes* in Montmartre.

Though I knew nothing about painting and had never visited an art museum, I was instantly attracted to this young man. From my perch in a café on the edge of the plaza I spent hours discreetly but obsessively watching him ply his trade. My attraction to him was unusual, as I was hardly given to romantic flights of fancy. I would much later try to analyze it, with the help of a professional.

Did that first magnetic pull spring from the way he scrutinized his subjects, as if trying to penetrate their psyches? Or did it have to do with the lyrical way he translated the lines and forms of a face into wispy dashes of color that danced across the surface of the paper? The truth was likely far more mundane, having more to do with his wavy brown hair, his wiry frame, and the fact that I was in Paris.

After observing the artist for the better part of an afternoon, while Annette toured the Louvre, I concluded I had nothing to lose by approaching him. It was not the sort of thing I had ever done, but I was convinced it was the kind of behavior being in Europe was all about. So, I waited until he finished a portrait, and then walked over.

"C'est trés jolie, cette peinture," I said timidly, hoping for the best from my one year of high school French, supplemented by a Berlitz phrase book.

He looked up from the box of pastels he was arranging and said, in perfect American English, "Thank you. But you might want to work on that accent." His own accent was decidedly Brooklyn. He smiled broadly and offered me his right hand. "I'm Larry Barnes."

I shook his hand stiffly while a burning sensation at the tip of each nerve in my face told me I was blushing fiercely. "I'm Lauren Towson," I said as calmly as possible. "I like your work."

"I figured that out. Your French isn't bad." He studied my face for a long moment, almost as if he were planning to paint it. "I'm finishing up here. Can I buy you a coffee?"

***

The coffee turned into a glass of wine, which led to several more glasses of wine, which led to a happy but inebriated call from me to Annette at the youth hostel to let her know she would be on her own for a day or two. I hung up before she had a chance to talk me out of staying with Larry.

I was smitten from the first sip of coffee. Larry had a way of focusing on me as if I were the most attractive person he'd ever seen, and of listening to me as if I had something worthwhile to say. The only people I had dated in New Jersey seemed more interested in how I would look as an accouterment to them, so this was a new experience, and an utterly seductive one.

The weekend that followed was straight out of Hollywood. We walked up and down the twisty, vertiginous streets of Montmartre, picnicked in the *Tuileries*, wandered the cool, green lawns of the *Parc Monceau*, window-shopped on the *Rue St. Honoré*, drank schnapps with the ninety-year-old proprietor of Larry's favorite bar in Montparnasse, and viewed Old Masters at the Louvre, Monets at the Marmottan, and drawings at the Museé Delacroix.

Larry made me privy to his own small but intensely exotic world. His Spartan eighth-floor garret was strewn with brushes, canvases, paints, pastels, sketchpads, dirty dishes, and dirtier articles of clothing; it was dank, dusty, musty and claustrophobic; it reeked of old cheeses, oils, and turpentine; I was completely charmed. To me it all represented a sophisticated world of art and culture that had previously existed only in books, an alien world as far removed from Bayonne as a place could be.

At the end of the weekend, I phoned Annette and asked her to meet me at the *Café Argentier* and to bring my backpack. I wanted to surprise her with my good news.

"Jesus, Lauren, you don't even *know* the guy." Annette leaned across the small metal café table and glared at me with the stern, schoolmarm-ish expression she held in reserve for this sort of occasion. "You can't just move in with him. That's *insane*."

I took a deep breath and tried to line up my arguments, but it was difficult because she had a point. It *did* seem sudden, but it was the sixties, I was in Paris, and life didn't often hand out such opportunities.

"I understand exactly what I'm doing." I paused for dramatic effect. "I love him." I spoke the three words softly, trying them out to see how they felt. I wasn't sure what romantic love was, never having experienced it, but the words felt right; I believed them. No one had ever before made me feel special, and maybe that's what love was about.

But I knew that wouldn't be enough for Annette. "It's like he's a part of me, my other half who's been floating around the universe and we've finally come together." This was a stretch, but I felt a classicist like Annette might respond to a mythological reference.

She rolled her eyes. "You sound like a B-movie. How many women do you think he's done this with?"

"You don't even *know* him."

Her shoulders dropped. She lit a Gitane, inhaled deeply, and exhaled a stream of sweetly acrid smoke. "That's why I'm worried."

I put my hand on hers. "Don't be. Larry is sweet…"

"He's your ticket out of Bayonne," she interrupted, not taking her eyes off her cigarette.

"That's not fair."

"Maybe not." She tipped the ashes into a black plastic ashtray advertising Pastis, "but how can I go to Rome and leave you here, all alone?"

"I've never been less alone." I took a sip of *café au lait* and held the bowl to my face so the warmth and milky mocha aroma filled my head. I felt very Parisian.

Annette took a last drag on her Gitane, crushed the butt into the ashtray, stood up, kissed me on both cheeks, and walked away without another word.

***

Larry referred to the pastel portraits he created at the *Place des Alpes* as "banal pieces of *merde*" and claimed he only made them to pay the rent. He did what he called his "real work"—painting in oils—after hours, but it never seemed to sell.

I loved to watch him paint. I was seduced by the way he applied pigments to canvas, slathered them onto the support and sensuously smudged them together using brushes, knives, and even his fingers. I was intrigued by the way he created three dimensions on a flat surface, and captivated by the way he would paint something realistic then systematically distort it for his own mysterious artistic purposes. And I loved to hear him talk about his work in the art lingo that tripped so easily off his tongue, though I rarely understood it.

Best of all was the passion he brought to the process. As the child of a bus driver and a refinery worker, I had never before considered that passion and work might in any way go together, nor that a person could spend a lifetime engaged in the creation of things that had no use or place in the world but to be pleasing.

***

Our days together developed a comfortable rhythm that suited us both. While Larry worked at the *Place*, I wrote very private and very bad poetry in my journal, shopped at the local produce market, made dinner, and waited for him to come home. My ability to succeed as half of a reasonably functioning couple gave me satisfaction that bordered on confidence.

The best part of each day came after dinner, when I would take my place on the hardwood floor of the garret's tiny studio area and watch Larry work, for at these times I felt like his muse. Though he didn't like to talk while he worked, he would often shoot me a wink and a grin, or simply mouth *I love you*. Once, he stopped painting abruptly and pulled me down onto the dirty throw rug, where we made frantic, agitated love. Just like that.

With each passing day of my Parisian idyll, I fell more deeply in love with this amazing artist. I knew beyond any doubt I had found the man with whom I would spend my life.

***

One August evening as we lounged in bed, perspiring from the August heat and a flurry of amorous activity, Larry lazily pulled a picture postcard from the drawer of his nightstand and held it up.

"This is what I aspire to."

The card featured a series of irregular black splotches against a white background. I had never seen anything like it and had no idea how to respond.

"Robert Motherwell's *Elegy to the Spanish Republic*." He lay on his back, holding the card and staring at it for a long time before handing it to me.

I wondered if this was a joke, but Larry continued to gaze at the card, his mouth open, looking like an awe-stricken holy figure in a Sunday school picture.

"It's lovely," I said, feeling the need to say something.

"You think so?" Larry took the card back and laid it carefully on the pillow. Turning onto his side, he leaned up on one elbow and looked down at it. He wiped a drop of perspiration from his face.

"Absolutely."

"I've never thought of it as 'lovely,' but I find it tremendously moving." He touched the card lightly, as if he were petting a small animal. "It speaks so clearly of love and hate. It's all encapsulated in those amazing oppositions. So simple, but so complex. Motherwell is a goddam genius."

"A genius," I said softly, happy to have dodged the bullet and held my own in the conversation. I ran my hand down Larry's damp arm, enjoying the sultry breeze that blew in through the window.

"I want you to visit this painting for me when you go back to New York next month. It's at the Met."

I missed only a quick beat before responding, "I will."

Then I turned away from him, afraid I would start to cry, for this was the first time I had any clue he expected me to go back home according to my original schedule.

"Once you've seen it, you'll never view art in the same way." He touched my shoulder, and I turned back to face him. "It changed my whole way of working." He took a half-empty glass of white wine from the table. "Motherwell is practically why I'm an artist." He put the glass to my lips, and I took a sip, feeling like a communicant being served by a priest.

When he noticed the tears on my cheeks, he smiled and brushed them away. "I told you it was moving."

And three weeks later, on the second of September, he dropped me off at Orly with a kiss, a tight hug, and the words, "It's been fun."

***

Elegy

Upon returning to the States, I landed the job of clerk typist at the Wylie and Wylie Literary Agency in Manhattan, a position I would never have tried for if Annette hadn't pushed me. It's a mystery to me why the agency took on the high-school-educated girl from Bayonne when most such jobs went to Sarah Lawrence English majors, but I believe it was due to the elder Mr. Wylie's rather obvious and embarrassing admiration of my physical attributes. I preferred to think it was because I was particularly well read and motivated.

Regardless of how or why it happened, I was delighted to live in Manhattan as part of the literary world. I was also thrilled to work close enough to the Metropolitan Museum of Art that I could get there on my lunch hour to visit Motherwell's *Elegy*. And I did. Repeatedly. Obsessively. I was certain that if I could figure it out, I would be reconnected with Larry.

The first time I saw it in person, I was reminded of the side of a cow, viewed at very close range. The second time, it looked like a Rorschach test. Once, I imagined I saw a pair of eyeballs, and another time, buildings collapsing in an earthquake. But the plain truth of the matter was I saw nothing but black marks on a white background. Nothing beautiful and nothing moving. But I kept returning, kept staring, kept trying, because it was Larry's favorite painting. I persisted because I knew it took time for things to work their way into your psyche.

***

Larry had told me that when we were studying Monet's giant water lily paintings in the *Orangerie*.

They were the most beautiful paintings I had ever seen. I was enchanted by the lush brushwork that formed a shimmering web of pink, blue, green, red and yellow that ran around the curved gallery walls. But I had learned to let Larry speak first. I didn't trust myself not to blurt out something stupid or naïve. So I enjoyed the swirl of colors while waiting for him to react.

"What do you think?" he finally said.

I shrugged and turned the question around. "What do *you* think?"

"I think they're as trite and saccharine as the last time I was here."

"So, why did you come back?"

"The brushwork. There's a flair to it, and enough abstraction to allow for the possibility that there could be something beyond the ordinary, materialistic obviousness of it all."

I nodded, keeping my eyes fixed on the paintings, afraid to look directly at Larry.

"I feel they're on the verge of speaking to me. Maybe they never will, but I have to give them a chance, because some things take time to work their way into your psyche."

***

But it wasn't working for me with the Motherwell at the Met. Though I continued to visit and faithfully reported to Larry, in my daily letters, that I loved *Elegy* more with each exposure, the truth was that after six weeks, I still had no idea what it was about, and finally decided to give up the enterprise.

On a cool October afternoon, I took a long, hard look at the familiar black and white mélange for what I thought would be the last time, and walked away. I moved tentatively, sadly, toward the door, glancing at the paintings on my right and left, incomprehensible works that had become as familiar as my own apartment walls. But when I was a step or two away from the door, a tall, slim man walked in, a man I instantly recognized as the one I had seen outside the Waldorf just weeks before.

He was accompanied by another gentleman, taller and more slender, who moved through the gallery with the casual air of a person at perfect ease with his surroundings, a manner I found astonishing in this imposing place. I peered over my right shoulder, pretending to be interested in a painting I had just passed, then turned casually and walked back toward where the two men were standing.

The man from the Waldorf stood directly in front of *Elegy* and gestured toward it as he spoke.

"Okay, Ben, give me some help here." He moved back, as if to allow the broad sweep of the painting into his line of vision. "You know how much I admire most of the Abstract Expressionists…"

The man called Ben nodded.

"…But I just don't respond to Motherwell."

"Maybe you're trying too hard." Ben's eyes remained focused on the painting as he spoke. "Maybe if you spend some time with it, it'll start to work on you. You've read up on Motherwell, haven't you?"

"Everything I can get my hands on, including what you sent. I even met him once. He was an impressive enough guy—articulate, concerned—but I'm still not getting it."

"So, maybe he's not your thing. Why are you pushing yourself so hard on this?"

"For Martha." The man called Charles spoke quietly. "She wants to buy a painting from the *Elegy* series—one over at the Gantry Gallery."

"I didn't know she was a Motherwell fan." Ben flicked a piece of lint off his dark blue jacket.

"She says he's hot."

"She's right."

"So, convince me. What do you see in him? What should I see?"

It was as if this man called Charles was asking the questions on my behalf. I stood still and listened carefully.

"You've got the play of opposites—opposing forces—the black and white, and the juxtaposition of rounded and linear shapes." Ben swept his arm in wide circles, then rapidly up and down, tracing the lines of the composition as he spoke. "Some people see these opposites as suggesting war and peace, love and hate, good and evil. He created this series in response to the Spanish Civil War."

"But what's he saying about it?"

"That's the beauty of the work—and of Motherwell. He suggests intellectual content but doesn't force it on us. He raises issues to engage us in a dialogue, but he doesn't direct us." Ben moved closer to the canvas and walked slowly along its length, scrutinizing it bit by bit. "He doesn't tell you what he's got in mind. He may drop hints through cues or clues imbedded in the paint, but he leaves *you* to figure it out."

"You say that as if it's an advantage."

"It is, if you're a thinking person." Ben backed up a few steps. "You could spend a long time with this painting and never get tired of it. You could carry on a discourse with it for the rest of your life. It's not like a little Dutch genre scene or some frou-frou Impressionist light study."

167

"That's below the belt." There was a light note in Charles' voice that made me think he was smiling.

"Your Impressionists created worthy paintings, but they play a different role in life. They're about aesthetics. This is about ideas. A man needs both."

"I'm just not certain all the satisfactions of my life have to come from the visual arts."

"Art does it for me."

"Which is why you're a curator. And because you're not a bad one, I'll take a chance on the Motherwell. He obviously has something to say to you, and it means a lot to Martha."

"Why don't you come up to my office and we'll talk specifics. Which painting are you thinking about buying?"

"I'll show you. I brought an image."

I watched as they walked out of the room, thinking how odd it was I should once again cross paths with this man, especially in front of the Motherwell. It seemed as if some peculiar force was playing around with my life.

***

Hanging onto the cool metal pole and swaying with the rhythm of the southbound subway car, I mentally composed my letter. I would repeat everything the curator had said, but without attribution; his opinions would become my own. I would impress Larry with my new analyses and ideas, all based, I would say, on "extensive observation" of the painting. I would close, as always, with a declaration of affection and a breezy request to *drop a line when you have a minute*. But I would say it without pushiness; guys hated pushiness.

It would be my best letter yet. Maybe good enough to provoke his first response.

Chapter Four
Blessedly Far From Bayonne

August, 1989

Now that I knew the contents of Charles' will, I wondered if I had been as dimwitted in my relationship with my husband as I had been with regard to Larry. Though I recognized such thoughts were ungenerous and unfair to Charles, I had no idea what to think about this Sydney Ray Jenkins, mysterious beneficiary of his literary largess.

I sat in the library, where I'd been since Gerald and Smithson left, and searched my memory for some tidbit that might relate to her. Surely Charles must have mentioned her, so I tried out the possibilities: *Syd, Sydney Ray, Ray, Sydney, Ms. Jenkins.* I tried to imagine the various permutations being spoken in Charles' voice: *I've just been to coffee with my friend, Syd... Ms. Jenkins has joined our Great Books discussion group... Lauren, I'd like you to meet Sydney, our new receptionist at the Foundation.* I desperately wanted one of these to have a familiar ring, because I was unwilling to consider the possibility that Charles had been seeing someone behind my back.

That was inconceivable; everyone knew Charles was devoted to me. Didn't they? We were a unit, a team. I was *Mrs. Charles Acheson*, and he was *Lauren's husband*; we had used each other to define ourselves for all these years. Hadn't we? There had been an immutability to our relationship. Hadn't there? We were perfect together. Everyone said so. And we looked good and acted right.

So, what was this Sydney Ray Jenkins all about?

I scanned the bookcases, as if the answer might lie inside these books he was giving away. I pulled a tattered copy of *Swann's Way* off the shelf and carefully turned its fragile pages, recognizing Charles' tiny, precise handwriting in the margins. I saw underlining. I saw question marks and exclamation points. But the words and the marks were like hieroglyphics I couldn't decode.

I dragged out a volume by Hannah Arendt and one by Karl Jaspars. These too were filled with marginalia, layer upon layer in different inks, as if Charles had read and re-read these words many times. Why had he spent so much of his time with them? I paged through Kafka's *Castle*, Camus' *Plague*, Ionesco's *Rhinoceros*, Plato's *Republic*, Joyce's *Ulysses*, Kant's *Critique of Pure Reason*, and Rousseau's *Social Contract*. All were annotated. Hemingway, Fitzgerald, Faulkner, Munro, Dickens, and Dreiser were dog-eared, as if they had been lovingly read and caressed over the years, but they bore few written marks. I pulled out more and more and more.

"Mrs. Acheson."

Daniel stood in the doorway.

"Can I can help you?" His voice was calm, but he looked alarmed.

I followed his line of vision to the floor where dozens of books were strewn about. It took me a moment to realize I was the one who had created this mess.

"No, thank you," I said as if nothing were amiss. "

He remained in the doorway.

"I'm fine. I don't need anything."

He walked away.

Disconcerted and frightened by my loss of control, I placed the books back on the shelves in no particular order. Each time I touched a volume, I felt a bit of Charles, as if he were lurking inside. I could smell his particular aroma in these books, and knew that if I could decipher the meaning of the scribbles, I would find something of his essence, something of his soul. Something that might make me understand what he had done. For his books had been his most treasured possessions, his constant companions, through all the years I had known him.

Why would he leave them to Sydney Ray Jenkins rather than to his wife of twenty-two years?

This is not to say I wanted them. If they had been mine I would not have allowed them to remain on these shelves, because they were an eyesore. I made a mental note to have Edward, my decorator, search for books with beautiful bindings, and nice porcelain pieces to intersperse among them.

Yes. That was it. I didn't *want* the damn books, and Charles knew it. That's why he didn't leave them to me. I brushed my dusty hands on my skirt and walked out of the library with an air of resolve that felt almost authentic.

I called Mitzi; I wanted to go shopping. I wanted something long and slinky, black and comfy, and not too formal. Something I could wear for the entertaining I was planning to do. Plenty of it. I was going to pick up the pieces of the mess Charles had left behind, God damn him, and make a life for myself.

***

"He left you in *charge*?" Mitzi said, as we made our way down Madison Avenue toward Jacques Bouvier's Boutique. "Of the whole Foundation?"

"According to Gerald, I'm Chairman of the Board. Absurd, isn't it?"

As we passed the Glorious Food catering company, I pictured my next dinner party. It would be soon. I felt unaccountably good and alive out here on my home turf. Even the occasionally garish glitz seemed bright, beautiful and good.

" Why would Charles think you'd want to get into the middle of all that?"

"I have no idea."

"So, what are you going to do?"

"Resign." I paused to examine a pair of pumps in a shop window. "Can you see me going to the office every day like Charles did? Can you imagine me in charge of all those grants? Please." I inhaled the aroma of cinnamon babka as we passed the Gold Coast Bakery.

"But he must have had a *reason* for leaving you in charge." Mitzi slowed her pace and slipped her arm through mine but kept walking.

"According to the lawyers, Charles thought it would be good for both of us—me and the Foundation—whatever that's supposed to mean."

"It means he had tremendous faith in you. The Foundation was his life."

"That and his books," I murmured.

***

I waited until cocktail time to open the mail so I would have a stiff drink in my hand when I faced the dozens of heavy cream envelopes I knew would hold condolence messages. Ironically, I had always fancied that the notes I had written to bereaved acquaintances over the years would have been so immensely welcome and appreciated. But now that the proverbial shoe was on the other foot, I knew the facts were otherwise.

I dreaded opening the mail. I knew every note would look and sound the same. Each would express sadness, sorrow, and sympathy; each would offer assistance; each would be written in black ink and composed in black tones with words that would fall heavily on the page, words that were meant for someone else. Not me. How could I be *the widow*?

Worse, each note would require an individual acknowledgment. I had seen the printed ones; God knows I had received plenty of them. But printed cards and social secretaries were cheating. The only proper response was a personalized, handwritten one, and I didn't think I would ever find the energy or requisite words for that project.

I poured myself a healthy dollop of Dubonnet and added three cubes from the crystal ice bucket Daniel had set out in the living room. I sat on the blue silk love seat, took a long sip of my drink, and picked up the first card. I slit it open with the antique silver letter opener Charles had given me for our eleventh anniversary.

My dear Lauren, no words can express the sadness we felt when we heard about Charles' passing. He was such a wonderful man and blah... blah... blah... *if there is anything at all we can do,* blah... blah... blah... *our thoughts are with you...* blah... blah... blah....

The next three notes were virtual duplicates of the first, both superficially and substantively, but the fourth envelope was different. It was not cream, but white; it was not heavy, but flimsy. It was cheap, and I was able to slit it open without applying the least bit of pressure. I pulled out a gaudy purple-and-blue flowered note card.

Dear Lauren,

I was so shocked to hear Charles had died. I saw the obituary in our local paper here in Bayonne. Are you okay? Do you need anything? Would you like to come stay with us for a while? You are always welcome.

The girls are doing well. Can you believe Sarah, our oldest, is going into her third year at Rutgers? June and Rachel are in high school. Freddie is still working at the GE plant, and I'm still teaching English, which I suppose I will be doing until they carry me out of the classroom.

I can't believe it's been so long since we've seen each other. I often think about our summer in Europe. I'm sure you've been back many times.

I mean it about coming out here if you need to get away. We would love to see you. I'm so sorry about Charles.

Love, Annette

I closed the card and examined the treacley images of violets and periwinkles.

It had been ages since I'd seen Annette; we had grown far apart quickly. While I had been immersing myself in the Upper East Side charity scene, redecorating the East Hampton house, and learning how to run a household, Annette had been finishing graduate school at Columbia, marrying her high school boyfriend, and settling down in Bayonne to teach and have babies.

Charles had urged me to invite her over. *She was always your best friend,* he would say. *Friends like that should be treasured. Why not have her over or go to New Jersey for the weekend? Or maybe she and Freddie would like to join us in East Hampton.*

Annette had invited me out to Bayonne any number of times those first few years, and had phoned whenever she came into the city. But I never accepted or reciprocated her overtures, and the contacts eventually stopped.

After I married Charles, we no longer had anything in common. At least, that's what I wanted to believe. As Mrs. Charles Acheson, I was a new person, a woman entirely separate and apart from Lauren Towson, a woman worthy of Mr. Charles Acheson's affection and unwilling to go back to where I had been.

Having always been a quick study, I had ingratiated myself into Charles's crowd and picked up the tricks of my new persona in no time, assimilating them as if they were my birthright. I had learned who the top decorators were, and how one got onto their waiting lists. I had learned how to dress, and where to shop. I had learned who the best caterers and florists were, and how to throw a party that would be written up in the *Times*. I had learned who ate what where, and which tables were considered prime and which Siberia. I had learned how to make a *maître d'* remember my name and use it. I had learned how to carry on a conversation at a cocktail or dinner party, and how to keep up with subjects likely to arise in each venue. I had learned enough about art, literature, theater, music, and politics to be good company, but not enough to be a bore or a boor.

I had worked so hard at it I almost lost touch with what it felt like to be my father's daughter or to be haunted by the ghosts of my mother and sister. I no longer recalled what it was like to care about an egocentric Parisian artist or to write amateurish poetry and hope it would someday be recognized. I had no clear memory of what it meant to be constantly fearful of what the future might hold and afraid it might be much too much like the present or the past. I had worked very, very hard to clean the slate.

Which is why I was so bothered by Annette's card. I hated the way the cheap white envelope looked against the piles of heavy cream, the way the flowered notepaper looked against the dignified cards that bore only stark black borders and discreet monograms. I hated the way the blotchy blue ballpoint script contrasted with the smooth flow of quality fountain-penmanship. I detested the note's cloyingly familiar tone and newsy tidbits. Most of all, I hated that Annette had the nerve to think I might ever want to return to Bayonne for any reason. I tossed the note onto the pile of opened letters and moved on to the next heavy cream envelope.

***

I stepped gingerly out of bed the following morning, careful to avoid any precipitous movements that might encourage the incipient headache that was skulking above my stiff neck, around the frazzled edges of my brain. I got into the shower, turned the water on high-heat and full-blast, and let it beat on the back of my neck and shoulders while I scrubbed with a loofah until my skin was as pink as the marble walls.

I looked up through the spray at the solid brass faucets, multiple shower heads, and crystal soap dish; I smelled the Florentine milk bath that cost sixty dollars a bottle; I told myself not to worry, Bayonne was far, far away. Then I scrubbed some more, as if I could buff away the vestiges of Annette's note.

After showering, I wrapped myself in a thick blue robe and went to my dressing room where I scanned the racks of clothes that ran along three walls. By way of rebellion against the whole notion of mourning, I selected a vivid coral dress, even though the color made my head hurt, then opened the wall safe to retrieve my Russian Rope bracelet and knot earrings. Though I hadn't worn jewelry since Charles' death, believing sparkle was incompatible with bereavement, I now felt ready. I peered into the safe in search of the familiar leather cases that held my favorite pieces, but a small, deep-blue box I had never seen before caught my eye. It was topped with a tiny envelope bearing my name, written in Charles' perfect script.

I took the box from the vault, set it on the chest of drawers and stared at it for several moments before opening the envelope. I pulled out a simple white card bearing a single sentence: *My dear Lauren, please forgive me.*

A note from a ghost.

The box contained a platinum channel ring filled with small diamonds, a piece I had recently admired at Harry Winston; I had hinted to Charles it would go nicely with my wedding and engagement rings. I removed the ring from its box and slipped it onto my left ring finger, along with the other two bands.

How long would I wear these rings, I wondered as I stared at my hand. How long would I remain "married" to Charles? The idea of dating was absurd, but the thought of remaining eternally alone was terrifying.

I placed the empty box back into the safe and closed it. I re-read the note, then tore it in half. I crumpled the two pieces together, gently at first, then harder, more roughly, finally ripping and crushing them into tiny bits of nothing before throwing them into the wastebasket.

***

I sipped my breakfast coffee, pausing to appreciate the Limoges cup in my hand; its delicacy and light weight, its luminosity and the refinement of its tiny, blue, hand-painted flowers comforted me. Yes, I was far from Bayonne. As I turned the cup to admire my new ring, Daniel came into the breakfast room to tell me Tom Smithson was on the phone.

I answered in a formal, curt tone, not wanting to encourage another visit or an extended conversation. "What can I do for you, Mr. Smithson?"

"I'd appreciate it if you didn't mention this call to Gerald."

I was not about to offer any such assurance.

"I'm calling about your role in the Foundation."

"I won't have a role for long." I rang for Daniel; I needed more coffee.

"I want you to know how much your husband wanted you to direct the Foundation. I don't think you understand the extent of his interest. Your husband told us you were an exceptionally capable woman and that you had a good sense of priorities and values."

"There are lots of capable people out there, many of whom are much more capable than I for this type of thing." Daniel poured a fresh cup of coffee, and I added a dollop of cream.

"That's not what your husband thought. Besides," he paused, "he said that since you'd been married you hadn't had the opportunity to utilize your extensive talents. He blamed himself for that."

"So, I'm *unproductive?*"

"No, please, you're taking this wrong. Or I'm saying it wrong. Your husband believed you would benefit as a person—his word was 'blossom'—if you took this on."

"And why aren't we sharing this with Gerald?" I enjoyed using the royal "we" when people were squirming, or when they should be.

"He's so…so interested in making sure you're happy that he's ready to let you do whatever you want." Smithson's voice was trembling. "He doesn't think we should to try to sway you if you want to resign. I don't either, if you feel strongly, but I thought you should know how Mr. Acheson felt before you make any final decisions."

***

I turned down lunch with Mitzi and the girls to spend the afternoon in Charles' library, though I was not sure what drew me back to this place I had studiously avoided for most of the past twenty-two years. I had always found it too dark, too cluttered, too musty, and too boring. But now I was attracted by the tidbits of himself Charles had left in this favored place. If I couldn't talk to him directly, I could seek his guidance through his leavings.

Still perplexed by yesterday's book-tossing performance, and mortified that Daniel had witnessed it, I was determined that today's visit would be more dignified. So, I pulled books out carefully, a single volume at a time, and slowly turned their pages, as I inhaled the smells, the flavors, and the words of Charles that lived inside them.

I deciphered the marginalia, and tried to comprehend its meaning. While I didn't understand much of it, I found comfort in the verbiage that sounded so much like Charles. Many of the notes were a word or two: *Brilliant! Nonsense! Makes sense. Re-read.* Others were thoughts or queries expressed in cryptic language. *Would Spinoza be considered a pantheist? Camus—a nihilist??* And some were elegant thoughts expressed in beautiful language. *A jewel in humanity's crown.* Those words were beside a statement from Martin Luther King, Jr.

When I opened a book of essays by Andre Dubus, I found a dedication inside the front cover—words written in a hand other than Charles': *I know this isn't the kind of book you'd normally pick up, but it's my turn to give you a tip for a change. Hope you love these as much as I did. I think he's a genius. XX Syd*

I flipped quickly through the pages then closed the book. I placed the hard cloth cover against my chin, bit my lower lip, and then replaced the book on the shelf. This was not something I was capable of dealing with at the moment.

I sat at the massive desk and looked at the range of items that seemed to define Charles' life. Two tickets for an upcoming Metropolitan Opera performance were stuck in the edge of the blotter—*Aida.* A crystal bowl held paperclips, rubber bands, a pair of onyx studs, a few loose stamps, and four tickets to a Yankees game. Pencils and fountain pens resided in a Venetian glass tumbler; Post-it Note pads were piled neatly next to an invitation to the Metropolitan Museum's Gauguin preview. A brown leather calendar lay open to the week of Charles' death.

I pulled out the heavy mahogany drawer on the lower left side of the desk, exposing a series of neat manila files, each marked with a subject related to the Foundation. I removed several and placed them before me, imagining myself reading the documents they contained, comprehending them, and acting on them. Creating them. I imagined myself doing what Charles used to do. There was such an enormous disconnect between the image and imaginable reality that I laughed and pushed the drawer back in, not noticing until it was almost shut the of files in front marked *Personal Correspondence*.

Chapter Five
Dear Charles

August, 1989

My hands trembled as I placed the four "Personal Correspondence" files on the mahogany desktop; I stared at them before opening the top one. It contained a sheaf of handwritten letters, most on blue-lined notebook paper, a few on fuchsia stationary, each written in the same bold, round penmanship as the inscription in the book of essays. I knew they would be signed by Sydney.

The letters were arranged in chronological order with one file for each year. The first contained eight or nine letters, all reasonably short, but each succeeding file folder was progressively fatter, filled with more and longer letters. This year's was overstuffed and bulky, though hardly more than half the year had passed when the correspondence ended, just before Charles' death.

Paging through the letters, I saw salutations that ran from *Dear Charles* to *Hi Charles* to *My Dear Friend*. Some lacked formal openings altogether, beginning with phrases like *I just finished the most amazing book* or *You won't believe the wacky play I saw*. The closings were similarly varied, with the early ones being in the nature of *Warmly* or *Fondly* or *All My Best*, while the later ones were signed *Love* or, in a few cases, *Much Love*. These were the important things—the openings and closings. The insides were filler. As I imagined the lovely young Sydney pausing over her paper, deciding on the right words, I wondered how and why *Warmly* and *Fondly* had changed to *Love*. Had the shift been a conscious decision or a matter of the relationship's evolution, or was it a response to language Charles had used in his letters to her?

I slipped the pages back into the files and went to the den to fix myself a drink.

***

After downing two Manhattans in rapid succession, I lay down on the sofa and thought about the word "love," in the context of a closing.

Surely, Sydney Ray Jenkins had used the term in a casual manner. Offhandedly. Without any special meaning attached to it. Yes, I was certain of that. I had to be. I knew Charles well enough to know that he would not have been comfortable with anything else.

But *did* I know Charles?

I got up, made myself another Manhattan, and took a sip of the warm amber liquid. I had always assumed I knew my husband well, but after his final action (I still could not bear to use the actual word, even in my thoughts), I wondered if something had lurked inside him to which I had not been privy. I took another sip, this one longer and deeper.

There was much about Charles of which I was certain. I knew that he was a greatly beloved man. The media had always described him as "generous," "benevolent," and "decent." They referred time and again to his intellectual pursuits and cultural passions, calling him "endlessly curious," and "a Renaissance man," one who had "not been spoiled by inherited wealth." He was portrayed as happily married and content with his role in the world, "uniquely comfortable in his own skin." We were portrayed as the perfect pair, sleek and elegant, healthy and handsome, the magical host and hostess who threw parties like no others and lived a life to be envied. Everything had been perfect.

Only *I* knew about those quiet times when he was so caught up in his thoughts that he seemed lost to reality, and about the brief interludes of melancholy when he would retire to his library for long hours, asking only to be left alone. But those episodes had been so rare and so frightening that I had never allowed myself to dwell on them.

I sat up and waited for my head to stop spinning; drinking three Manhattans in the middle of the afternoon was not my habit. Thus fortified, or numbed, I returned to the library.

***

Perhaps Charles and Sydney had had some kind of code, for after reading through at least twenty letters, I had gleaned absolutely nothing of interest beyond the minimal intrigue of the salutations and closings.

The vast boring bulk of each letter was devoted to books Sydney had read, lectures she had attended, writers with whom she had spoken, and ideas about which she had written or was pondering. It was clear she was a writer, apparently of essays. She alluded to literary and scholarly journals that had published her work, and thanked Charles for advice or referrals to editors and for his "astute comments," and "excellent critiques" of her work. She frequently thanked him for sending her books.

Beyond the literary chitchat, she occasionally related things that were happening in her life. "I've moved into a new loft." "I'm applying for a fellowship to Yaddo." "I'm off to Berkeley to do some research." I wondered what tidbits of his own life Charles had offered up in return.

I quickly lost interest in the pile of tedious verbiage, which revealed no tawdry innuendoes, no declarations of undying devotion, and no suggestion of impropriety. While relieved, I was also disappointed that there was nothing here to explain who this mysterious woman was, why Charles had never mentioned her, and why he had left her his books.

Before calling the whole thing quits, I flipped to the last letter in the last file. It was dated a week before Charles' death and began with the words *Dearest Charles*, one of a handful with such an opening. It went on:

I don't know anyone else who insists on tormenting himself over the big questions of life the way you do. It's not that I don't take these things seriously. You, of all people, know that. The things you and I think about, the questions most people are happy to live without ever addressing, are the things that make life interesting and meaningful for us. Everything you talked about in your letter—Why are we here? What are we supposed to accomplish? Is there a reason for any of this, or are we part of some big cosmic joke?—boils down to one big question: what the hell is it all about? Isn't that what all our reading, seeking and questioning come down to?

The quest to find an answer is an elusive enterprise, but it gives me a reason to wake up each day. Without the quest, what is there? Another day, another paycheck, another party, another meal, and another and another and another until there are no more. But, my friend, when the quest becomes torture, when the inability to find a conclusive answer results in the kind of debilitating existential pain your letter hinted at, it's time to step back and seek perspective.

Your contention that you have never done anything of consequence is absurd. The fact that you have never had what you call a "real job" is utterly irrelevant. You do so much for so many with your foundation and the way you live your life. Your existence is filled with the significance that comes from fostering art, music, beauty, literature and, most important of all, thinking and exploring and creating—the things that give life meaning. To say that you are merely "a rich old man who attends parties and benefits for people who don't need them" is absurd.

I stand as an example of the many people whose lives you have affected beyond measure. You have made my life meaningful; you have, in fact, made my life possible. Never minimize that.

All my love,

Sydney

Though I didn't fully understand the context or import of what she was saying, I understood enough to be bothered that Charles had turned to this young woman rather than to me to discuss these so-called "big questions." I thought back to when Charles and I were first becoming acquainted. Had our relationship ever looked anything like this one, or had it sprung from something else altogether? If so, what?

***

The first time Charles and I spoke to one another was in October, 1966, two weeks after the auspicious visit to Motherwell's *Elegy to the Spanish Republic,* when I had eavesdropped on him and Ben.

Though I had not received a single communication from Larry since my return to the States, not even in response to "my" brilliant thoughts on *Elegy,* I continued to believe that he loved me as much as I loved him. To have believed anything else was beyond my capacity. He was too busy to write, or couldn't afford the stamps. Maybe he wasn't the corresponding type.

But something happened that October which made Larry's lack of contact more troubling. It began when I walked into a downtown doctor's office in search of a tidy label for the constellation of flu-like symptoms from which I was suffering and crystallized when I walked back out into the cool October twilight with not a cure but only a sense that my life had taken one of those sudden, veering turns that can reroute the course of the planets.

***

I called in sick the morning after that appointment, and headed up to Morningside Heights to meet Annette at her favorite coffee shop. Seated at a rocky, linoleum-topped table, I looked around at the crowd of Columbia students whose greatest concerns seemed to be tests, grades, and procuring the latest Beatles album. While I had been as untroubled as they the day before, I now viewed the world through a gauzy veneer that dulled sensation and colored every element of my past, present, and future.

Annette rushed in, lugging a pile of books. "Sorry I'm late." She dropped the books on the table with a noisy crash and sat down in the rickety chair across from mine. "I'm meeting my advisor at eleven. What did you want to tell me?" She brushed a stray hank of hair off her face and leaned forward on the scratched green linoleum tabletop, setting up a wobbly wave action that nauseated me.

I took a sip of water to settle my stomach and pondered how best to present my news. There had to be words for this situation that were more apt than the obvious ones, but I didn't know what they were.

I peered around to make sure no one was listening then whispered, "I'm pregnant."

It was the first time I had spoken the words. They had been spoken *to* me, as in *I'm afraid you're pregnant, Lauren.* I had *contemplated* the words and their implications relentlessly over the past twelve hours. But I had not spoken them, and hearing them articulated in my own voice made me dizzy.

The color drained from Annette's face, and her eyes grew round. "Jesus. Are you sure?"

"I'm sure." I shot a nasty look at a nearby woman who had turned our way at the sound of Annette's question.

"Have you been to the doctor?" Annette now spoke quietly.

"Yesterday."

"How pregnant are you?"

"Two and a half months." I said the words to the scarred tabletop.

"Larry?"

"Of course." I scratched the table with my thumbnail.

Annette inhaled deeply and exhaled slowly. "I can't believe this. What are you going to do?"

I shook my head and shrugged, at which point a heavyset, red-haired waitress dressed in a green uniform and a badge that said HI, I'M DORIS appeared at my side.

"What can I get you girls?"

"I'll have a bagel," I said, relieved to engage in a pretense of normalcy. "No cream cheese."

"I'll have...I don't know...I'll just have coffee," Annette said. "Black." She turned back to me but was silent until the waitress was beyond earshot. "How can you be so *calm*? What are you going to do? Have you told Larry?"

"He's there, I'm here. What's the point?"

"He's the father," Annette said through pursed lips.

"I'm not sure I'm going to need a father."

"Gallant, but stupid." Annette's hands curled into fists. "You can't do this alone."

"I'm not sure I'm going to do this at all."

"You're going to give it up for adoption?"

"No, I mean I may not do this *at all*."

Annette looked quizzical, and then her eyes opened wide. "You're not saying... you might not *have* the baby?"

I shrugged again. "There are options."

"But... where would you go? Sweden or something? How would you pay for it?"

"I've heard about places here in New York."

Doris dropped the coffee and bagel in front of us. "Enjoy, ladies."

"That's incredibly dangerous, not to mention illegal."

"No more dangerous than having the baby. What about my job? And what about Larry?" I tore my bagel into little, doughy pieces. "He told me he's not interested in *ever* having kids."

Annette rolled her eyes and took a long drink of coffee so hot she had to suck in air to cool her mouth. I knew she was doing it to avoid saying what she wanted to say about Larry. "How can I help?"

The diner's door opened, letting in a gust of cool air along with something else that grabbed my attention. It was the man from the Waldorf, from the museum, the man called Charles. He wore a tweed sport coat and khaki pants, carried a couple of thick books, and was accompanied by two younger men who looked twenty years his junior, around my age. They sat down a few tables away.

"What are you staring at?" Annette asked.

I nodded in Charles' direction. "I've seen that man before."

Annette snuck a peek over her shoulder. "Who is he?"

"I don't know, but I keep running into him, which seems weird in a town this big."

Annette turned around for a better view. "Jeez," She whirled to face me. "That's *Charles Acheson*."

"Who's he?"

"A big philanthropist. He runs a foundation. Gives away tons of money—mostly to artists. His picture's in *The Times* every other day. Mostly at parties. Society stuff."

"What kind of artists?" I popped a mangled piece of bagel into my mouth.

"I don't know, why?"

As I stared at him, the nutty thought taking shape in my mind made me grin. "I happen to know an artist who could use some money."

"Oh God, Lauren," Annette groaned.

"If I could get Larry hooked up with someone like that, he might feel better about settling down—maybe even with a baby." I spoke quickly, feeling a charge of energy. I smiled as I indulged in a brief flight of fancy in which Larry, the baby, and I strolled through the *Tuileries* on a clear Paris morning. I placed my hand, as if by instinct, on my still-flat belly.

"Hold on, a minute ago you weren't going to *have* the baby."

"I said I *might* not." I tossed another piece of bagel into my mouth and took a sip of Annette's coffee. "If I could offer Larry a way of supporting us...."

"Stop *staring*, and come back to reality. You have to decide what you're going to do about this baby."

I kept my eye on Charles. "Maybe my running into him like this, over and over—especially now—is fate. If Larry and I had some money, this whole thing could work out."

"You're crazy. This isn't fate, it's a delusion. You haven't heard from Larry since you left Paris. How can you *think* about raising a baby with him?"

Maybe it wasn't fate, but in my desperation and my ridiculous, callow youth, these serendipitous meetings seemed like something worth paying attention to. I stood up, squared my shoulders, and started toward Charles' table.

"*Lauren!*" Annette grabbed my arm. "Don't be crazy."

I shook off her hand and kept my eyes trained on my prey. I walked like an automaton, but the sick feeling in the pit of my stomach had been replaced by euphoria, a nothing-to-lose feeling not unlike the one I had experienced when I first approached Larry in Paris.

"Excuse me," I said to the man. "Are you Charles Acheson?"

He stood up. "Yes, I am."

"I'm Lauren Towson." I stuck out my hand.

He took it with a firm grip. His fingers felt coarse but practiced, seasoned, as if he'd shaken many hands and knew exactly how to do it. "A pleasure. Should I know you? You look familiar but, forgive me, I can't make the connection."

"There isn't one," I said with a charitable smile, "but I saw you at the Metropolitan Museum recently, talking with someone about Motherwell's *Elegy*."

"Ah, the Motherwell. What do you think of it?"

"I love the opposing forces." I was proud of the way the statement rolled off my tongue. "I find it quite moving."

"Then maybe you can explain it to me sometime." He chuckled. "I'm *still* not sure I get it."

"Motherwell's not for everyone," I said easily, wondering where *those* perfect words had come from. As I acted out the scene, I felt like an admiring member of the audience, for I had never possessed anything remotely resembling that quality my boss would call *chutzpah* and my father would have called *balls*.

"What can I do for you, Lauren?"

"I understand you give grants to artists."

"My foundation does."

"I have a friend in Paris who's a talented painter. I wonder if he might be eligible to apply."

"Unfortunately, we restrict our grants to New York-based artists."

"He's from New York," I said quickly.

"Then he might be eligible. I can send you our guidelines."

"Is there someplace I could pick them up? I'd like to get the process started."

"You're welcome to stop by our office in Midtown."

"Perfect. I work in Midtown." That seemed like another sign.

He handed me a business card. "Here's the address. Ask the receptionist for guidelines and an application."

"Thank you." I touched the engraved black letters.

"You're welcome. It was nice to meet you."

"Same here." I nodded to the two young men at the table.

"Excuse my rudeness," Charles said when he saw me acknowledge his companions. "My wife always tells me I'm terrible about introductions. These are my friends, Joel and Steve. They're in my Humanities class at Columbia."

I nodded again to the two young men, and then turned my attention back to Charles. "You're a student?"

He grinned broadly. "A perennial student, actually. I felt the need to renew my acquaintance with the classics, so here I am at Columbia."

"Did you go to college there?"

"No, Princeton."

"Oh, I'm from New Jersey. Bayonne."

"Been through it many times."

I smiled. "Anyway, sorry to have interrupted you."

"Not at all. It was a pleasure." He sounded as if he meant it.

I started to walk away but turned back. "Did you buy the Motherwell?"

"You're bold, aren't you?"

"Sorry, it's none of my business."

"You're right, it's not. But I did. For my wife."

"She's a lucky woman. My boyfriend would love to have a Motherwell."

"Is that why *Elegy* 'moves' you?" He smiled. "Be honest now."

I returned his smile before turning to walk away, having no idea how I had pulled off such an impressively cool non-response.

"God, Lauren," Annette said when I sat down. "I can't *believe* you did that."

"He's a nice guy." I thought about his grin and my own smart, flirty attitude. For a few delightful moments, I had completely forgotten about my problem.

Chapter Six
A Dark, Out-of-the-Way Place

October, 1966

The day after I met Charles Acheson in the coffee shop, I walked up Madison Avenue on my lunch hour to the building that housed the Acheson Foundation's offices. I stepped off the elevator into a reception area that featured a series of hard-edged abstract paintings in pure primary tones. I had learned the expression *hard-edged* from Larry, who explained that the strongly contoured, geometric style was the newest thing, though he personally dismissed it as "fatuous." A tall, reed-thin young woman dressed in gray slacks and a black cashmere sweater sat beneath one of these paintings at the reception desk, reading a newspaper.

"I'm here for a grant application," I said.

"What type of grant are you interested in?" She barely glanced up from her newspaper.

"It's for a painter."

"Visual artist. Have a seat."

I did as instructed and flipped through a copy of *ARTNews*, amazed at how the drip-, splash-, and clump-covered pictures made Motherwell's *Elegy* look Old-Masterly.

"I'm going to lunch now, Shari."

I knew that voice, and looked up to see Charles Acheson breeze by.

"Hi, Mr. Acheson," I said.

Judy Pomeranz

With his hand on the elevator button, he looked back over his shoulder with a quizzical expression that slowly turned into a smile. "It's Lauren, right? Here for that application for the man who likes Motherwell?"

I nodded.

He walked back into the waiting area. "What's your friend's name?"

"Larry Barnes."

"I'll watch for the application. I can't make any guarantees, but I can assure you I will pay particular attention to his submission."

The receptionist presented me with a large brown envelope and a suddenly gracious smile. "Is there anything else I can do for you?"

I shook my head, stood, and walked into the elevator Charles held open.

"You work in the neighborhood?" he asked as we descended from his twentieth-floor offices.

"Yes, I'm a typist at the Wylie and Wylie Literary Agency."

"Ah, a literature person." Charles said. "Who are your favorite writers?"

I found the question odd. "I like Tennessee Williams, John Updike, Iris Murdoch, Christopher Isherwood…"

"You do read eclectically."

I blushed. "But I like poetry best."

"What kind?"

"Kenneth Koch, Frank O'Hara…"

"New York School. I try reading those fellows in the *New Yorker*, but most of their work leaves me cold."

"Like the Motherwell." I tried out a small grin.

He smiled and nodded. "But I'm generally more comfortable with modern painters than modern poets."

"I wish I could say the same."

Charles stepped aside so I could exit the elevator ahead of him. "Maybe one day you can teach me about modern poetry, and I'll tell you what little I know about modern painting."

I had no idea what the appropriate response to this come-on might be, so I said nothing.

"Are you a poet yourself?"

I studied the lobby's granite floor. "I write some, but I wouldn't say I'm a poet."

"What's a poet, if not someone who writes poetry?"

"Someone who gets it published."

Charles stopped and faced me. "History has shown that not all artists—not even most—are accepted by the establishment during their lifetimes. That does *not* diminish the importance of their art." He ushered me into the revolving door and out onto the sidewalk. "I'm going to grab a sandwich. If you'd like to join me, I'd love to hear what you have to say about modern poetry, including your own work. We give grants to literary artists, too."

***

The maître d' at the Seldrake Club showed us to a window table overlooking Central Park and handed me a brown leather menu featuring foods that were surprisingly plain for this world of ornate wood paneling, chandeliers, and hunting scenes.

"So, tell me about your poetry." He settled comfortably into his armchair.

"It's really not worth talking about." Though intrigued, I was baffled and embarrassed by this stranger's interest in me and my poetry.

"Do you enjoy it?"

"Very much."

"I'd love to be a writer. What a privilege to have that kind of release. The greatest and most honest art—visual, as well as literary—comes from probing self-analysis. You shouldn't dismiss your art or demean it as unimportant just because you do it for yourself."

No one had ever taken my writing seriously. My high school teachers had always treated me as an amusing amateur. So, what was I to make of this man? What did he want?

"Do you ever let people read your work?" he asked.

"Not really."

Our food arrived, and I stirred my soup slowly, noticing the heaviness of the silver spoon as it dragged through the noodles and chunks of chicken. I took a small bite.

Charles stared out the window. "I love Central Park, don't you?"

"It's lovely."

"Do you spend much time at the Metropolitan Museum?"

191

"I have since I got back from Paris."

"You were visiting your artist friend there?"

I nodded and tried to return the little smile he gave me, but it didn't work. Thinking about Paris brought back the immediacy of my problem. I took a large, scalding bite of soup. Penance.

"Must have been a bohemian summer. The painter and the poet."

"Larry doesn't know I write poetry. He doesn't notice much outside of his art." I hadn't had that thought before I said the words.

"Most artists are self-centered. That's why they're so good at self-expression. Artists are wonderful for the world, but can be disastrous as friends or partners."

"Sounds like you know a lot of them."

"I'm a collector, so I know a few."

"You don't like them?"

"I didn't mean to imply that. I like some very much. But they can get so wrapped up in their own worlds, I'd be reluctant to rely on them, if you know what I mean."

I did.

"The deepest thinkers I know, with the most interesting and original ideas, are artists. They play a special role in helping us understand what life's about and why it's worth living."

I felt like a character in a French film.

"Poets do that too," Charles continued. "Sometimes when I'm reading Yeats or Frost I feel like they've been inside my head, like they have access to thoughts I didn't know I had until they articulated them."

"I thought you didn't like poetry, or didn't get it."

"It's *modern* poetry I have trouble with. I don't know what to watch for, how to parse it, or how to go about reading it. I've been told it's not so different from abstract expressionist painting, except that the painter reduces the world to line, color, and shape while the poet reduces it to words. A whole universe in twenty-six letters." He spoke slowly, groping for his point. "I'm often at a loss."

"The way I feel when the world's reduced to line, color, and shape," I admitted.

Charles chuckled. "No one gets it all." He put his hands flat on the tabletop and leaned toward me, his eyes as alive as those of a child with a new toy. "Have you seen the new Rauschenberg combine at the Museum of Modern Art?"

"I've never been there."

"Oh, you must see it. It's the kind of work a poet would love. See, it's all about images and how they play in your mind. Profound, evocative. Almost narrative. I'd be delighted to take you to see it sometime, if you're interested."

I didn't know what to say. His blue eyes were clear and appeared guileless, but I was having a hard time taking all this at face value.

"Listen." Charles raised his hands as if to show he was unarmed, "I'm sorry if that seemed forward. I didn't mean to scare you."

"No, I didn't mean— I'm not scared. I wouldn't want to inconvenience you."

"I do have an ulterior motive." He grinned slyly.

Just as I suspected.

"I'm hoping you'll let me read your poetry."

If he was hitting on me, I was flattered, but spooked. If he wanted to read my poetry, I was charmed, but too embarrassed to let him. Either way, it was bizarre, so I smiled weakly.

"Why don't we leave it at that you'll give me a call if you want to go," he said.

***

Much to my surprise, I found the nerve to do just that. And what an eye-opener the museum was.

I was alarmed by the agitated surface of De Kooning's *Woman I;* I relaxed into the languid female form captured by Modigliani in *Reclining Nude;* I smiled at Dubuffet's childlike image of the *Corps de Dame;* and I scrutinized Picasso's *Girl Before a Mirror.* All the while, I listened to Charles' theory of how one could gain insights into an artist's world-view by comparing his depiction of a subject with that of other artists.

We had moved way beyond Rauschenberg.

"Are you familiar with Gustav Klimt?" Charles asked as we strolled toward a painting filled with tiny brilliant bits of color, like a mosaic.

I shook my head and moved closer, then stepped back as the image resolved itself. It was a woman with full, white breasts, and a large belly, wrapped in a patchwork quilt. She was pregnant. A series of bowed female heads echoed the woman's own as it dipped toward her womb as if in prayer for her child-to-be. A human skull hung menacingly near the woman's stomach.

"Do you like it?" Charles asked.

I studied the figure and scanned the canvas for clues to the drama's outcome, seeking a hint about the baby's fate, or the mother's. Was that really a skull? If so, what did it signify?

"What do you know about this picture?" I asked.

He looked at the label. "It was painted in 1907, so it would have been toward the end of Klimt's career—"

"No, not about the artist, about the subject."

"It's painted in a characteristic style—"

"No," I insisted, staring at the painting. "The woman. What do you know about her?"

Charles paused. I could feel him looking at me. "Nothing."

I couldn't take my eyes off the painting.

"Are you okay?" Charles asked.

"Not really," I murmured.

He took my elbow and led me across the room to a bench. We both sat down.

I bit my lower lip until it hurt, and took a deep breath. I looked down at the floor, afraid to look back at the Klimt and too embarrassed to look at anything else. I sneezed, and Charles slipped a linen handkerchief into my hand.

"I'm sorry," I whispered.

"There's no need to be."

I wiped my nose with the handkerchief before remembering it wasn't mine. "Sorry."

"I wish you'd stop apologizing," Charles said. "I have more handkerchiefs where that came from. All I need to hear is that you're okay."

I thought about it, then nodded and looked up at him. His attention was fixed on a simple line drawing across the room. A Matisse, I would learn much later.

"Tell me what you'd like to do." He looked back at me and touched my shoulder. "Do you want to talk? Do you want me to put you in a cab to take you home? Do you want to be left alone?"

"You're amazing."

"Hardly."

"I'd like to get out of here." I wiped my nose with the balled-up handkerchief and let him guide me through the museum to the front entrance, feeling like an old woman with her devoted son.

We walked up Fifth Avenue in silence, passing flashy shop windows and fashionable people. Stable people. I felt dowdy in my gray wool skirt and sweater; I also felt crazy and possessed after my behavior in the museum. Why would Charles Acheson, who could surely have any woman he wanted, choose to be with *me* right now? It made no sense.

"Would you like a drink? Or dinner?"

"A drink might be nice, if you don't have to get home."

"No, my wife's in the Hamptons, so I'd enjoy the company."

"I'm not exactly great company tonight."

"Not the worst I've ever had." Charles smiled.

"What's your wife doing in the Hamptons?"

"We have a home there, an old place that's been in my family for years."

I'd never known anyone with a second home. "Where do you live when you're in town?"

"Up the street, right across from the Met. And you?"

"Near Grammercy Park."

"That's a beautiful neighborhood, and handy to the New School. I've taken great courses there."

"What kind of courses?"

"Mostly literature and philosophy. I took a psychology course there once, for fun."

"Why do you take all these courses?"

"I'm a dilettante. Always dabbling." He said it rather sadly.

We passed The Plaza and turned onto Central Park South.

"Where are we going?" I watched a carriage driver lure a handsome young couple into his coach.

"To a favorite little dive of mine, if that sounds okay to you."

"Whatever you want." I was so relieved and pleased to be away from the Klimt, walking down the street carrying on a conversation like a normal person, I boldly tucked my hand into the crook of his arm.

"This place is nothing fancy, just a friendly hole in the wall. Kind of out of the way. Good place to talk."

"Dark?"

He considered the question. "I guess. Reasonably dark."

"Dark and out of the way." I removed my arm from his. "Did you choose this place so no one would see us if I get weird again?"

He looked at me with an amused grin. "I believe my psychology professor at the New School would have called that remark a classic indicator of paranoia."

***

"I'm pregnant."

I blurted it out shortly after we sat down at a corner table in the Moonglow Bar. There was no smooth segue into the subject, no rational transition. I made the confession by way of explaining my behavior at the museum, partly because I had someone I could talk to, someone who was kind and wise and old enough to have had sufficient life experience that he might have something useful to contribute. Most importantly, he was someone I didn't really know and wasn't likely to see again, so my confession would be private and anonymous, like talking to a priest or someone on a train.

"I had a feeling that might be the case." He said it as calmly as if I had told him I wore a size six shoe.

"Why?"

"The way you reacted to the Klimt. Is this a good thing or a bad one?"

"I'm trying to figure that out."

"The artist is the father?"

"Yes."

"He doesn't know?"

I shook my head and watched the red and white glow of the *Budweiser* sign reflect off the varnished wood of the bar.

"You're afraid it might scare him away?"

"Why do you say that?"

196

"I had a daughter. I learned a few things about how young women think." He flipped through the metal pages of the small jukebox affixed to the wall beside our booth.

"You *had* a daughter?"

"She died." He stopped flipping pages and stared at the song titles.

"My God. I'm sorry."

We were silent as the waitress placed drinks in front of us. Rum and Coke for me, single malt Scotch on the rocks for Charles.

"What happened to her?" I asked after the waitress left.

"Car accident." He stirred his drink with a yellow plastic spear. "Her boyfriend was driving."

"Oh, God. How old was she?"

"Twenty-one. She had graduated from Smith and was supposed to have her coming-out party the week after the accident." He went on, as if reliving it. "The party was going to be at the Maidstone Club in East Hampton, and there were other parties leading up to the big one." He ran his finger along the ridge of a deep gouge in the wood tabletop. "She was on her way home from one when it happened. Her boyfriend—her fiancé, as she called him—was killed instantly. Chelsea lived for three days, but never woke up." He sipped his Scotch. "For the best, the doctor told us. She wouldn't have been the same. Wouldn't have had any kind of life."

I remembered hearing those same words spoken with regard to my own sister, and I knew how much they hurt. I also knew what one was expected to say. "Then it was better for her."

"But not for me. I'd give anything to say goodbye or sit by her bedside and hold her hand." He stared at two men seated at a nearby table, then turned back to me. "I'm sorry to burden you. I don't know what got me started."

"I got you started, by asking questions. I'm sorry."

"Why do we keep apologizing to each other?" he said with a tired smile. "I like talking about her. I never want to lose the memories or forget the intensity of that relationship. There's no one on earth like your own child, as you'll soon know."

"Maybe."

"You mean you may not keep the baby?"

"I may not *have* the baby," I said firmly. I wanted to accustom myself to the idea, and saying the words aloud as often as possible seemed a good start.

"You're not considering an abortion, are you?"

I nodded. "I'm considering it."

"Where would you have it done?"

I shrugged. "Here in New York."

"That's not safe." Charles spoke slowly, sounding like a concerned father. "Besides, it's irreversible. You might be haunted by that someday."

This was not the absolution, objective sounding-board, or moral support I had been seeking. "I might be more haunted if I *have* the baby."

Charles was quiet for a while. "Promise me you won't go to some sleazy, back-alley place in New York. Go someplace where it's legal."

"I don't have to promise you anything."

He took a sip of his drink. "You're absolutely right. Forgive me."

He seemed so chastened, I softened my tone. "I appreciate the advice, but I can't run off to Sweden or wherever people go for these things. I don't have the money."

"I understand. I just don't want you to do something dangerous or something you'll regret later."

I finished my drink and set the glass down. "I'd better get home."

Chapter Seven
A Brief Silence

October, 1966

The day after our visit to the Museum of Modern Art, I was shown to the same window table in the Seldrake Club that Charles and I had shared a week earlier.

"Thanks for coming." Charles stood to greet me.

I nodded and sat. I still wasn't sure I should have come.

"I'm sorry I offended you last night."

"You didn't."

"Or if I hurt you."

"You didn't do that either."

"Or if I overstepped my bounds."

I looked out the window at a chubby blond child toddling beside his nanny along a path in the park.

"I know you're going through a rough time, and I didn't mean to put more pressure on you, but I hate to see anyone make a decision on the basis of money." He spoke quietly. "If you want the baby, you should have it. If you don't want it, you should go to a place where you can terminate the pregnancy safely."

"I hear what you're saying." I turned to face him. "But you come from a completely different world than I do. Money *is* a factor for me, a big one. I can't afford to go halfway around the world to get this taken care of, and I can't afford to lose my job, which I will if I have a baby without a husband. That's my reality."

"I'll give you the money to do whatever you want."

The offer caught me off-guard, and frightened me. I looked across the table into those light blue eyes, trying to read a motive.

"I'll give you money for a safe abortion or set up a trust for raising the child, whichever you want. I'll pay your way to Paris if you and Larry want to raise the child together, though I frankly think that might be a mistake."

"Why?" I had so many questions I wasn't sure which my *why* was directed at.

Charles paused. "Because he doesn't know you're a poet."

"What?"

"If he isn't interested enough to know that you write poetry, he may not be interested enough to be a good husband or father."

My hands clenched into tight fists. "How would *you* know? You don't know him. You don't even know *me*, for God's sake."

"You're absolutely right, and if I were smart, I'd end the conversation right here. But I want to say one more thing."

I coiled my heavy white napkin around my fingers, weaving it in and out, pulling it tighter and tighter.

"You seem afraid to tell him about the baby—"

I allowed the linen to unravel.

"—which might mean you're not ready for a serious relationship."

"What do you think we *had*?" I balled the napkin up, threw it on the table, and leaned forward. "Why take me to lunch, to drinks, to the museum? Why offer me money? What do you *want* from me?"

"I don't want anything."

"Then why are you doing this?"

Charles looked out the window. "I liked your style, your spunk, that day we first met in the cafe. I liked the way you approached me without fear and without groveling—you'd be surprised how rare that is. I liked the way you wanted to help your friend." He looked at me. "I like that you write poetry and work in a literary agency. I like your modesty about your poetry. I like that you could admit what you didn't know about Motherwell and modern art."

"That's it?"

He turned his attention back to the scene outside the window. "I also like that you remind me of my daughter."

"Jesus." I felt like someone had knocked the wind out of me.

"That's why I invited you to lunch and the museum. It was as if I could have a piece of her back again, as if I could make up for some of the things I didn't do for her or say to her. But then I started to like you as you, not as her. I like the you that has Chelsea's beauty, courage, and spark of life, but I also like the you that's nothing like her, the down-to-earth you, the you that wasn't afraid to expose your fear. The you that didn't feel the need to impress me. You're refreshing." He peered around the room as if he was lost. "That's it. I'm sorry I've been so pushy about your situation, but I can't stand the thought of another beautiful young woman sacrificing her life."

***

As I lay in bed that night, Charles' words ricocheted inside my head. *I can't stand the thought of another beautiful young woman sacrificing her life.* I pulled the thin foam pillow over my head to keep the demons out, but Jessica was already in there, and she wouldn't go away.

I saw my older sister's shining, auburn hair; her pale, flawless complexion; the thick, pouty lips the boys found sexy but Jessica hated. I saw the smile that started in her green eyes and traveled to her mouth but always remained mildly melancholy.

I clenched my jaw and squeezed my eyes more tightly shut, trying to keep out the new picture that was emerging—not of Jessica when she was fully alive, nor when she lay in her coffin like a beautiful plastic saint. This was Jessica, age sixteen, lying in the rented hospital bed that dominated her pink bedroom with the force of a living presence. She was surrounded by bottles, jars, syringes, pills, smells, and zombie parents who sat by her bedside while a malignant tumor burrowed its way through her brain, making the organ look like an ant farm.

I turned on the light, hoping the glare would erase the image, but all it did was send the tape reeling forward to the place where I saw myself walk into that pink bedroom and ask my parents for a ride to Annette's slumber party.

"Maybe you should stay home tonight." My mother stroked her comatose daughter's long hair. "Jessica might need you." My mother's eyes were bloodshot, surrounded by dark, puffy circles.

I nodded and turned to walk away, as I had each time I had been denied something over the past several months, but then I stopped, spun around, and shouted, "Why should she need *me* when she has both of *you* twenty-four hours a day? What about *me*? Who do *I* have?" I glowered at my weary mother and skewered my father with a piercing look. "She's a *fraud!*" I screamed. "She's *faking!*"

Jessica's eyelid twitched, as if she had heard me.

My mother stood up, unfolding her limbs carefully, as if she had not moved in days and was afraid they might shatter or crack. "I'll drive her," she said to my father.

Jessica died while my mother and I were on our way to Annette's.

She was laid in an open casket for the funeral. All through the service, I gazed at the coffin but was unable to think of the beautiful body as my sister.

The night after the funeral, when the fact of Jessica's death threatened to slither into my consciousness, I ran to my parents' bed and burrowed against my mother's tightly curled body. I forced her to hold me and rock me like a baby.

"It's all right, Jessica," she said to me. "It's all right."

She didn't even know which of us was left.

We never spoke of Jessica after that. We went on living our lives, pretending that nothing had changed. Everyone remarked on how well we were doing—*remarkably well, all things considered*—until my father left home one morning and didn't return. I never saw him again, which was not a bad thing since I was always fearful he might try to do to me the things he had done to Jessica, the things we all knew about but never mentioned.

My mother died a year after he left. The doctor said the wounds were self-inflicted.

But I had perfected the role of *doing remarkably well.* I lived with Annette's family until I finished high school, after which I devoted myself to creating a life that would bear no resemblance to the one I had known in Bayonne. I cast myself as an ordinary girl from an ordinary background who sought the things such a girl might seek—a grand tour of Europe, a career in New York, the thrill of independence. I never let on that I had already had far too much independence. I played the role so convincingly I was able to fool myself. Most of the time.

That's why this vivid vision in the night was so disturbing.

I can't stand the thought of another beautiful young woman sacrificing her life.

I got out of bed, wrapped myself in my fuzzy blue bathrobe, took a bottle of Schlitz from the refrigerator, turned on the Late Show, curled up into myself on the sofa, and tried hard to forget.

***

The next afternoon, I had twelve rejection letters to type for the older Mr. Wiley and was having trouble completing even one. I felt queasy and dizzy; my abdomen and back ached, and tiny, sharp contractions let me know that the baby, almost three months in gestation, was no happier than I was. I shifted in my chair in a vain attempt to seek a comfortable position.

At three o'clock, the younger Mr. Wiley tossed another letter into my in-box, but instead of breezing past as he usually did, he stopped and looked me up and down. "You're awfully pale. Are you sure you're over that flu bug?"

I had lied about my reason for missing a few days of work.

"Maybe I'm not."

"Why don't you go home. Get some rest."

Far too uncomfortable to protest his offer, I stuck my full in-box in a drawer, slipped the plastic cover over my IBM Selectric typewriter, pulled on my white cardigan, and dragged myself out into the cold October afternoon, where I made an unprecedented investment in a cab ride home.

As the taxi crept through traffic toward Gramercy Park, I felt increasingly lightheaded, and uncomfortable in the lower reaches of my torso. This pregnancy was far more difficult than I had imagined possible; I was not sure I could go through with it even if I wanted to.

But I never had to make the decision, for I barely made it out of the cab and into my apartment before the baby decided for itself, exiting my body in a trickle of blood.

Other than wrenching cramps, the experience was neither terribly painful nor dramatic. My reaction, once I understood what had happened, was relief that my body had taken decisive action when my mind had been unable to do so.

As I cleaned myself with a warm, damp washcloth, my body grew limper and limper and finally relaxed. My muscles uncoiled from neck to shoulders and on down into my lower back, thighs, and calves. My mind, for the first time in weeks, was at perfect ease. I was floating. I truly believed that my body's rejection of this child—or was it the child's rejection of me?—had produced the perfect result.

***

I spent the next few days in bed, letting my body recover from the physical trauma and letting my psyche generate a new framework around which my life could now be built, a framework that included neither a baby nor an abortion. While this prospect was initially exhilarating, my relief turned into unease, and my unease into a bone-crushing depression that left me indifferent to the world and everything in it. I wanted nothing but to lie there. Eternally.

Annette spent what time she could with me to cook, cajole, and try to make me talk about what had happened. One needed to express one's feelings, she said. She reassured me that what happened had been for the best. But nothing could penetrate the heavy curtain woven of weariness, guilt, and sadness that had descended over me.

"I'm responsible for this baby's death," I finally told her, almost too weak to say the words. "I've killed a child."

"That's ridiculous. You miscarried. It's no one's fault."

"The baby knew it wasn't wanted."

"Oh, Lauren, please be real."

To me, it *was* real. Way too real. I had let this child know, just as I had once let Jessica know, that I wanted it out of my life. And then it happened. "I have to tell Larry."

"What's the point?"

There was no point. No point to that and no point to anything else. It was all too exhausting. I lay back in my bed and explored the terrain of the dirty white plaster ceiling. I was finished talking.

***

Two days later, while Annette was preparing a can of tomato soup on my tiny gas stove, the phone rang.

"You'd better get that. It might be your office." She had earlier told the older Mr. Wylie I was still suffering from the flu and would be out a few more days.

204

I turned my head sideways on the pillow and looked at her. It was the third day of my siege of silence, and Annette looked devastated. None of her jokes, threats, pleas or admonitions had made any difference. I was unable—or unwilling—to say a word.

We both listened to the high-pitched ring until Annette picked up the receiver and said hello.

Her mouth dropped. She gripped the phone so tightly her knuckles turned white. "It's *Charles Acheson*," she whispered, hand over the mouthpiece. "He's *worried* about you, for God's sake. He called your office, and they told him you were sick."

I turned my head toward the wall.

"I'm afraid she's not feeling up to talking right now. I'll give her your message."

She slammed the receiver down. "Jesus, Lauren, I can't believe you would stiff Charles Acheson. What's *wrong* with you?"

I closed my eyes and re-entered the peaceful dark place inside my head.

***

The phone rang again the next morning while Annette was in class.

For a time, I was content to let it ring, but the jangling noise ultimately carved a jagged fissure in my skull, which made me drag my limp body over to the phone. I lifted the receiver.

"Good morning." I recognized Charles' voice. "Are you okay?"

I held the receiver out and gazed at it as if it were a foreign object of only mild academic interest. I wasn't *stiffing him*, as Annette would say; I simply had no words.

"Is there anything I can do?"

I hung up and went back to bed. I had come to recognize the simple beauty inherent in a life of nothingness. If I didn't speak, didn't leave the apartment, didn't do anything but watch television, I would have nothing to worry about and no one to harm. This was how life was meant to be lived. If I'd never left the apartment in the first place, never gone to Europe, never met Larry, I would never have gotten pregnant, and never have killed his child.

I lay back on the bed and let the gentle nothingness wash over me.

***

When I resurfaced, it was dark outside, but a small light shone in the room, a lamp which illuminated a book Charles Acheson was reading. The book was mine; it contained poetry by Kenneth Koch, a writer whose loose and easy imagery I had always admired.

I stared at Charles as he read silently, watching his lips move. His eyes moved from side to side and line to line behind his tortoise shell reading glasses as he slouched in my armchair, his long legs stretched in front of him, crossed at the ankles. His graceful hands held the book low, and his chin almost touched his collarbone as his head bent down. He turned the page with a tender touch, as if showing respect for the very paper the book was printed on.

A fine spray of wrinkles radiated from his eyes: three deep lines in his forehead suggested concentration. Or worry. But his features had a perfect regularity and precision of articulation.

As he turned another page, he looked over to where I lay watching him. He returned my gaze without smiling or speaking.

"Why are you here?" I don't know why I chose that moment to break my silence.

"Your friend Annette let me in. I was concerned about you."

"Why would you care?"

He rested the open book upside-down on his thigh. "For the past few days, I've been trying to figure out why I care, why I'm so smitten."

I'd never heard anyone use that word before.

"You're a beautiful young woman. You're bright, sweet…"

No one had ever spoken to me like this before.

"I want to know if I can do anything to help."

"There's nothing to be done. The baby's gone."

"Annette told me. Have you seen a doctor?"

"I don't need to. And I don't need help from you. Would you please leave me alone?"

He removed his glasses, put them in his jacket pocket, and stood. "You know where to find me if you need anything."

As I watched him leave, I remembered that he too had lost a child, one he'd gotten to know far better than I had mine. I didn't know if my child was a son or a daughter, though I felt sure it was a boy. A sweet little boy with Larry's brown hair and dimples, Larry's artistic style and talent, Larry's taut, sinewy body.

***

At some point, I began to live again.

I rose from my bed—at first for five or ten minutes at a time—and talked with Annette. Then I put on a clean robe and had a light meal. Within a few days, I donned an old pair of jeans and a sweatshirt and stepped outside. One fine morning, I sat on a park bench and watched my breath come out in white puffs. Within a few weeks, I was back at work.

I was once again operating within the realm of what people would call "normal." But nothing was the same. I no longer went to bed with fantasies of Larry and our life-together-someday-in-Paris dancing in my head; I no longer dreamt of the day when I would be a widely-published, critically-acclaimed poet; I no longer wrote or read poetry at all. I no longer mapped out my strategy to become an agent rather than a typist; and I no longer felt a subtle thrill of satisfaction and pride that I had attracted the interest of one of the city's most important philanthropists, a worldly sophisticate, decades my senior.

All my energy was devoted to getting through each day, one at a time. I went to work and came home. I ate meals, talked to Annette, and occasionally read a magazine or went to a movie. I watched television and slept. That was my life, right through the holiday season. I was relieved, when I turned off the lamp on my bedside table each night, to have crossed one more day off the calendar.

Judy Pomeranz

Chapter Eight
A Common Language

January, 1967

On the first Saturday of the New Year, I dragged myself out of bed at ten, flipped on the TV, and curled back up to commune with the cartoon characters who had become my constant weekend companions. Dressed in my dingy blue bathrobe, my hair straggly and unwashed, my face streaked with yesterday's mascara, and my bloodshot eyes rimmed with dark circles and puffy pouches, I was a pathetic sight, but could not have cared less. Not about that or anything else.

Which makes it particularly surprising that I responded as I did when an inane cartoon character—a chubby, loud-mouthed, red-haired girl in a checked pinafore—took her dog Spot to visit the local art museum. As they wandered amongst the Rembrandts and Renoirs, Davids and Degas, Copleys and Cassatts, giggling and chattering stupidly, I experienced a peculiar, unexpected urge to visit Motherwell's *Elegy*.

I fought the urge. It was insane to take cues from cartoon people. No good could come of an enterprise that risked rekindling feelings for Larry, which I had successfully put aside, along with all other feelings. I preferred to stay here in my bathrobe, as I had for more weekends than I cared to remember.

But the compulsion kept niggling at me, prodding me, and I was finally forced me out of bed, out of my robe, into my jeans, and onto the bus, which I rode uptown without observation or contemplation, staring straight ahead until I disembarked a block from the Metropolitan Museum. From there I made my way to the Motherwell.

The painting was larger than I remembered, or else I was diminished. I stood and stared until its presence overwhelmed me and I had to turn away. I sat on a bench facing the opposite wall and tried to concentrate on the soothing sky blue tones of a large color field painting, but *Elegy*'s dark shapes and pale background stayed in my mind, making me feel like I was swimming in a sea of black and white.

Even without looking at the picture, I felt the push and pull of the contrasts, the energy of the brushwork, the calm of the meandering black drips, the harshness of the carefully-delineated edges, the softness of the feathered edges, the primal force of the biomorphic forms. The black spoke of the hole into which I had sunk; the white hinted at something brighter: hope. I turned back to it.

Yes, there were elements of something universal, something I couldn't define but that resonated on an intensely personal level. I sensed that Motherwell had captured a fundamental part of me and committed it to canvas with a loaded brush. The feeling was both comforting and disquieting, also embarrassing because I had always been pragmatic and was not given to new-agey experiences. I felt vulnerable, stupid, and exposed.

***

It was late afternoon when I left the Met and walked out into a dark, blustery day. As I stood on the museum steps and gazed across Fifth Avenue at the series of elegant apartment buildings marching up the street, I remembered Charles had once told me he lived in this neighborhood.

I crossed the street and walked down the Avenue, barely aware of the cold wind that made my face hurt and my breath freeze. I peered into each chandelier-lit, wood-paneled lobby, wondering if it might be his. I examined each fur-clad woman on the street, wondering if it might be his wife. I looked into each long, black limousine parked on the street, wondering if it might be waiting for him.

***

When I got home, I pulled out a piece of my best pink stationary, determined to write Larry and tell him about my experience with the Motherwell while it was still fresh in my mind. This time it would be my *own* experience, my *real* experience, not an analysis appropriated from someone else. I removed the top of my Shaeffer cartridge pen, smelled the deep, inky aroma I had always loved, and poised the nib over the paper to write.

But no words came.

I was unable to explain what the painting meant to me. The more I tried to put it into words, the more convinced I became that doing so would cheapen or obliterate the experience. But there was another problem, a larger one:

I had nothing to say to Larry.

Nonetheless, the nib ultimately pressed down on the paper and flowing ribbons of black ink emerged from it, forming letters. But rather than beginning *Dear Larry*, the letters spelled out *Dear Charles*.

I was at the Metropolitan Museum of Art today, and I admired the Motherwell painting once again. Or, more accurately, for the first time. You did the right thing buying a Motherwell for your wife. She's a lucky woman.

I'm sorry I worried you last fall. I was going through a rough patch, but things are better now. You were kind to me, and I appreciate it.

I struggled over a conclusion. *Sincerely* was too formal and *Love* was too personal. *Very Truly Yours* sounded like a business letter and *Best Wishes* like a greeting card. I finally settled on *Fondly*, an expression I had never liked but was the best I could come up with. I wished I were enough of a poet to express what I wanted to say to Charles, or to understand it.

***

A long stretch of days passed after I sent the letter to his foundation's office, days that turned into a month. On each of those days, I came home from work and ritualistically unlocked my flimsy metal mailbox at the foot of the stairs. Each day I pulled out a small pile of envelopes, turned them facedown, and walked up to my apartment without looking at them. Each day, I changed into jeans and an old sweater and made myself a cup of tea before sitting at my tiny dinette table to open the mail. I wanted to be in a state of perfect comfort when I read Charles' response.

Judy Pomeranz

But by the end of the fourth week, I resigned myself to the fact that there was not going to be one. And why should there be? I was merely reaping the harvest I had sown with my own thoughtless actions. I jotted the ridiculously stale metaphor down in my journal with the thought that I might one day incorporate it into a poem about a lovely but fleeting relationship and its sad but predictable ending. But, thankfully, that maudlin poem never got written, because, on the last day of the first month of 1967, Charles phoned me at work.

"Would you like to meet for lunch at the club?" He asked the question as casually as if we lunched together every day.

"I... I... of course I would."

"12:30?"

"Okay... Yes. 12:30."

***

I arrived at the Seldrake before Charles, and the maître d' greeted me as if I were an old friend. He showed me to the same table we had occupied on our two previous visits, but when I looked out the window, I saw a different landscape than the one I remembered from the fall. The trees were now stark, spidery and leafless, etched against a wintry gray sky. The scene stood in sharp contrast to the warm-toned, leafy landscape I had observed from this vantage point before.

"Sorry I'm late."

I looked up at the sound of the familiar voice and smiled as Charles pulled out the chair across from mine.

"I'm sorry for the way I treated you," I blurted out before he had a chance to sit down.

"Are we going to spend another lunch apologizing to each other?"

"No, not to each other. Just me to you."

He shook his head. "No..."

"I was afraid I'd never hear from you again," I interrupted, surprised to hear the words tumble from my mouth. Where was the suave, smooth woman I had planned to be at this reunion?

"I told you I wouldn't torment you anymore, and I meant it," he said.

"I wasn't ready to deal with anything. I needed time."

"It must have helped. You look great."

212

"Why did you wait so long to respond to my letter?"

Charles half-smiled, as if pleased I'd noticed. "I was in Paris."

I could feel my neck and shoulder muscles tighten. "Business?"

"Mostly pleasure."

"You're lucky," I said in a polite deadpan. "What did you do there?"

"Museums and galleries, and terrific meals with good friends. I treated myself to long, lazy afternoons at the *Café Deux Magots*, and squandered too much time and money at my favorite bookstores in the Latin Quarter. I made a pilgrimage to Gertrude Stein's home on the *rue de Fleurus*."

"Sounds wonderful." I concentrated on drawing patterns in the condensation on my water glass.

"I also saw a show of your friend's paintings."

I stopped playing with the glass and looked up at him. "Larry's?"

"Yes." He looked cautious, as if he didn't know how I would take this.

"How did that happen?"

"It was all quite coincidental." He glanced down at the menu of daily specials as he spoke. "A friend who owns a gallery mentioned this young American painter who had shown up on the Parisian scene out of the blue. He said the young man worked in an abstract style my wife might find interesting. It turned out the artist's name was Larry Barnes."

It was odd hearing that name articulated by Charles.

"He was having a show—his first one-man exhibition—so I dropped in at the opening."

"Did you like his work?" I tried to sound casual, as if this was a purely academic matter, but my mouth was dry. I took a sip of water and opened the menu.

"It was interesting."

"But did you like it?"

"I need more time with it before I can say for sure. But he is developing a following in Paris. Important critics have noticed him."

So, it seemed much had changed on both sides of the Atlantic. "Did you see him?"

"I spoke to him briefly."

This whole thing was bizarre. I wondered if Charles could be making it up, or if he might have engineered the whole thing. "What did you think of him?"

"Interesting fellow," he said without inflection.

I was becoming impatient with his repeated use of the same ambiguous characterization. "Did you like him?"

"It was quite a mob scene, and we only had a few words with each other."

Having resisted for as long as I could, I finally let loose with the question I'd been wanting to ask all along. "Did you say you knew me?"

"I did."

"And?" I rested my elbows on the menu and leaned forward.

"He said he'd spent time with you when you were touring Paris last summer."

"That was *it?*"

"It was terribly crowded, and there were people coming at the poor guy from all sides. It wasn't the time for an intimate chat."

I stared at him.

"I told him you were a poet," Charles said quietly.

"And?"

"He was distracted. He didn't really hear me, there was so much going on…"

"Did he ask you to say hello to me? Or anything?"

"No."

We sat for a long while in awkward silence as I tried to absorb the final coda to what I had once envisioned as my life's story. Looking at the gray day outside the window gave me a chill, and I buttoned the fake brass buttons of my navy blazer.

"So, tell me what you've been up to all this time," Charles finally said in a forced-upbeat manner. "I've thought about you a lot."

"I've been working." I concentrated on the trees outside.

"You're feeling better?"

I nodded.

"You're tough to have come through that experience intact."

I smiled weakly. "So, did your wife like Larry's paintings?"

"She hasn't seen them. She wasn't with me."

"She doesn't like Paris?"

"We're separated. She lives on her own now, over on Park Avenue."

"I'm sorry."

"Thank you. She never got over what happened to our daughter." He studied the menu, as if buying time to think. "She blames me. She says she knows it's unfair, but she can't help it. She can't see me without thinking about Chelsea and getting sad and angry."

"Why?"

His eyes stayed on the menu as he spoke. "She never liked Chelsea's boyfriend, never thought he was good enough. He wasn't from an old family, didn't go to the right schools, wasn't on track to become a millionaire by inheritance or earning power." He took a sip of water. "She tried to interest Chelsea in other boys. She fixed her up with people we knew in East Hampton, people from the club, friends here in town."

"But why does she blame *you*?"

"Her boyfriend was driving when she was killed."

"Why is that *your* fault?"

"Because I never helped her convince Chelsea to drop him. I liked him. I found him refreshing—like you. He was pleasant and unassuming, bright and clever in a street-smart way, and well educated, too. Not Ivy League, but he went to a good school—Rutgers—and took his studies seriously. He was working on a graduate degree in English Literature when they were killed."

"Both of them?"

"Both of them."

"I liked what he did for Chelsea. He made her happy, in a natural way. She was content and centered in a way I had never before known her to be." He brushed a breadcrumb off the tablecloth. He took a deep breath and exhaled broadly. "She could be high-strung, intense. I'm afraid she was spoiled—I take full blame—and a snob. But Jeffrey loosened her up and made her more generous, more forgiving, more fun." Charles picked up his knife and systematically slid the blade between each set of tines on his fork. "She was great fun." He ran the blade of the knife across the white tablecloth as if trying to scrape up a spill.

"But I still don't see why your wife blames *you* for the accident."

215

"She's sure that if I had supported her we could have convinced Chelsea to stop seeing him. Then the rest would never have happened." Charles carefully arranged his silverware back into a proper place setting. "She may be right."

"That's absurd." I wanted to grab his arm to shake sense into him or comfort him. I wished I had the nerve to touch him. "When did your wife move out?"

"In December. Right before the holidays."

"When did your daughter die?" I knew my questions were personal, but was emboldened by the abrupt role reversal that had taken place, with me being the priest and he the penitent; me the strong, rational one and he the one in need.

"Last May."

I opened my mouth but had no words. I had assumed her death was an event from the dim past.

"Remember the day you saw me at Motherwell's *Elegy*?"

I nodded.

"I was there because my wife wanted one of his paintings."

"I know that."

"It was part of my reconciliation effort. It's tawdry, to think I could buy her back." He paused. "She had wanted an important Motherwell ever since he became fashionable, but we had a rule that we would only buy art we both loved, and I vetoed Motherwell." He took a slow sip of iced tea. "When I heard there was a good one on the market last September, I thought if I bought it for her it would help us. Pathetic, right?"

"Not at all. Sweet."

"Pathetic or sweet, it didn't work. She moved out and filed divorce papers."

"I'm sorry I brought it up."

"Here we go again with the apologies." Charles forced a small smile. "This is no way to start a relationship."

I wasn't sure what that meant, *start a relationship,* but I liked the sound of it.

Chapter Nine
Is This Love?

May, 1967

Charles and I began spending time together. Our meetings were intermittent and tentative at first, but increased in frequency and ease as the weeks went by. Though I never stopped feeling off-balance, and could never fathom why *he* would have chosen *me*, I adapted to the rhythms of my new life.

We attended poetry readings in the Village, concerts at Carnegie Hall, and operas at Lincoln Center. We spent weekends at MoMA, the Guggenheim, the Whitney, the Frick, the Asia Society, the Morgan Library, the Met, and the Cloisters. We discussed the smallest details of our lives and the grandest literary themes, but it was not until May that Charles invited me to his home.

"It's a dinner party a week from Saturday, if you're free." He said it so casually. "It'll be a chance for you to meet my friends."

***

On the afternoon of the party, I tried on a succession of outfits in front of my cloudy full-length mirror. It was a ritual I had often carried out with Annette. We would assess each option with a lengthy commentary and given each a rating. We would arrive at a consensus on which ensemble made me look sexy but not cheap, voluptuous but not fat. We would end the afternoon with a makeover in which

Annette would pull my hair into a pile on top of my head or coil it into a French twist, then brush bright blue eye shadow onto my lids.

But Annette was not with me that afternoon; she would have been out of her depth. Ever since I had begun spending time with Charles I had been conducting research and now preferred to proceed on my own, trusting my new, hard-earned sense of style. I had read fashion magazines at the public library and scrutinized mannequins in shop windows along Fifth Avenue. I had walked Madison Avenue in the seventies and eighties, observing women on the street and attending to the fine points of hair, clothes, make-up, demeanor, facial expressions, and gait. I now felt ready to make these my own.

I ran through the possibilities with a trained eye. The A-line skirt and sweater were too school-girlish, the cocktail dress too frou-frou, the royal blue knit sheath rather dowdy, and the mini-skirt a tad risqué, so the black wool pants and pink cashmere top carried the day. It was now okay to wear pants, I understood, even in the evening. It was daring, defiant, and plucky. That's what *Cosmopolitan* said. Plucky. I liked the way that sounded. I put on the pants and sweater then added a string of fake pearls. Upper East Side women always wore pearls. Single-strand.

I dabbed on brown eye shadow, less than I would have instinctively, and brushed on a heavy coat of mascara. I used no foundation, having read that the natural look was in. I ran a gloss of pale pink over my lips, then scrutinized my face in the mirror.

Not bad, but the cheeks were too rosy. They were more "milkmaid" than "fashion model"; none of the women on Madison Avenue had bright pink cheeks. So I applied powder to tone down the blush, then brushed out my newly cut hair and let it hang loose, close to my head, with a curve inward at the ends.

***

I arrived at Charles' building at seven-fifteen for the seven o'clock dinner party. I had learned that people in such circles never arrived on time. A uniformed doorman, whose hat reminded me of my father's transit authority cap, ushered me into the lobby and asked my name. He checked it against a list and showed me into a small elevator.

I was surprised when he followed me in. He placed a key in a slot in the brass wall-panel, then pressed a button. As the walnut-paneled lift ascended at a leisurely pace, a light fixture composed of dangling crystals tinkled softly. When the elevator opened, the doorman wished me a good evening, then disappeared, leaving me in a foyer furnished with a console table, a chair on either side, and a single door. I had never before been in a building with only one apartment on a floor. I pressed the simple brass doorbell.

When Charles came to the door, I let out a long breath I hadn't known I was holding in; it was a relief to see a familiar face in these alien surroundings. Best of all, he looked pleased to see me.

"You look lovely." He kissed my cheek. He took my coat and handed it to a man who materialized out of nowhere. "I'd like you to meet my friend Daniel, the man who keeps me organized." Charles turned to the short, stocky man dressed in a black tuxedo. "Daniel, I'd like you to meet Lauren."

Daniel nodded cordially, but did not speak, nor did he smile. I followed suit but tempered my nod with the smallest hint of a grin, sensing this was the way one responded to servants.

***

Charles had invited three couples to the party. And me. I wondered if that meant the party would consist of four couples, or three couples, a host, and an odd woman out. As the other guests arrived, I stood close by Charles' side, shaking hands, making small talk, smiling (but not too broadly), and nodding. I did a lot of nodding. Every so often, Charles would drape an arm around me or place his hand casually on my forearm. The gestures seemed proprietary. I felt like a hostess.

Mitzi Stone and her husband Paul were the last to arrive. Mitzi was five foot ten, and as thin as a London model. Her dark brown hair was pulled tightly into a compact configuration at the nape of her neck. Her complexion was pale and translucent, and her eyes were as dark as her hair. Her lips were rouged in clear red, and she was dressed entirely in black.

Daring, defiant, and plucky. I had never seen anyone who could so properly be called striking. She was not classically beautiful; her features were a millimeter too large for perfection and on the edge of horsey, but she epitomized my idea of *chic*. Without glitz or glitter, she exuded *breeding*. She spoke without any apparent accent, in a round voice filled with soft vowels and smooth consonants that formed mellow tones. But the most interesting thing was that she appeared my own age, a fact worthy of note because everyone else in attendance, including her husband Paul, was substantially older.

Paul, whom Charles introduced as his oldest and closest friend, had silvery hair, regular but craggy features, and a warm, crinkly smile. He and Charles had known one another since Princeton, where they had both studied art history.

"Mitzi's quite an art expert," Charles said with evident affection. "She majored in art history at Smith and grew up with one of the world's great collections of Baroque art. It's now at the Met, thanks to her late father's generosity."

Mitzi smiled modestly but did not bow her head and gaze at the floor as I might have done in a similar situation. It was a fact I carefully recorded.

In the course of the idle chitchat early in the evening, Charles referred to me more than once as "my good friend," a designation that struck me as intentionally ambiguous. It wasn't as good as "oldest and dearest friend," and certainly not as good as "girlfriend," but it was better than "friend," the word he used in connection with Daniel, the servant.

"Have you and Charles known each other long?" Mitzi asked.

"Several months," I replied casually, though I was disappointed that Charles had not mentioned me to his friends.

"We met at the office," Charles said. "Lauren was picking up an application for an artist friend of hers."

Mitzi nodded. "Do you live around here?"

"No, downtown."

"Lauren lives in a great part of town, just off Grammercy Park," Charles said.

I wondered why my neighborhood needed preemptive defending.

"She's been teaching me about the modern poets." Charles moved the group out of the marble foyer into the living room. "She's a poet herself."

"Really," Paul said. "I met Allen Ginsberg the other night at one of those horrible literary events in the Village with people crammed on top of one another, and too much cheap wine and angst."

"What was he like?" I asked.

"He droned on about sex, war, and drugs. I had no idea what he was talking about, and I don't think he did either."

I chuckled at Paul's story, following the lead of everyone around me, though I found it more sad than funny.

**

Throughout the evening, I observed the scene as an astute student might, picking up on the rhythms and flows that defined its character. I noticed that, during the cocktail hour, the conversational floor was passed successively from one man to the next. One would hold forth for a time on, say, his golf game, the stock market, his political views, or a trip, and then, as if in a relay race, he would smoothly pass the conversational baton on to the next. The women chimed in from time to time with brief remarks or quips related to what the most recent male speaker had said, but never changed the subject.

The pattern shifted during dinner. While the men focused on eating, the women kept up a steady patter. I found it surprisingly easy to uphold my end of this unwritten social contract, throwing in the occasional word about how delicious everything was, how much I loved the new exhibit at the Met, or how mediocre Thursday night's symphony performance had been—a tidbit I had gleaned from the Mr. Wileys.

After dinner, the conversational shift-over was completed. When the group retired to the library for drinks and smokes, the women took over entirely, for the men had eaten and drunk so much they all seemed drowsy. Their wives chattered amiably and animatedly, each making sure her husband was required to chime in every so often, probably to ensure he stayed awake.

"Isn't that right, dear?" one would say, or "Where *were* we when that happened? Was it Paris or Lyons?"

So I gave it a try. "Charles, what was the name of that artist who painted the elongated Madonnas at the Met?" Worked like a charm.

But then Mitzi asked the question I had dreaded and fervently hoped to avoid: "Where are you from, Lauren?"

There was no way of pretending you were well bred if you were from Bayonne. "Just outside New York."

"Me too. I grew up in Greenwich."

"That's where Charles' brother lives," I said. "Do you know him?"

"Findlay lives down the road from my mother."

And thus the conversation turned to Greenwich and Findlay. I sat back and grinned, pleased that my diversionary tactic had succeeded. Mitzi glanced at me with an expression between wise and admiring, an expression that suggested she was not entirely taken in by my ploy but was impressed enough to not blow my cover. I was beginning to like her.

***

After the last of the guests had left, Charles put his hands on my shoulders. "You are truly beautiful. Everyone loved you."

He lifted my chin with two fingers. It was like a slow-motion scene out of a movie. I didn't turn, didn't move my head, and didn't blink. I simply parted my lips ever so subtly, allowing him to kiss me.

That was the first night we spent together.

***

Before I left the next morning, Charles asked me to join him the following weekend in the Hamptons. Though I had never been to the far tip of Long Island, I knew the area's reputation, and spent the week imagining myself as Daisy Buchanan.

When the time came and we drove down Southampton's Main Street, making our way toward East Hampton, I found the small, old-timey shops sweet, but disappointingly ordinary. The neighborhoods beyond Main Street, filled with white frame homes, old-growth trees, and perfect lawns, were pristine and spruced up as if for a special occasion, but far from posh. It wasn't until we approached the ocean that the residences grew into structures that could properly be called mansions, most of them partly obscured by the towering boxwood hedges that lined their front yards. That's when I felt I was in the legendary Hamptons.

"Privacy." Charles nodded at the boxwoods. "The Village doesn't like fences, so the hedgerows substitute. They're marvelous. So old and dignified."

"They're lovely," I said, though I had as much trouble understanding the concept of dignity in bushes as I had once had finding meaning in the Motherwell. By now I understood that, in this world, simply acknowledging the validity of someone's position was far more important than understanding it.

"This is our street," Charles said as Jimmy turned the black Lincoln onto Lily Pond Lane.

I wondered what "our" referred to. Did it refer to me and Charles, or to Charles and his estranged wife? Maybe it referred to Charles and Jimmy, or maybe it was the possessive form of the "royal we"?

Jimmy turned again and drove down a driveway that ended at an enormous, weathered brown-shingle house with forest-green shutters and trim.

"It's beautiful," I said.

"I'm so glad you like it," Charles said, as if it mattered to him.

When Jimmy opened the Lincoln's back door and I stepped out, Charles watched me, gauging my reaction. He smiled nervously, but when I responded with a generous grin, his shoulders and face relaxed. I sensed the extent of my power.

"I'm so glad you you're here with me." He touched the small of my back and ushered me through the front door.

The entry hall was two stories high and lined with dark wood paneling and a tall wall of windows beyond which the ocean lay like a broad blue ribbon set atop a line of low, reed-covered dunes. The first floor had so many rooms I lost count, each one larger and more decorous than the last, but the atmosphere was too heavy for my taste. The furniture was too large and the colors too dark until we got to the sunroom that ran along one side of the back of the house—a wicker-filled, glass-enclosed space into which the golden afternoon light and blue water were welcome décor. That was a room I could live in.

The second floor was filled with bedrooms and sitting areas. All were for guests, Charles explained, except the master bedroom, and Chelsea's room, a place that particularly intrigued me. It was like a shrine; it looked as if its occupant had just stepped out and might return at any moment. Three small impressionist seascapes hung on the wall over a double bed, which was covered with a fresh blue cotton coverlet. Ready for use. A porcelain container filled with pencils and pens, and three carefully stacked locked diaries sat on an open rolltop desk. Bookshelves were filled with the detritus of an affluent young woman's life: two tennis trophies, a slew of silver-framed photos, a propped-open Valentine card, and an assortment of memorabilia and trinkets so dense I couldn't take them all in. It was a room frozen in time. Charles had a hard time walking away from it, but when he finally did, he shut the door and showed me into the master suite.

It consisted of a sitting room decorated in dusty rose, an enormous pink marble bathroom, and the bedroom itself, which was larger than my efficiency apartment. I found the suite impressive but overbearing with its mahogany furniture and gray-toned pinkness. I imagined myself re-decorating these rooms, brightening them up. I wondered what Mitzi Stone would do with them.

Charles put his arms around me and drew me so close I could smell his lemony aftershave. "I can't believe I have you to myself for the entire weekend."

***

After a long afternoon walk on the beach, we sat down to dinner at a small round table in the sunroom. A maid served us grilled swordfish, herb-roasted new potatoes, the sweetest green peas I had ever put in my mouth, and a bottle of Sancerre, followed by raspberries with cream, and tiny cups of espresso. As I took my last sip of the steaming coffee, Charles walked around the table and stood awkwardly beside my chair. He put his hand in the left pocket of his sport jacket and pulled out a small gray suede box.

"I didn't intend to spring this on you for a while." He gently touched the soft pile of the suede. "If I were a more cautious man, I would wait until we knew each other better. If I were more romantic, I would do this on Christmas or Valentine's Day." He handed me the box. "I know this is sudden, and I'm afraid of scaring you away, but I can't wait." He kissed the top of my head. "It's so perfect having you here. So perfect."

I held the box, enjoying its softness, unable to think about what was inside for fear I would be proven wrong.

"Aren't you going to open it?" He was anxious, like a small boy.

I lifted the lid and looked in. It was a diamond. A single enormous diamond in a platinum setting.

"My God," I whispered.

"Take all the time you need to think about it," Charles said quickly. "Take a year, take a decade, if you want. I just had to give it to you."

"Are you asking...?" Maybe it was superstition, maybe it was insecurity, but I couldn't bring myself to say the words. I had to hear them from him.

"I'm asking you to marry me."

I stared at him.

"I love you, Lauren."

When I was finally able to make words come out of my mouth, I repeated his. "I... love... you." I formed each one slowly and carefully, as if I was just learning the language or was drunk and afraid of slurring. I said them again. "I love you, Charles." This time, they came out more easily, more strongly.

But as I spoke them, I wondered if the words were true. I loved the way Charles made me feel—important, bright, and worthy. I loved the way he lived and the things he had, the things that could now become mine. I admired his philanthropy and kindness, and I respected his knowledge. I loved the way I acted and felt when I was with him. But whether all that translated into the cosmic thing people called "love," I had no idea.

"I love you very much." I repeated the words once again, testing their feel in my mouth, hoping to make them fit.

When we made love the previous weekend, I had been comforted by his strength, his gentleness, the way his long body wrapped around my smaller one. There had been a sweetness, a loveliness to the experience, but none of the fiery passion I had felt when making love to Larry, none of the feral intensity.

But this man *loved me*. Of that, I was certain. He would take care of me. Always. Not like Larry, not like my father, not like my mother, not like Jessica. I didn't know if I was *in* love, but I was most assuredly *loved*, and that was so much more important.

Charles gave me a long, tender kiss on the lips. When we finally drew apart, I whispered in his ear, "Yes."

"What?"

"I said yes, I will."

"Yes, you will—?" It was as if Charles was now the one reluctant to say the words.

Judy Pomeranz

"Yes, I will marry you."

Chapter Ten
An Ordinary Marriage

September, 1967

When Charles asked me, a week after our engagement, where I wanted to be married, I didn't hesitate.

"The Waldorf-Astoria."

"Are you sure?" He seemed surprised. "You don't want a church wedding? We can do it anywhere you want. The Maidstone Club in East Hampton or here in town at the Plaza, the Carlyle… you name it."

"I'd prefer the Waldorf."

"That's fine with me. I didn't know you were such a fan."

It wasn't until two weeks before our September wedding that I confessed to Charles why I had chosen the Waldorf. When I told him the story of how he had caught my attention and imagination on that rainy day, weeks before we met, he smiled. When I admitted how taken I had been by his self-assurance, his good looks, and his Gucci shoes, he laughed. When I told him I believed there had been an element of fate at work in our encounter that day, along with the greatest good luck, his eyes filled with tears.

***

We agreed it would be a small affair with few guests and two attendants. Charles selected his brother Findlay as best man, and I asked Mitzi to be my matron of honor. She and I had become surprisingly close in the short time since the engagement, which I attributed to her relief at having someone her own age poised to join her social circle. She had given me so much help in planning and preparing for the wedding that offering her the position seemed the least I could do, or that's what I told myself. The fact was, I had no one else to ask other than Annette, and that didn't seem right.

But I did invite her to the wedding, along with her boyfriend, Freddie Spitzer, a gesture that made me feel magnanimous. The only other guests on my side of the aisle would be my favorite neighbor in the Gramercy Park building, along with the two Mr. Wylies and their wives.

"You're sure there's no one else you'd like to invite?" Charles had asked.

"I'd prefer to keep it small." In truth, there was no one else I could think of.

***

All the local papers and many magazines ran news of the upcoming marriage in flashy feature stories, gossipy tidbit columns, or as straightforward society dish. They talked about the break-up of Charles' first marriage and speculated on its relationship to the "tragedy the couple had endured in the loss of their beautiful and promising daughter." They talked about our twenty-year age difference and our relatively recent acquaintance. They compared me with the first Mrs. Charles Acheson, complimenting my "beauty and unassuming charm," and only occasionally pointing out my resemblance to Charles' late daughter.

Thankfully, the press showed little interest in the details of my past. They were satisfied to parrot the official word Charles' staff had put out at my direction: that I was a poet, that I had grown up as an only child in the New Jersey suburbs, and that my parents had both died years before. Period. I found writing my own biography, exactly as I wanted it, to be exhilarating. I was beginning to appreciate what money could buy.

***

I chose a long, clingy, cream silk wedding dress of plain lines and devoid of surface decoration—No lace, no beads, no fake pearls, no embroidery. None of the things I would have looked for in a wedding dress had I been on my own. The choice was Mitzi's.

"You don't think it's too plain for a wedding gown?" I had asked.

"Not at all. You want sophistication. You're young, and you're marrying an older man. You don't want to look like a baby doll, you want to look as if you've been around. And you want your sense of style to come from within, not from a gaudy exterior."

***

The wedding went exactly according to plan.

The presiding judge, a friend of Charles', offered a ceremony that was brief, secular, and to the point; total elapsed time was six minutes. I had no religious convictions, nor did Charles insist on incorporating any of his own. After the groom kissed the bride, we all adjourned to an adjacent room in the hotel for cocktails and dinner.

Everyone told me how beautiful I was, including members of the society press, who snapped photos in the hallway before and after the ceremony. When Mitzi overheard one photographer's gushing compliment, she shot me a thumbs-up to acknowledge the success of our joint effort. But the sweetest praise came from Charles as he offered a toast.

"This beautiful and talented woman has made me the happiest man alive." A cliché, but so transparently sincere no one could object. "Lauren brought a brilliant spark into my life when I needed it. A few months ago, the 'rest of my life' seemed unendurably long; today, it's far too short. I want centuries, rather than decades, to spend with you, my wife." He smiled and raised a glass in my direction.

Mitzi grinned and raised her glass as well. Annette sobbed. Paul said, "Hear, hear!" and Freddie Spitzer shouted, "That's our gal!"

Which made me cringe, but I did what I knew Mitzi would have done: I raised my glass, looked Charles straight in the eye, and mouthed "thank you," with the smallest of smiles on my lips.

***

Judy Pomeranz

We honeymooned at the Hotel Excelsior in Florence in an endless, airy suite overlooking the Arno. We wandered cobblestone streets, visited churches and museums, admired medieval architecture and Renaissance art, sipped steamy cappuccino at piazza cafes, and peered into storefront workshops where furniture and frames were handcrafted just as they had been centuries before. We did all these things that Charles loved.

But mostly we shopped.

At first, Charles had to encourage me in this endeavor. "If you love that so much, why don't you buy it?" he asked one day as I stared at a white fox coat in a furrier's window on the Lungarno.

"I could never afford anything like that," I said, unable to take my eyes off it.

"Yes, you can."

It took me a moment to understand what he was saying, but as I absorbed the meaning of his words, I smiled broadly. So I could. It was a life-changing moment.

"Why not try it on?"

We marched into the shop as if we had a right to be there. I wrapped myself in the satin-lined fur coat and found that it fit perfectly. As if custom-made. As if intended for me. As if fate were once again intervening on my behalf, which was all the encouragement I needed.

"I'll take it."

And thus it began. Once I broke through the shell of insecurity with that white fox coat, shopping became easy, natural, and necessary. I shopped at Gucci, Pucci, and Farragamo; I bought Valentino, Adolpho, and Armani. Thanks to Charles' generosity and my own newly adopted but quickly honed free-spending ways, I became friends with all the shopkeepers on the via Tornabuoni. At least, it felt like friendship.

***

We spent our Florentine evenings at sparklingly chic restaurants, trendy new bistros, and modest, local trattoria. Charles' knowledge of the latter put him in a select class of tourists who moved in circles beyond those defined by the guidebooks. Thus, I learned to approach these casual eateries that appeared to have come right out of

230

the Italian equivalent of Bayonne as discoveries or adventures rather than disappointments.

Late at night, we opened our bedroom windows, let in the soft, humid breeze and musky scent of the river, and made love. These nights reminded me of that sultry summer in Paris with Larry.

"Florence is the most romantic city in the world," Charles said one night as he held me.

"It's lovely." I felt warm and safe, nestled in that sumptuous bed and in Charles' embrace. Different from passion, other than ardor, it was pleasant.

"I haven't seen you write a word in those beautiful leather books you bought. I should think this town would be a poet's dream." He untangled his body from mine, propped himself up on an elbow and looked at me. "Am I monopolizing you? Would you like me to give you some time to write?"

I shook my head. "I like being monopolized by you."

I smiled as the line tripped off my tongue, though I didn't know if it was true. What was true was that my interest in writing had been completely displaced by the consuming project of learning to live this new life. I had only bought the leather books because they were pretty and because Charles had pressed me to. He said he liked to think they were the kind of books Dante might have written in, or Boccaccio. But I had no desire to put pen to paper. I now had better things to do.

"Speaking of poetry, would you like to see my favorite statue of Dante, outside *Santa Croce,* tomorrow morning?"

"I'd love to, but I have to go to Gucci for alterations."

Charles nodded, rolled onto his back, and studied the ceiling.

We never made it to Santa Croce.

Judy Pomeranz

Chapter Eleven
A Marriage, in a Nutshell

1967–1989

I returned from the honeymoon confident of my status and eager to take my place alongside my distinguished husband on Manhattan's social A-List. I was pretty, young, and fresh, or so they said, and he was Charles Acheson; nothing more was required.

While I adored the whirl of parties and thrived on my new position in the Upper East Side ecosystem, I could see that Charles was dubious about our social schedule. He and the first Mrs. Charles Acheson had lent their presence only as necessary to please friends or aid in favorite causes; they had not engaged in anything remotely resembling the frenetic schedule of engagements I arranged for us.

"I have to get to know your friends," I told Charles when he timidly mentioned this might be too much. "I need to become part of the group."

"If that's what you want, I'm happy to do it," he replied, sounding weary. "But I'd be as happy to stay home or go out with *your* friends. I don't want you to feel cut off from your old life."

"That's no problem," I said in grand understatement, since I had no old life worth mentioning. "I want to be part of *your* life. That's what makes me happy."

Charles would smile when I said things like that, but once he added, "I'd like to be part of your life, as well."

***

"Why don't you write poetry anymore?"

We had been married two years when Charles asked the question.

"I'm too busy," I said, not wanting to discuss it.

"But it used to mean so much to you."

"What I'm doing now has more meaning: my charity work, my friends, collecting art with you, going to the theater and the opera. That poetry nonsense was a phase. Everyone writes poetry when they're young. It embarrasses me now."

"I thought I married a poet," Charles said wistfully.

"What's *that* supposed to mean?"

"Nothing. I just don't want my lifestyle to keep you from doing what's important to you."

"Don't ever worry about that." I graced him with a brilliant smile. "I love our life."

***

Nearly all the women in our social circle had children, and I quickly learned that the existence of these little ones bound one to other mothers. It mattered not whether the offspring were tiny or fully-grown, mothers had a common set of interests, conversational topics, and points of reference. Mitzi and I, the outliers, were ourselves bound together by our exclusion from this aspect of society, and proudly so.

That's why I received the news of Mitzi's pregnancy with mixed feelings.

"I'm so happy," she told me. "We've been trying for so long."

This was the first I had heard of these so-called attempts, and I was hurt by the revelation. But I simply responded, "That's wonderful!" and threw my arms around her. I pulled back from our embrace and looked her in the eye. "I'm *thrilled* for you."

The truth was quite the opposite. I knew many women became so involved with their children that they had little time for their friends, and I couldn't imagine life without Mitzi. No matter what I told Charles about 'my friends,' I had only one worth the title, and I was terrified of losing my only ally in this child-obsessed world. While it had been fine being one of two childless women, it would be less than

234

fine being the only one. *Is something* wrong *with her?* people would wonder. *Surely she wants children, doesn't she? Is there some… problem?*

Now I alone would be excluded from the privileged, coded conversations about the inner workings of infants, the best pediatricians, the top schools, good and bad nannies, F.A.O. Schwartz, spit-up, drool, and diapers. I would be the only one not shopping at the baby boutiques lining Madison Avenue. I would be needle pointing pillows while everyone else stitched primary-colored wall samplers.

***

The subject of children had arisen only once between Charles and me, shortly after we were married.

"If you want children, I'll be happy to consider fatherhood again," he had said one day as we were walking together in Central Park.

"Is that what you want?"

"This one's up to you." He stopped, turned to me, and touched my shoulders. "I'm almost fifty years old; I'm well past needing this. But I love children and would be happy to raise them with you if that's what you want."

"I don't. Not right now."

Ever since my miscarriage, I had harbored dark feelings about pregnancy. While I had tried to overcome my concerns by smiling at cuddly babies and thinking about all the frilly, soft things I could buy, I could not imagine pregnancy or motherhood as something with a happy ending. It had certainly not done much for me or for my mother.

Besides, I liked things as they were, and feared the intervention of any force that might provoke change. I was walking on eggshells, and harbored anxiety that the house of cards could come tumbling down and I would find myself back in Bayonne. I was also fearful of the image of a small, helpless being in Charles' arms, eating up the affection, time, and attention that were now all mine.

But that changed when Mitzi became pregnant.

***

It came as a surprise to Charles when I said casually at breakfast one morning, "I'd like to rethink the baby thing."

He looked at me over the top of the *Wall Street Journal*, which he lowered to the table. "Is this because of Mitzi?"

"I would *never* make a decision like that just because someone else is doing it." I bit into cracked wheat toast.

"Children are consuming. Your time won't be your own anymore.

"I know." I was annoyed that he gave me no credit for having thought through the implications of the idea. "I *am* capable of sacrifice."

"I know, darling. I meant you should consider the consequences." He measured his words. "If you're approaching it as a sacrifice, you might be unhappy going through with it."

"You've always said you'd do whatever I wanted on this."

"I will. I just want to be sure you know what you want."

I sipped my coffee and placed the cup back onto the saucer with deliberate calm. "Is there some reason you think I wouldn't be a good mother? Have I changed so much since the last time we discussed this?"

The tiny pause before his response said far more than his words. "You'd be a wonderful mother."

***

Mitzi's baby, Alexandra, was born in June, a perfect time for strolling the neighborhood and showing her off. As godmother, I sometimes strolled with them, but veered off when the screaming began.

Over time, I watched Mitzi scrape spit-up off her suede jackets and formula off her shoes. I heard her coo and sing tuneless ditties. I smelled nice things, like baby powder, on her cocktail dresses, along with disgusting things I didn't want to think about. I saw my friend's formidable command of language and subject matter diminish to dissertations on cribs, pacifiers, and poop.

I watched Mitzi's universe contract into a tiny place with room to accommodate only herself and her baby. It was not that Mitzi was never out and about; she handsomely upheld her end of the social contract. But no matter what she was doing, her mind was on

Alexandra. This disappointed me, but it also frightened me because I remembered how my mother's focus had always been on her beautiful daughter, and I knew what had happened when that daughter was no longer there for her.

No, it was not healthy. Babies were undependable. I couldn't do it.

And that was that. From then on, Charles and I drifted along with our lives, not pausing to examine the whys or wherefores. Or, at least, I did. And as long as the house of cards remained standing, that was fine.

***

Our life together fell into a rhythm to which it would beat until he died. We developed the patterns, modes of operation, methods of coping and means of going about the business of living that couples do to ensure life is predictable, if not necessarily stimulating.

Summers were spent in East Hampton and the rest of the year in Manhattan. I developed a steady routine of shopping, lunching, decorating, planning, and attending social events. Charles spent his days engaged in Foundation matters, admiring and buying art, auditing classes, and closing himself in his library with his books. We both traveled, sometimes together, sometimes not.

We did continue to go out together nearly every evening, though we spent less and less time in each other's company. I never viewed this as a problem, since it was common for spouses to socialize independently at parties. Besides, we had less to talk about than we had in the early years, a phenomenon I assumed to be perfectly natural. Once you get to know the other person, how much is left to say?

***

Charles' book obsession grew. Each year, he sank further into the abyss of literature. He didn't read his books, he consumed them. The floor-to-ceiling, wall-to-wall bookcases, which had been full enough from the day I moved in, became stuffed with volumes that spilled out onto the desk and tabletops.

During the early years of our marriage, Charles had talked to me about his books. He attempted to draw me into discussions of philosophy, literary deconstruction, and poetic interpretation. I found it easy to answer him as I had answered Larry about the Motherwell: "That's lovely, Charles," or, "That's most interesting."

While my reflexive responses rarely failed me, I grew weary of the charade and made my boredom known through a discreet yawn, a roll of my neck or shoulders, or walking away. Reasoning that I was more productively engaged in the real world and that Charles was better off understanding that, I ignored the sadness in his eyes when I declined to participate in his flights of intellectual fancy.

Eventually, he stopped trying to talk to me about anything other than mundane details of life. The deep chasm that separated my interests from his became part of the rhythm of our lives. I never considered this a good or bad thing. It was just the way it was.

Chapter Twelve
The Least She Could Do

November, 1989

Despite the distance that had grown between us, my marriage continued to define me, even three months after his death. I was *Mrs. Charles Acheson*, a person bearing no resemblance to Lauren Towson. Though I reminded myself in the weeks and months after the funeral that I was a *single woman*, that designation had no more reality for me than *widow*, an appellation that bordered on surreal.

The press still referred to me as "Mrs. Charles Acheson," and so did my mail. Charles' homes were still mine, his brother was still my only family, his lawyer was still my counsel, his household staff still worked for me, and the dozens of philanthropic organizations he had supported still kept in close touch.

The shape of my days was essentially unchanged since Charles' death. I still worked out with my trainer, ate lunch with my friends, shopped Madison Avenue, strolled through museums, chatted on the phone, and planned charitable functions. I even began an entire redecoration of the apartment.

The evenings, however, were different. Charles and I had always been in great demand, routinely turning down five or six invitations for each one we accepted. We had dined, danced, drunk, and schmoozed with everyone we cared to and many people we didn't, and I had thrived on it. Whether as hostess or guest, I was at my best arriving on Charles' arm at an evening affair.

Now the invitations were few and far between. No one needed a single woman; as a hostess, I knew that first-hand. But it hurt to realize that the invitations I had received in the past were not the result of my brilliant and determined efforts or my clever social skills, but had come my way only because I was married to Charles.

I gratefully accepted the handful of invitations that still arrived, but I was uncomfortable attending parties alone. I was forced to recognize that, when I had been a star, it had been as half of a duet, or, worse yet, as an accompanist. I was ill equipped to perform solo.

So, I stayed in at night. I watched television, needle pointed, drank wine, and slept, but none of these pursuits satisfied me. One night, in a weak moment, I tried to write poetry in a soft leather blank book Charles had brought me from Venice, but the results were so amateurish that I ripped out the pages and threw them into the fireplace, then tossed in the book, to guard against the temptation to try again.

***

On one of those solitary evenings, while I sipped Merlot and watched *Dallas* on TV, Gerald Bailey phoned.

"I wanted to check in, to see how you're doing."

"I'm fine. Why?"

"We haven't talked in a while." He spoke in an unusually upbeat tone, as if we were old friends. "I also wanted to let you know we've got things well under control at the Foundation. God knows we miss Charles, but we're carrying on. We're moving in the direction he'd want us to go." He paused as if observing a moment of reverent silence, or waiting for a response. "By the way, your name came up at today's meeting."

"My name?"

"Some of the Board members wondered when you would formalize your resignation. They're skittish about procedure—crossing the t's and dotting the i's. No one wants to pressure you. We know you've got other things on your plate. But we can't formalize the Board membership until you write a note resigning the position of Chairman. We know it's coming, so we're operating as if we've already received it. I can have a letter delivered to you in the morning. All you'll have to do it sign it, and we'll have this thing off our dockets once and for all."

First 'our plates were full,' now it's 'our dockets.' I hated his stupid metaphors. "That won't be necessary. I'll take care of it."

"Excellent. And Sherry and I would love to have you over for dinner when you have a free evening. How's your schedule?"

"I'm afraid I'm awfully busy"

"Maybe we can catch you next month."

"Maybe. Does that young man still work for you, the one who came here to talk about the will?"

"Smithson? No, he left the firm. Didn't fit in. Bright boy, just not a good match."

"Where is he now?"

"Out on his own. Why?"

***

I called Directory Assistance the next morning and got a business listing for Tom Smithson. He answered the phone himself.

"Mrs. Acheson, how nice to hear from you." The words were fine, but he sounded cautious. "What can I do for you?"

"I need to know the real reason you phoned me about my position with the Foundation."

"I wanted you to understand how much it meant to your husband."

"Why did you want to keep our talk a secret from Gerald?"

Smithson answered slowly, as if weighing his words. "He didn't want me to meddle."

"So why did you?"

"Because I didn't think you'd made a decision. You hadn't had a chance to think about it. Gerald made the decision."

"Meaning?"

"He didn't want you to take the job."

"Why would he care?"

Smithson breathed audibly in, then out. "He cares about the Foundation. He's invested time in it over the years. He..."

"Would you please say whatever you're trying to say."

"Maybe he thought you'd be in over your head."

"Maybe I would be."

"That's not what your husband thought." Smithson cleared his throat. "Also, Gerald thought of himself as heir apparent to the chairmanship." Smithson spoke more confidently.

"Why? He has no stake in the Foundation."

"The Chairman has considerable power. He—or she—distributes millions of dollars a year; that buys a lot of influence and visibility in this city."

I wondered if Smithson was angry over being asked to leave the firm. Maybe this was sour grapes.

"I suppose you've resigned by now," he said.

"No."

"Think about it before you do. Charles—"

"I know."

"He said you'd be perfect."

***

I took a sip of wine and looked at Mitzi. "You think I should do it?"

I had invited myself over to her place to discuss the matter.

"I told you a long time ago to give it a shot."

"It seems so consuming."

"What *else* do you have to consume you?"

I didn't have an answer. My eyes scanned the Cy Twombly painting that hung on her living room wall—a mass of crayon scrawls, pencil marks, and thick smudges of flesh-toned oil paint that echoed my muddled mental state.

"You can always give it up if you don't like it. What have you got to lose?"

"I've never done anything like this before." I poured myself another glass of Petit Syrah from the bottle on the coffee table.

"You've organized and run plenty of things." Mitzi paused to pour herself a refill, then looked me in the eye. "You need to move on." She leaned forward. "Charles is gone, and so is the life you had with him. Now you can do something that's all your own."

"Jesus Christ," I whispered. I set the delicate, long-stemmed glass on the table and leaned back into the soft upholstery. "What if I don't *want* to leave Charles behind?"

"Then this could make you feel closer to him. Maybe you'll discover more about his passions, about what made him get up in the morning."

"What would you do if Paul died?" I knew the question was cruel, but didn't retract it.

"God only knows. I'd be a basket case."

"I'm sorry I asked."

"No." She waved her hand, "I deserved it. I'm not saying I'd handle it any better than you are, probably far worse, but I know what you're capable of, and I can't stand to see you waste yourself."

"That's apparently what Charles said, or implied." I turned my attention to a small Rembrandt etching of a peaceful rural landscape. "He told his lawyers that since we'd been married I hadn't had an opportunity to channel my talents in a 'productive way'."

"I rest my case." Mitzi smiled and took a sip of wine.

Judy Pomeranz

Chapter Thirteen
Cacophony

December, 1989

On the morning of my first Board meeting, I checked myself in the mirror. The navy blue gabardine suit, ivory silk blouse, gold button earrings, businesslike Baume and Mercier watch, light hose, and low-heeled navy Farragamo's were all in order. My hair fell sleekly and simply, and my make-up was heavy enough to disguise my fatigue but subtle enough to suggest sobriety and discretion. There was nothing more I could do.

I shoved my papers into the shiny new Mark Cross briefcase I had bought for credibility, and snapped the clasps shut. Charles had never asked anything of me before; giving it a shot seemed the least I could do.

***

I had spent three weeks studying the pile of grant applications that were up for consideration, analyzing each in terms of the mission statement Charles had written when he established the Foundation. Since it was his money we were spending, it seemed right to spend it as he would have. That was the only touchstone I could come up with.

The funds requested by the twenty-five grant applicants added up to five times the amount the Board was authorized to disburse. We would have to be selective. Six proposals were from writers, three from musicians, twelve from visual artists, one from a pop-psychologist with a weight-loss plan, one from a man who wanted to start up a circus troupe, one from a political philosopher who held the answer to world peace, and one from a rabbi who wanted to conduct a study of the effects of art on religion.

Four were easy to dismiss, since they fell outside the Foundation's mandate of assisting "promising or established New York artists," but the other twenty-one were on the table, since each was from an artist within a broad definition of "promising or established," mostly the former, and each made a reasonable case that the funds would be put to good use.

Making decisions was surprisingly tough.

I, who had never paid the least attention to this process, finally understood what Charles had been doing all these years, and why. I had intended to undertake the minimum work necessary in this job, and rely on the process running without my help. But while going through the applications, I became caught up to a degree I would never have predicted.

While the form was the same as the one I had picked up all those years ago for Larry, the arts were vastly different now. Only three of the visual artists in the pack were painters and three were traditional sculptors. The remaining six worked with new and peculiar mediums, odd techniques and even odder concepts.

The literary applicants were more traditional, including a much-published novelist who needed a stipend while finishing a book, two poets who needed to pay the rent, and two authors of short stories. The only offbeat character was a self-described experimentalist who created poetry by cutting words and phrases from books, tossing them in the air, and pasting them onto a page in the order in which they fell. The resulting creations had a surprisingly snappy humor and entertaining liveliness.

The musicians were all composers, two who worked in jazz and a third who identified himself as a "classicist in the nature of John Cage."

I read each proposal several times; I viewed the slides, listened to the tapes and read the poetry and prose. I found myself unwittingly spending eight or ten hours a day on the project. I canceled lunch dates, neglected shopping, and some days did not set foot outside the apartment. I asked myself why in the name of God I was doing this and what was in it for me. I never came up with a good answer, but was unable to take the task less seriously.

I struggled with my decisions, considering and reconsidering my positions until three o'clock on the morning of the Board meeting. After I crawled into bed, the images, words, and music of these artists ran relentlessly through my mind.

***

Although I was fifteen minutes early for the meeting, I was the last Board member to arrive. I found the others carrying on a spirited discussion, which halted abruptly when I entered the room.

"Lauren," Gerald greeted me warmly, "it's a pleasure to have you with us." He gave me a peck on the cheek. "You know everyone."

I looked around the long rosewood table and nodded. Through Charles, I knew each of these men by name, face, profession, and reputation, but none beyond that.

"Please—" Gerald moved his briefcase and papers away from his seat at the head of the table "—sit here. This is where Charles sat. It's reserved for the Chairman."

I wondered why Gerald had been sitting there, but I kept my counsel. I felt a peculiar brand of insecurity here that made any show of warmth—even Gerald's artificial hale-fellow-well-met variety— appealing. So I nodded and waited for him to move out of my way.

"I hope I'm not late." I looked pointedly at my watch. "Have I missed anything?"

"Not at all. You're right on time. We were just chatting."

I took my seat at the head of the now-silent table, hoping I looked like one of those terribly confident, powerful "new women," but feeling like a frightened child. I placed my briefcase on the table, popped its clasps open, and pulled out the sheaf of applications, along with my notes. I closed the briefcase and placed it beside my right foot on the hardwood floor. Though each noise I made echoed throughout the silent room, I took comfort in these small moves, which I hoped would make me appear practiced, seasoned. But when my chair screeched loudly across the parquet floor as I pulled myself closer to the table, I blushed and grinned stupidly at the six people whose eyes were trained on me. I folded my hands and waited for something to happen, until I realized the others were waiting for *me* to make something happen. I was the Chairman, and I was not off to a good start.

"We should discuss these proposals," I said in a shaky voice.

"Good idea. Would you feel more comfortable if Bill or I directed the discussion, since you're new at this?"

I was not sure how to respond. I most certainly would have felt more comfortable, but had a nagging sense it was not a good idea.

"I've been through six or seven hundred of these in my years with Charles," Gerald said. "I'd be happy to kick things off, to show you how we operate."

I turned from Gerald to the others around the table, who were all still staring at me. "That would be fine. Thank you."

And that was that. Once he started, he didn't stop.

He ran through the first several proposals at a rapid clip, disposing of each by presenting a brief summary of the application and his recommendation for action, and then, in a *pro forma* manner, opened the floor for discussion and closed it almost immediately. No one else had anything to say.

While Gerald's recommendations coincided with my own views on the first few applicants, such was not case for long. We disagreed on the case of the automatist poet, whose application Gerald recommended denying.

"Would you explain your reasoning?" I asked.

He looked surprised that I had spoken, but hesitated only an instant before responding. "Charles never felt experimental poetry was valid, and we respected his opinion."

I couldn't bring myself to point out that Charles had once loved reading experimental poetry, because the last time I had discussed the subject with him was over twenty years ago. "I see."

My view differed from Gerald's on the novelist's application, as well. He recommended approval, while I contended that writers in greater financial need should be given preference.

"Charles did not believe desperate poverty should be a requisite for receiving one of our grants." Gerald adopted the demeanor of a teacher patiently tutoring a slow student. "He felt good artists deserved to earn more than a bare subsistence, and that successful artists should be freed of having to worry about whether their success would persist. He always said that if he truly believed in an artist, he would support him or her as fully as he could. He did not favor simply doling out funds to those in greatest need."

While that was all probably true, I was not sure it was relevant here, since there were other *equally worthy* applicants who needed the money more. But with everyone at the table looking at me, and no one else pressing the point, I simply responded, once again, "I see."

In the end, the Board accepted, by tacit consensus, Gerald's recommendation in each of the twenty-five cases. As the new member, I deferred to the unanimity of the group, especially since Gerald had consistently defended his recommendations with the reasoning that "this is what Charles would have wanted." But none of it felt right.

After the last application was disposed of, Gerald leaned back in his luxuriously padded leather chair and beamed. "Well done," he said to the group at large. "We handled that with admirable dispatch and spent all the allotted funds. Is everyone satisfied?"

Each person at the table nodded, but no one said a word.

Judy Pomeranz

Chapter Fourteen
Trust

December, 1989

When I got back to the apartment after the meeting, I stripped off my in-charge suit and silk blouse, ripped off my pantyhose, and dropped the whole works on the closet floor. I told myself that the meeting hadn't gone badly; I hadn't fainted, cried, screamed, or made a complete ass of myself—that was a moral victory—and three of the eight artists I would have funded were given grants, which wasn't terrible. But I wasn't buying my own pep talk; it had been a disaster.

Fighting the urge to climb into bed, pull the duvet over my head, and not re-emerge until cocktail time, I pulled on black wool leggings and slipped a green chenille turtleneck over my head. It was hardly a fashion statement, but more appropriate than the nightie I wanted to get into.

I felt like I did when floundering to create a place for myself in the world, after Jessica and before Charles. I recognized the hazy aura that glowed like a halo around everything in sight, the knowledge that nothing was certain or reliable, and that I lacked standing to operate in my own universe. I wanted to dump this whole Foundation enterprise and return to being who I was.

Whoever that was.

Yes, I would get on with my life, my real life, not this idiocy. I would stop thinking about the Foundation and get on with it.

Whatever *it* was.

I went to the solarium and flipped on the TV, hoping a soap opera would put my plight into perspective or make me forget it, but I couldn't stop thinking about that damn meeting. What bothered me most was not that Gerald had rejected my views and railroaded his own positions through, but that I had let him do it. I was Chairman of the Board, and I had allowed him to run the meeting as if I had not been in the room.

I turned off the TV and went to the library, a room in which I had spent so much time over the past few weeks that I thought of it as *my* library rather than Charles'. I buzzed Daniel on the intercom and asked for a pot of tea, though I really wanted a vodka tonic, then I dumped the contents of my briefcase onto the desktop and shuffled through the pile of grant applications and hand-written notes. Why did I bother with this? It's not as if there was anything in it for me.

Or was there? Much as I hated to admit it, these past three weeks had been oddly satisfying, even gratifying. I had enjoyed pondering the philosophy and quality of different types of literature and learning about the new forms of visual art being created these days. It had been fun to pick up tidbits about music, a field about which I knew virtually nothing, despite the scores of season ticket cycles I had blindly run through. I had enjoyed puzzling through the quandary of who would benefit most from the money.

Okay, it *had* been entertaining, but the cost was far too high. Why should I torture myself? Why spend the time, only to be railroaded by Gerald? The heaviness in my stomach was not depression or insecurity, but humiliation. Gerald had marginalized me. So had his colleagues. If they didn't want me there, then fine. I'd quit. I stacked the applications and dropped them into the leather wastebasket.

I squeezed a slice of lemon into my tea and stared at the empty bookcases lining the room. The humiliation combined with anger as I realized I was as much to blame as Gerald. I had let it happen. I slapped the desktop. It hurt, but in a good way. I did it again, harder. I took a sip of scalding tea, and stared at the stack of papers in the wastebasket.

***

Later that afternoon, I called Joanne, Charles' secretary at the Foundation, and asked her when the applications for the next quarter's grants would be available. It was idle curiosity, I told myself. I intended to be gone long before the next quarterly meeting.

"We have some here already. I can send them right over, and get you the others as they come in, if you want."

"Fine. Why didn't that happen last time? I got the whole pile a few weeks ago."

"Gerald told me not to bother you. He thought it was inappropriate, right after Mr. Acheson's passing. Besides, he assumed you would resign the position."

"I see."

"But when I heard you were planning to chair the meeting, I went sent them over."

"You mean Gerald didn't ask you to?"

"He said you would be a figurehead."

"So why did you send them?"

There was a long pause. "You should be the one to make that decision."

"Thank you. "And from now on, send me the applications as soon as they come in. I want as much time as possible to review them." Sensing I had found an ally, I addressed the bigger question.

"The Board has a mind of its own. A surprisingly unified mind. And they have an eloquent spokesman in Gerald." I waited for a reaction, but Joanne said nothing. "Is this how it was when Charles was chairman? Did Gerald run the show?"

"Not at all. He deferred to Mr. Acheson on everything. The whole Board expressed their own views, but if there were differences or a tie to be broken, what Mr. Acheson wanted governed."

"Why?"

"It was his money. He was the founder, he knew best what the Foundation was all about, and they respected that. Besides—" She stopped.

"Besides what?"

"The Board members knew Mr. Acheson could get rid of them if they didn't respect his views."

"Would Charles have *done* that?" This was a completely new concept; the Charles I had known was so agreeable, so benign.

"He did on a couple of occasions."

"He *fired* people, to get his way?"

"It wasn't like that. He created an outside Board because he honestly wanted other opinions, especially on proposals that were beyond his areas of expertise. But there have been members who didn't share or respect his approach. They had their own agendas." She let the words sink in. "Each removal made sense."

"Must have been nice being the founder," I murmured to myself.

"Mr. Acheson agonized before asking each of those men to resign."

"At least he could do it."

"Fixing the Board's composition is the prerogative of the Chairman," Joanne said slowly and deliberately.

"Yes, but—" Then I got it.

Neither of us spoke for several seconds.

Joanne broke the silence. "Did you know they met before you got in this morning?"

"I noticed they were all there before me. I didn't know why."

"Gerald asked them to come in at 7:00." Joanne's voice was uninflected; she delivered information but carefully avoided editorializing.

"Why them and not me?"

"He wanted to get everything worked out ahead of time— especially on any controversial cases—so you wouldn't have to sit through the whole process."

"So thoughtful of him."

"I'm sorry."

"Forget it."

I hung up and rubbed my green chenille sleeves so hard my hands got hot. Gerald had excluded me. Whether his motives were evil or benevolent, he had plotted against me. This was worse than a stupid soap opera. I poured another cup of tea and took a long drink. I allowed myself to imagine how warm and dark it would be upstairs under the duvet, how silent, how peaceful.

I shook my head and focused, knowing that if I allowed myself to fold now, I would never again emerge. I thought about Gerald and his oily ways. I thought about what Joanne had said about how the Chairman possessed the authority to determine membership of the Board. Then I pulled the applications out of the wastebasket.

Why had Charles wanted me to do this?

I placed my hand on the telephone receiver but couldn't bring myself to pick it up; this was like diving into a pool so deep the bottom was indiscernible. I inhaled deeply, as if preparing for the jump, then asked myself how Charles would have handled a situation like this.

He had often spoken of "the profound importance of trust" in working relationships. Trust and loyalty. He once told a television interviewer: "one should surround oneself, to the extent possible, with individuals whose ideals and spirit coincide with one's own." That sounded important, and relevant. Especially the part about that elusive thing called "trust."

***

"You heard me, Mitzi." I spoke sternly into the phone but tapped my fingers nervously on the desktop.

"But... a *Board* member? I've never done anything like that. I don't even know what a Board member does."

"Neither did I, but recall *you* told me that serving on the Board wouldn't involve any skills beyond those we use everyday." I paused for effect. "That *was* you, wasn't it?"

"Very funny. Anyway, I was talking about *you*, not me."

"So, are you with me?"

"Why would you *want* me to be?"

"Because you know more about art than anyone I know. You're a collector, a scholar."

"Oh, please, art history was my college major. That hardly makes me a scholar."

"It's more than that. You know artists, you know the market. You watched your father collect, you catalogued his collection before it went to the Met. And you care about it all."

"That makes me an art *lover*, not a scholar, and certainly not a Board member."

"I trust you," I said, trying out the concept. I made an effort to sound calm, but I scrawled angular, black scribbles across the blank page in front of me. I watched the jagged lines form, as if of their own accord, melding together to form a wicked-looking web.

"To do what? What's that got to do with—"

"Everything." I set the pen down on the blotter.

"Are you sure?"

"Now you're fishing for compliments. I wouldn't have asked if I wasn't."

"I don't know…"

"Listen, I need people on the board I can trust, who know the arts, who understand what Charles would have wanted. You fill the bill." I brushed a bead of perspiration off my forehead.

"I don't know what to say."

"Say you'll do it."

***

"But Ms. Acheson, I'm a secretary," Joanne said after I made my proposal. "I've never done anything like this before."

The argument sounded familiar. "That's not true." I looked at my reflection in the mahogany desktop as I spoke into the receiver, and tried out a look of authority. "You've done *exactly* this for the past twenty years. You know more about the operation of the Acheson Foundation than anyone. Most importantly, Charles trusted you implicitly—he told me that—and I know you were always loyal to him and his interests."

"You're kind to ask, but—"

"I'm not asking out of kindness. I don't do that. Ever. I'm asking because I need you. You know the process, and you understand exactly what Charles wanted the Foundation to do." I tucked the receiver between my neck and shoulder and strung together a chain of paperclips.

"I'm flattered, but I don't know anything about art, and I'll never be as passionate as Charles was. I'm not made that way."

"I'm not looking for erudition, and no one will ever match Charles for passion. I'm looking for judgment. And I'm looking for someone I can trust."

"Why would you trust *me*? You hardly know me."

"Charles trusted you." I put down the paperclips and drew circles across the paper, on top of the jagged lines. "But mostly I trust you because you're the one—the only one—who told me what Gerald was up to. And you let me know what I could do about it."

"That was nothing."

"It was something to me." I examined my face again in the desktop, searching for changes, for I felt like a different person.

"Let me give it some thought."
"What is there to think about?"

***

Those two went reasonably well, but the next would be the riskiest of all. I held the receiver tightly and spoke with as much courage as I could muster. "Mr. Smithson, this is Lauren Acheson."

"How nice to hear from you. Please, call me Tom. What can I do for you?"

I cleared my throat. I was taking a huge flyer here, operating straight from the gut, as my father would have said. I barely knew this man. "How would you like to serve on the Board of the Acheson Foundation?"

"I beg your pardon?"

"You heard me."

"I don't understand why you're asking me."

"I can trust you, and I have a feeling Charles trusted you." I enjoyed the sound and the feel of that word, *trust*. I had used it more in this one day than I had in all my previous days combined. "I also know you tried very hard, to your own professional detriment, to protect Charles' interests. I admire that." I rarely dispensed such broad-based praise, but it seemed warranted.

"Thank you, Mrs. Acheson, I appreciate the sentiment—"

"Please, call me Lauren."

"Touché. But I hadn't heard there was an opening. Is there?"

"There will be soon."

***

After giving the matter a great deal of thought over several more days, I was unable to come up with even one more person I wanted to invite to serve on the Board. Having only three people I could trust, two of whom I barely knew, might say something about me—or about the way I had lived my life. But I couldn't worry about that. With my three new colleagues chosen and now firmly committed, I went to the Foundation office to get Joanne's advice on which of the current members, besides Gerald, I should get rid of to make room for them.

"It's not my place—" Joanne shifted in her chair.

"It *is* your place as a prospective Board member, particularly if I say it is." I regretted the last words as soon as I said them, and apologized, admitting, "this whole thing makes me nervous."

"Don't worry about it."

"Can you tell me which members Charles respected the most?"

"He respected them all."

"Tact is one of your best qualities," I smiled wryly, "but let's rank them. Who did he rely on the most?"

Joanne hesitated, then named Jacob Epstein and Rovier Alexander as men whose expertise and judgment Charles had relied upon especially heavily. The first was an artist himself, the second a successful businessman and professor of literature who collected rare books. I knew both only superficially and had no independent opinion, but I was in the mood for action.

"That's good. I need one more."

Joanne said nothing; she was clearly uncomfortable with ranking people; it was a quality I admired.

"Jonathon Pauley," she said slowly, referring to the Met's curator for Italian Renaissance painting. "Mr. Acheson always wanted to know what Mr. Pauley thought before he made up his own mind."

"Okay, and which were more...extraneous?"

***

Under Joanne's tutelage, I prepared letters to three members of the Board, including Gerald, requesting their resignations. Joanne had convinced me that asking for resignations was kinder and more professional than unceremoniously unseating the members, which I, in the case of Gerald, would have found far more satisfying.

A week after the letters went out, I learned from Joanne that Gerald had asked her if I had "gone off the deep end." When she tried to explain that I was taking a fresh approach and needed new blood, adding that she herself would be serving on the Board, Gerald responded with a harsh laugh, saying that he was glad to be spared the chore of "training a bunch of rookies."

I too enjoyed a good laugh, after Joanne related the conversation to me, when I sent another letter, terminating Gerald's retainer as counsel to the Foundation.

***

Once the resignations were signed and formalized and the new appointments were in place, I felt ready to deal with one more item of business I had to put behind me before I could move on with my life—the disposition of Charles' books.

Three months had passed since I had read the correspondence from Sydney Ray Jenkins, and two and a half since I had the books packed for shipping. But the boxes remained in place. Each time Gerald's secretary had phoned to see if they could be picked up for "shipment to the legatee," I had demurred.

My hesitation had nothing to do with a desire to read the books and little to do with a desire to keep them out of the hands of Sydney Ray Jenkins, whoever she was. Instead, my inability to act stemmed from an irrational but powerful feeling that these books were the final remnant of Charles. To send them away was to banish him from the apartment, to scatter his ashes.

Dozens of brown cartons were stacked in orderly rows on the library floor. Neatly wrapped, taped, and tied, the books were inaccessible. I could not see them, nor could I touch them or smell their bindings. So, what was the point? Though I had asked myself that question countless times and knew there was no point, it was not until now—now that I had something else of Charles to hold onto, less tangible but more solid—that I was able to let the books go.

I pulled open the bottom desk drawer and removed the four files marked "Personal Correspondence." I placed them in an empty brown box, which I sealed with tape. I marked the box with Sydney Ray Jenkins' name and placed it with the crates of books.

I imagined the room without boxes. Perhaps it was time to make it *my* room. I could fill the shelves, as I had always wanted to, with Lalique figurines or Limoges boxes, English enamels, Meissen, or Sevres, or the tiny Faberge picture frames I had collected over the years from *A La Vieille Russie*. Maybe I would put my favorite photos of Charles in the frames, so that he could continue to inhabit his favorite room.

I picked up the phone to call Gerald's secretary.

Judy Pomeranz

Chapter Fifteen
Her Own Place in the World

August, 1991

"Your work is spectacular," I told the young artist.

The man barely nodded as he reflexively wiped his brush on his dirty jeans before using it to apply a scumbly dash of yellow to the plaster object in front of him. He was painting a cast of his own head with graffiti. As he worked, the jagged, slashing lines morphed into an electrical storm against a night sky, which might represent the chaos or energy in the artist's mind.

The cavernous Bowery studio was filled with cast-plaster body parts painted with dramatically distorted or disturbingly naturalistic imagery. There were still-lifes on arms, eerie landscapes on torsos, and tiny, ghastly portraits on fingertips. Some of the casts were melded together into larger pieces, others stood on their own; each work seemed to carry a message, though not a clearly defined one. The artist was like Motherwell that way. This timid, awkward man might be a genius.

But he was utterly inarticulate; he had completed only the ninth grade and was achingly shy. He hardly spoke a word to me.

And that was exactly why I was here. I had come to look at his work in connection with a grant application he had filed. His slides were impressive, but the application itself had bordered on incomprehensible, making this a textbook case for a studio visit.

Over the past year, I had made these visits part of my standard operating procedure. I saw them as a way of overcoming the inherent unfairness of judging visual artists—whose favored medium of expression was not, after all, words—on the basis of the prose in their applications. And the process was working well. In some instances, my visit would confirm an artist's worth; in others, it would reveal inadequacy.

So, although Jimmy was reluctant to drop me off in neighborhoods like this, Mitzi said I was crazy to visit questionable places to meet with people I didn't know, and Joanne said my approach was unprecedented and "awfully time-consuming," I persisted. The system worked, and I enjoyed it.

***

I expanded the concept so that I now attended readings, galleries, and musical performances involving our applicants. I encouraged other Board members to do the same, but most demurred, leaving me in my new favorite position: the driver's seat. The Board deferred increasingly to my recommendations, because no one could compete with my research and growing expertise.

"You're becoming too wrapped up in this," Mitzi warned me. "It's an obsession. You don't see anyone, you haven't been to the Hamptons in months, and you don't do anything but work. I'm worried about you."

While I couldn't explain it to Mitzi, or understand it myself, I had something I never had before: my own place in the world. I neither feared exposure as a fraud nor felt pressure to perform for an audience. It was a space I filled perfectly.

It was far from selfless charity. I had begun this enterprise to get in touch with and get over Charles. I had stayed with it to get back at Gerald. And I had ratcheted up the level of engagement to avoid thinking about the existence of a person called Sydney Ray Jenkins.

It was a project born of avoidance, reared on retribution, and fed with denial, but I found myself performing a service no one else could perform, and I was learning to trust my taste and my judgment. For the first time in my life, I understood what had kept my late husband going—for a while, anyway.

Chapter Sixteen
A New Tradition and a New Life

August, 1991

On the third Saturday in August, the day Charles and I had once religiously set aside for the dreaded Great Gatsby Picnic, my Manhattan living room was filled with people entirely unlike any that had ever been assembled there before. They were young and dressed in black. Some sported body-piercings in the most amazing places, others were tattooed. Hair ran from short and spiky to long and frizzy. Combat boots and flip-flops were the footwear of choice.

The party was in honor of all the artists who had received grants from the Foundation during the nearly two years I had been running the show. Every recipient was invited, as were all members of the Board, so they could get to know and appreciate the others. I planned to do this annually, from now on.

At the same time, I was letting go of old traditions: the Gatsby party, Monday lunches at Lutèce, Tuesday tennis, daily personal training sessions, and the Cancer Ball which went on this year and brought in as much money as it always had, confirming my once deeply-suppressed fear that I might not be indispensable to the Upper East Side charity circuit.

***

After cocktails and dinner, my guests retired to the library for coffee and *digestifs*, then dispersed to several rooms for "show and tell."

The writers would read from their work, the visual artists would display and talk about their creations, and the musicians would demonstrate their performance or compositional talents. Then each one would respond to questions.

This was not a party without an agenda; I had never given one of those and was not about to begin now. My first goal was to compel the artists to get to know one another and share their work, as I had become a great believer in cross-fertilization among creative people. My second aim was to encourage the grant recipients to become more articulate about their work and less fearful of talking with people who could help them. Self-promotion was, unfortunately, everything in the art world. I wanted to push my artists off the margins and into the mainstream.

I cared about these people. I had acquired a small stake in their lives, an entirely new and curious phenomenon for me. I wanted to see them succeed.

As I listened to one of my favorite young poets read in the library, I realized that this room was no longer Charles'; it was now fully mine. But where I had once visualized Sevres, Baccarat, and Faberge on the shelves, there were once again books, along with small sculptures made by grantees. And the few walls not covered by bookcases were crammed with post-modern canvases created by my painters.

The living and dining rooms were still hung with works by Whistler, Renoir, Johns, Pollock, Rubens, de Kooning, Monet, Hartigan, and Rauschenberg. Out of respect for Charles' memory, those paintings and drawings retained places of honor, for he had purchased them out of love, just as I had purchased these. But my walls no longer displayed the works I once insisted Charles buy because they were chic, trendy, or recognizably valuable—a second Motherwell, the Twombly, the minor Picasso etchings, and the O'Keefe still life. I had sold those and donated the proceeds to the Acheson Foundation.

***

"That was a terrific party," Mitzi said the next day over brunch at the Plaza. "The food was perfect, the flowers were gorgeous. You have *not* lost your touch."

I smiled. "Do you think everyone had a good time?"

"Absolutely, after they warmed up." She smiled wickedly. "Our fellow Board members—and their spouses—found themselves in different company than they're used to, but it was good for them. They certainly amused one another.

"It felt good to give a party again." I warmed my hands over my coffee cup.

"So, why don't you do it more often?" I could see she was excited at the prospect of bringing me back into the world. "Why not revive the Gatsby tradition? You could do it in the fall, it wouldn't matter." She leaned toward me as she spoke. "Everyone in East Hampton misses that get-together. How about it? I'll help you."

"I don't have time." I concentrated on the Pollock-inspired swirls I was making with my sunny-side-up egg yolk.

"Oh, come on. I'll call the florist, the caterer, and the calligrapher. Whatever you want. You won't have to do a thing. Just show up and be the perfect hostess."

"I mean I don't have time for East Hampton. I'm thinking about selling the house."

Mitzi's fork dropped onto her plate with a clang. "You're *what?*"

"I've talked to an agent. I don't use it anymore."

"Don't rush into this. Don't do something you'll regret."

"I'm hardly rushing. The house has been virtually empty for two years."

"But you've always—"

"My life isn't what it always was. Everything's different now."

Mitzi wiped the corners of her mouth with her napkin, then placed it back on her lap. She looked me straight in the eye. "You're taking all of this too seriously."

"It's just a house. I can buy another one if I change my mind."

"It's not just the house—its everything. You're so into this Foundation, you don't have a life. It's not healthy."

"For God's sake, I'm fine. Better than fine. I love what I'm doing."

"You're escaping."

"Have you been reading Freud again? What am I escaping *from?*"

"Charles' death… that whole Sydney Ray Jenkins thing… being on your own. Pick one. You won't slow down so you don't have to deal with it."

"I am fine" I said, enunciating each word. "And don't forget who talked me into taking this job in the first place." I gave her a broad, smug grin, then took a sip of coffee to end the conversation.

"Okay, so blame me, but don't sell the house yet. Give it another summer. It's been in Charles' family for so long… they *built* it, for God's sake."

"There's no one left in the family except Findlay, and he doesn't want it."

Chapter Seventeen
A Small Island

September, 1991

I got the call moments before I heard it on the evening news: Rovier Alexander III, "scholar, industrialist, and longtime member of the Acheson Foundation Board of Trustees," as the anchor described him, was dead of a heart attack at the age of seventy-one.

I stared out the solarium windows at the clouds scudding across the gray evening sky, and wondered why it always took a loss to make me see that what I had had was so real and so precious. I pictured Rovier's face: somber and thoughtful, wrinkly, papery and pale. He wore horn-rimmed glasses he forever pushed up the bridge of his nose. Sometimes aloof, he was kind and gentle, with a crusty sweetness.

An old-school gentleman who had fallen in love with modern literature at Yale in the early 1940's, Rovier had carried on a love affair with books that had never waned. Though he ran his family's textile business throughout his adult life, he devoted hours each day to the simple pleasures of reading and discussing what he read. He and Charles had met at a course taught by Mortimer Adler at the University of Chicago. They knew they were soul mates when each discovered the other had come from New York to spend a semester living in Chicago's Hyde Park to sit at the feet of the revered master of the Great Books.

This man whom I had once perceived as a dry, professorial type, had become a trusted ally. A mentor, he had taken the time and trouble to educate me. Rovier had been the Board's literary expert, and I had put great stock in his views and his wisdom.

***

I arrived at the office the next morning to find a tall stack of faxes and endless voice-mail messages awaiting my attention. Nearly all were from people interested in filling Rovier's position on the Board. There were academics, historians, curators, business owners, renowned writers, museum directors, even a university president. The scavengers were already circling the body.

"I don't understand why all these people want to be on the Board," I said to Joanne. "The pay is nil, the work is grueling, and there are no perks."

"Prestige. Snob appeal. It's one of the best-endowed philanthropies in the city, and it has the caché of Charles' name. People want to be associated with that name—and with yours."

"Hardly."

"I mean it. You've developed a reputation; you're too busy to notice. Many of our recent recipients have made big names for themselves. Everyone wants to be a king-maker; it's like playing God."

"That's a stretch."

"Things look more glamorous from the outside."

I smiled at how much Joanne had grown in sophistication— and cynicism.

"So, how do we replace Rovier?"

"The Board's composition is entirely up to you. You can recruit someone you know, or you can interview outsiders. You'll have plenty of folks to choose from. This is just the beginning." She gestured to the piles on my desk. "It happens every time we lose someone."

I thought about my last Board choices: Joanne, Mitzi, and Tom. They had turned out to be perfect selections, but only by the grace of God. I had chosen them with no real knowledge of what the job would entail, no vetting, no interviewing, and practically no rational thought. *Seat of the pants* was the expression my father would have used, or *gut instinct*. But it had worked.

***

To avoid dealing with the mountain of resumes, I turned to the grant applications that had arrived in the morning mail. I glanced at the cover page of each one, enjoying the way the familiar documents felt in my hands. Unlike the pitches from people who wanted to join the Board, I knew exactly how to approach these. Holding them made me feel competent.

There were five applicants: a poet, a fiction writer, and three visual artists. Ever since one of our painters had been awarded a MacArthur Foundation Fellowship, applications from visual artists had been pouring in.

I sat back and stared out the window, recalling the day the young painter had won that prestigious award. She had phoned me as soon as she heard the news, and told me she would never have gotten to this point without the Acheson Foundation's support. That was why I no longer went to the Hamptons or lunched with the girls; that was why my home was half-decorated chaos and my clothes were out of date. And that was why it was all okay.

***

I read the poet's application first. He was fifty-five and a lawyer by day. His poetry employed traditional metric and rhyme schemes, and sounded, on a quick read, sappy and trite. But he had been published in important literary journals, which made me think I was missing something. It was exactly the kind of case in which I would have sought Rovier's judgment.

I dropped the application into my in-box and moved on to the next, which was from the fiction writer. This man worked in an original, experimental style. Claiming to be an acolyte of Jorge Luis Borges, he wanted to take the style of the Latin American genius "giant leaps further" and "run amok," which struck me as pretentious but interesting. I again longed for the wisdom Rovier would have brought to the table.

I remembered how Annette had studied and admired Borges. Her Masters thesis had critiqued one of his grand themes, though I had no idea which. She had been so enthused she had planned to do her Ph.D. dissertation on Borges. I didn't know whether she had ever completed that degree, but an idea began to take shape in my mind, one that was derailed when I noticed the name on the next application in the pile:

Larry Barnes.

I stared for several minutes. It couldn't be the same Larry Barnes. No, it was a common name. But I read on to learn that he was the same age as my Larry Barnes. *My* Larry Barnes; what an odd way of thinking about him. And this painter had exhibited in Paris at the time Charles had seen Larry's work there. A lifetime ago. I leaned back in my chair and read through the application slowly and carefully.

***

Larry Barnes had lived and worked on West Eighth Street in lower Manhattan since his arrival back in New York from Paris five years ago. I blinked, took a deep breath, and read on.

Judging by his exhibition history, he had achieved success in Paris, a streak he sustained for nearly a decade, until the exhibitions gradually dried up. He went from two or three major shows a year to one every year or two, then ultimately to none. The application offered no explanation for this pattern, but it was not unusual in the notoriously fickle art market.

It was possible that Larry's star had fallen for reasons beyond his control. Perhaps his style no longer appealed to the market. Perhaps economic factors had contributed to a decline in his popularity. Perhaps he had been overtaken by newer, younger talent. Or maybe he had brought the decline on himself by changing his style, toying with a successful formula, or overplaying a well-tested one. It might even have been voluntary. I knew artists who had done stranger things than refuse shows.

My hands trembled as I read on.

The reason for his return to New York was also left unstated. Had he been driven home by economic need? Did he hope to find new markets here? Was he seeking fresh inspiration in a new environment, or coming back to work with someone here? Maybe his return was prompted by personal factors. Maybe homesickness. Maybe seeking his roots.

Maybe an American wife.

I looked into the windows of the office building across the street. I saw, as I did every day, hundreds of people hunched over computers, talking across desks, pacing office floors. I had watched these people for years but had no idea who they were, nor did I care. Despite the swarms of humanity that inhabited this city, or because of them, it was easier to be anonymous in New York than anyplace else on earth. There was no privacy and there was complete privacy, all at the same time. One could be simultaneously conspicuous and invisible. But it still seemed inconceivable that Larry Barnes could have been living on this small island for the past five years without my knowing it.

If I had known, would I have sought him out?

There was a gentle irony to the notion that this man who had once cast me aside as unnecessary ballast was now coming to me for support. How sweetly different from that long-ago summer when I was apprentice and he was master, when I begged and he withheld. He appeared not to know at whose doorstep he had come begging; the envelope was addressed not to me but to the Acheson Foundation.

I had to force myself to resist the temptation to tear the application into tiny pieces and flush them down the toilet. Even though I didn't want to resurrect my past or risk letting old feelings resurface, I had to treat him as I would any other applicant. I had to be better than my instincts, better than I was.

I lined his slides up on my lighted viewing board and scrutinized them, one by one. The works were expressive but prosaic, bland, sadly uninspired. Masses of slashing strokes. They were also remarkably similar to the paintings he had done when I knew him. Did this mean that, while I had evolved into someone entirely new, he had remained exactly the same?

Judy Pomeranz

Chapter Eighteen:
End of an Era and a New Beginning

October, 1991

I awoke with a start. It was 4:30. My entire system was buzzing. I had a ten o'clock appointment with Larry Barnes.

***

I had Jimmy drop me at Washington Square so I could walk the short distance to Larry's studio. I needed to wring out a solitary moment before encountering my past.

Larry's building was a nondescript four-story structure with battered trim, peeling paint, and a Korean grocery store at street level. I entered a door beside the grocery and stared at the four buttons on the buzzer panel before pressing the one next to a scrap of yellowing paper on which the name BARNES was scrawled.

"Come on up," A familiar voice yelled down the stairs. "I'm on four."

The steps were steep, and the stairway smelled of urine and alcohol. The gray walls were gouged and sprayed with lively, figurative graffiti. As I slowly took the steps, I instinctively avoided touching the railing, paused at the second floor, then the third, and then forced myself to proceed with the final flight.

Dressed in blue jeans, a black tee shirt, and dirty white running shoes, Larry looked like a seasoned version of his old self. His hair was thinning and streaked with white, a small paunch was evident under the tee shirt, and unfamiliar lines radiated from the corners of his mouth, but essentially he was Larry, and for an instant I was Lauren Towson from Bayonne.

"Ms. Acheson." He stuck out his hand, "I'm Larry Barnes."

His failure to recognize me made me feel as if I had an edge.

"Hello, Larry." I gave his hand a firm shake. "How nice to see you again."

He looked at me closely, and I could see the recognition slowly dawn. "Jesus Christ," he whispered. "Lauren?" He ran his eyes up and down the length of my body, from head to foot and back again.

I nodded.

"Jesus Christ."

I relished my supremacy and his bewilderment. "It's been a long time."

"Yes it has." His mouth hung open as if the last word wouldn't quite leave it.

"May I come in?"

"Of course. "I was... I am... I didn't realize you were... I mean... you're... involved in the foundation?"

"It was my husband's. I'm Chairman of the Board of Trustees."

"Your husband is—"

"Was. Charles Acheson."

"I had no idea—"

"Why should you?" Now I was the kindly superior making excuses for my muddled subordinate.

"I... right... how could I be expected..." Larry closed the door behind me as I entered the studio. "Can I take your... your..."

"My shawl," I said, as if teaching English to a foreigner. "No, I'll keep it." I wrapped the blue pashmina tightly around my arms and shoulders, hoping it would protect me.

The studio was dominated by three large sash windows. Two paintings rested on easels and dozens more were propped against the walls. A small table held a can of brushes, a mustard jar filled with clear liquid, and a palette covered with fresh globs of paint. Brick-and-board bookcases crammed with painting supplies lined the walls, and a small, rusty refrigerator stood in a corner. Seating options were limited to rickety card-table chairs and an old green sofa.

Larry gestured toward the sofa. "Have a seat."

The brown stains on the green fabric made me opt for a chair. Larry remained standing, shifting his weight from foot to foot, his hands clutching his upper arms.

"Can I get you something to drink? Water? Beer? Coke?"

"I'm fine, thanks."

"Would you like to see my work?"

"That's what I'm here for."

He scurried around the studio, gathering five or six canvases, which he leaned against the sofa. Once all were assembled, he began his exposition.

"I did this one in Paris after my dad died." He pointed to a painting that featured slashes of black paint over fine veils of gray and brown. "I don't consciously paint autobiographically, but the colors and the slow sweep of the strokes reflect my state of mind."

Larry had entered his milieu. Talking about his art, as if from a script, calmed him. He had probably given a similar pitch to many a gallery owner over the years.

He moved the painting to reveal one beneath it, a figurative work inspired by Picasso's *Frugal Repast*, then a small painting composed of greens and pinks that had had its genesis in a minor work by Monet at the *Musee d'Orsay*.

"What about the Monet 'Water Lilies' at the *Orangerie?* You were studying them intently when I last saw you."

Larry gazed at me. "You have an amazing memory."

"Did the water lilies ever 'work their way into your psyche?'"

He smiled broadly. "You are amazing."

I feared I might be won over and completely disarmed by that smile, but I persisted. "Did they?"

"No, they never did."

Then he held up a work that was different from all the rest. It was a brilliant primary-toned painting that featured a clown-like image. Thick with impasto, the figure's oversized mouth smiled out from an egg-shaped head. It was signed and dated sixteen years ago and was, unlike the others, original and appealing.

"Let me guess. Inspired by Dubuffet?"

"No." He grinned. "Inspired by my first child."

"I don't think so." My response was automatic.

"What do you mean?"

I took in the details of his features and his expression as I pondered my response. I imagined telling him I had carried his first child; I imagined giving an emotional and purgative rendition of the whole story. Then I imagined the exquisite relief that would flood over his countenance when I told him I had miscarried.

"Nothing. Do you have any other paintings like that one?"

"No. That was a one-time thing."

"Like having a first child."

He stared.

"Listen, I've taken enough of your time. I'd best be—"

"Would you like to have dinner? I've thought about you so often."

Same old Larry, enterprising and full of what my father would have poetically called 'bullshit.'

"I don't think so, but thanks for letting me see your work." I stood.

"Do you want to go out for coffee? Get reacquainted?" The pitch of his voice hinted at desperation.

"No, thanks." I pulled the shawl more tightly around myself. I offered him my hand, which he shook awkwardly.

As I went down the long, steep steps, I felt sad about Larry's uninspired painting, his shabby quarters, and his frantic desire to please me, now that I had money to hand out. I was melancholy that this chapter of ancient history had come to a close. But my most pronounced feeling was one of deep tranquility. After all these years, it was finally over.

Chapter Nineteen
En Route to Hog Heaven

October, 1991

With the Larry episode safely behind me, I mustered the energy and focus to fill Rovier's Board position. I called in the most impressive of the high-fliers who had sent in their credentials, and those who had been recommended by other Board members. I interviewed and scrutinized them, pumped them for scholarly insights, and toyed with them to see how they would react under pressure. I had planned to have Tom Smithson, whom I trusted implicitly, interview my top choices, but I didn't have any. While these people were bright, clever, accomplished, and undoubtedly worthy, I was not comfortable with any of them.

As I sat at my desk, fretting over next steps, I glanced at the grant application on the top of my in-box, the one from the writer inspired by Borges. A crazy thought crystallized. Not long ago, it would have made me laugh or sneer.

I asked Joanne to find the phone number for Annette Spitzer in Bayonne. As soon as she did, I punched it into phone, not wanting to give myself time to change my mind or agonize over an approach. When Annette answered, I blurted out, "Annette, it's me, Lauren." They were words I would have used thirty years ago.

"My God, it's great to hear your voice." Annette still sounded naïve and sweet, and she still had that New Jersey twang.

After pleasantries and updates on both sides, I worked around to the point. "The Foundation has been short one Board member, since Rovier Alexander died."

"I know. What a terrible loss."

"You've heard of him?"

"We studied together at Columbia. He was doing post-grad work when I was working on my Ph.D. We used to lunch together. He was wonderfully interesting."

"Yes, he was." I was so stunned I could think of nothing further to say.

"He was kind enough to speak to my high school class about literary criticism. The students loved him."

"You mean, he came to *Bayonne*?"

"A few weeks before he died."

I tried to imagine the worldly Rovier Alexander III in the stultifying, stifling world of Annette and Bayonne. "Were you close?"

"Not really, but we spoke every few months. I was a fan."

"Me too. Did you ever complete your Ph.D.?"

"Finally." She laughed. "It took years, but I did it, and I hated to see the thesis process end. I was so happy living in the mystical world of Borges. It was an escape, and a delight."

"Escape?"

"You did it your way, and I did it mine."

It had never occurred to me that Annette might have felt the need to escape Bayonne, nor had I contemplated that one might make the escape without leaving.

"Would you like to replace Rovier on the Foundation Board."

"Me? I've never—"

"That doesn't matter. I don't need someone with foundation experience, I need someone with literary expertise." I paused before adding, "and I need someone I can trust, which makes you perfect for the job."

***

Annette arrived for her first Board meeting dressed in a floral cotton shirtwaist and black pumps. Her gray-streaked brown hair was tied in a bedraggled hank with a limp blue ribbon. Her tortoiseshell glasses were now bifocals, but the frames looked exactly like the ones she wore thirty years ago.

"You look terrific!" She threw her arms around me in an enormous hug, which I found embarrassing but also strangely comforting.

Throughout the meeting, Annette was circumspect in voicing her opinion. Though she was prepared with responses when asked and showed she had given all the applications a great deal of thought, she didn't volunteer much. But when it came time to discuss the literary applicants, she was downright effusive.

"I adored this man's work," she said about the Borges fan. "His stories moved me to tears, made me laugh out loud. Not one left me indifferent. His writing not only shows a spark of Borges, but it has the depth and intellectualism of Garcia-Marquez."

In short, Annette was opinionated, outspoken, and extravagantly demonstrative when she cared about something. Her style was decidedly different from that of the other Board members, but she was damn good.

***

After the meeting, I invited Annette to spend the next weekend with me in East Hampton.

I was tired. The trauma of losing Rovier, the effort I had poured into replacing him, and the experience of resurrecting Larry had all taken a toll. For the first time in ages, I needed to get away, and nothing sounded better than a few days at the beach.

Asking Annette to join me was inspired. We soaked up the healing Indian Summer sun, we read, we listened to the ocean, we laughed, and we talked and talked and talked as if no time had passed since the days when we were inseparable. Talking to Annette was uniquely purgative; it had been many years since I had spent time with anyone who knew from whence or from whom I had come. With Annette, no pretenses were necessary or possible.

We talked about Larry, about the miscarriage, about college, about life on Fifth Avenue and life in Bayonne. We talked about Annette's husband, Freddie, and about their children. We talked about my mother and father and my sister. I talked about Tom Smithson, who had become as good a friend to me as Mitzi, or as Annette herself had once been. And we talked about Charles.

"I was so hurt by his suicide." It was the first time I had said the word out loud. "For the longest time I didn't think about how *he* must have felt. I could only think about what he had done to *me*."

"How could you be expected to think about someone else at a time like that?"

"I hardly knew him. I never tried to understand him or figure out what he needed." Admitting that to myself was another first. "It never occurred to me that he needed *anything*."

Annette didn't respond.

"Or maybe it did occur to me," I said quietly. "Maybe I didn't want to take the time to find out or be bothered. Maybe I knew I wouldn't be able to handle it. Or maybe I didn't want to mess with my perfect life." I closed my eyes. "That possibility torments me."

***

On Saturday afternoon, as we lounged beneath a brilliant yellow sun, I told Annette about Sydney Ray Jenkins.

"I don't believe Charles had an affair," Annette said. "He loved you so much."

"How could you know that? You haven't seen him in years."

"Admittedly. But I knew him when he fell in love with you, and it doesn't seem like something he would have done."

"I agree, it doesn't. I came up with good reasons why he might have left her his books, reasons I could live with. It wasn't until I learned that he had used Foundation funds to support her that I allowed myself to believe it."

"But why the charade? He had plenty of money he could have given her, so why go to the trouble of faking a grant application?"

"I decided I wasn't going to dwell on it. Why he did what he did is not relevant." I spoke in a voice intended to close the discussion, a voice that belonged to Mrs. Charles Acheson of the Upper East Side, not Lauren Towson, or even Lauren Acheson.

Annette watched the whitecaps on the ocean. "Are you sure you're being fair to him?"

***

"I envy you this place," Annette said the next morning as we ate breakfast on the deck. She sipped coffee and looked over the ocean. "It's Utopia. I feel completely rejuvenated."

"It is peaceful." I bit into a lemon-ginger scone. "Did I tell you I'm planning to sell it?"

"Why?"

"I don't have time to come out here. I'm lucky to make it a few weekends a year."

"That's better than nothing."

"But it's a waste, letting it sit empty most of the time."

"Couldn't you work here? You don't have to be in Manhattan all the time —"

"I don't want to get back into the Hamptons lifestyle. The parties, the club, the obsessive tennis, the civic nonsense. It's all a huge, addictive, time-and-money-sinkhole."

"So, why not do *this* once in a while? "Sit on the deck, enjoy the sound of the ocean, read the books in that marvelous library upstairs, sip coffee and wine, take a swim now and then. Forget the social stuff. I'd love to have a place like this to write," she said dreamily. "I'd sit by that window in the library—the one that faces the water. I'd set up my pile of books and a laptop, and be in hog heaven."

"For a literary luminary, your choice of words is as crude as ever."

"Can't take Bayonne out of the girl." She chuckled. "I'd take up poetry if I had a place like this, or painting. You've got unbeatable subject matter for both. Look at that ocean."

"There are a lot of artists around here."

"I know, all the big names. It's too bad the younger ones who need the time and space the most can't afford the Hamptons."

"I could give this place to a young artist," I mused, as we nibbled at our scones and raspberries and flipped through the *Times*. "One of our grantees."

"That's a generous thought," Annette said, "but how could they afford to keep it up?"

I shrugged.

Annette lifted a spoonful of berries to her mouth, but stopped in midair. "What about an artist's retreat? You could make this a place like Yaddo. You could have six or eight people here at a time." Her eyes widened. She leaned forward and spoke quickly. "They could stay for a month or two, whatever they need. You have the staff here anyway. They could provide meals, keep things running, and make sure the house doesn't get trashed. You could have painters, sculptors, writers, and musicians. They could each have their own space to create during the day and then they could socialize at night, share ideas. It would be perfect. Best of all, you wouldn't have to give the place up. You could set aside as much of the house as you want for your own use."

"Nice of you to let me keep a room or two."

"It would be wonderful. You'd be an impresario."

***

When I got back to Manhattan, I called Tom Smithson to tell him about Annette's idea.

"It's a fascinating concept, and it might be a good solution to your problem of what to do with the house. Your friend Annette's quite a pistol. That was some performance she put on at the Board meeting."

I was pleased by his words and chose to interpret them as a personal compliment. "So, how do we make this retreat happen?"

Chapter Twenty
What's It All About?

November, 1991–July, 1992

Annette and I plotted logistics and developed criteria for granting residency fellowships while Tom fought to convince the East Hampton zoning board that having a houseful of artists was not the same as having a houseful of convicts.

I kept a bedroom and sitting room for my own use, as well as two guest rooms and the library. The artists in residence, a maximum of eight at a time, would have free run of the rest of the house. Our long-time staff would stay on to provide cooking and cleaning services.

Thanks to more miracles than I can count and the kindness of innumerable strangers, within eight months of its conception, the Charles Acheson Artists' Retreat was ready to do business.

***

During the flurry of preparations leading up to the opening, I often thought about the weekend Annette and I had spent in East Hampton. My mind drifted back to Sydney Ray Jenkins. Though I admonished myself that revisiting the issue would be unwise, unhealthy, and painful, Annette's question haunted me. *Are you sure you're being fair to Charles?*

***

> *Dear Ms. Jenkins,*
> *I would like to meet with you.*
> *Please let me know if and when that would be possible. I will be happy to come to Los Angeles, unless you would prefer meeting here in New York.*
> *Sincerely,*
> *Mrs. Charles Acheson*

Having drafted and redrafted a dozen lengthy and variously sarcastic, nasty, pandering, or noxiously polite iterations, I settled upon short and simple. I reviewed the draft before copying it onto a sheet of heavy, ivory stationary, making one change: I signed it *Lauren Acheson.*

***

> *Dear Ms. Acheson:*
> *I would be delighted to meet you. Charles always spoke so lovingly of you, and I have long wished we could become acquainted, though in the aftermath of his tragic death it didn't seem appropriate to present myself. I know you had many things on your mind far more important than meeting Charles' "literary correspondent," as he used to call me.*
> *I will be in New York next week for a conference at the Waldorf. Perhaps we could meet for a drink at Peacock Alley. Say five-thirty on Tuesday? Leave me a message at the hotel desk if that's not good for you. Otherwise, I'll look forward to it.*
> *Sincerely,*
> *Sydney Ray Jenkins*

***

I reread the typed note, looking for sarcasm. Though I found nothing overt, I could hardly believe she would be "delighted" to meet me. Uncomfortable with the idea of meeting on her turf and her terms, I left word at the Waldorf that I would prefer meeting at my place. Tuesday was fine, I added, though 6:00 would be better than 5:30.

Yes, I can be petty.

***

I got home from the office at 5:00 that evening and hopped into the bathtub with a glass of Chardonnay. As I soaked, I wondered whether Daniel would recognize Sidney Ray Jenkins when she arrived. Had Charles had her here at the apartment when I was in East Hampton or somewhere else?

I threw on a pair of forest green gabardine pants and a light wool twin set. Casual seemed right. Casual complemented nonchalance, and that was the effect I was going for. It had been a while since I had worried about such things.

When the doorman called to announce that Ms. Jenkins was on her way up, I went to the library, curled up on the sofa, and opened a book, trying to create a tableau that would suggest I was so wrapped up in my reading I had forgotten company was due. I did not want to be present when Daniel opened the door. If there was to be a happy reunion between the two of them, I wanted no part of it. And no knowledge of it.

"Mrs. Acheson," Daniel said as he stepped into the library. "Ms. Jenkins to see you."

"Oh, yes, of course," I said, pretending to be startled at having my reading interrupted. I took my time marking my place, then finally looked up.

"Ms. Jenkins." I didn't know what to say next. I, the unflappable hostess, master of the poker face and quintessential conversationalist, was thrown off guard; I was not sure of the proper greeting was for a woman who might have been my husband's mistress. "So nice to meet you," I finally said. I stood and shook her hand.

She was young, as I had known she would be. And she was attractive, as I had suspected. But with her short, spiky black hair, rhinestone-encrusted glasses, and butterfly-tattooed cheek, she was hardly the woman I had been imagining. Hardly Charles' type. That assessment made me feel better, until I remembered, sadly, that I didn't know what Charles' type might have been.

"Please, come in." I shifted my weight from one foot to the other, as Larry had done when I arrived at his studio.

"Thank you." Sydney Ray Jenkins sailed in and took a seat on the sofa. "It's such a pleasure to finally meet you. Charles spoke of you so often."

"I'm glad you could make it." I sat stiffly in a wing chair.

"As am I."

"Can I get you a drink?"

"I'd love a glass of wine." She smiled a sweet smile, which created a dimple in her cheek that made the tattooed butterfly flutter. "I need it after the tedious papers I've listened to today—my own included."

"You were here for a conference, you said?"

"An academic meeting. Very dull. Trust me, you don't want to know about it," she said with another smile, this one quite brilliant. "One of the things I loved about Charles was that he put up with me droning on—in letters—about my work and academia. I was on the other side of it then. I was a student when we first became acquainted."

"And now?"

"I'm an associate professor at UCLA."

I nodded, increasingly unsure what it was I had to say to this woman.

"I wanted to thank you for the books, but the time didn't seem right, so soon after his death, and then—"

"There's no need to thank me. They were Charles' books, and entirely his gift. I was not aware of that provision of his will."

"That could have been a shock, huh?" Sydney Ray chuckled. "Here's this *woman* you've never met, and your husband's leaving her his books!" She laughed heartily. "I assume Mr. Bailey explained who I was before you heard about the bequest."

"Mr. Bailey?"

"Gerald Bailey, Charles' lawyer."

"I *know* who Gerald Bailey is," I said too snippily, "but what did *he* have to do with this? What would he have told me?"

"You mean he didn't tell you who I was?"

"Not really." There was not much to be lost by frankness.

Sydney Ray shook her head. "Not long before he died, Charles told me he was amending his will to leave me his books. He said he wanted to do it because I'd appreciate them." She glanced up as if to gauge my reaction. "He assured me you wouldn't want them, that it would be a favor to you—you wouldn't have to dispose of them." She paused, but continued before I could interject. "I couldn't afford many books then, couldn't afford much of anything. That's why I applied for the Foundation grant. You knew about that, didn't you?"

I nodded. "But only recently."

"That's how I got to know Charles. After I got the grant, we started to correspond. He would send me books and ask what I thought about them. We had a mail-order book discussion group." She smiled at me quickly. "We loved the same authors, hated the same politicians, almost thought the same thoughts."

"How did you meet?" I asked, unaccountably saddened by what I had just heard.

"We never did—not in person."

"I beg your pardon?"

"God." Sydney Ray shook her head and let it drop into her hand. "He swore to me his lawyer would explain to you who I was."

"Why didn't Charles do it himself?"

"I honestly don't know. I can't believe Mr. Bailey never said anything. He promised... what did you *think* all these years?"

"What do you mean you and Charles never met?" I asked, ignoring her question.

"I never saw Charles, and he never saw me. I applied for the grant, and he wrote to tell me I'd been approved. He told me he was intrigued by my ideas and wanted me to be able to follow my dream of writing and teaching at the university level. I was star struck. I was so amazed this important person would notice what I was trying to do."

I recognized that feeling.

"So, I wrote to thank him. And that was the beginning of what turned out to be a four-year-long correspondence. Purely literary in nature."

"You never saw him, and he never saw you?" Annette's words echoed in my mind: *Are you sure you're being fair to him?*

"No, and I regret that deeply. I felt such kinship with your husband, such a profound intellectual bond, that I felt horribly cheated when he died before I could meet him. I lost a dear friend without ever seeing him." She looked up at me.

"I'm sorry." And I was; I was sorry for Sydney Ray, sorry for Charles, and, most of all, sorry that I hadn't bothered to know my husband well enough to notice what kind of companionship he needed.

"What were you thinking all this time? About me..."

"Never mind."

"Shit," Sydney Ray said quietly, shaking her head. "Shee-it!"

"Whatever," I said with a small grin.

"What the hell is *with* Gerald Bailey?"

"Gerald had his own agenda." I spoke the thoughts as I had them, and it all made sense. "He didn't want me left with kind feelings toward my husband because he didn't want me to carry on Charles' work. He wanted me to be angry at Charles so I would want nothing to do with the Foundation."

"What an asshole."

"That's an accurate characterization."

We chuckled. Both of us. Quietly at first, but soon we were laughing so loudly that Daniel peeked in the door to see if everything was all right. We laughed so hard and so long my sides ached like I had never laughed before.

When we quieted enough to catch our breath, Sydney Ray said, "I was crazy about your husband." She spoke quietly. "He was my intellectual soul mate, to borrow a phrase from the sixties. And while a part of me wanted so badly to meet him, mostly I was afraid of that happening."

"Why?"

"When something is perfect, you hate to mess with it. I was afraid if we met the magic might disappear."

"You must have been good for him."

"Do you think so?"

I nodded. "You were someone he could talk to about things that mattered to him."

"Not that he needed that. He had you."

"He needed that, believe me." I debated before asking the question I really wanted to ask. "Do you know why he killed himself?"

She shook her head and brushed away a tear left over from the laughter. "I don't. I wanted to ask you."

"I saw your last letter to him. He seemed tormented by something. What was it? What was going on?"

"I didn't fully understand it, but I think Charles' fatal flaw was caring too much. You know?"

I shook my head.

"Most of us have so much going on in our lives that we don't take the time to think about the bigger issues.: why we're here, what the world is all about, what our role is, what we're supposed to do with our lives. But Charles was obsessed with his *raison d'être*, and he devoted endless hours to reading and studying to try to get a grip on it. He was the most curious person I've ever known, but his curiosity had a deeper, frightening edge to it. My guess is that he could no longer handle not knowing what it was all about."

I should have known. I should have seen.

Maybe I had, but didn't want to acknowledge it. I was so proficient at denial that I had been happy to believe everything was in place in my world and operating exactly as it should. To have thought otherwise would have required resources I didn't have—or was too selfish to expend.

"I'm glad you were there to help him."

I meant that. I only wished I had been there as well.

Judy Pomeranz

Chapter Twenty-One
Perfectly Good

August, 1992

By the end of the summer, the Charles Acheson Artists' Retreat was alive with activity. With a composer, three fiction writers, a poet, two painters, a print-maker, and a sculptor in residence—as well as Tom Smithson and myself, who were there for the weekend—it was all exactly as I had hoped.

After dining with the group, Tom and I excused ourselves and retired to the small deck off my sitting room for a cognac.

"It seems like a great group." Tom sipped his Courvoisier.

I nodded, looking out into the darkness that hid the sea.

"I love the salt air," I said, apropos of nothing. "I love the smell of it." I leaned back in my chair and savored the serenity of the moment. It was lovely being out here with Tom. Though he and I had become delightfully comfortable with one another as colleagues and friends, we seldom had time together to sit and relax.

"It's healing," Tom said quietly. "The sea has great healing properties. Aren't you glad you didn't get rid of this place?"

"Very."

"What'll happen to the house when you're gone?"

"You'll take care of it for me," I said, though I'd never thought about it. "You're my lawyer."

He chuckled. "What if I'm not around?"

"I can't worry about that."

He nodded. "Maybe we'll set up an endowment to run it in perpetuity."

I fetched a small leather notebook from the sitting room. I jotted a few words of verse that had occurred to me. They were lines about the sea and about history. I was pretty sure they were my own words, but they might have come from something I'd read. It didn't matter; I liked them and wanted to remember them.

"Charles would love it if he knew you were writing again."

"Maybe in concept he would, but probably not if he could read what I've been writing. I'm not exactly the Belle of Amherst."

"That's not the point, is it? Being the Belle of Amherst."

"I don't know the point."

He smiled.

"I don't know the point of anything. That's what killed Charles, you know."

"What killed Charles?"

I loved Tom for the way he went along with the stream of consciousness binges I occasionally indulged in these days. He didn't act as if I was crazy, or eccentric, but tried gamely to conjure what sense he could from it all.

"What killed Charles was wanting—no, needing—to know the point." As I spoke, I made marks in my notebook, and pondered my metaphors. Then I laid the pen across the page. "We can't know the point, and we have to understand that there might not be a point."

"That's a depressing thought."

I pulled my shawl more closely around my shoulders against a gust of sea air. "Why is that any more depressing than thinking there *is* a point that we're not privy to? I'd prefer to believe that what we see is what we get. What's there is there, and what we make of it is what we make of it."

"I can live with that." Tom interlaced his fingers behind his head and leaned back.

"Charles couldn't. He couldn't put the "why's" aside or see them as an intellectual game. He was tormented by them, and I was oblivious to it all. I never helped him."

"Did you love him?"

I looked at Tom, but he was staring straight ahead. I thought for a long time before answering. "I loved the way he made me feel— protected, safe, treasured, smart. I loved the way he took me away from what I needed to escape and put me into a place where I could lose my old self and become whatever I wanted to become."

"And did you?"

I looked at the blackness where the ocean belonged and jotted more words in my notebook. I turned to Tom, trying to find his eyes. "Not while he was alive. I became someone I thought was quite extraordinary, and I was pleased with that person. It took me a long time to realize that that person was neither extraordinary nor who I wanted to be. Charles made me the person I wanted to be, but only after he died."

"So, did you love him?"

"I don't know what that means."

Tom nodded slowly. "Do you miss him?"

"Not really. I shouldn't say that, but we were so removed from one another when he was alive—or I was so removed from him—that his death didn't leave me missing him. It left me scared, it left me lonely, it left me at sea, and it left me feeling terribly sorry for myself and unsure how to behave or think as a single person. It left me without an identity. It left me missing the place in the world that he had carved out for me. I was Annie without Daddy Warbucks. But it did not leave me missing him."

"And now?"

"I'm sad that I wasted the opportunity to know him, and I'm sad he didn't get to know me the way I am now. I'm sad when I think of him, but it's not the same as missing someone. There are few people I've ever cared about enough to miss. I'm good at avoidance." I set the book on the table beside me and smiled at Tom. "It's one of my greatest talents."

"Avoidance?"

"Does that unsettle you?"

"Hardly. It's no surprise." He placed his hand over mine on the table that separated us. "But you're missing a lot."

"I like having your hand on mine. It's comfortable."

Tom smiled but still didn't look at me.

"Do you think you'll ever fall in love and get married?" I asked.

He shrugged. "Who knows?"

"Maybe *we* should get married," I mused. "I'm due for a younger man, and we're damn good together."

"My God, the salt air certainly does things to your mind." He took a deep breath of the dampness. "But we *are* good together, aren't we?"

"We are."

"So, what do you think?" He grinned broadly. "Shall we go to Vegas?"

"It wouldn't last a day. I'd eat you alive."

"That's for damn sure. You'd chew me up and spit me out."

"Anyway, why ruin a perfectly good thing?"

"*Perfectly* good," he whispered.

THE END

Elegy

Judy Pomeranz

BREAKING NEWS

"So, to recap, in case you're just tuning in, Delta flight five-two-five, en route from New York's Kennedy Airport to London Heathrow, crashed in a ball of fire on the east coast of the Gaspé Peninsula in Canada at 6:05 this evening." The CNN correspondent looked soberly into the camera. "Two hundred and fifty-three passengers and a crew of fourteen were on board the airliner. Early indications suggest that there are no survivors.

"According to investigators here on the scene, wreckage is strewn over twenty-five miles, on land, and in the water." He paused. "Thank God this is a sparsely populated region."

***

Pamela stared at the TV and tugged on the gold chain around her neck so hard it dug a ridge into her skin. There must be dozens of flights from New York to London, she told herself over and over as she watched the coverage. Yes, the odds were he was flying on another airline altogether. He might have even gone from LaGuardia. Did London flights leave from LaGuardia? Just because he had a Delta mileage credit card didn't mean he was flying Delta. It was a business trip—his firm's travel department would have made the arrangements. He could have been on any airline. He could have left from any airport. Maybe even Newark. Besides, she had no idea what time he had left; he might have left much earlier in the day, or later. He was probably safely in the air right now, or still at the airport. Maybe he was in London by now, or maybe his plane had been diverted because of the accident.

She punched his mobile number into her cell phone again. Her call log noted this was the fourth time she'd tried in the last ten minutes. Once again it went directly to voicemail. She put her phone down, not wanting to leave another message. She didn't want him to think she was obsessing. He would know from the first three messages that she was concerned. That was enough. He didn't like her calling at all. Too risky, he had said. He had given her the number only when she insisted she should have it in case of emergency.

"What kind of emergency?" he had asked, looking concerned.

"Don't worry, I won't use it," she had promised. "I just need to know I have it." This was months ago.

She clutched the Tiffany heart that dangled from the chain around her neck and poured herself a third glass of Chardonnay.

***

After midnight Pamela finally forced herself off the sofa. She had to sleep; she was scheduled to conduct her first solo deposition at eight o'clock the next morning. Besides, there was nothing she could do but wait.

Not counting the calls to Justin's mobile, she had picked her phone up a dozen times over the course of the evening, wanting desperately to talk to someone. She had thought about calling the airline but knew they wouldn't release passenger names. She had thought about calling the National Transportation Safety Board but knew she wouldn't get anything more than she was getting on CNN. She had thought about calling Justin's office to see if they had any information but knew that would be reckless. She had even thought about calling his home phone to hear whether the voices at the other end sounded frantic or fine, but that would be insane.

She had to wait. She had no standing to ask for information or seek comfort from anyone.

***

She went to her bedroom without turning off the TV. She took off the silk blouse and charcoal gray pencil skirt she had worn since morning. A lifetime ago.

She tried to remember what morning had felt like. She had eaten her shredded wheat and banana, downed three cups of coffee while reading the Times, and walked to the subway, enjoying the warm, sunny spring day and sweet memories of the night before.

She had been melancholy, knowing she wouldn't see Justin for the next ten days and that communication would be impossible. But she had looked forward to the freedom their separation would bring. She wouldn't be tied to the phone. She could make plans with friends, without worrying that she'd miss an opportunity to see him if he had free time. Planning ahead was not something she and Justin had the luxury of engaging in. It was all about grabbing opportunities when they arose, maximizing those rare moments when he could break away.

So yes, she had felt sad this morning, but light and unencumbered as she walked through the tree-lined streets of the Village and across Washington Square. She had run into her friend Maria, a woman she had known since Columbia Law School but rarely saw, and had spontaneously asked if Maria was free for dinner tomorrow night. She was. They made a plan to meet at Bar Boulud, on Broadway across from Lincoln Center. It was that easy. Pamela had stepped onto the crowded subway car, marveling at how simple life could be and wondering whether the trade-offs inherent in her non-traditional relationship were worth it.

Now, she hung up her skirt and pulled on the orange silk nightie he had given her. He referred to it as persimmon; he was always specific about colors. She loved his keen visual sense, which, like his interest in gardening and his love of art museums, she read as a special, feminine sensibility and a fascinating and lovely counterpoint to his tough, back-slapping, hard-drinking, hale-fellow, senior partner persona. Persimmon made her know the trade-offs were worth it, especially since he assured her they were temporary.

She checked again to make sure her cell phone's ring volume was on high and placed the phone on her nightstand. She turned the bedroom TV on to CNN, then went into the bathroom.

She stared at her image in the mirror as she brushed her teeth. She looked awful. An utterly different person from the fresh-faced woman who had walked to the subway this morning. Her eyes were ringed with red from the wine and from crying. Dark, puffy circles hung beneath them, and her complexion was blotchy and dry. Even her hair looked like straw. It was as if all the oxygen and hydration had been sucked out of her system.

She pulled an orange plastic bottle of Ativan from the medicine cabinet and took one with a glass of water. One tablet, the label said. As needed. For sleep. The prescription bottle was dated November 24 of last year. Exactly one month after they first got together. That was the first time in her life she had ever had trouble sleeping. And now she was on the last refill. She popped one pill more into her mouth and swallowed it.

***

The Ativan took the edge off, so Pamela drifted through the next few hours, floating, but she remained continually aware of what CNN was reporting.

Wreckage was still strewn over a 25-mile radius, there were still no likely survivors, there was still no known cause for what had apparently been a mid-air explosion, and there was still no public roster of passengers who had been on board. Not a single new detail was revealed until 3:30 a.m., when CNN announced a phone number family members could call for information.

Pamela grabbed her cell from the nightstand and punched in the number. Though her tongue felt thick and she had trouble articulating words, she managed to tell the woman who answered that she had a friend who might have been on board.

"I'm so sorry to hear that," the woman responded. "I do hope he or she wasn't on this flight."

"I do too. If I give you the name can you check?"

"I'm sorry, but we can only deal with family members at this point."

"But how am I supposed—" Pamela couldn't finish the sentence without crying, so she stopped.

"I'm sorry, but the passenger manifest should be released to the press within the next twenty-four hours."

"*Twenty-four hours?*"

The woman might as well have said twenty-four years.

"How can I—?"

"There are confidentiality issues involved," the woman continued, betraying impatience. "And besides," she added in what

Pamela thought was a tone laced with accusation, "surely you can understand we have to take care of *family members* first."

The statement landed with a thud. She buried her head in the big down pillow on which she could still detect his scent.

Maybe he wasn't calling because he hadn't gotten her messages. Maybe his phone didn't work overseas so he had no idea she was worried. Maybe he assumed she knew what flight he had been on and that his plane had arrived safely. Or maybe he had gotten the messages and was angry at her for calling, for using his number when she knew he didn't want her to. And maybe he figured calling back would reinforce her bad behavior. She could imagine him thinking that way, and she tried to get angry about it.

Why hadn't he told her where he was staying in London? Why hadn't she asked? Or had she? Had she evaded the question? That might have been the case, but she couldn't remember. It didn't matter. All that mattered was that he would be okay—he had to be okay—and the next time he went away, she would know where he was staying so she could get in touch with him if she couldn't reach him on his phone.

She tried to get angry at him for relegating her to a tiny compartment in his life where she didn't have access to basic information like where he was staying. She tried to get angry at herself, an otherwise confident, talented professional woman, for being in a pathetic state and for allowing him to control her life. Even in her drugged stupor, she knew anger would be so much easier to handle than the gut-churning fear, the crushing sadness, and the horrible feelings of helplessness and impotence.

She tried to get angry about the time he had scolded her like a child for saying she'd like to tell one of her friends about their relationship.

"How could I ever trust you again if you did that?" he had asked.

"But I didn't do it, and if I had, what would it have to do with trust?" she had asked. "I want to share this amazing part of my life with people I care about."

"You're sharing it with me," he had said. "Isn't that enough? And how could I trust you if you breached the sanctity of the most important secret I have in my life?"

"It's my life too," she had murmured.

"If you're going to talk about this with your friends, I'm gone. I can't take that risk."

"Would it be that easy for you to walk away?" she had asked, trying to keep her voice from quivering.

"I didn't say it would be easy," he answered softly, pulling her closer to him and kissing her gently on the neck. "I love you so much. I couldn't live without you."

That had been the last time she had talked about sharing her secret, but not the last time she had thought about it. With no one to talk to, she didn't know the rules of engagement in this human drama—how one should or should not behave or feel in different situations, the wonderful ones and the crazy-making ones—so she never knew whether her instincts and emotions were rational or completely off base. She did, however, in her most honest moments, know that her friends would consider the relationship toxic.

"A married man?" Liz would say. "Are you nuts?"

Pamela also knew that, in the abstract, she would have agreed with Liz.

But this situation was not abstract, nor was it about reason or logic. It was about love. That's what she had to believe to make sense of it. She was madly in love with a man who could have had any woman in town and had chosen her; it was a madness around which she had built a whole life, a life that excluded the people she had once cared most deeply about. She was only able to abide the madness because it was temporary. Soon they would be together.

"It'll happen, babe," he had said. "I just have to work out the details,"

"Are you sure you want this?" she had said, not wanting to get too invested in something that might not happen.

"More than anything." He gazed at her with a wounded look. "How can you even ask that?"

"You *are* still married," she ventured.

"Oh, sweetie," he had sighed. "Lynn and I don't have a real relationship."

"What do you mean?"

"We're comfortable enough, but not at all devoted to each other, and certainly not in love. It's nothing like what *we've* got." He directed the full force of his sparkly green eyes at her. "It ended a long time ago, babe. I just have to make it official. Then it'll be *our* time."

***

She made it through the deposition, though without any recollection of what the opposing counsel had asked her client, and by noon she was back in her office, watching CNN and flipping through websites covering the crash, which was now referred to in screaming black italics as *Disaster at Gaspé.*

Wreckage was still everywhere, in the smallest of shards. There was still no known cause and still no sign of survivors. How could eighteen hours go by without anything new to report? Pamela pounded her desk so hard her fist stung, then ached with a sharp intensity she had never before experienced. She pounded the desk again and again, then dropped her head onto the slick walnut surface.

Why the hell didn't he call?

A CNN reporter noted that families of the victims were beginning to gather in the vicinity of the crash. Pamela lifted her head and looked at the screen.

A young blonde woman looked shell-shocked as she walked with two towheaded toddlers toward a tent that had been set up to minister to the families' needs. A stoic and grim gray-haired man allowed an aid worker to lead him by the arm to a table set up with tea and cookies. Three lanky teenage girls graced with the sweet, rich beauty only the young possess talked quietly with their haggard mother, who sat on a folding chair outside the tent. A heavy-set middle-aged woman, all alone, wept openly, noisily, and without shame.

Pamela envied them all.

She wished she could be there with them. She wished she could mourn for a man she knew was on that plane rather than wonder about one who had disappeared into a vacuum. She wished she could scream and cry or display her grief with quiet dignity. She wished the whole world could watch her on TV and know what she was going through. She wished her family and friends or even anonymous aid workers could help her through this horror show. She wished she knew her place in all this. She wished she *had* a place in all this.

Then she heard the breaking news from CNN. There would be no further search for survivors. It was official. Investigators had determined that no one could have survived this crash. Everyone on board, all 253 passengers and fourteen crewmembers, were officially dead. The airline would release a passenger list as soon as all the families had been notified.

"No one would want the families of these victims to learn about their fate by reading it in the paper or seeing it on TV," one reporter remarked quietly.

"Oh God, no," said another. "That would be a horrible way to learn it. Not that there is any good way."

The first reporter looked mournful, and shook her head, "You're right. I feel so badly for the families."

***

It was another fifteen hours before the passenger list was posted online, fifteen hours of staring at CNN, fifteen hours during which Pamela had neither eaten nor slept and had come to feel nothing at all. All the sadness and fear, even the attempts at anger, had been wrung out of her.

She was empty, left with nothing but a sense of inevitability as she gazed at the computer screen while the names scrolled by in alphabetical order. She didn't even have the energy to react when **Lynn Vandermaar**'s name passed by just before his. It would be a long while before that would that would sink in.

But when his name, **Justin Vandermaar,** appeared in bold, black print, she felt like she had been slapped in the face. Seeing his name on her computer screen brought back the early days when they would email each other, the days after they met at a bar association luncheon at which he was the keynote speaker, the days when they were simply colleagues and friends, the days before he became afraid to email her and asked her to stop as well. Seeing his name brought to mind the twinkle in his eye when he watched her open the card attached to the first of the carefully-chosen Hermès scarves he loved to buy her, the card he gave her before he became afraid to sign cards. Seeing his name made her think of how sweetly right it had felt to see his monogrammed cufflinks lying beside her earrings on the bedside table at the Peninsula the first night they had spent together.

She could feel his hand in hers and see the funny, excited smile that would cross his face each time he undressed her. She could hear the gravely tone in his voice when he first told her he loved her. All the difficulties that had attended the relationship fell away and Pamela was left with nothing but an enormous, fiery ball of love—or something like it—that grew so quickly and so dramatically inside of her that, begging for an outlet and finding none, threatened to explode and demolish her entire being.

But it didn't explode, nor, sadly, did it demolish her. Instead it fizzled out and gave way to the weary, listless state that had preceded it, a state Pamela understood she would inhabit for a long time to come.

Maybe the rest of her life.

Judy Pomeranz

ANGELS AND GHOSTS

"Take these, my sons, and hold onto them." Father O'Malley handed Sam and Willie each a tawny wood cross upon which hung an emaciated, white plastic Jesus.

Sam gazed down at his cross then looked over at Willie, who smirked and rolled his eyes.

Father O'Malley placed one open palm firmly upon Willie's head. "They will bring you comfort." Father smiled as he gently and pushed a wisp of hair off Willie's forehead.

***

Throughout the endless service, Sam stared at Jesus's twisted yet oddly graceful body and the heavy head that dangled limply off to one side. He ran his hand over the back of the cross, finding a measure of comfort in its satiny smoothness. But the awkward figure frightened him. He was unable to reconcile the peaceful expression on Jesus's face with the blood that dripped down his forehead from beneath the crown of thorns and stained his hands where they were pierced by nails larger than any Sam had ever seen in his father's workshop.

***

After the funeral mass, Sam, Willie, and their dad climbed into a long, black car and lined up along the back seat, miles behind the driver. Sam and Willie wore their Sunday School clothes: blue blazers, gray pants, and white shirts. Their dad wore a dark gray suit. Sam had wanted to wear his favorite tie, the one with the little Santas on it, but his father made him wear the blue-and-white striped one instead.

As the big car crawled slowly through the familiar streets of Westchester County, no one said a word. Sam wanted to ask his dad about the car: who was driving it, where it had come from, why they were using it, why they were all in the back seat, and if they could keep it forever. He wanted to show his dad the cross he clutched in his fist and ask all the questions that swam around in his head about the figure on it. He wanted to ask why the long white car in front of them was filled with flowers.

But most of all he wanted to ask about his mother. Willie had told him their mother was gone for good and would never come back. Uncle Jimmy had told him his mother was going to heaven, and Father O'Malley had agreed. Sam wanted to ask his dad how far away heaven was and whether his mother could get there in the white car, but he especially wanted to ask why they couldn't all go with her. Why would she go without them, and was Willie right that she wasn't coming back? Sam was bursting with questions but knew he was not supposed to talk right now.

"She is an angel now," Father O'Malley had told him last night.

Sam himself had played an angel in the Christmas pageant a week ago, so he knew angels had haloes and wings. He also knew, because his mother had told him, that angels were sweet and good and that they always behaved. That part made sense to Sam because his mother was indeed sweet and good, and he was sure she always behaved, even though she was sometimes so sad.

She was also beautiful. Sam loved touching her long, blonde hair, feeling its shiny softness, and he loved sitting on her lap and burrowing his whole self into her. That made him feel cozy and safe, no matter what was going on. He felt certain she would be even more beautiful with a halo, but he wasn't at all sure what she would do with the wings.

"Will she be able to fly?" Sam blurted out, unwittingly breaking the silence in the car.

Willie rolled his eyes and pursed his lips, the way he did when Sam said something stupid. His dad looked at him without responding or even smiling, then his lower lip trembled, which was more frightening to Sam than the crucifix or his mother's absence.

So he looked back down at the cross and tried to think about his mother.

"She will be with Jesus," Father O'Malley had told him.

Given the shape Jesus was in on the cross, Sam didn't like that idea at all. But as he thought more about it he remembered the pictures of Jesus in his Sunday School classroom, pictures in which he was neither bloody nor hanging on a cross, pictures in which he smiled sweetly and was surrounded by a golden glow. That Jesus looked handsome and infinitely serene, and he had hair as soft and flowing and beautiful as Sam's mother's, though his was brown instead of blond. That Jesus wore a white robe like an angel's, not a scrap of cloth like this Jesus on the cross. That was the Jesus Sam would think of his mother spending time with.

"Can we go to Jesus with her?" Sam had asked Father O'Malley.

"No, Sam, I'm afraid we can't, not right now." Then he had stooped down and looked Sam directly in the eye, which had made Sam so uncomfortable he gazed at Father O'Malley's white collar rather than his face. "This is something she has to do by herself. You must stay here and look after your father, who will miss her very much."

Sam noticed a smudge of dirt on Father O'Malley's collar and was almost as unsettled by that as by the notion that he had to look after his father. That wasn't the way it was supposed to work. "He can't go with her, either?"

"No, Sam. But one day, if you are good, you will all be together. You and Willie and your mother and father. And when that day comes, you will have all eternity to spend together in heaven."

"Bullshit," Willie had mumbled into Sam's ear.

"What did you say, Willie?" Father O'Malley asked kindly.

"Nothing, Father."

**

When the big black car came to a stop, Sam, Willie, and their dad remained silent and in place for a long, uncomfortable time as their friends, family, and neighbors got out of other cars and walked into the cemetery. Then the three of them got out and made their way past a sea of dirty stone markers and a few towering monuments toward a place where a big hole had been dug in the ground. A pile of black dirt sat on one side of the hole, and an enormous wooden box as golden and smooth as the back of Sam's crucifix hung from a metal frame over the top of the hole. Willie had told Sam at the church that that box would "supposedly" take their mother to heaven.

"How can you go somewhere in a box?" Sam had asked.

"That's exactly my point, pal," Willie had said, then shushed him before he could ask any more questions.

Sam, Willie, and their father approached the box in front of the hole. Sam shivered as a cloud passed over the sun and the wind picked up and rustled the bare branches of the trees. Even though everyone had said it was a warm day for January, Sam wished he had his blue puff jacket on and knew his mother would have made sure he was wearing it when he left the house.

He looked at his aunts and uncles and grandparents and cousins, people he usually saw only on holidays; he looked at his neighbors and the people from the church; he looked at his parents' friends and the people his dad worked with. Everyone except his mother was here, which made Sam sure Willie was right about her being in the box. She was almost always around wherever he and Willie were, and she would certainly never be absent at a time like this, when everyone she liked was right here in one place.

Although she *had* missed Christmas Eve dinner, Sam remembered. She had been home, just not at the table. Earlier in the day, she had helped Sam glue sequins on felt ornaments, put red and green sprinkles on vanilla-scented cookies, and sponge stencil decorations on the windows. She had been there, all right. She felt sad and tired, the way she sometimes did, when the company arrived for dinner, so she had gone to bed. But she had been there; she was always there. No, she would never miss a day like this with everyone around.

Standing in front of the wooden box, Sam believed Willie might be right; she might not be coming back. That would explain why everyone was so sad. He understood that heaven—if that's where she was—was very, very far away and a place where only the angels could go. He might never see her again, despite what Father O'Malley said about eternity.

He became more afraid of the future than of the crucifix, and as empty as if someone had drilled a hole through him.

His eyes filled with tears, but he didn't want to cry in front of all these people. He didn't want Willie to call him a baby, but he couldn't keep the tears from running down his face.

He bit his lip so hard it hurt, and he looked down at the crucifix that he still clutched in his right hand. He tried to be as peaceful as Jesus. He told himself his mother would be in heaven and that heaven was a wonderful place, as Father O'Malley had said. He told himself his mother would be with Jesus, and while that was supposedly a good thing, he still didn't understand why she should prefer Jesus to him and Willie and their father. He told himself he had nothing to cry about; he wasn't bleeding like Jesus. But when he wiped the tears from his face he found blood on his hand from where he had bit his lip, which made him cry harder.

***

By the time Father O'Malley finally stopped talking, Sam's shoulders had stopped heaving and his tears had dried up. The hole still pierced his center, but he didn't hurt. He felt nothing as he watched the box that held his mother being lowered into the ground.

"I am the Resurrection and the Life," Father said. "May her soul and the souls of all the faithful departed, through the mercy of God, rest in peace." He sprinkled holy water into the hole that held Sam's mother. "Amen."

Sam leaned forward and watched the water fall like tears onto his mother's box, along with dirt. She wouldn't like that; she didn't like dirt on herself or anyone else. Suddenly Sam didn't much like Father O'Malley.

He took the crucifix Father had given him, rubbed its smooth back one more time, and kissed the figure of Jesus. Then he tossed it into the hole on top of the dirt which lay on his mother's box. He wished he could jump in after it.

"Yes, Sam," Father O'Malley said with a small, twisted smile. He took Sam's hand in his own big, rough one and pulled him away from the precipice. "Your mother is now with Jesus, and that was a sweet and appropriate offering."

But Sam had not intended to make an "offering." He had merely intended to throw his mother a kiss, the way he did when the yellow bus picked him up each morning for school; the crucifix was the only vehicle he had for delivering the kiss now that she was in a box in the ground. Still, he was glad to have Father O'Malley's approval, especially since he had made his own father cry and made his brother shake his head and look at him as if he were a stupid baby.

"Bless you." Father O'Malley placed his hand on Sam's head where it stayed until everyone but the four of them had left the gravesite.

***

As he sat on the green sofa in the family room that afternoon, Sam wanted badly to take a nap. It was the first time he could recall wanting a nap, and now no one in this whole houseful of people seemed interested in putting him to bed.

With his little finger, he absently traced the outline of the stain on the sofa where he had spilled the cherry Kool-Aid last summer. He ignored the people who milled around him, people he knew and people he didn't, way too many people. If he couldn't be with his mother, he wanted to be in his own bed with his eyes tightly shut; he wanted to be quiet and have it quiet around him. But people kept talking to him, tousling his hair, touching his shoulder, sitting beside him, and hugging him. Some of them smiled sadly; others had tears in their eyes when they talked to him. It all made him very, very tired.

He finally slipped off the sofa and wound his way through the forest of towering grownups into the hallway and toward the stairs. If no one else would put him to bed, he would do it himself.

"Come on, pal." Willie grabbed his hand. "Let's get the hell out of here."

Sam didn't know where Willie had come from or where he was taking him, but he let himself be dragged along as Willie cut a path through the people into the kitchen and over to the basement stairway.

"This stuff sucks," Willie said quietly. "The whole thing sucks."

"Yeah," Sam agreed, without knowing exactly what he was agreeing to. Willie was ten years old and often used words Sam didn't comprehend, but he usually got the general idea.

Willie looked around to make sure no one was watching, then he flipped on the basement light and let Sam go ahead of him down the stairs, before quietly closing the stairway door.

When they reached the bottom of the stairs, Willie took Sam by the hand and walked him into their father's workshop, a small space that smelled of oak and pine and paint and varnish, and was lit by two bare bulbs screwed into the ceiling. Filled with heavy metal tools and tiny drawers that held nails and screws and washers and nuts and other things Sam liked to dump out and play with, the workshop felt cozy and safe. Sam loved watching his father repair things and make things out of wood, and he loved looking at the faded old calendar that hung in the room, which featured girls in bathing suits his father called pinups. His mother had given the calendar to his father when he first set up the workshop, saying it was an appropriate decoration for "a guy's playroom."

Willie sat on the cold concrete floor, facing the workbench, and leaned against the wall. Sam sat beside him.

"Why'd you throw your cross into Mom's grave?" Willie asked.

"I don't know. I felt like giving her something." He was embarrassed to tell Willie he was throwing her a kiss.

Willie nodded. "It wasn't about Jesus, right? Or about Father O'Malley?"

Sam shook his head.

"You know that stuff's a crock, right?" Willie looked at him with resolve, but his voice shook.

Sam nodded because he sensed it was the right thing to do.

Then Willie walked to the workbench; he hoisted himself up onto the tall stool, reached into the pocket of his blue blazer, and pulled out the crucifix Father O'Malley had given him. He placed it on the workbench, then turned back to Sam and stared at him. His features softened. "You should get out of here. Yeah. Go back upstairs."

"I don't want to," Sam said. "I hate all those people."

"I hear you, pal. I wish they'd leave and never come back."

"Why are they here?" Sam asked.

"They're supposedly helping us get over Mom."

"What do you mean?"

"It's bullshit. It's all unfair bullshit." Willie's face crumpled as if he were about to cry. But he drew a deep breath and pulled himself together. "If you won't get out of here, promise me you won't watch."

"Watch what?"

"Just close your eyes, and keep them closed."

So Sam lay on his side and gratefully shut his eyes, thinking maybe he could finally go to sleep.

But when he heard a soft clank of metal on metal, he opened his eyes a tiny bit and saw that Willie had taken their father's biggest hammer down from its hook on the wall. He turned it over in his hands, feeling its cold hardness and measuring its heft. He looked back at Sam, who quickly closed his eyes.

But he opened them again in time to see Willie raise the hammer and aim its heavy metal head at Jesus's torso. Willie slammed the hammer down onto the crucifix, then pounded and pounded and pounded until it dissolved into a million sharp little pieces.

When he stopped pounding, he turned to his brother and stared for a long moment. "It's all bullshit," he said, and sobbed.

As Sam sat up and stared at Willie, he could feel tears creeping down his own cheeks.

"She's not coming back," Willie said. "Not ever."

"But Father O'Malley said we'd see her—"

"Father's full of it. There's no heaven, there are no angels, and we're never going to see her again."

"But what about eternity?" Sam whispered.

"There's no eternity. There's only now, only this. Sorry, pal."

"Why did she leave us?" It was the question Sam had been trying to ask for the past three days.

"She didn't go on purpose. She's dead. No one will say that. Why do they all keep pretending it's going to be okay?" Willie wiped the tears from his face. "It's not okay. It won't ever be okay again." He sat down beside Sam. He took Sam's hand, gently pried open the fist it had clenched into, and held it tightly as he gazed straight ahead. "Promise you'll never leave me, pal."

Sam was silent as he realized that was a promise he couldn't make. He clutched Willie's hand and gazed at the wood and plastic shards as he leaned back against the cold, hard concrete wall.

THE GREEN FELT HAT

Audrey steadied her trembling hand as she applied black eyeliner to the shadowed rim of her wrinkled upper lid. It had to be perfect this time. Slowly, ever so slowly, she painted the thick, inky mark, which would give her that alluring, wide-eyed-yet-worldly appearance she knew became her. She moved back from the mirror and squinted to focus on her handiwork. The line was jumpy in a couple of places, but overall fine. With her brightly rouged cheeks and pearlescent emerald lids, now highlighted by the new black lines and heavy gobs of mascara—which she momentarily had forgotten was generally better applied *after* the liner—she resembled a china doll, which was good. It was the way it should be.

For Audrey was preparing to meet her first love. She would dine tonight with the man who, when she was only nineteen, had swept her off her feet, as they would say in the movies she loved. She had been Bacall to his Bogie, Hepburn to his Tracy, Hellman to his Hammett. Theirs had been a perfect romance, marred only at the end by his marriage to someone else. Or had he been married all along? Hard to recall.

But it didn't matter. She would think only about the good times, about the Eden her existence had been while Jack had been part of it. It wasn't as if things had been so bad since. Not at all. For Audrey too had married well and happily, if not exactly passionately. Matthew had run an investment bank in the days when that had meant something. It had given him the means to offer Audrey, their three daughters, and their five or six grandchildren every material thing they could possibly want.

And there was security, because Matthew was solid and reliable, and there was something like love, because Matthew doted on her.

But the whole thing with Jack, whom she hadn't seen since college, was different. It was a true love story. Tonight was a brand new chance, the kind that doesn't come often in life, the kind one lets pass only at one's peril. But one had to be discreet, which was why Jack was not picking her up at the co-op but would meet her at their old favorite bar, Peacock Alley at the Waldorf Astoria. Audrey was certain that's where they had gone on their first date, back when she was at Barnard.

Peacock Alley would be fine. It was public, exposed, but none of Audrey's friends went there, so it seemed safe enough. And best of all, it was close by; she was confident she could remember how to get there.

There was a time when Audrey knew how to get everywhere. Uptown to downtown and eastside to west, she walked all over Manhattan. But because Matthew had recently become so protective, she hadn't gone anywhere on her own for some time. She missed her independence. She often pleaded with him to let her walk, but he insisted she use their driver, saying the streets were unsafe, "not like they used to be."

She dusted her face with sweet-smelling powder and smiled into the vanity mirror. She pulled a brush through her silvery hair and placed the beautiful felt hat on her head, the same green one she had worn that first night at Peacock Alley. How many years ago was that? She should figure it out before she saw Jack. But it was so hard to keep track these days.

She removed her make-up smock and finished dressing. It was a shame she hadn't thought to do that before putting her hat on, but it didn't matter; she managed to pull her dress over her head without too badly disturbing the hat. She put on her signature triple-strand pearls, which, unlike Jackie's, were real. Then she snapped on her favorite diamond earrings from Harry Winston, Matthew's favorite jeweler, and did a slow turn in the full-length mirror. She wondered if Jackie was still alive. Hadn't her husband died?

On a whim, Audrey slipped off her wedding and engagement rings. She smiled at her deception as she gently turned and tugged at the diamond solitaire. It moved up to her knuckle and stopped. She yanked at the big diamond, trying to get it past her knuckle, then tugged at the platinum band, but neither ring would budge beyond that point. She pulled on them more, working until her knuckle was red and raw. This was how Matthew kept her in line, she realized with a flash of ire. He made her wear rings that couldn't be removed. Just like a slave.

But that wouldn't stop her. She slammed the bedroom door as she walked into the hallway, forgetting the need for discretion. Then she moved quietly toward the foyer, listening for footsteps. Matthew was not home; he never was at this time of day. It was Constance, her so-called companion, and Nina, the maid, she had to watch out for.

"You look lovely, ma'am." It seemed Constance had been summoned by the slamming door. "Do you have something special planned?"

Audrey hated Constance's condescending tone, but replied, sweet as could be, "I felt like a lift, so I put on my favorite clothes."

"You look beautiful."

What an inane little person, Audrey thought, still annoyed about the rings. "Would you be good enough to brew me some tea, dear? Nina always makes it too strong. Yours is so much better." Audrey knew Constance loved a compliment. "Would you mind?"

"Of course not." Constance smiled.

"I'll wait here in the solarium."

"That's fine, ma'am. I'll be right back."

"No rush, dear."

As Constance went off to attend to the tea, Audrey moved as quickly as she could toward the front door, grabbing her cane, coat, and sunglasses from the hall closet. Then she slipped out the door and onto the elevator.

When the door opened into the building's small, paneled foyer, Audrey peeked out.

Perfect, that substitute doorman was on duty. He wouldn't know her.

"Taxi, ma'am?" he asked.

"No, thank you," she said proudly. "I'll walk."

She looked across the street at the big park whose name now eluded her. She breathed deeply and smiled. How lovely it was to be out here on her own; it was like being released from prison. She walked to the left, then turned left again, and crossed the next street, which she thought was Madison Avenue, before turning right and walking down it. She would have liked to drop in on her best friend Jeannine, who lived somewhere around here, but she had no time. She had something much more important to do.

But, what was it?

She paused, leaning on her cane, and adjusted her green felt hat. Of course, she was going to meet Jack at Peacock Alley. She moved on as quickly as her arthritic hip allowed. She felt wonderful, like she was nineteen, and she knew that, with the green felt hat, she looked it, too.

As Audrey walked past the canopied entrance to the Hotel Carlyle, she remembered all the times she and Jack had listened to Bobby Short there. Or was it she and Matthew? Oh dear, she needed to clarify that before she saw Jack. She must not make any blunders that would mar this magnificent afternoon and her one chance for a perfect future. When had she seen Bobby Short here? She marched in the door and found her way to the concierge desk.

"When did Bobby Short perform here?"

"He was here for years, right up until he died."

"Yes, but from when to when? Was he here in…" Audrey tried to calculate what years she had been with Jack, but she couldn't do it. "Would he have been here when I was in college?"

"When would that have been?"

"If you don't know the answer, just say so," Audrey said, annoyed that one couldn't get good service anywhere these days. She walked back out the door.

Audrey didn't have time to fool around with incompetent staff. She had to get to the Plaza before it was too late. So she walked back over to the park and turned left, feeling confident that was the way to go. She continued on for a long, long time, so long that her feet were sore, her legs weary, and her clothes wet with perspiration, before she finally arrived at *A la Vielle Russie*. She knew she was getting close now. That was where Jack—or Matthew?—had bought her the Faberge cigarette case.

And sure enough, there was The Plaza, across the street. Audrey limped into the intersection, leaning heavily on her cane. Perspiration made her sunglasses slip to the tip of her nose. She must not be late. He might leave.

Then she paused, in the middle of Fifth Avenue and Fifty-ninth Street. She looked up at the elaborately carved limestone façade of The

Plaza. It didn't look right. She couldn't picture Peacock Alley in that building. It didn't fit.

Before she knew what was happening, horns blared, cars swerved around her, brakes screeched, and someone grabbed her by the elbow and hustled her across the street. She nearly choked with fear, realizing this was what Matthew meant about the streets not being safe. She couldn't breathe. The man dragged her to the curb, her feet useless beneath her.

"Jesus, lady, watch out, would you?"

Shaking, she pushed her glasses up on her nose and looked at the man who still held her by the elbow. He was a policeman.

"You just about caused an accident, about got yourself killed. Watch the goddam traffic lights, would you?"

She looked into his eyes, which held both anger and concern. Such language from an officer; it shouldn't be allowed.

"Do you need help?" he said more quietly. "Can I call you a cab?"

Audrey shook her head.

"You sure?"

She nodded.

He gave her a once-over, then left her on the sidewalk at the corner of Central Park where a group of horse-and-buggy drivers awaited their passengers. Her elbow ached; her whole arm felt bruised where the policeman had yanked on it. She rubbed it as she pondered what to do next.

She wondered if the horsemen were Amish and asked a passing stranger, who didn't respond. "I was once in Pennsylvania Dutch country, many years ago. They all rode horse buggies," she told another passerby, who gave her a curious look and kept walking. People were not as polite as they used to be.

Standing in the middle of the sidewalk, Audrey was bumped and jostled by people in a hurry, who gave her haughty looks and asked her to move out of the way. But she couldn't move; she was exhausted. Her feet were sore, her bunions throbbed, her hip ached, and her head felt like it was spinning around and around.

What was she doing out here? Where was Constance? Where was Matthew? Where were her girls? Why did they leave her out here alone?

A tear crept down her cheek and slipped into her mouth. The traffic noise, construction jackhammers, and general din hurt her ears and made her feel bombarded. She longed for the silence of her co-op but had no idea how to get there. So she hobbled into the park, which looked green and sunny and cool, and tried to sit down beneath a tree. But her hip wouldn't allow it, and she couldn't walk all the way over to one of the benches, so she stood beneath the tree. That was better.

Why would Matthew leave her out here? And why would Constance desert her? Then it all made sense. Matthew and Constance must be lovers. They must have plotted to do away with her, to leave her out here like a helpless pauper. Well, she would show them. She would take up with Jack. That would teach them a lesson.

Oh, yes, of course. Jack. That was where she was going. She was on her way to meet Jack at Peacock Alley. He was waiting for her, and she mustn't be late. She tried to run but could only hobble slowly back over to the sidewalk.

"Excuse me, sir, which way is Peacock Alley?"

"Not a clue, lady."

"Ma'am, could you please direct me to Peacock Alley?"

"I don't know if it's around anymore, but it used to be at Waldorf. That way."

"Thank you."

Audrey headed toward the crowded, wide sidewalk that would take her to Jack. With armies of people moving this way and that, it was hard to keep a sense of direction, so she tried to follow a man in front of her who looked like he might be going to the Waldorf. But she soon lost track of him.

Just when she thought she couldn't take another step, she saw Saks Fifth Avenue across the street. Audrey pulled off her green felt hat and looked at the yellowed label inside. *Saks Fifth Avenue*. She crossed the street, careful to stay with the crowd this time, and walked into the giant department store, where she was overwhelmed and frightened by glitter and flash and colors and potions and creams and lotions and sprays of cologne.

"Can I help you? Interested in a quick make-over?"

Audrey breathed again. The young woman seemed nice. "Thank you, dear, but I'm afraid I haven't time. I have to meet Jack at the Waldorf-Astoria."

"Jack?"

"My boyfriend, dear."

"Cool! Enjoy!"

When Audrey caught a quick glimpse of herself in the young woman's mirror she wished she had had time for that makeover. Her shimmery green shadow and dark mascara combined to make bruises beneath her eyes. Her rosy cheeks were streaked with wet powder and rouge. But no matter. Jack would love her regardless, especially in her green hat.

"Could you direct me to the Waldorf-Astoria?" she asked the young woman.

"Sure. It's out that door and down to the right."

Audrey panted as she walked the last long block that would finally bring her to the Waldorf and Jack. When she saw the soaring Art Deco structure come into view, she felt a shiver run down her spine, just as they said in the movies. That's where she would meet Jack. She could only imagine where that would lead and what the shape of her new life would be.

She picked up her pace and crossed Park Avenue. Yes, she remembered this street well. As she walked past a line of black limousines toward door of the Waldorf, someone called her name.

"Jack?" She twirled around, smiling broadly as she sought the source of the voice.

"Audrey, dear, it's me." Matthew took her sore elbow and guided her gently toward the car. "We have to go home now."

"I can't, Matthew. I have to meet someone here."

"Audrey, you can't meet him," Matthew said quietly.

"Jealousy doesn't become you," she said with a flash of annoyance.

Matthew's eyes were red-rimmed and ringed with puffy circles. "Come on," he said wearily, trying to move her toward the car. "Let's go home."

"Leave me alone!" She tried to scream the words, but they didn't come out loudly. She tried to shake Matthew's hand off. "I have a date. I have to meet Jack." There. She'd said it.

Matthew didn't seem surprised.

"How did you find me?" she asked, still trying to shrug off his grip.

"Constance said you'd been talking about Peacock Alley since last week. You've had quite a walk, my dear."

"Yes I have, and now I have to go in and meet Jack, if you'll kindly take your hands off me." She tried to keep her feet glued to the ground, but Matthew kept her walking.

"Audrey, Jack's dead."

"Stop it. That's an evil thing to say."

"He had a stroke last week. You read the obituary yourself, my dear. Remember?"

"That's a horrible thing to say." Tears filled her eyes, and she tried to slap him but he backed up to evade her attack.

"I'm sorry, Audrey." Matthew looked her squarely in the eye.

As she stared back, she wondered for a terrifying instant if it could be true, if Jack could be dead. No, of course he wasn't; they had a date. But Matthew looked so tired and sad that Audrey realized how deeply hurt he must be to have made up this cruel story.

"Of course he's dead," she finally murmured quietly, humoring him. "I forgot for a minute. It's a shame, isn't it?" She smiled up at Matthew, hoping to make him feel better, but he still looked so unhappy, so ineffably weary. "Let's go home." She would call Jack from there and explain everything. Their date would have to wait. Matthew needed her.

Luke opened the car door, and Matthew put his hand on Audrey's shoulder, carefully easing her into the back seat. But her green hat was knocked off in the process and carried on a gust of wind down the block.

"My hat!" Audrey cried as she watched it tumble and sail away.

"Don't worry, my dear. It's such an old one." Matthew stepped aside so Luke could shut the door. He walked around the car and got in on the other side of the back seat. "I'll buy you a new one," he said with a brilliant smile, "any hat you want. We'll stop at Bergdorf's on the way home. Would you like that?"

Audrey nodded and tried to force a smile. She owed it to Matthew.

"Luke," Matthew said, settling into his seat, "take us to Bergdorf's."

Audrey brushed a tear off her face and stared out the window at the Waldorf-Astoria. "Yes," she said bravely, "to Bergdorf's."

POSTCARDS

Charlie Donovan lived in one room at the Empire Arms Hotel. He had a hot plate instead of a kitchen, hooks on the wall instead of a closet, a walk down the hall instead of a bathroom. A veteran of World War I, Charlie bore a mark of that conflict that dazzled me as a boy: he had only one leg. Where the other belonged was an empty pant leg folded over twice and secured with a large safety pin.

My family used to visit Charlie, a distant relative of my father's, every year at Christmastime. Mother saw the annual trek from our Long Island suburb to his home in the Bronx as fulfilling a charitable duty. Dad hated going and always tried to talk Mom out of it, but my sister and I loved the visit because Charlie had the world's greatest collection of postcards.

I learned about the Washington Monument, the Corn Palace, Las Vegas, the Tetons, Grauman's Chinese Theater, the Grand Canyon, and Yosemite through Charlie's cards. I got my first glimpse of Mount Rushmore and the Great Salt Lake. I learned about Grossinger's in the Catskills and the Beverly Hilton in California. I particularly favored the cards featuring people, like the Mexican sporting a sombrero or the fleshy, bikini-clad woman Charlie called a "Florida bathing beauty." He would wink at me each time he pulled that one out.

It wasn't only the postcards that kept my sister and me enthralled for so many years. We also loved watching Charlie's tall, lanky frame dangle like a marionette from his crutches, and we loved staring at that pant leg, trying to figure out exactly where his own leg ended and what it looked like under there.

***

The last time I saw Charlie was in 1964. I was fourteen years old and had to be talked into making the trip that year, as I had recently learned to resent all intrusions on my time, especially those involving family. I sulked in the back seat of our charcoal gray Oldsmobile Ninety-Eight as we rode into town.

"Look at those lovely Christmas decorations." My mother looked out the window at a passing shop.

"Why can't we have decorations like that, Dad?" my younger sister Nan whined. "Why can't we have a lit-up Santa on the roof or a flying reindeer?"

"How tacky," I murmured from my corner of the tufted black leather seat. I considered my sister ridiculously unsophisticated and saw right through my mother's chatter as a pathetic effort to get us enthused about our sorry mission of mercy.

Nan slapped the sleeve of my quilted ski jacket; I responded with a punch in the thigh.

"Why can't we get into the spirit of the season like we used to?" Mother said. "Remember how we all loved to cut the tree, then come home and drink cocoa?"

Dad's sideways look across the front seat indicated he had never found that particularly entertaining.

But I vaguely remembered that I once had, and was embarrassed by the memory. "How long do we have to stay at Charlie's? I've got stuff to do."

Dad looked at Mom as if wondering the same thing.

"We'll stay as long as he wants us to," Mother replied. "You can afford to give up one afternoon to bring some pleasure to Charlie. Besides, you used to love going to see him."

"That was when I was too stupid to know better," I said.

No one responded, which made the remark less satisfying than it should have been. I settled into my seat and stared out at the used car dealers, graffiti-covered warehouses, and abandoned storefronts that signaled we were getting close to the Empire Arms.

We parked around the corner from the hotel's front door. Dad told us twice to make sure we locked our doors, that this was not the kind of neighborhood where you left your car doors open. He said, as he did every year, that he didn't want to come back and find the car gone. "Then we'd have to move into the Empire Arms," he said with a laugh—as he did every year.

I used to hope our car would be stolen and we'd move in with Charlie. I liked the idea of looking at those postcards day after day, and thought sharing a bathroom with a bunch of old men would be a kick. Besides, I might catch a glimpse of Charlie's stump if we lived there.

But this year the idea of being stranded at the Empire, worlds away from my buddies and my new hi-fi system, stuck with godforsaken old codgers who had nothing better to do than hang out in the seedy front room they called a lobby—though it bore no resemblance to a lobby in any real hotel—was abhorrent. I made sure my door was securely locked.

The four of us trooped up the Empire's front steps. My mother, dressed in her navy blue cashmere coat, "because you wouldn't wear fur in this neighborhood," headed the line. She carried two large tins of cookies and one smaller one of fudge. Nan marched behind her, looking prim and prissy in her red stretch pants, blue jacket and Santa lapel pin. Dad went next, wearing corduroys and a tweedy jacket with an Aran sweater underneath. I brought up the rear, slouching along in my jeans and dirty blue ski jacket covered with patches from places my family had spent ski vacations over the years—Vail, Aspen, Snowmass, Lake Placid, Killington, Banff, and Kiel.

Mother stopped at the front desk and slapped the button on the silvery domed bell, which summoned a stocky, gray-haired woman in a cotton, floral-patterned housedress from the back room. She looked us over and told us to "Go on up—Charlie's expecting you." She stared at us as we marched toward the stairway, and the old men in the lobby looked up from their card games to gape as well. No one spoke; I was aware of each and every creak in the floor planks.

"Those coots give me the creeps," I said when we reached the stairwell.

"Be quiet," my mother said in a loud stage whisper.

Nan crossed her eyes at me and stuck out her tongue.

Dad said nothing.

"It smells like piss in here," I said, as we mounted the steep, concrete steps.

"You're gross," said Nan.

Mother shot me a threatening look.

Dad did nothing.

325

We emerged from the narrow steps into the third-floor hallway. The patterned carpet was brown and stained. The wallpaper was so faded its pink roses had become nearly indistinguishable from the once-ivory background. The odor of old tobacco hung in the air, along with something decidedly less pleasant that I couldn't put my finger on and didn't care to.

Mother knocked on Charlie's door. I could hear the rubber tips of his crutches plunk-plunking in our direction, stopping when they got close. I imagined him putting both crutches under one arm to free up a hand to open the door. Which he did.

"Merry Christmas, Charlie." Mother touched his shoulder and kissed the air near his hollow right cheek.

Dad stuck out his hand. "Happy holidays, Charlie." He glanced back and forth between the floor and Charlie's face.

"Same to you both." Charlie smiled. Then he turned to Nan and me. "Who are these big shots?" He said that every year.

"Charlie, it's *us*." Nan gave him a big hug and a wet kiss on the cheek.

"Hey old man," Charlie said to me, sticking out his hand. "How's my buddy?"

I limply shook his hand, releasing it as quickly as possible. I remembered how I used to hug him and practically climb all over him; now I could hardly stand to touch his powdery, wrinkled fingers, which felt like they would disintegrate if I grasped them too tightly.

After we were all in, Charlie shut the door, moved his crutches back into position under both arms, and swung in behind us. "Put your coats on the bed." His voice was thin and tinny.

Mom and Nan did as they were told, neatly laying their wool coats on the white chenille bedspread that had tiny holes I figured were made by moths. Dad and I kept our jackets on.

"Here you are, Charlie. All your favorites." Mother opened one of the cookie tins and passed it under his eyes.

"They look delicious, as always, Marjorie. Awful pretty too." Then he winked at me. "How 'bout passing those to my buddy over there."

"I don't want any," I said before Mother could move in my direction. I felt nauseous and didn't even want to smell them.

Mother glared at me.

"I'll have one," Nan said.

I wondered if she would ever grow up.

"Sure we can't interest you in a cookie, John?" Charlie said. "I seem to recall these chocolate ones here are your favorites."

I shook my head, then turned to stare out the window at the body shop across the street.

"So, you all look like the world's treating you right," Charlie said.

"Yes, Charlie," Mother said. "We're all doing fine."

"Fine," Dad said quietly.

"I got five A's on my report card, Charlie," Nan said, "and I gave a report on the Statue of Liberty. I told them about your postcard and what you said about the French sculptor who made it."

"Good for you, honey," Charlie said. "I suppose you want to take another look at that old card, huh?"

"Of course I do!" Nan said.

I was ashamed to have her as a sister.

"And what about your brother?" Charlie looked at me. "Think he wants to take a look at that bathing beauty, or maybe the gal in the grass skirt?"

Everyone was silent, waiting for me to answer. I pretended to be so fully engrossed in the streetscape out the window that I didn't hear the conversation.

"Well, let's you and me take a look," Charlie finally said to Nan. "If Johnny wants to join us later, he can."

I hated being called Johnny.

The old oak bureau that held the three boxes of postcards stood against the wall down from my window. Out of the corner of my eye, I saw Charlie lean his crutches against the side of the chest and slowly bend over to open the bottom drawer. The pinned-up gray pant leg dangled when he stood up and paused to regain his balance. "Here, honey," he said to Nan. "You take these over to the table for us."

Nan took the boxes, one at a time, then sat at the table with Charlie and Mother. Dad sat in a forest green easy chair with his head back, staring at the ceiling. Nan munched on cookies and shuffled through cards while Charlie told her about the places they depicted, like Key West, "A little island at the bottom of Florida," and the Tetons, "great horseback-riding country."

I wandered over to the bureau, so I could look in the mirror at the pimple I had popped in the car on the way over here. It was ugly

327

and red and oozed clear liquid. The bump on my nose, from where I had broken it in a game of touch football, seemed more prominent than ever, as did the freckles, which I detested as much as the pimple. But what startled me most was the hostility I saw in my eyes.

I looked away and tried to concentrate on the memorabilia stuck in the mirror's frame. There was a picture of my family from our Christmas card three years ago and old school photos of Nan and me smiling broadly. A couple of old birthday cards were stuck in the frame, as well, decorated with flowers and brown with age.

And there was that wrapping paper, as always. A neatly folded rectangle of silver foil that said CHARLIE in multicolored glitter. It had caught my eye when I was young, probably because of the sparkle. I asked Charlie back then where it had come from.

"It's from a gift," he had said.

"It's beautiful," I said.

"Yes, it is."

I stared at it now, noticing the dust, the creases in the paper, and the way the glitter looked so dry it would probably crumble right off if anyone touched it.

"Charlie," I said.

"Yes, John? You want to join us, buddy?"

"No. Tell me about the wrapping paper."

"There's not much to tell."

"Why have you kept it all this time?"

"Because it's pretty. Don't you think?

"Maybe it once was, but not anymore."

"John, don't be rude." Mother turned to Charlie. "It's festive, Charlie, decorative."

"The boy's right," Charlie said. "It's not as pretty as it used to be, but it's special to me."

"Of course it is, Charlie," Mother replied.

It occurred to me that my mother treated Charlie more like a child than she did Nan or me, as if he were mentally stunted or incapable. While he never seemed to mind, I suddenly knew as clearly as I knew anything that Charlie was at least as smart as she was and probably smarter.

"Who made it for you?" I asked.

"It came on a gift."

"I know," I said impatiently. "Who gave you the gift?"

328

In the mirror, I saw Dad look over at me, then at Charlie.

"It was from a friend," Charlie said, "a lady I knew a long time ago."

I had never before considered that Charlie might have had friends. "What lady?" I persisted for reasons that are no longer clear to me.

"That's enough, John," Dad said. "It's none of your business."

"It's okay, Jack." Charlie turned back to me. "A lady I knew before the war. Her name was Stella." He almost whispered the last sentence.

"Before the war? You mean this is *that* old?"

"No, not quite." Charlie smiled. "She gave me this when I came back home. But it's still pretty old." Then he turned his attention to Nan, resuming commentary on a picture of Niagara Falls.

The walls of that room became horribly confining. I was unutterably depressed by the old, brown cards stuck in the mirror and the ones Charlie and Nan were going through. I was sickened by the smell of mildew and chilled by the cold drizzle outside. I hated the anguished coughing I heard through the wall and the slow padding of feet in the hallway. I hated the beige sweater Charlie wore over the white shirt that was now nearly transparent, and I hated that it was the same sweater and shirt he wore every year. I hated the cup for his teeth that sat by the bed, and I hated that missing leg. All that had captivated me before suddenly repulsed me. Most of all, I hated that Charlie was a relative of mine and that he lived this way and in this place and that all of this was therefore connected to me.

I turned away from the mirror and looked at my family. "Can we leave now?"

"We just got here, John," Mother said. "What's the matter with you?"

"Nothing, I just can't stand it here."

"God damn it, John," my father bellowed. "What the hell is wrong with you?" But I knew he knew exactly what I meant.

"You creep," Nan chimed in.

Charlie looked at me through his flimsy wire-rimmed glasses, his watery blue eyes staring straight through me, piercing my heart. "No one's keeping you here, Johnny," he said quietly. "You can go anytime your family's ready."

We didn't leave right away; my parents had a point to make about me not getting my way by being rude, and they were going to make it. We probably stayed longer than we would have had I not said a word. Dad went back to staring at the ceiling, Nan and Charlie went back to their cards with Mom looking on, and I gazed out the window, keeping an eye on the Olds Ninety-Eight to make sure no one stole it.

As it turned out, that was our last visit with Charlie. We never saw him again. He became one of those holiday traditions that fell by the wayside, like a box of old ornaments or cutting our own Christmas tree. It probably had to do with the way I behaved that day, but I'm not sure. We never talked about it. Charlie was, quite simply, forgotten.

***

Nearly twenty-five years later, I received a call at the office from a lawyer, informing me that Charlie had passed away two weeks earlier. He had died at the age of 96 in his room at the Empire Arms Hotel.

"He left you a bequest," the lawyer said.

"I can't imagine he had anything to leave," I said.

"It's not much. Just a collection of picture postcards."

"It's all he had?" I asked.

"As far as we can tell."

"How long did you represent Charlie?" I was making conversation while trying to digest the fact that Charlie had been alive all these years. I had no idea.

"I didn't really represent him," the lawyer said. "I met him when I was visiting my uncle who lived at the Empire, and he asked me to draw up a simple will."

"That was nice of you."

"No big deal," the lawyer said. "Charlie really wanted you to have those cards."

I didn't know what to say or think. "Did he have any other relatives?"

"As far as I know, it was just you and your sister."

"Did he have any friends? Anyone to arrange a funeral or take care of his things?"

"The funeral home took care of the burial—cremation, actually. I asked them to hold the ashes for you." The lawyer sounded apologetic. "It took me a while to track you down."

"No, I mean, that's okay. Thank you for taking care of it." I was trying to get my mind wrapped around the notion that a relative of mine had died without having anyone other than the nephew of the man down the hall to attend to anything. "I'll be glad to pay for whatever services you rendered to Charlie."

"That's not necessary. Charlie gave me something out of his Social Security check. He insisted. Anyway, it was a *very* simple will." He chuckled. "You've heard the sum total of it."

"Thank you."

"I left the postcards for you in Charlie's room," the lawyer said. "I thought you might want to go through his things."

"His things? I hardly knew him —"

"If you're not comfortable with that, the hotel will take care of it. I can have the cards delivered."

"No, I—I'm okay with it."

I cleared my calendar for the rest of the day, and left for the Empire Arms; I went alone, since I had never mentioned Charlie to my wife. I parked my black BMW in the same block where Dad had always parked the Olds.

The neighborhood hadn't changed much, except that more of the storefronts were empty, more of the warehouses abandoned. The liquor store on the corner was still in business, and young men huddled in packs on the sidewalk outside. The body shop was gone, but the sign remained: *WE TREAT THE BEST CHASSIS IN TOWN AND WE TREAT 'EM BEST.*

The Empire Arms looked the same too, but the mood was different. Quieter. A couple of withered, wispy men sat in torn chairs in the lobby, but there were no card games, no conversations. I approached the desk and hit the bell that still sat on the counter. An old woman walked slowly out of the office.

"You must be here about Mr. Donovan."

"How did you know?"

"His lawyer said you were coming. We don't get many visitors." She looked at me with rheumy, red-rimmed eyes. "I remember when you used to visit Charlie."

I stared at her without recognition. "That was years ago. You have an exceptional memory."

"I have an exceptional memory for years ago, but don't ask me about this morning." She tried to smile but her lip cracked and bled. She turned to take a key off the pegboard behind her.

"Have you got a new tenant moving in?" I asked.

She handed me the key and shook her head. "Nobody moves in—only out. You remember how to get up there?"

"Yes." I walked toward the stairs.

"You know, your uncle was a fine man."

I turned back toward her. "Charlie wasn't my uncle."

"Great uncle?"

I shook my head.

"What then?"

"I'm not sure," I said. "I never knew how we were related."

"Why didn't you ask?"

I didn't have an answer.

The claustrophobic stairway looked the same as always, but the smells were different. More medicinal. Less smoky. Staler, if that were possible.

I turned the skeleton key in the lock of Charlie's door, number 4D, and went in. The white chenille bedspread had been replaced by an orange synthetic blanket. Otherwise, it all looked the same. Charlie's crutches leaned against the wall next to the bed. The cup on his bedside table was empty; I was glad someone had remembered his teeth.

I walked to the dresser and looked at the mirror that still held a measure of Charlie's life. I was stunned to see Nan's and my school pictures still stuck in the frame, and those age-darkened birthday cards down below. And the silver wrapping paper. CHARLIE. The name was defined now more by glue than remnants of glitter.

An empty Old Spice bottle, a black comb missing several teeth, a small pearly button, and an open cardboard box filled with large safety pins—the kind Charlie used to pin up his pant leg—lay on the dresser top. I opened the top drawer and found four pairs of gray trousers, neatly folded, and two white shirts with frayed collars and cuffs. The second drawer held rolled-up black socks and dingy underwear.

I opened the bottom drawer slowly, less afraid of what I would find than of how I would react to it. The three familiar shoeboxes were all in place, along with one I had never seen. I took a long look at those three boxes before taking them out, putting them on the table and lifting their lids.

I dumped the cards out ceremoniously, each box in turn, and shuffled through the piles. The Grand Canyon, the Statue of Liberty, Las Vegas, they were all still there. I thought of all the business trips I had made throughout Europe, Africa, and Asia and wondered why it had never once occurred to me to send Charlie a card.

I went back for the fourth shoebox and dumped its contents alongside the postcards. Fragile envelopes, pastel-colored stationary, and flowery greeting cards, all faded with age, fell out of the box. Each one featured the same spidery, elegant script, made with a fountain pen and filled with swirls, flourishes, and sinuous trailing lines. It was a feminine hand, not easy to read but lovely to look at.

I pulled a thin, white sheet out of an envelope. The paper cracked at the crease and tore when I unfolded it.

My dear Charlie, my soldier hero, the letter began, *I read your letters over and over, and I stare at your picture from morning to night. You are everything to me.* The letter went on in this vein for a few sentences, then turned to news of the woman's life, of her family, and of the town in which she lived—Oil City, Pennsylvania, the same town, it appeared from the context, in which Charlie had lived. Why hadn't I known that? The letter closed with the following words: *You are my life, my dear Charlie. All I think about is holding you once again, as I will in a few short weeks. Your loving Stella.*

I pieced the stationary back into place as well as I could and tucked it into the envelope. I thought I smelled perfume emanating from it, but it had to be my imagination. I perused more letters, all addressed to *Private Charles Donovan* in care of a U.S. Army regiment. Each was written during the war by Stella, the woman plainly destined to become Mrs. Charles Donovan; she often referred to their wedding plans. But the last letter was addressed to Private Donovan in care of the Veteran's Hospital in Pittsburgh.

My dear Charlie,

After giving much thought to the conversations we had at your hospital bedside, I have sadly concluded that you are right. We are not meant to be man and wife.

My father says that what happened to you is a sign from God. He says that even if I think I could live with a man missing a leg, God does not intend it to come to pass. Nothing like this happens for nothing, he said, and we should not ignore such signs. I am young and whole and alive, he said, and need a man who is, as well.

This does not mean you have no life in you, Charlie. Not at all. Only that we are no longer right for each other. You will find another woman, and our lives will go on, and we will live in God's finest graces.

I wish you all good things, Charlie. I still regard you with great fondness and esteem, but I must ask you not to continue our correspondence, as any further contact might weaken our resolve.

With all kind thoughts, greatest respect, and deep love,
Your Stella

I stared at that delicate paper, admiring the beautiful penmanship, the carefully constructed letters, before folding it and placing it back in its envelope. I had intended to put it back in the box, but found myself crumpling the envelope into a tight, disintegrating ball, as small as I could make it, and throwing it across the room.

My stomach churned, as it had the last time I was here, and my head pounded. I had never met this Stella, but felt as if I knew her altogether too well. I stared up at the foil wrapping paper on the mirror and wondered how Charlie could have looked at it every day of his life, this gift from a woman who could see no further than the air where his second leg belonged.

For Stella, too, he had been as easy to discard as a box of tattered Christmas ornaments.

I took my coat off, loosened my tie, unbuttoned my collar and opened the window to let in the wintry air. Then I sat with the other three shoeboxes and read each and every postcard.

As I looked out at the darkening sky, I wondered, for the first time, what Charlie had done in this room for all those years. How had he made the far-too-many hours of each day go by? What did he care about? Did he ever love another woman after Stella? Did he have any friends? Would anyone, other than the woman at the hotel desk, remember he had even lived?

I carefully took the piece of once-shiny wrapping paper from the rim of the mirror and placed it in the box with Stella's letters, all except the last one. Then I put on my coat, stuck my tie in my pocket, picked up the four shoeboxes, and drove home, to the same town I had grown up in.

Judy Pomeranz

PEOPLE DON'T FLY

People don't fly. That was my first supremely inappropriate thought when I saw Mr. Jacobson shoot past the window on a downward trajectory. *People don't fly.*

I remember being surprised, maybe even shocked at the time, but not horrified like I should have been. I've replayed the scene a thousand times now, and it's always the same. I'm sitting at my desk in my BVD's, getting ready to write a check for the minimum balance due on my VISA bill, when I catch a glimpse of this red and black thing zooming past my window.

The window was grimy, so I didn't have a clear view. Besides, I wasn't really looking. I've thought a lot about this lately—way too much, actually—and I've concluded that the brain does something weird to avoid making sense of this kind of thing, because it doesn't want to. But, at the same time, you know kind of what's happening. So, I think I knew it was a body—or a person—and I may have even known it was Mr. Jacobson wearing those stupid black jeans he was much too old for and that silky red shirt that reminded me of Wayne Newton.

Yeah, I knew from the get-go what was going on, but it didn't *strike* me. I saw it and thought, *that couldn't be Mr. Jacobson, because people don't fly.*

It was a couple seconds later—maybe a half-second—when I bolted out of my chair and ran to the window to see what he would look like splattered on the ground. So, I must have known what it was—and who it was—because when I ran over there, I knew what I was going see on the pavement.

I stared; that's all I could do. I just stared at that mess of a person who resembled a pile of doll parts. It wasn't gross; I didn't see much blood, though it would have been hard to say, considering the red shirt. It's not like there were brains splattered all over the place. He mostly looked messy. And unhappy.

***

I first saw Mr. Jacobson the day I moved into the building, right after I split up with Amanda. When she and her new inamorata (her word) took over the rent-controlled one-bedroom she and I had shared on Columbus Avenue, I moved down to the East Village because it was cheap and as far away as I could get from the two of them.

I didn't have much to move, and had managed to get what I had into the back end of my buddy Jeff's pick-up. I kept thinking about the lead-in to those old Beverly Hillbillies reruns as we drove that damn truck through Manhattan, with a mattress, a huge torn khaki duffle bag, my puke-green armchair that smelled like stale beer, box springs Jeff had scared up from his group house in Brooklyn, and fifteen boxes of miscellaneous crap in the open truck-bed behind us. We even sang the theme song as we drove.

We parked on the street in front of the building, in the *No Parking: Entrance* zone spot, carried the stuff through the so-called lobby and shoved it into the freight elevator, which is actually an ordinary elevator that's more dented and scratched-up. As we were trying to cram the mattress into the elevator car, I saw old Mr. Jacobsen behind me.

He watched us as we maneuvered and manipulated the way-too-large thing into the way-too-small space. We were pushing and shoving and sweating and swearing and yelling and grunting and making a big fucking deal about this project, and all the while Mr. Jacobson—whose name I didn't know at the time—stood there watching.

"Jesus *Christ*, man," Jeff finally said to him, "either help us out here or get out of the way."

The old man was not actually in the way, but he was giving Jeff the creeps, the way he stood there staring into space and at us, and not saying or doing anything. Mr. J shuffled to the front door and walked out. He wasn't mad, wasn't anything. Basically vacant. Nobody home.

"Asshole," Jeff muttered.

"Yeah."

***

I didn't see him again until months later, nor did I think about him. He's not the kind of guy you think about.

I had come in from work; we'd gotten off early because of a freak snowstorm that paralyzed the city. I was in the elevator and the doors were beginning to close when I heard this voice say, "Hold it!" It was a Minnie-Mouse voice. Not squeaky, but high-pitched and funny. I stuck my hand into the space between the doors, and when they snapped back open, the owner of the voice joined me in the car.

"Thanks." She pulled off a red and blue knit stocking cap. Her sneakers— old Keds, not the new *athletic footwear*—were soaking wet and made squishy noises when she shifted her weight. She smiled up at me. "Even with cold feet, I love snow."

"I hate it," I said, just to be perverse.

"I'm from Minnesota," she said, as if that explained everything.

I nodded, and the doors opened onto the sixth floor. My floor.

"We're practically neighbors," she said with ridiculous excitement since what did she *think* we were, for God's sake, living in the same building. "I'm in 7G."

"I'm in 6F," I said.

"I'm going make some cocoa. Want to come up?"

I'm not a cocoa fan, but I liked the way she looked. Blonde and tiny and cute in a pug-nosed, Gidget way. Spunky. I don't often hang out with spunky people, but she looked good to me. It was nasty and gray outside, my apartment would be cold, I was pissed from being bossed around all day at work, and this little red-cheeked person who was making cocoa appealed to me. It's not something I can explain.

So, I said sure. "Let me drop off my coat." I started down the hall toward my apartment. "I'll be right up."

"7G," she repeated, as if I'd already forgotten.

***

Judy Pomeranz

When I got upstairs, I knocked on her door, trying to "rap smartly," a line I remembered from an English whodunit. I do read from time to time, even though most people I know find that hard to believe. I figured a spunky individual would appreciate a "smart rap." And sure enough, she opened the door with a big smile.

"I'm Loretta Homer." She stuck out her hand as I walked into her apartment.

"Lance Barker. Nice to meet you."

Then she looked past me, out into the hall, and craned her neck to the left. "Mr. Jacobson, how nice to see you."

When I looked to see who she was talking to, I saw the crazy guy Jeff and I had seen in the lobby. He didn't respond, didn't even acknowledge her.

"Mr. Jacobson, this is Lance," Loretta said.

I nodded in his direction, but he still didn't respond. He stared at me, the way he had before. Maybe he nodded; it's hard to say.

"Would you like cocoa?" Loretta asked him.

This spunky thing was turning spooky now. What was the *deal* asking everyone in sight if they wanted cocoa. He didn't answer.

"I'll bring you some," she said.

Then he went into an apartment across the hall, just above mine, and we went into Loretta's, where she made that cocoa. After delivering the promised mug to Mr. Jacobson, she demonstrated that chocolate-making farm girls from Minnesota are not necessarily the virginal prudes you might imagine. It was a good evening.

***

After that, I spent a lot of time with Loretta. She was an artist; she had a studio in an old warehouse in the Brooklyn, where she made huge paintings of things I was never able to recognize or respond to. Still, I used to tell her how much I liked them.

But what I really liked was *her*. She was sweet, and spunky, and, most of all, lonely. She had been in New York for six or eight months and had met few people. She said I gave her a nice, warm feeling, and she gave me one. She was only twenty-five, but had this grown-up, confident way about her. She was easy with herself and with people. She honestly, genuinely liked people, which made her different from me.

340

To me, most people are in the way. They're in line ahead of you; they're in cars creating gridlock and driving like maniacs; they're buying the last onion bagel; they're kicking up a fit because you're double-parked; they're texting in the movie theater; they're asking stupid questions; and they're jostling you in the street; they're screaming for you to work twice as hard and fast as any human being possibly can.

But to Loretta, people were magical. All these damn people. She used to tell me how each one had a value and a spark (that's the word she used, a spark) all their own. She liked to talk to people and see where they were from, what they were interested in, what they liked. She even liked to "incorporate their spirits" into her paintings. She got a kick out of that, though I never understood it. I'd rather have a good TV show and a beer than a conversation.

But I did like talking to Loretta, and I especially liked what we did after we talked.

***

"Why do you bother with him?" I asked her one night when she was making spaghetti for dinner. Loretta wasn't much of a cook, but she did do a few things well, and spaghetti was one of them.

"Bother with who?" She ladled red sauce over the pasta and covered the whole thing with tin foil.

"Mr. Jacobson."

"He's sweet."

"He's never said a word to you."

"He doesn't have to talk. It's in his eyes. He has lovely eyes."

"He has vacant eyes," I said, pleased with my choice of words. It was rare for the right one to pop into my mouth. "He has eyes like a dead person. He doesn't talk, he doesn't react, he doesn't do anything but roam the halls and stare at people. He gives me the creeps."

"He's lonely," she said, as if that ended the conversation, then she left the apartment to deliver Mr. Jacobson's spaghetti dinner

***

Loretta talked to old Mr. J like you would talk to a person in a coma. She would chatter on about the weather, her work, the Mets, whatever. She would talk and talk and never expect a word in return. She brought him dinner now and again, not every night, just once in a while. And if she didn't see him for a few days, she would tap on his door to see how he was doing. He would open the door, grunt, and she'd go home happy.

I was at her apartment, watching the evening news one night, when she did just that. "I'm going to check on Mr. Jacobson. I'll be right back."

I nodded and kept watching TV.

She came back to the apartment and sat on the ottoman in front of my chair. She was blushing and smiling as big a smile as I'd ever seen on her.

"What's up?"

"He talked." She said it breathlessly.

"He *talked?*" I felt like we were in that part of Heidi where she drops her crutches and walks. "Jesus Christ, What'd he say?"

"He thanked me for the spaghetti."

"He said all those words?"

"Yes."

"What brought it on? Why would he talk all of a sudden? And, if he can talk, why didn't he do it before?"

"I don't know, but I'm so excited he did."

"Why?"

"I always believed there was someone inside that body, but I wanted proof." She turned her little elf face toward mine and fixed those big blue eyes on me. "Does that sound crazy?"

"A little." I pretended to be joking, but I meant it. It was a little crazy, but it was so *her* that it was also cute.

"If I ever leave here, will you take care of him?" she asked, suddenly serious.

"Where are you going?"

"Nowhere," she said quickly. "I just meant in case. I can't stand thinking of him all alone here, with no one to visit him."

"What did he do before you came along? He got by, right?"

She pondered the question. Finally she nodded. "He did."

And so I managed to end the conversation without having to make a commitment.

***

Loretta did leave. She moved back to Minnesota six months after we met. She decided she didn't like New York, even though her art was going places and she was getting noticed, which was what she had hoped for when she moved here. But she didn't like it. "It's not me," is the way she put it. That made me wonder what place would be *me*. It was a new concept, this idea that there might be me-places and not-me-places. I thought you were where you were and made do with it.

When I look back, her leaving was inevitable. She was one of those people who pops into your life like a fly or a mosquito, and then buzzes out again. One of those people who leaves a little mark on you, like a bug leaves a welt, a mark that goes away as fast as a mosquito bite, even though the bug-juice might hang around in your system longer. The bottom line is these people don't stay. And she didn't.

***

After Loretta left New York, I saw a lot of Mr. Jacobson, not that I wanted to. He wandered more than ever; he'd lost his only visitor. I would see him on the sidewalk in front of the building, standing there, staring. I would see him in our sorry excuse for a lobby, the grubby little place outside the elevators. I saw him in the park across the street, sitting on a bench, watching kids play. I even saw him on *my* floor, the sixth, where he had no business being. I never knew whether he was lost or lurking.

I never spoke to him. I'm not the kind of guy who smiles at someone, or winks, or says a friendly or witty thing. Whenever I saw him, I'd try to get out of the vicinity before he could spot me. When he did catch sight of me, he'd stare, as usual. I never found those eyes kind, the way Loretta did. Just spooky.

***

The last time I saw him, not counting the day he went flying, he was standing next to the elevator on the ground floor when I came in the door. Something about him made me think of my father, who is not a guy I have good feelings about—and that's putting it mildly. The way he hung out there reminded me of my old man, who also used to hang out while my mother worked and I went to school or did whatever the hell I did in those days. My dad would hang out on the sofa with a brew, or with a fifth, if times were good. He would stare too, like Mr. J, but at the TV, so it wasn't as bizarre. He was watching something, as opposed to watching nothing.

I walked past him the way I always did, and he stared at me, the way he always did. But he looked at me more carefully than usual, if that makes any damn sense. He didn't seem so vacant. It was like he was about to say or do something.

I didn't hang around to find out if he would. I didn't want it to happen because I didn't want to have to deal with it. I might have smirked or looked disgusted, because I was. I hated the guy. He represented everything about New York that sent Loretta back to Minnesota, and that pissed me off. It's not like I expected her to be here forever, but without people like Mr. J around this hellhole, she might have lasted longer. So I might have shot him a dirty look, but not on purpose.

***

A couple hours later, he flew past my window, and all hell broke loose. The cops came by and talked to everyone, including yours truly:

"Did you know him well?"

"Did he have family or friends?"

"Did he seem unhappy?"

"Do you think he would have jumped? Any reason to think he might have been pushed?"

My answers were: "no," "no," "not anymore than anyone else," "yes," and, "no."

He wasn't pushed. Who the hell would bother? There was no one on this earth who cared enough about Mr. J to have pushed him. Or to have saved him. Sure, he might have jumped. Why the hell not? What did he have going on here that would have made him want to stick around? What do any of us have going on here?

He had Loretta for a while; so did I. She was the kind of person who made a difference in things like this. But I wasn't about to get into that with the cops. She was long gone, and it wouldn't have been fair to bring her into this.

344

I actually started to wonder if she'd ever really been here. There was no trace of her—it's not like she had left anything behind. Maybe she was a mirage-thing, like something from the *Twilight Zone*, or one of those visions people at Bellevue have. Maybe I'm as nuts as old Mr. J.

I finally told one of the cops, the third one who came by asking the same stupid questions, to butt out. I told him that Mr. J did what he did. No one did it to him, and it was no one else's business. Anybody has a right to jump out his window. As I said it, I realized I admired the old bastard for taking matters into his own damn hands and doing something with his life. He was a lot gutsier than I'd given him credit for being, a hell of a lot gutsier than I was, or anyone else I knew. *Gutsy or nutsy,* I thought, and chuckled to myself at my poetry.

***

The next day, I looked at the weather forecast for Minneapolis in the *Times.* That made the place real to me, and made me feel like Loretta might be out there somewhere. After Mr. J took his flight, I wanted to believe she was somewhere in the world, though I felt like a complete asshole for thinking that and would never have said it out loud. Don't get me wrong, mostly I still think people are in the way.

I never heard anything more about Mr. Jacobson, and I don't care to. I don't know if he had a decent burial or if he had any family. I don't know where he came from or how he ended up here. I don't know why he did what he did, and I don't need to know; I never made any commitment.

The crazy thing is, he was probably less in the way than most people. But still, it's kind of a funny thing to think about and kind of makes the whole thing about him a little sad.

Judy Pomeranz

ALL THE RAGE

"…exquisite. These are truly breathtaking."

"Conceptually, this one is provocative."

Maya wandered though the cavernous, white-walled rooms of the Gavinski Gallery's new space in Chelsea, admiring once again the installation of her *Tales of Hoffman* series. The twelve enormous canvases were hung such that they spoke to one another, played off one another, released each other's energy. Yes, the installation she and Larry Gavinski had finally agreed upon created a synergy that made the whole series much more powerful than the sum of its parts.

"She's a splendid formalist."

"What the hell are these all about?"

"…so retro! The expressionistic style takes me back to the fifties."

As Maya was particularly interested in hearing the candid comments of people observing her new work, she insisted Larry not introduce her at the exhibit's opening. She preferred roaming anonymously through the gallery, sipping wine, listening.

"…strikingly new. I've never seen anything like it."

"My dog could have done this."

"These are so ordinary, so banal."

"…been done before. Derivative."

Uncertainty made Maya crave feedback. She wouldn't call it creative insecurity; that was a cliché. No, it was simpler than that, and far less dramatic. Maya worked alone, without regard to or much knowledge of what others in the New York art world were doing or what they might think of what she was doing. So, she never had the slightest clue how her work would be received until she released it into the world.

Maya's equanimity in the face of this uncertainty, and her ability to listen as an objective third party to both positive and negative critiques of her paintings, stemmed from her new status as a foolproof commodity. Ever since her exhibit at the Cappelli Gallery, where Jock Morganstern famously paid four times the asking price for the privilege of buying each and every item before the show opened to the public, Maya had been golden. While she didn't know if her works were good, she did know they would sell, and for much more money than they could possibly be worth.

"Hey Maya!"

She saw Jake Farnstein from *Art Times*.

"Shhh. That's her."

"That's the artist?"

"She's lovely, isn't she?"

Her anonymous eavesdropping was over for the night.

"Hello, Jake," she said to the plump man dressed in dull khaki tones that matched his skin.

"Maya, you've outdone yourself. This is gorgeous stuff."

"You think?" she said modestly.

"Best ever, and you'll come up with something even better next time. I can't get over the way you keep evolving. These are Twombly, Frankenthaler, and Diebenkorn all thrown together, maybe even a hint of Pollock."

Talk about derivative, she thought.

"You've nailed the best of all of 'em," he raved. "Terrific stuff."

"Thanks." She drained her wine glass. She nodded to Jake and moved toward the bar for a refill. The high praise would have been pleasant if it had come from anyone other than Farnstein. He was such a sycophant. The moment an artist was discovered by the right collectors, Jake would shower the creative soul with high praise, as if he had been the one to make the discovery. Jake had ignored Maya until Morganstern came along.

"Hello, I'm Fred Barger." A middle-aged, balding man stuck out his hand to Maya. "I just want to say how much I admire your work. There's a drive to it that resonates with me."

Maya smiled and mouthed her thanks, even though she knew he was the one who had called it "phony."

"You're a true colorist," said a skinny woman dressed all in black. "These are ethereal."

Funny, Maya thought, *the woman's earlier word was "banal."*

***

By the end of the evening, all twelve paintings had red dots on their labels. A sell-out. Of course. Maya leaned into an Eames chair in the gallery's back room, kicked off her stiletto-heeled shoes, propped up her thin feet, and sipped wine.

Larry Gavinski raised his glass in her direction. "You've done it again, Maya. They couldn't put their money down fast enough. I couldn't hold on to anything of yours if I wanted to."

Maya smiled, wondering how long the buzz of the wine and the buzz of her fame would last.

"Do you really think they're good, Larry?"

"Are you kidding? We had a bidding war on *The Diva*. Some guy I've never dealt with before wanted it so badly he paid three times the price to get it away from Meyerhoff."

"Crazy," she said softly, shaking her head. "But do you think they're good art? Do they *mean* something to the people who are buying them?"

"Why else would they spend the money?" Larry looked at her as if she weren't making sense.

***

The next morning, Maya climbed the three flights of stairs to her SoHo studio. She breathed in the smell of oil and turpentine that permeated the air as she neared the fourth floor. Those smells were among the few things that made her feel like a real artist these days.

Entering the studio, she looked at the remnants of *Tales of Hoffman*. She had worked on the canvases right up until Tuesday morning when Larry insisted they *had* to begin installing. Her paint-filled palette was still on the rickety square table next to the wall where she propped her canvases; the floor was dappled with viridian green and cerulean blue she had used in the final painting in the series; an almost-empty bottle of Chardonnay sat on the floor near the spot where she had stood for way too many hours on Tuesday afternoon looking at her huge canvases, agonizing over whether they were worthy.

Whatever that meant.

She tossed the bottle into the garbage can and scraped paint off her palette. She liked to start each new series fresh, preferring not to be distracted or influenced by colors that remained from the previous one. She ran the palette knife over the smooth wood surface, lifting globs of pigment and wiping them onto a heavy cloth, pondering what she might try next.

The period of transition between exhibitions used to be a time of intense intellectual challenge for Maya. It was often wrenching, difficult, but ultimately satisfying. Before beginning something entirely new, she would sketch, draw, and play with clay; she would read literary works, Greek philosophers, or New Age mystics; she would allow lines, shapes and colors to tumble around in her mind; she would study old and new masters at the Metropolitan Museum and MoMA; she would watch films to get ideas about narrative, light, and energy. She would allow her formal and conceptual notions of time and space to gel. Only after that, often many months later, would she begin to paint. She would slowly push her brush in the direction of her thoughts. Each color had a meaning; each stroke was a means to a pre-conceived or fully considered end. Each painting was a supreme act of faith.

But that was before the Capelli show. Since the Morganstern purchase, Maya's working method had changed gradually but dramatically. Her primary goal had become putting paint on canvas at a rapid enough rate to fill the many galleries around the country and abroad for which she had committed to do shows. The contemplative approach had become a lost and much-lamented part of her history.

So now, knowing her next exhibit—a one-woman show at the Pietro Gallery in Beverly Hills—was only a month away, she squirted thick globs of random hues onto the clean palette, propped up a pure white canvas, and started painting.

***

Within two weeks, Maya had turned out fifteen new canvases. She called them *Great Expectations*, because that was the first title that jumped out at her when she turned to her studio bookshelf. They were finished; she didn't even feel the need to work them over. She didn't care to look at them.

Fifteen in two weeks. A record. She had never done anything close to that before. She had slapped the paint onto the canvas with brushes, slathered it with her palette knife, dripped it off a stick, and smudged it with a cloth. She even pressed her fingerprints into a few spots, remembering a conservator at the Met once told her that fingerprints left in old paintings could help determine attribution. It was soothing to pretend that, hundreds of years from now, someone might care.

***

"...spectacular energy!"

"There's a clarity of vision here I've never seen in Maya's work before."

"...glorious use of light and color."

L.A. audiences were easier to please than New Yorkers. The people who came to openings here thought it showed their sophistication if they understood and appreciated what the artist was trying to do, if they "got it," whereas New Yorkers proved their *bona fides* by criticizing. So, Maya took the remarks she overheard at the Pietro Gallery with a larger grain of salt than usual.

But she couldn't ignore the money. The money spoke loudly in validation of her new approach. Giorgio Pietro had talked her into pricing her paintings in the low seven figures, much more than her earlier works had sold for, even the Morganstern paintings. And once again, by the end of the opening evening, all fifteen works displayed red dots. Three had been the subject of bidding wars.

As Maya sipped a drink with Giorgio at the Four Seasons on Doheny, she reflected on what an odd business she was involved in.

"Did you ever feel your own life was happening *to* you," she said to Giorgio, "instead of *because* of you? Like it's all happening in *spite* of you?"

"Sure. "Been there."

"Really?" Maya was excited to have someone with whom she could share her concerns, someone who understood. "When I was thirty, I was doing my best work, and I was lucky to sell four or five paintings a year. At thirty-five, I'm mass-producing, and I could sell any piece of crap I signed my name to. It doesn't make sense."

"Destiny's a funny thing." Giorgio downed a handful of nuts and leaned toward her earnestly. "Complicated. I was confused about the whole karma business myself until I went to this phenomenal place near Big Sur. I recommend..."

That's when Maya remembered she was in California, and tuned out.

***

After the Pietro show, Maya's confidence grew with her success. She was interviewed by art journals and the popular press; she was the subject of photo spreads in fashion magazines and profiles on network news shows. She was in such demand socially, she couldn't even respond to all the invitations. She was a personality, and she played the role with a panache that surprised her.

When asked about her working methods, Maya pled privacy and superstition. She explained that she didn't like talking about her personal creative process, fearing that such talk might interfere with its effectiveness. As luck would have it, she was an important enough figure now that interviewers didn't press her for answers she didn't want to give; they didn't want to jeopardize their access.

Maya lost interest in eavesdropping at openings; she knew what people would say. Besides, she was beyond the point where anonymity was an option. She attended openings briefly, accepted the kudos, and bowed out early.

The buzz went on and on. Maya could do no wrong.

***

Then something strange happened.

Maya arrived in her new, high-priced studio in Chelsea one fine spring morning, ready to slap paint on canvas as she had done the day before. She had a London show coming up in three weeks and was determined to finish ten paintings in two days, to allow herself time in the Hamptons before the exhibit.

She opened a bottle of wine and turned on the soundtrack to *La Cage Au Folles*; listening to *We Are What We Are* always energized her and encouraged her painting arm to fly. She picked up the palette, which she had covered tightly the night before, and pressed a large, square-tip brush into brilliant red paint. The oil smelled delicious; the paint felt thick, gooey, and sensuous. Maya twisted the brush around in the glob of paint, enjoying the sensation of its heavy weight against her brush. She remembered how she used to have such respect for her materials. And for her art.

But this was unproductive thinking. She admonished herself to quit messing around and start painting so she could get to the beach. She inhaled deeply, then moved the square brush from red into a stunning yellow, creating an orangey mass of swirls and streaks on the palette. She moved into cobalt blue, on to slate gray, and finally to black, white, ocher, and a horrible violet color she had specially created in quantity because it was a crowd pleaser. She never lifted the brush from the palette, couldn't bear to violate the huge, virgin canvas. She idly pushed the brush around until the palette was filled with mud.

When the CD played the final rendition of *The Best of Times Is Now*, Maya realized she had wasted an hour. She remained paralyzed, strangely incapable of putting paint on the canvas. Desperate for help, she moved over to her bookcase and scanned the titles, as she had done in the dim and distant past. She set the palette and brush on the floor and pulled out catalogues that featured the work of her heroes from the Renaissance to the 1990's.

She plopped down next to the palette, took a long drink of wine straight from the bottle, and flipped through the volumes of reproductions. As she turned pages and sipped wine, she recalled how each of these artists had once influenced her style. She paused when she got to DeKooning's energetically painted *Woman V*. She stared at it for a long time, took the last drink from the wine bottle, then used her paint-filled brush to emulate De Kooning's slashing, slathering strokes right on top of the picture. She turned to a copy of one of Whistler's *Nocturnes* and brushed thin veils of color, like Whistler's, onto its surface.

She opened a book of Old Master paintings and took great care to meticulously reproduce the wonderful brushwork Titian had used to create the luminosity of human flesh on top of *Venus with a Mirror*. Maya then returned to modernism, squiggling away on the surface of Van Gogh's *Olive Orchard*, before passing out on the floor.

**

When she came to, she was ashamed and sickened by the mess she had made of her favorite books. Worse yet, she remained incapable of approaching the white canvas that hung low on the wall in front of her.

Her hand shook as she picked up the phone to call her agent. "Jason, you've got to do something for me."

"Whatever you want, babe."

"You've got to cancel my next three shows."

"What the hell—? What's wrong?"

Maya wiped perspiration off her forehead. "I can't work this way anymore. I can't do this phony stuff anymore—"

"Phony? Maya, you've been doing great stuff. Better than ever. Look at your record—"

"They sell, Jason, but they're not good, they're not even real. They're just paint on canvas, and I can't do it anymore."

"For God's sake, Maya, all paintings are just paint on canvas. What do you want?"

"I want to do what I did before. I want to create something that has meaning."

"What you do has meaning for your public."

"No, it doesn't, Jason. I'm a commodity. I'm hot because Capelli and Morganstern made me that way, not because of my art."

"So what? Jesus, Maya, you're going nuts here. Pull yourself together—"

"Cancel the shows, Jason."

"It's too late, babe."

"Jason, you have to—"

"Can't be done. Just keep doing—"

Maya hung up the phone.

She wandered back to the bookshelf and pulled out a volume of Sartre and one of Spinoza, remembering the paintings she had once done under the inspiration of existentialism, then pantheism. She thought back to another series she had done after reading Plato's *Republic*. Few of those paintings had sold, but she knew they were among her best works. Touching the spine of Nietzsche's *Beyond Good and Evil*, she told herself that perhaps her recent series were inspired by nihilism, but she knew that was a contradiction in terms, as well as simply untrue. Her recent series were inspired by nothing, and that was not the same at all.

She opened another bottle of wine.

***

"It's unbelievable."

"She's never been better."

"Brilliant! She's a genius."

Maya overheard remarks as she slipped into the Ganson Gallery in London. As soon as she removed her sunglasses and long coat, they were all over her.

"You've entered a whole new conceptual phase, Maya."

"These have an intellectual content greater than anything since surrealism."

"The formal qualities are overwhelming."

Maya nodded her thanks, grabbed a glass of wine, and walked through the gallery, admiring the installation. The new works did interact beautifully with one another. Yin and yang. They spoke, they danced, they played together," Maya thought. Or did the wine make them do that?

In the end, it didn't matter. She finally understood that. If they thought it was genius, then genius it was. Maya smiled modestly as she watched red dots go up on the labels of her brand new small-scale works on paper. *Smudged De Kooning*, *Whistler in the Mud/Nocturnal Mire*, and *Venus Gets Down and Dirty* were among the first to go. She looked on with pride as Jake Farnstein and the new critic for the *London Times* raved over the stark beauty and formal genius of *White Canvas I, II, III,* and *IV*.

Maya had come full circle; she had weathered the crisis and was back on a roll, one that could go on and on or end as suddenly as it had begun. Maybe she'd consider that place in Big Sur, after all. She raised her glass to Ted Ganson, the gallery owner, as he stuck a red dot on *Dirty Olive Pickers, a/k/a Violated Van Gogh.*

Judy Pomeranz is an art critic and fiction writer, based in Chicago. Her articles have appeared in a wide range of magazines and newspapers, and her short stories in a variety of literary magazines. Her first novel, *Love Without Asterisks*, was published by Miniver Press.

Cover Image: Cafe Latte, by Jean Beebe, oil on paper Our thanks to Jean Beebe and Jean Davis for allowing us to use it.

Miniver Press publishes non-fiction and selected literary fiction, specializing in lively and informative print and eBooks. For more information, visit us at miniverpress.com